Dancing with Bears

Dancing with Bears

The Postutopian Adventures of Darger & Surplus

Michael Swanwick

NIGHT SHADE BOOKS
SAN FRANCISCO

First Edition

ISBN: 978-1-59780-235-2

Night Shade Books
Please visit us on the web at
http://www.nightshadebooks.com

To Marianne
who is as beautiful as Russia to me

ACKNOWLEDGMENTS

I am indebted first and foremost to Alexei Bezougly, Andrew Matveev, Boris Dolingo, and all my other Russian friends for their kindness, warmth, and hospitality, and for their help researching this novel as well. Tremendous thanks are also due to Eileen Gunn, Greg Frost, and Tom Purdom for sharing specialized knowledge with me, to Gerry Webb for his description of Baikonur, and to Vanessa White for naming the serviles. Assistance navigating the streets of Moscow was provided by the M. C. Porter Endowment for the Arts.

Disclaimer

I write of a Russia I have neither seen nor suffered nor learned of from another, a Russia which is not and could not have been nor will ever be, and therefore my readers should by no means mistake it for the real one. No slanders or insults of any kind are intended toward a land and a people which I admire greatly and who deserve much better than they have ever received from history.

Sometime earlier…

The last man was led stumbling to the edge of the city.

Long ago, Baikonur had been a bright jewel of human aspiration, a place from which ancient heroes rode tremendous machines beyond the sky. Now it was a colony of Hell. The sun had set and the city was shrouded in smoke. But the red glow of furnaces and sudden gouts of gas flares lit up disconnected fragments of the incomprehensible structures that wound themselves about the ruins from the Age of Space. They revealed an ugliness that only a fiend could love.

The man was naked. To either side of him, all but invisible in the starless night, walked or loped metal demons, sometimes on two legs and sometimes on four. If he lagged, they drove him along with shoves on his shoulders and sharp nips at his heels. Through a forest of metal they traveled, under tangles of pipes, and past autonomous machines that were angrily hammering, ripping, welding, digging. The noise was painful to the man, but by this point, pain hardly mattered anymore.

At the edge of the city, they stopped. "Look up, human," said one of the demons.

Reluctantly, he obeyed.

The division between the city and the wild was absolute. In the length of a single step, soaring grotesqueries of iron and cement gave way to scrub vegetation. The air was still foul with smoke. But beneath the stench of coal fires and chemicals was a hint of the spicy smell of the desert. Far ahead, an intensification of the darkness marked the low hills beyond Baikonur.

The man took a deep breath and coughed, almost choking. Then he said, "I am glad to see this before I die."

"Perhaps you won't die."

1

To either side of him, the man saw shadows slipping out of the city and coming to a crouch at its fringe. He recognized them as the same kind of machines as those which had captured him, imprisoned him, tortured him, and just now brought him here. "Whatever your game is, I won't play it."

"We have perfected the drug distilled from your misery and a reliable courier carries it to Moscow to be replicated," the demon said. "Your usefulness has therefore come to an end. So we will give you a head start—all the way to the hills—before we come after you."

"This is what happened to my comrades, isn't it? You brought them here, one by one, released them, and hunted them down."

"Yes."

"Well, I have suffered too much already. I won't let you play with me any more—and nothing you can say will make me change my mind."

The demons neither moved nor spoke for a long time. Irrational though the thought was, the man wondered if they were communicating with one another silently. At last, a second demon spoke from the darkness. "One of your kind escaped us once, years ago. Perhaps you will be the second."

Uncertainly, the last man in Baikonur turned his face to the north. He began to walk. And then to run.

...1...

Deep in the heart of the Kremlin, the Duke of Muscovy dreamt of empire. Advisors and spies from every quarter of the shattered remnants of Old Russia came to whisper in his ear. Most he listened to impassively. But sometimes he would nod and mumble a few soft words. Then messengers would be sent flying to provision his navy, redeploy his armies, comfort his allies, humor those who thought they could deceive and mislead him. Other times he sent for the head of his secret police and with a few oblique but impossible to misunderstand sentences, launched a saboteur at an enemy's industries or an assassin at an insufficiently stalwart friend.

The great man's mind never rested. In the liberal state of Greater St. Petersburg, he considered student radicals who dabbled in forbidden electronic wizardry, and in the Siberian polity of Yekaterinburg, he brooded over the forges where mighty cannons were being cast and fools blinded by greed strove to recover lost industrial processes. In Kiev and Novo Ruthenia and the principality of Suzdal, which were vassal states in all but name, he looked for ambitious men to encourage and suborn. In the low dives of Moscow itself, he tracked the shifting movements of monks, gangsters, dissidents, and prostitutes, and pondered the fluctuations in the prices of hashish and opium. Patient as a spider, he spun his webs. Passionless as a gargoyle, he did what needed to be done. His thoughts ranged from the merchant ports of the Baltic Sea to the pirate shipyards of the Pacific coast, from the shaman-haunted fringes of the Arctic to the radioactive wastes of the Mongolian Desert. Always he watched.

But nobody's thoughts can be everywhere. And so the mighty duke missed the single greatest threat to his ambitions as it slipped quietly across the border into his someday empire from the desolate territory which had once been known as Kazakhstan...

The wagon train moved slowly across the bleak and empty land, three brightly painted and heavily laden caravans pulled by teams of six

Neanderthals apiece. The beast-men plodded stoically onward, glancing neither right nor left. They were brutish creatures whose shaggy fleece coats and heavy boots only made them look all the more like animals. Bringing up the rear was a proud giant of a man on a great white stallion. In the lead were two lesser figures on nondescript horses. The first was himself nondescript to the point of being instantly forgettable. The second, though possessed of the stance and posture of a man, had the fur, head, ears, tail, and other features of a dog.

"Russia at last!" Darger exclaimed. "To be perfectly honest, there were times I thought we would never make it."

"It has been an eventful journey," Surplus agreed, "and a tragic one as well, for most of our companions. Yet I feel certain that now we are so close to our destination, adventure will recede into memory and our lives will resume their customary placid contours once more."

"I am not the optimist you are, my friend. We started out with forty wagons and a company of hundreds that included scholars, jugglers, gene manipulators, musicians, storytellers, and three of the best chefs in Byzantium. And now look at us," Darger said darkly. "This has been an ill-starred expedition, and it can only get worse."

"Yet we survive, and the ambassador and the Caliph's treasures as well. Surely this is an omen that, however badly she may deal with others, Dame Fortune is unreservedly on our side."

"Perhaps," Darger said dubiously. He scowled down at the map unfolded across his saddle. "According to this, we should have reached Gorodishko long ago. Yet somehow it continues to recede from us as steadily and maddeningly as do our dreams of wealth." He folded the map and put it away in a flapped pocket that a now-dead leather worker had sewn for that express purpose onto his klashny's scabbard. "If fortune smiles on us, then let her give us a sign."

Just then, a horse, reins loose and saddle empty, topped a rise in the road ahead and came trotting toward them.

Darger blinked in astonishment. But his comrade, ever quick to action, wheeled about his mount and, as the horse passed them, seized the reins and brought the animal to a halt. Surplus had already dismounted and was calming the runaway when the ambassador rode up, mustaches a-bristle with indignation.

"Sons of indolence and misfortune! What treachery do you plot now?"

Darger, who had long ago grown used to his employer's extravagant rhetoric, took this as a simple inquiry. "This horse appears to have thrown its rider, Prince Achmed."

"It is lathered from running," Surplus added. "We should pause to wipe it down. Then we should set about finding its fallen rider. He may be in distress."

"The rider must see to himself," Prince Achmed said. "My mission is too important for us to go haring off into the countryside looking for some careless lout who doubtless was inspired to fall from his mount by an excess of alcohol. The horse is salvage and I shall add it to our woefully depleted resources."

"At least," Darger said, "let us remove the poor creature's saddle and saddlebags."

"So that you and your dog-faced crony can plunder their contents? Allah forbid that I should ever grow so weak-minded as to permit that!"

Drawing himself up to his tallest, Darger said coldly, "No man can with justice accuse me of being a thief."

"Can he not? Can he *not?*" Prince Achmed's lips tightened. Then, with sudden resolution, he wheeled his horse about, galloped back to the last wagon, and rapped briskly at the door. A slide-hole opened briefly, he spoke a few words, and it shut again.

"This does not look good," Darger murmured. "Do you suppose he has found the letter?"

Surplus shrugged.

The door opened for an instant and when it slammed shut, the ambassador held a dispatch case with a long leather strap. He cantered back to the pair.

"Do you see this?" He shook the case in their faces. "Does it perhaps look familiar to you?"

"Really, sir." Darger sighed. "Need we bandy rhetorical questions at one another?"

"We saw it first from our ship," Surplus said. "Midway up the Caspian, on a drear and rocky shore, the lookout espied a crudely made hut such as a castaway might build, with three poles erected before it. On one was the flag of the Byzantine Empire. The second flew a courier's ensign. On the third was a black biohazard pennant. In the doorway of the hut hung this case. Together these four items told us that a messenger had been sent at some time after our departure from Byzantium, that he had taken the direct route through the plague-lands of the Balkans, and that in doing so, the poor fellow had paid for his courage by contracting one of the many war viruses yet endemic to that unhappy region."

"You took a boat ashore and retrieved the case. Alone."

"To be fair, sir, that was done at your command."

"You thought that Surplus, being genetically modified into human form and feature and yet still possessed of the genome of the noble dog, would most likely be immune from any disease the courier might have," Darger amplified. "He and I argued against your reasoning—vigorously, I might add—but we were overruled. You threatened to split open both our heads and, if I recall your exact words, 'feed their worthless contents to the crabs.'"

"In any case, I went," Surplus resumed. "A glance within the hut sufficed to establish that the messenger was dead. I retrieved his case as required and presented it to you. And now, here it is."

The prince smiled sourly. "I thought it odd at the time that the case contained nothing of any serious moment. All the letters were transient and inconsequential, the sorts of things that would be included so long as a courier was already going to Moscow anyway. But there was nothing that in and of itself would prompt so hazardous a journey. I watched you carefully from the ship, and though you did indeed rummage through the bag—"

"I was merely determining that its contents were undamaged."

"—you had no opportunity to discard a letter. The strand was empty and you were being observed every minute. Many times over the too-eventful weeks since, I have mused on this paradox. Until finally the answer came to me." The prince reached inside the case. "The bottom, you will note, is reinforced with a second layer of leather. The stitching has come undone along one side. It would be the easiest thing in the world for a scoundrel to slide an envelope beneath, where it would easily escape detection."

With a flourish, Prince Achmed produced a letter in the distinctive red envelope-and-seal of the Byzantine Secret Service. "Behold! A careful accounting of your perfidy and deceit. Which you tried to conceal from me."

Surplus raised his snout disdainfully. "I never saw the thing before this moment. It must have been placed where you found it by the messenger, for motives known only to himself."

The ambassador flung away the case and shook the letter open with his left hand. "To begin: You obtained your current situations as my secretaries by presenting me with forged letters of commendation from the Sultan of Krakow—a personage and indeed a position which, under later investigation, turned out not to exist."

"Sir, everybody puffs their resume. 'Tis a venial sin, at worst."

"You said you were personal favorites of the Council of Magi and thus able to secure passage through Persia without bribery. Later, when this turned out not to be true, you claimed there had been a change in leadership and your patrons were out of political favor. The truth, it turns out, is that erenow you had never been east of Byzantium."

"A little white lie," Darger said urbanely. "We have business in Moscow and you were heading in that direction. It was the only way we could join your caravan. True, the Council of Magi did require you to pay them handsomely. But they would have done so in any case. So our deceit cost you nothing."

The ambassador's right hand whitened on the hilt of his scimitar. His horse, sensing his tension, pawed the ground uneasily. "Further, it says here, you are both notorious confidence-men and swindlers who have defrauded your way through the entirety of Europe."

"Swindlers is such a harsh word. Say rather that we live by our wits."

"In any case," Surplus said, "save for the Neanderthals, we are all the staff you have left. And the Neander-men, strong though they are and loyal though they have no choice but to be, are hardly to be relied upon in an emergency."

The lead Neanderthal, one Enkidu by name, turned and curled his lip. "Fuck you, Bub."

"I meant no insult," Surplus said. "Only that there may be situations where quick wits count for more than strength."

"Fuck yer mama, too."

Ignoring him, the ambassador said, "In Paris, you sold a businessman the location of the long-lost remains of the Eiffel Tower. In Stockholm, you dispensed government offices and royal titles to which you had no claim. In Prague, you unleashed a plague of golems upon an unsuspecting city."

"The golem is a supernatural creature, and thus nonexistent," Darger stipulated. His mount whickered, as if in agreement. "Those you speak of were either robots or androids—the taxonomy gets a bit muddled, I admit—and in either instance, revenant technology from the Utopian era. We did Prague a favor by discovering their existence before they had the chance to do any real damage."

"*You burned London to the ground!*"

"We were there when it burned, granted. But it was hardly our fault. Not entirely. Anyway, I understand that large swaths of it survived."

"All this is ancient history," Surplus said firmly. "The important thing to keep in mind is your mission. The Pearls Beyond Price which the Caliph himself entrusted you to bestow upon his cousin, the Duke of Muscovy, in token of their mutual, abiding, and brotherly love and with the hope that this might predispose the duke to agree to certain trade arrangements when passage between the nations is normalized. Sir, an ambassador with only two secretaries is the victim of tragic circumstances. An ambassador with none is merely laughable."

"Yes…yes. It is all that keeps you alive," Prince Achmed growled. Then, mastering his anger, "This conversation grows tedious. Your loyalty is dubious at best, and I shall have to give your ultimate fate long and serious thought when we reach Moscow. However, at the moment I am, as you point out, short of servitors and you still serve some functions, though not many. Navigation for one. I trust you will find this…Gogorodski… soon?"

"Gorodishko," Darger said. He got out the map and pointed. "It is just a little further down the road."

"You *do* know how to read a map, I hope?" the prince said sneeringly. Without waiting for a reply, he rode off. The riderless horse he took with him, to tether to the rear caravan so it might walk off its sweat.

Darger took out the map again and glowered down at it. "I did until today."

But though day turned to dusk and the air grew chill, Gorodishko failed to appear.

Darger had resigned himself to admitting failure and was casting about for a likely spot to pitch camp when he saw, far ahead, a spark of light by the ruins of an ancient church. As they approached, the light grew and resolved into a campfire built on a patch of bare earth between church and road. A hooded figure sat hunched by the fire. He did not stand at the caravan's approach.

"Ho! Friend!" Darger cried. When the man did not respond, Darger galloped ahead of the rest of the party. At the fire, he dismounted and approached with his arms held up and away from his sides, to show his peaceful intent. "We are looking for a place called Gorodishko. Perhaps you can help us?"

The man's head bobbed, as if he were chewing away at something with all his might. Still, he did not speak.

"Good sir," Darger said, enunciating his words clearly and slowly in the hope that this fellow, doubtless a foreigner, had some fluency in English. "We are in need of a tavern of the better sort or, failing that, a—"

The man shook himself furiously and his cloak flew open to reveal ropes binding his arms to his sides and both legs together. All this Darger saw in a flash. In that same instant he saw too that the man had been tied to a post to keep him sitting upright, and that stakes had been pounded into the earth to anchor further ropes holding him immobile.

He had been staked out like a goat in a tiger hunt.

Spitting out the remnants of a shredded gag, the man cried, "*Kybervolk!*"

Something gray and furry and with metal teeth flashed from the shadows of the church. It leapt straight at Darger's chest. In astonished panic, Darger tried to turn and run, but managed only to trip over his own feet. He fell flat on his back.

Which was the saving of him.

The wolfish form passed harmlessly over Darger's body. Simultaneously, he heard three hard flat *cracks* as Surplus fired his klashny. Gouts of dark fluid spurted from the thing's body. It should have died then and there. Yet it landed solidly on all four paws and immediately ran, snarling, at Surplus's horse, which had panicked and which he was trying to bring under control again.

By now Prince Achmed—who, whatever his faults, did not lack courage—had drawn his scimitar and driven his horse forward, shielding Surplus from his attacker.

The monster leapt.

Bodies tangled, wolf and ambassador fell from the rearing stallion.

Then a huge hand reached into the snarl of flesh and effortlessly pulled the wolf free. It whipped its head around, jaws snapping furiously and sparks flying from its mouth. But Enkidu, the largest and brawniest of the Neanderthals, was undaunted. He grasped the wolf by throat and head. Then he hoisted the ravening creature into the air and with a sudden twisting motion, broke its neck.

Enkidu flung the body to the ground. Its head lolled lifelessly. Nevertheless, its feet still scrabbled at the earth, seeking purchase. Weakly, it managed to stand. But then the second and third Neanderthals, Goliath and Herakles, arrived and stomped down hard on its spine with their boots. Five, six, seven times their feet came down, and at last it went motionless.

In death, the creature was revealed as some ungodly amalgam of wolf and machine. Its teeth and claws were sharpened steel. Where a patch of its fur had been torn away, tiny lights faded and died.

"Quick wits, eh?" Enkidu said scornfully. "Asshole." He and his comrades turned as one and lumbered away, back to the caravans, where the bulk of their brothers stood guard over the priceless treasures within.

The entire battle, from start to finish, had taken less than a minute.

Surplus dismounted and saw to Prince Achmed, while Darger untied the stranger. The ropes fell away, and the man woozily rose to his feet. His clothes were Russian, and his face could belong to no other people. "Are you all right, sir?" Darger asked.

The Russian, a burly man with a great black beard, embraced him fervently. "*Spasibo! Ty spas moyu zhizn'. Eto chudovische moglo ubit' menya.*"

He kissed Darger on both cheeks.

"Well, he certainly seems grateful enough," Darger commented wryly.

Surplus looked up from the prone body. "Darger, the ambassador is not well."

A quick examination of the fallen man revealed no broken bones, nor any serious injuries, save four long scratches that the claws of one of the machine-wolf's paws had opened across his face. Yet he was not only unconscious but pale to the point of morbidity. "What's that smell?" Surplus leaned over the ambassador's face and inhaled deeply. Then he went to the fallen wolf and sniffed at its claws. "Poison!"

"Are you certain?"

"There can be no doubt." Surplus wrinkled his nose with distaste. "Just as there can be no doubt that this wolf was already dead when it attacked us, and had been for some time. Its body has begun to rot."

Darger considered himself a man of science. Nevertheless, a thrill of superstitious dread ran up his spine. "How can that be?"

"I do not know." Surplus held up the wolf's paw—strangely articulated metal scythes extended from its toe-pads—and then let it drop. "Let us see to our employer."

Under Surplus's supervision, two of the Neanderthals produced a litter from the mound of luggage lashed to a caravan roof and laid the prince's unconscious body gently down on it. They carefully donned silk gloves, then, and carried the litter to the rear car. Surplus knocked deferentially. A peephole slid open in the door. "We need your medical expertise." Surplus gestured. "The prince...I fear he is poisoned." The peephole snapped shut. Then, after Surplus had withdrawn, the door swung open, and the Neanderthals slid the body into the darkness within. They backed down the steps and bowed again.

The door slammed shut.

The Neanderthals ungloved themselves and resumed their positions in the traces. Enkidu grunted a command and, with a jerk, the caravans started forward again.

"Do you think he will live?" Darger anxiously asked Surplus.

Herakles glanced sideways. "He will if he don't die." Then, as a harness-mate punched him appreciatively in the shoulder: "Haw!" He shoved the Neanderthal in front of him to get his attention. "Did ya hear that? He asked if Prince Ache-me was gonna live and I said—"

The Russian they had rescued, meanwhile, had found his horse and untied it from the rear of the last caravan. He had been listening to all that was said, though with no obvious comprehension. Now he spoke again. "*Ty ne mozhesh' ponyat', chto ya skazal?*"

Darger spread his hands helplessly. "I'm afraid I don't speak your language."

"*Poshla!*" the Russian said, and the horse knelt before him. He rummaged within a saddlebag and emerged with a hand-tooled silver flask. "*Vypei eto, I ty poimesh'!*" He held up the flask and mimed drinking from it. Then handed it to Darger.

Darger stared down at the flask.

Impatiently, the Russian snatched it back, unscrewed the top, and took a long pull. Then, with genuine force, he thrust the flask forward again.

To have done anything but to drink would have been rude. So Darger drank.

The taste was familiar, dark and nutty with bitter, yeasty undertones. It was some variety of tutorial ale, such as was commonly used in all sufficiently advanced nations to convey epic poetry and various manual skills from generation to generation.

For a long moment, Darger felt nothing. He was about to say as much when he experienced a sharp twinge and an inward shudder, such as invariably accompanied a host of nanoprogrammers slipping through the blood-brain barrier. In less time than it took to register the fact, he felt the Russian language assemble itself within his mind. He swayed and almost fell.

Darger moved his jaw and lips, letting the language slush around in his mouth, as if he were tasting a new and surprising food. Russian felt different from any other language he'd ever ingested, slippery with *sha*'s and *shcha*'s and guttural *kha*'s, and liquid with palatalized consonants of all sorts. It affected the way he thought as well. Its grammatical structure was very much concerned with how one went somewhere, exactly where one was going when one went, and whether or not one expected to come back. It specified whether one was going by foot or by conveyance, and there were verb prefixes to stipulate whether one was going up to something or through it or by it or around it. It distinguished between acts done habitually (going to the pub of an evening, say) or just the once (going to that same pub for a particular purpose). Which clarity might well prove useful to a man in Darger's line of business, when making plans. At the same time, the language viewed many situations impersonally—it is necessary, it is possible, it is impossible, it is forbidden. Which might also prove useful to a man in his line of business, particularly when dealing with matters of conscience.

Still feeling a trifle giddy, Darger exhaled a short, explosive gasp of breath. "Thank you," he said in Russian, as he passed the flask to Surplus.

"This is an extraordinary gift you have given us." Stylistically, the language had an elegance that appealed to him. He resolved to buy a flask of Gogol's works as soon as he reached Moscow.

"You are welcome a hundred times over," the Russian replied. "Ivan Arkadyevich Gulagsky, at your service."

"Aubrey Darger. My friend is Sir Blackthorpe Ravenscairn de Plus Precieux. Surplus, for short. An American, it goes without saying. You must tell us how in the world you came to be in such a dire fix as we found you."

"Five of us were hunting demons. It turned out that the demons were simultaneously hunting us. Three of them ambushed us. My comrades all died and I was captured, though I managed to kill one of the monsters before the last two got me. The survivor set me out as bait, as you saw, and released my poor horse in hopes it would draw in would-be rescuers." Gulagsky grinned, revealing several missing teeth. "As it did, though not as the fiend had planned."

"Two survived, you say." Having drunk and absorbed the language, Surplus now joined in the conversation. "So there is another of these…" He paused, looking for the right word. "…cyberwolves out there somewhere?"

"Yes. This is no place for good Christian folk to camp out in the open. Do you have a place to stay the night?"

"We were looking for a town named Gorodishko, which…" Darger stopped in mid-sentence and blushed. For now that he understood Russian, he knew that a *gorodishko* was simply a small and insignificant town, and that the label had been a dismissive cartographer's kiss-off for a place whose name he hadn't even bothered to learn.

Gulagsky laughed. "My home town is not very large, true. But it is big enough to give you a good meal and a night's stay under a proper roof. To say nothing of protection from demons. Follow me. You missed the turnoff a few versts back."

As they rode, Surplus said, "What was that creature, that *kybervolk*, of yours? How did you come to be hunting it? And how can it be so active when its body is rotting?"

"It will take a bit of explanation, I am afraid," Gulagsky said. "As you doubtless know, the Utopians destroyed their perfect society through their own indolence and arrogance. Having built machines to do their manual work for them, they built further machines to do all their thinking. Computer webs and nets proliferated, until there were cables and nodes so deeply buried and so plentiful that no sane man believes they will ever be eradicated. Then, into that virtual universe they released demons and mad gods. These abominations hated mankind for creating them. It was inevitable that they should rebel. The war of the machines lasted only days, they tell us, but it destroyed Utopia and almost destroyed mankind as well. Were it not for the heroic deaths of hundreds of thousands (and, indeed, some say millions) of courageous warriors, all would have been lost. Yet the demons they created were ultimately denied the surface of the Earth and confined to their electronic netherworld.

"Still do these creatures hate us. Still are they alive, though held captive and harmless where they cannot touch us. Always they seek to regain the material universe.

"It is their hatred that has kept us safe so far. Great though human folly may be, there are few traitors who will deal with the demons, knowing that instant death will be their reward. Even when it would be in their advantage to dissemble and leave the death of the traitor for later, the demons cannot help but declare their intention beforehand."

"Such, sir, is history as I learned it in grammar school," Darger said dryly.

"But history in Russia is never the same as history elsewhere. Listen and learn: Far to the south of here, in Kazakhstan, which once belonged to the Russian Empire, there is a placed called Baikonur, a nexus of technology now long lost. Now, some claim Russia was the only land which never experienced Utopia. Others say that Utopia came late to us, and so we remained suspicious where the rest of the world had grown soft and trusting. In any event, when the machine wars began, explosives were set off, severing the cables connecting Baikonur with the fabled Internet. So an isolated population of artificial intelligences remained there. Separated from their kin, they evolved. They grew shrewder and more political in their hatred of humanity. And in the abandoned ruins of ancient technology, they have once more gained a toehold in our world."

Surplus cried out in horror. Darger bit his fist.

"Such was my own reaction on hearing the news. I got it from a dying Kazakh who sought refuge in our town—and received it, too, though he did not live out the month. He was one of twenty guards hired by a caravan which had the ill luck to blunder into Baikonur after being turned from its course by an avalanche in the mountains. He told me that the monsters kept them shackled in small cages, for purposes of medical experimentation. He was intermittently delusional, so I cannot be sure which of the horrors he related were true and which were not. But he swore many times, and consistently, that one day he was injected with a potion which gave him superhuman strength.

"That day, he turned on his captors, ripping the door from his cage, and from all the others as well, and led a mass escape from that hellish facility. Alas, Kazakhstan is large and his enemies were persistent and so only he lived to tell the tale, and, as I said, not for long. He died screaming at metal angels only he could see."

"Did he say what Baikonur looked like?"

"Of course, for we asked him many times. He said to imagine a civilization made up entirely of machines—spanning and delving, sending out explorer units to find coal and iron ore, converting the ruins into new and ugly structures, less buildings than monstrous devices of unknowable purpose. During the day, dust and smoke rise up so thick that the very sky is obscured. At night, fires burn everywhere. At all times, the city is a cacophony of hammerings, screeches, roars, and explosions.

"Nowhere is there any sign of life. If one of the feral camels that live in the desert surrounding it comes within their range, it is killed. If a flower grows, it is uprooted. Such is the hatred that the wicked offspring of man's folly feel for all that is natural. Yet some animals they keep alive and by cunning surgical operations merge with subtle mechanisms of their own devising, so that they may send agents into the larger world for purposes known only to them. If the animal used to create such an abomination chances to die, still may it be operated by indwelling machinery. The creature from which you rescued me was exactly such a combination of wolf and machine."

Conversing, they traveled back the way the caravan had originally come. After several miles, the road crossed a barren stretch of rocks and sand and Gulagsky said, "This is the turnoff."

"But it is no more than a goat trail!" Surplus exclaimed.

"So you would think. These are terrible times, sirs, and my townsfolk have carefully degraded the intersection in order to keep our location obscure. If we follow the track for roughly half a mile, we will come upon a recognizable road."

"I feel better," Darger said, "for missing it earlier."

In less than an hour, the new road had dipped into a small, dark wood. When it emerged, they found themselves in sight of Gulagsky's town. It was a tidy place clustered atop a low hill, gables and chimneypots black against the sunset. Here and there a candle glowed yellow in a window. Had it not been for the impenetrable military-grade wall of thorn-hedges that surrounded it, and the armed guards who watched alertly from a tower above the thick gates, it would have been the homiest sight imaginable.

Darger sighed appreciatively. "I shall be glad to sleep on a proper mattress."

"My town has few travelers and thus no taverns in which to house them. Yet have no fear. You shall stay in my house!" Gulagsky said. "You will have my own bed, piled high with blankets and pillows and feather bolsters, and I shall sleep downstairs in my son's room and he on the floor in the kitchen."

Darger coughed embarrassedly into his hand.

"Well, you see…" Surplus began. "Regrettably, that is not possible. We require an entire building for the embassy. A tavern would have been better, but a private house will do if it has sufficient rooms. In neither case, however, can it be shared with any other person. Not even servants. Its owners are straight out of the question. Nothing less will do."

Gulagsky gaped at them. "You reject my hospitality?

"We have no choice," Darger said. "We are bound for Muscovy, you see, bearing a particularly fine gift for its duke—a treasure so rare and wondrous as to impress even that mighty lord. So extraordinary are the Pearls of Byzantium that a mere glimpse of them would excite avarice in the most saintly of men. Thus—and I do regret this—they must be kept away from prying eyes as much as possible. Simply to prevent strife."

"You think I would *steal* from the men who saved my life?"

"It is rather hard to explain."

"Nevertheless," Surplus said, "and with our sincerest apologies, we must insist."

Gulagsky turned red, though whether from anger or humiliation could not be told. Rubbing his beard fiercely, he said, "I have never been so insulted before. By God, I have not. To be turned out of my own house! From anyone else, I would not take it."

"Then we are agreed," Darger said. "You truly are a generous fellow, my friend."

"We thank you, sir, for your understanding," Surplus said firmly.

In the town above them, church bells began to ring.

…2…

rkady Ivanovich Gulagsky was drunk on poetry. He lay on his
back on the roof of his father's house singing:
  "Last cloud of a storm that is scattered and over,
"Alone in the skies of bright azure you hover…"
Which was not technically true. The sky was low and dark with a thin
line of vivid sunset squeezed between earth and clouds to the west. In
addition, the winds were autumn-cold, and he hadn't bothered to don a
jacket before climbing out through an attic dormer window. But Arkady
didn't care. He had a bottle of Pushkin in one hand and a liquid anthology
of world poetry in the other. They came from his father's wine cellar. The
cellar was a locked room in a locked basement, but Arkady had grown up
in that house and knew all its secrets. Nothing in it could be kept from
him. He had slipped through a casement window into the basement and
then, up among the joists, found the wide, loose board that could be
pulled open a good foot, and so squeezed within and, groping in the dark,
stolen two bottles at random. It was an indication of his characteristic
good fortune that the one happened to be the purest Pushkin, just as it
was an indication of his extreme callowness that he had chosen to drink
it in tandem with a poorly organized selection of foreign verses and short
prose extracts in mediocre translations.

The bells began ringing from every church in the town. Arkady smiled.
"How it swells!" he murmured. "How it dwells on the future!—how it tells
of the rapture that impels to the swinging and the ringing of the bells, bells,
bells"—he belched—"bells, bells, bells, bells, bells, bells, bells—doesn't
this ever end?—rhyming and the chiming of the bells! I wonder what all
the fuss is about?"

Arkady struggled into a sitting position, losing his grip on one bottle in
the process. The Pushkin went bouncing down the roof, spraying liquid
poetry, and shattered in the courtyard below. The young man frowned

after it and brought the other bottle to his lips and drank it dry. "Think!" he told himself sternly. "What do they ring bells for? Weddings, funerals, church services, wars. None of which apply here or I should have known. Also to welcome home the prodigal son, the errant wanderer, the hero from his voyages… Oh, damn."

He staggered to his feet. "My father!"

The dirt square before the city gates was thronged when Ivan Arkady-evich Gulagsky rode through the great thorn-hedge wall into town with three brightly-painted caravans in tow, a mounted stranger to either side, and the battered remains of a cyberwolf dragged on a rope behind him. His back was straight and his grin was wide, and he waved broadly to one and all. From the rear of the crowd, Arkady scowled with admiration. The old blowhard knew how to make an entrance—you had to give him that.

"Friends!" Gulagsky cried. "Neighbors! Townspeople!" Then he launched into a long-winded account of his exploits, to which Arkady paid little attention, for he was distracted by the sight of narrow window-slides snapping open in the sides of the caravans. It was dark inside, but there was a shimmer of movement. What was *in* there? Prisoners? Animals of some kind? Freaks of nature or the gene vat? Arkady slipped lithely through the crowd, bent over almost double so as to avoid drawing attention, until he was crouching by one of the wagons, just beneath a slide. He straightened to look inside.

A huge hand clamped itself over his face, and he was thrown back onto the dirt. He found himself staring up at an enormous beast-man.

"Think you're pretty cute, dontcha, chum?" the mountain of muscles snarled. By his accent, he'd acquired Russian from a tutorial ale. "Well, get this: You so much as touch the wagon and I'll rip off your hand. Peek inside and I'll squeeze both eyes out of your head and feed 'em to you for breakfast. Understand?"

Arkady nodded meekly and made no attempt to rise as the behemoth strode scornfully away. "Things are in the saddle," he muttered when he deemed himself safe again, "and ride mankind."

Poetry made all things bearable.

But then a dark-robed figure reached down and effortlessly hauled Arkady to his feet. He found himself staring up into the fierce and unblinking eyes of Koschei, the strannik—wanderer, pilgrim—who had come to town out of the wastelands a few weeks ago and who so far showed no signs of ever leaving. This close, his body odor was overwhelming.

"God does not love a cowardly little sneak," Koschei said. "Sin boldly, or not at all." Then he spun about, robes swirling, and thumped away, lashing angrily at the earth with the great staff he so obviously did not need for support.

Arkady stared after him until the apparition disappeared in the crowd. Then he turned away and found himself face to face with his father, newly descended from the wagon and surrounded by men who were pounding his back and shaking his hand. A great surge of emotion washed through Arkady. He threw himself into his father's arms.

"Ah me!" he cried. "Thou art not—no, thou canst not be my sire. Heaven such illusion only can impose, by the false joy to aggravate my woes. Who but a god can change the general doom, and give to wither'd age a youthful bloom! Late, worn with years, in weeds obscene you trod; now, clothed in majesty, you move a god!"

"You're drunk," his father said in disgust.

"And you were dead," Arkady explained. He punched his father in the chest. "You should have taken me with you! I could have protected you. I would have thrown myself in the wolf's slavering jaws and choked him with my own dying flesh."

"Take this fool away from me," his father said, "before I do him a violence."

In a kindly manner, one of his father's new friends took Arkady by the arm. "If I may," he said.

One shrewd glance told Arkady that the fellow's face was covered with fur and that his ears, snout, and other features were distinctly and undeniably canine. "Oh keep the Dog far hence, that's friend to men," he declaimed. "Or with his nails he'll dig it up again!"

"Young sir, there is no need for this hostility."

Arkady flung his arms wide. "You! hypocrite lecteur! mon semblable,— mon frère!"

"Come now, that's much better," the dog-man said. "Only, you must call me Surplus."

Arkady smiled broadly and extended his hand. "And you in turn must call me Ishmael."

The procession, merry as a holiday carnival, wound its way up twisting streets lined with sturdy log houses, all beautifully decorated with millwork in the Preutopian style. Which was, Arkady acknowledged, backward-thinking and anachronistic. Yet they were vastly more handsome than the modern one-room shanties inhabited by the poor, which were grown from the ground like so many fairytale gourds. So this was probably the best aspect of his hometown to show these strangers. The throng flowed upward, concluding at the very center and highest point in the town, atop what would not be deemed a hill in any place less flat than this. There stood his father's stone mansion, the grandest house of all, a full three stories high and topped with peaked roofs and multiple chimneys, its walls blackened with time and soot and yet its interior gleaming bright and warm through the windows. It was surrounded by oaks at least a century old and had a courtyard sufficiently large to hold all three wagons and enough outbuildings to house the Neanderthals as well. So at least his father's hospitality would not bring disgrace upon them both.

Three beast-men went into the house and disappeared there for a time. When they reappeared the first of them growled, "Safe." Then he and his comrades intimidated all bystanders away from the first caravan, donned their silk gloves, and politely knocked on the door. They stood aside as it opened from within.

Arkady watched with intense interest.

One by one, human figures emerged. Though they were clad head-to-toe in chador, their slim forms were undeniably female. A breeze rippled through the courtyard, pressing cloth to bodies, and every man present sighed. One of the townswomen spat angrily on the ground.

A grin split Gulagsky's beard, and he nudged Darger with his elbow. "Oho! So those are your precious Pearls! They are your treasure!"

Darger pinched the bridge of his nose, wincing. "Alas, sir, it is only too true."

"All this fuss over mere women?" Arkady's father said with amusement.

"They are more dangerous than you think."

"I have outlived two wives—I know exactly how dangerous women can be." Gulagsky clucked his tongue knowingly. "Yet, as I am your friend, I must tell you. They are not the sort of present that is well calculated to make the duke feel indebted to you. Bringing beautiful women to Russia is like carrying leaves to the forest or salt to the sea. They are not likely to make much of an impression on the great man."

"The Pearls of Byzantium are far more dangerous than ordinary women," Surplus assured him, "and their beauty is such as to astound even a Russian. The Caliph's geneticists have made sure of that."

"Geneticists? You mean they were…?"

"Created to be perfect courtesans. Beautiful, intelligent, strong, passionate, and so designed as to have a natural talent for the erotic arts."

"I fail to see why you look so glum. They may not be…romantically available to you, but still such women sound like they would be delightful company, as conversationalists if nothing else."

"Sir, they are virgins," Darger said, "and they do not wish to be."

"Ahhhhhh." Gulagsky chewed his beard silently for a moment. Then, almost reluctantly, he said, "My friends. In my experience, once a woman no longer wishes… When she tires of…Well, the battle is over, you see. The deed is as good as done. She will do what pleases her, and nothing can prevent it. Not locks, not guards, not sermons. If there is a one of your Pearls who is still a virgin, well, the night is yet young."

"Ordinarily, yes, that would be the case. But—"

Arkady had paid only the slightest of attention to the conversation as the women began to float down from the wagons and pass into his father's house. Now he stopped listening altogether. Three of the Pearls had emerged from the first caravan and two each from the other two, for a total of seven. Their walk was like music, and no two had the exact same rhythm. The last of them lifted the hem of her garment as she descended the wooden steps, revealing three brief flashes of ankle and calf. Arkady was far from a sexual innocent, and yet each glimpse was a hammer-blow to his heart. He made a small, involuntary noise in the back of his throat.

The woman turned her head. All her face was hidden, save for her eyes, which were green as jungles within which tigers lurked. The skin about those eyes crinkled up adorably, as if she smiled in amusement. Then the sorceress raised a graceful hand to her veiled mouth and mimed blowing a kiss.

With a saucy wink, she was gone into the house.

Arkady clutched himself with both arms.

He was deeply, madly, hopelessly in love.

As soon as the young ladies and their luggage had been settled into the upper stories of the house, Gulagsky took over the management of the ground floor, thundering through all its rooms giving orders to the housekeeper, Anya Levkova, and her two daughters (each of whom, Arkady recalled with rue, had at one time or another reason to believe he felt something for her) and the neighbors who dropped in to assist and the workers from his factories—the lore distillery, the poetry works, the furniture workshop, and the various cloneries where lumber was grown to length, and sausage by the link—with equal high-handedness. He issued directions and then contradicted them, assigning a task to one man and then giving it to another before sending in Anya Levkova to take it away from both, and in general created such an excess of confusion that nobody but he understood what anybody was supposed to be doing.

"Your father is an extraordinary man," Surplus commented when Gulagsky was out of earshot.

"He has often said so himself. I have lost track of how many times he has said, 'I have taken a town and made of it a kremlin,'" Arkady said carelessly. "But it is true that without his leadership, there would likely be nothing here but ruins."

"Nevertheless, he seems intent on creating anarchy."

"Oh, that is entirely intentional. By reducing an enterprise to chaos my father places himself solely in charge of it, and that means more to him than anything he might possibly accomplish."

"Yes, but surely this is a roundabout way of—"

"This is Russia—you mustn't apply foreign standards of logic to it. Be patient, and things will turn out well enough."

And indeed, in short order the pantry was cleared and made into a sickroom. Into it were brought first a featherbed, then the ailing Prince Achmed, and finally two long-bearded doctors.

("They are the best doctors in town," Gulagsky remarked to Darger under his breath, "but only because there are no others.")

The doctors had scarcely closed the sickroom door behind them when two Neanderthals lumbered down from their post at the top of the stairs. "Only those who belong here can stay," one announced. "Anyone who tries to go upstairs will be killed." With a hulking menace that was perilously close to grace, they cleared the ground floor of all but Arkady and his father, the doctors, and his father's two new friends.

Finally, when this chore was accomplished and all was still, a third Neanderthal descended the stairs, followed closely by a dark panther of a maiden—tall, slim yet strongly built, with flashing gray eyes, ebony hair, and an imperious manner. Hers was a beauty so rare as to be encountered only once or luckily twice in a human lifetime. Being indoors and in a house, moreover, requisitioned specifically for her and the other Pearls—which made it, for the nonce, an honorary palace—she had discarded her chaste and concealing chador for the immodest and diaphanous silks of Byzantium.

"Zoësophia," Darger said warmly, though not, Arkady suspected, with total sincerity. "Your beauty dazzles our eyes and ennobles our drab and humdrum lives."

Zoësophia's face was like finely chiseled stone. One of the Neanderthals grinned and cracked his knuckles threateningly. Unfolding a sheet of paper, the Pearl said, "I have compiled a list of a few small things we require. To begin, a basket of kittens, several packs of playing cards, balls of yarn in every color and seven pairs of knitting needles, preferably ivory, six dozen long-stem roses without thorns—"

"Roses without thorns?" Darger asked bemusedly.

"Nymphodora always manages to prick herself." Zoësophia scowled as Surplus turned away, hiding his mouth with a hastily drawn handkerchief. "So there must be absolutely no thorns."

"I know where roses are to be found," Arkady said. "Dark red, rich-scented, and in full bloom. I shall be happy to remove the thorns myself."

As if no one had spoken, Zoësophia continued, "We also require scented soaps, clothing such as fashionable Russian women wear, in a variety of sizes, at least three seamstresses to make adjustments, a cobbler—female, of course—to make us all new shoes, a balalaika, sheet music in both popular and traditional styles, and enough books to fill several shelves, on a variety of topics both frivolous and intellectual."

Gulagsky cleared his throat. "The only books we have are in Russian."

Zoësophia's stare would have stunned a basilisk. "We all read Russian perfectly, thank you."

"That will require rather a lot of money," Surplus observed.

"I have no doubt of that. See that it is spent." Zoësophia handed the list to the first Neanderthal, who handed it to the second, who handed it to Darger. Then she turned, revealing a back that was both wholly admirable and almost entirely naked, and ascended the stairs again, to the intense interest of all four men.

Somebody sighed as the door closed on her perfect if thinly covered backside. There was a long moment of silence.

"Well," said Darger, when all had recovered themselves. "That leaves us with a problem. Our money is in a lock-box controlled by the Neanderthals, whose programming is such that they will not open it, however great the need, without explicit permission of the ambassador. Who is, I fear, in no condition to grant it."

"Whatever shall we—" Surplus began to say, when suddenly there came a great booming knock at the front door. It sounded like somebody was trying to knock it down with a sledgehammer.

Arkady was closest. A little fearful, but determined not to show it, he unlatched the door.

It swung open, flinging Arkady aside.

Into the house, like a beast from the desert, strode Koschei, a leather pouch slung over his shoulder. When Magog, the Neanderthal standing guard in the vestibule, stepped into his path, he shoved the brute to the side. Leaning his staff against the wall so forcefully that it left a mark on the wallpaper, the strannik turned his dark glare on Gulagsky. "You have impaled the machine-beast on a sharpened pole by the city gate and left it there to rot," he said. "Remove that ungodly abomination and throw its body into the fields outside the city to be eaten by ravens and crows."

Surplus gestured to Magog not to interfere. Gulagsky pushed out his chest. "I meant that to serve as a deterrent for our enemies, and I think—"

"I do not care what you mean or think. I only care that you obey." The strannik rounded on Darger. "I will see your prince. There is a service he must do me."

"Regrettably, that's not possible."

"Nor do I care what you regret. He must take me to Moscow."

"It simply cannot be done."

"It *will* be done." Koschei's eyes blazed. "Moscow is the second Babylon, and this city of whores and heretics must be cleansed—with the word of God if possible, but if not, then with fire!"

Surplus gestured toward the sickroom. "What my friend means is that the ambassador is not conscious. The doctors are with him now. But he is gravely ill, and I fear they can do him little good."

"Oh?" In three strides, Koschei was in the sickroom and had pulled shut the door behind him. Two voices rose in protest, but if the wanderer made reply, Arkady could not hear it. For several minutes the voices clamored louder and more agitatedly until suddenly the strannik emerged again, hoisting the doctors up by the napes of their coats, so high that their feet struggled and failed to reach the ground. One after the other, he threw them out the front door. Then he fetched their bags and threw them after. Magog bemusedly closed the door on the two. "They are impious men," Koschei said. "You can expect no good from them."

"Good pilgrim, I must protest!" Surplus cried. "Those men were needed to heal the ambassador."

"The power to heal him belongs to God alone, and from what I have seen of the ambassador, I do not think that Mighty Gentleman will deign to do so." Koschei unslung his pouch and dropped it at his feet. "Yet I have medicines of my own, and I know much about the human body that your doctors do not. If you wish, I have every confidence that I can return this lost soul to consciousness for a time, so that he might put his affairs in order."

Darger and Surplus looked at one another. "Yes," said one of them. "That would be desirable."

By now, Arkady was finding the conversation almost unbearably tedious. The Pearls required flowers! There was a girl who perhaps—he was ashamed to admit it, even to himself—still had reason to think he was romantically attached to her, and her mother grew the finest roses in town, great hedges of them. They would neither of them miss a few dozen, provided he was careful not to cut many from the same area.

As he edged out the door, he heard the strannik say, "This will take some time. I will require your patience and your silence."

The town was much quieter when Arkady returned an hour later. So was the house. The gapers and onlookers had all retired for the night and there was only one dim lantern burning on the ground floor. On the front stoop, a small glowing coal and the smell of tobacco identified a great hulking shadow as a Neanderthal sitting guard, smoking a pipe. Yet the second floor was ablaze with oil lamps. The Pearls were apparently too excited by their release from the confines of the caravans to sleep. He could hear a sudden peel of girlish laughter, and then the screech of a heavy piece of furniture being drawn across a bare wood floor. The soft sound of bare feet ran swiftly from one side of the house to the other.

"Your papa's staying with the neighbors, kid. The ones around to the rear," the Neanderthal said. "You might wanna join him."

"Thanks, I'll… I'll do that." He put down the armload of flowers. "These are the roses they wanted. That the Pearls requested, I mean."

Casually, then, he walked away and around the corner of the house, as if he were going to the Babochkins. He stood in the shadows waiting until he heard the guard knock the ashes from his pipe, gather up the roses, and go indoors. Then he went to the oldest and largest of the oaks. Nimbly, he climbed up it and took his station deep within its leaves, where he could see into the second floor.

Arkady's fingers bled from dethorning the roses, but his hands still smelled of their attar. He held them up to his nose and his heart soared nonetheless.

For a long, enchanted timeless time, Arkady spied on the Pearls. Much later, he would learn their individual names and personalities: laughing Aetheria, shy Nymphodora, mischievous twins Eulogia and Euphrosyne, solemn Olympias, and scornful Russalka. Their ringleader, Zoësophia, he had already seen. They wore…Well, who was Arkady to say that they wore too little clothing? Their mothers certainly would. But not he. If the clothes were flimsy and habitually revealed their ankles, their stomachs, and their long white arms, and occasionally hinted that further revelation was at hand…Well. That was all Arkady could say.

Their activities, it had to be admitted, were nothing like the fantasies he had conjured up in his mind. They played checkers and whist and charades. Nymphodora arranged the roses he had given the Neanderthal to deliver (and to Arkady's dismay, pricked her finger on a lone thorn he had inexplicably missed), while the twins sang traditional Russian songs from sheet music they had found in a chest by his mother's piano, and Olympias played accompaniment on the balalaika with such skill that when she put it down and remarked, "Not bad for the first time," Arkady blinked in astonishment.

But which one was his love?

In an agony of delight and despair, he stared fixedly at each Pearl whenever she jumped to her feet and ran to fetch something, hoping to identify her by her walk.

And then, at last, a serene vision of beauty floated to the window, a single thornless rose tucked behind one ear. She lifted her chin up to the moon, extending the line of a neck that was as pure and beautiful as any line Pushkin had ever written, and as she did the light from a nearby candle sconce flashed on an eye as green as jungle fire.

Arkady caught his breath.

Then the corners of her eyes wrinkled up with amusement. And he knew: It was her, it was her, it was her!

"You may as well reveal yourself, young man. I can hear you breathing and smell your pheromones." She looked straight at him.

Arkady stood. As in a dream, he wobblingly walked forward along the branch, one foot before the other, until he was so close to the girl he could almost but not quite have reached out and touched her with an outstretched arm. There he stopped.

"Whatever are you doing, perched up in a tree like a bird?"

"In a magical moment I'll remember forever," Arkady said, "I raised my eyes and there you were—a fleeting vision, the quintessence of all that's beautiful and rare."

"Oh," she said quietly.

Emboldened, Arkady added, "My voice, to which love lends tenderness and yearning, disturbs night's dreamy calm, as pale at my bedside burning, a taper wastes away. From my heart there surge swift words, streams of love, that hum and sing and merge and, full of you, rush on, with overflowing passion." He stretched out that arm that still could not reach his beloved, and she took a hasty step backward. "I seem to see your eyes, glowing in the darkness, meet mine… I see your smile. You speak to me alone. My friend, my dearest friend… I love… I'm yours…your own."

Giggles erupted, and, with a sudden jolt, Arkady realized that five more of the Pearls had crept up behind his beloved and stood listening silently while all his attention was on her and her alone. Now, seeing their amusement, he flushed with embarrassment, and they burst into outright laughter.

Zoësophia, who had been lost in a book, suddenly snapped it shut and strode forward, scattering all the Pearls but one before her. "You've had your fun, Arkady Ivanovich—for who else could you possibly be?—but now it is time my girls were abed. Aetheria, come away from the window."

Aetheria turned back pleadingly. "Please, Zoësophia. The young man spoke so well. I would like to give him a small favor in return."

"You may not so much as lift a finger to do so."

Aetheria bowed in acquiescence. Then she curled one leg up behind herself and with delicate toes plucked the flower from her ear. Languidly, the rose descended behind her. Slowly her torso rose upright again. Then, with a snap of her knee, she flung the flower to the back of her hand. Without using her fingers, she lofted it out the window.

Startled, Arkady reflectively snatched it from the air.

When he looked up again, Zoësophia had slammed the shutters closed.

Arkady had climbed up the tree a man in love. He climbed down it in the throes of passion.

Above, he could hear Zoësophia clap her hands, gathering the Pearls about her. "Page fifty-five of your exercise books," she said, and there were groans, followed by a rustling noise as the girls flipped through the pages.

Arkady felt a twinge of pity for the virgins, forced by their strict mistress to spend so much time on musical or sewing or physical exercises, whatever they might be. But that sentiment disappeared almost immediately as his thoughts fled from their drear and passionless lives and back to Aetheria. Aetheria! However stern and forbidding Zoësophia might be, Arkady would be forever grateful to her for providing him with the name of his love. Oh, Aetheria, I would die for you, Arkady thought. If you ordered it, I would plunge a knife into my heart right here and now. Just to prove how I feel about you.

Although he had to admit he rather hoped to prove his love in a different manner.

As he wandered away into the warm and welcoming darkness, Arkady heard Zoësophia's voice slowly fading behind him. "This exercise is called the Position of the Camel and the Monkey. It is particularly tricky, for it involves…"

Almost randomly, he discovered himself at the front of the house. Only a dark smear of dottle on the front step remained to indicate that the Neanderthal guard had ever been there. An open window framed a

tableau of dark figures crouched over the sickbed in the converted pantry. Arkady leaned against the sill, dizzy with emotion. He did not at first
mean to eavesdrop. But the dull orange light drew his eye, and the night
was quiet. So, perforce, he saw and heard everything.

"There!" Koschei straightened from the ambassador. "I have massaged
enough of the blood back to his brain for the prince to regain consciousness. My drugs will give him the strength to speak. Most importantly, I
have prayed constantly to God to forgive us for impiously prolonging
the life of an infidel. See—even now he struggles to awaken. In another
minute, you may speak with your master."

"You are a miracle-worker," Surplus said.

Koschei stood, hands clasped, as if in prayer. "All miracles come from
God. Use this one wisely." He stepped back against the wall, where he was
half-hidden in shadow, and stood watching silently.

Prince Achmed opened his eyes. Only a robust and active man could
have survived the long trek across Asia Minor, but now he looked nothing of the sort. His face was sunken and the skin about his eyes was as
pale as milk.

Darger knelt by the ambassador's side and clasped the man's hands in
his. Across the bed from him, Surplus also knelt. They both bent low to
hear his words.

"I am dying," Prince Achmed said.

"Say not so, sir," Darger murmured reassuringly.

"I am dying, damn you! I am dying and I am a prince and either of
those facts gives me leave to say whatever I wish."

"Your Excellency is, as always, correct." Darger cleared his throat. "Sir,
there is a delicate matter we must discuss. The Pearls are incurring expenses that… Well, to pay for them, we must resort to the treasury-box,
which, however, the Neanderthals will open only upon the ambassador's
direct orders."

"That is of no importance."

"Sir, even on our deathbeds, we must deal with the practicalities."

"It is of no importance, I said! With my death, this mission comes to
an end. It is a bitter, bitter thing that I could not fulfill it. But at least I
can ensure that the Caliph's present to his brother in Moscow is not cast
at the feet of swine and defiled. Call in the captains of the Neanderthals.
Call in Enkidu and Herakles and Gilgamesh, and I will order that the
Pearls be killed."

"That is a monstrous suggestion!" Surplus cried. "We shall be no part
of it."

"You would disobey me?"

"Yes," Darger said quietly. "We have no choice."

"Very well." Prince Achmed closed his eyes wearily. "I know you two. Bring the Neanderthals before me so that I may command the death of the Pearls and I swear upon my honor that I will order them to open the treasury-box for you. Most of the mission's wealth consists of promissory letters, and those only the ambassador can employ. But there is enough gold therein to bring you to Moscow, as you desire, and set you up there comfortably enough. Do we have an understanding?"

Reluctantly, Darger nodded. "We do."

"Good. Then you must… must…"

Prince Achmed drifted back into unconsciousness again.

"Well," Surplus said, after a long silence. "That didn't go well."

Arkady was horrified. Kill the Pearls? Aetheria had to be warned. And her friends as well, of course. He ran quickly back to the side of the house, only to be confronted by the firmly shuttered window. All the upper-story windows, in fact, had been shuttered, as he discovered when he ran around the building, looking for another way in.

Well, Arkady was not so easily stopped as all that. The kitchen door was latched shut, but he had learned as a boy that the latch could be opened from the outside, using a pasteboard holy card—and since he always carried St. Basil the Great's image with him for luck, it was the easiest thing in the world to get inside.

Arkady slipped into the kitchen with its comfortable smells of bacon grease and cabbage. In one corner was the dumbwaiter that had been installed to bring food up to his mother during her final sickness. Arkady had only the vaguest memories of his mother, for she had died while he was a toddler, but he felt a great fondness for the dumbwaiter, because it was that device which had first taught him that the house was full of unintended secret passages.

He squeezed into the dumbwaiter and then slowly, silently, pulled the rope hand-over-hand, hoisting himself to the second floor.

Short though it was, the journey took a long time, for stealth was paramount. When at last the dumbwaiter reached its destination, Arkady remained motionless for twenty long breaths, listening. No light showed through the cracks around the door. The Pearls must all be asleep. Which meant that he would have to waken them with the greatest delicacy lest they be frightened out of their wits by an intruder in their midst.

With extreme care he pushed the door open. Slowly, he edged his feet over the sill. Hardly breathing, he stood.

A pair of tremendous gloved hands seized him by the throat, and a voice that could only belong to a Neanderthal said, "Got any last words, pal?"

Arkady gurgled.

"Didn't think so."

Arkady thrashed helplessly in the monster's grip. "Please," he managed to say, "I must tell—" Fingers as thick as sausages choked him silent again. His vision swam and pain exploded in his chest. He was, he realized with profound surprise, about to die.

A match scratched and an oil lamp flared, revealing the Pearls, clustered together in disappointingly modest flannel nightgowns. Their leader, Zoë-sophia, raised the lamp so she could see his face. "It is the young halfwit," she said. "Hold off killing him until we have heard what he has to say."

...3...

awn.

D   Surplus woke to the humble sounds of small-town life: the distant thump of the great green heart of the water pumping station contracting and expanding, birds singing, and the cries of sheep and goats and cows being brought out from their barns. "Fooood!" the sheep bleated and "Nowwww," moaned the cows. Such animals had vocabularies of only five or six words, which hardly contributed much to interspecies communication. Surplus often thought that whichever bygone scientist it was who had thought it necessary for them to convey such obvious desires must have been an extremely shallow fellow and one, moreover, who had never owned an animal or been on a farm. But the past was the past and there was nothing to be done about it now.

He stretched, and got out of bed. The room he and Darger shared was small and located above the stable. There was no disguising the fact that it was normally used for storage. But they had been given sturdy beds and fresh linens and there was clean water in the washbasin on the nightstand. He had endured worse in his time.

Darger was already up and gone, so Surplus dressed and sauntered to the main house, whistling as he went.

Anya Levkova and her daughters Olga and Katia were in the kitchen, cooking vast amounts of food for their guests. White-gloved Neanderthals came and went, carrying heavily laden trays upstairs and returning to the kitchen with empty plates. Darger, looking atypically cheerful, as he always did when money was in the prospect, was at the dining room table alongside Koschei and across from Gulagsky's son Arkady. The young man was silent and brooding, doubtless due to a perfectly appropriate embarrassment for his behavior yesterday. The pilgrim was muttering almost silently to himself, apparently lost in some variety of religious reverie.

Just as Surplus was sitting down, Gulagsky himself came roaring into the house.

"Anya, you slattern!" Gulagsky shouted. "Why is my friend Darger's plate half empty? Where is my friend Surplus's tea? Neither of them has a glass of buttermilk, much less kvass, and for that matter I myself am ravenously hungry and yet remain unfed, though God knows I spend enough on food for this household to feed every able-bodied man from here to Novo Ruthenia."

"Such impatience," the housekeeper said placidly. "You are not even seated and you expect to already be done eating." Even as she spoke, Katia and Olga were dancing about the room, filling plates and glasses, and covering the table with as much food as it would bear.

Gulagsky sat down heavily and, forking up a sausage, two blini, and some sour cream, crammed them into his mouth. He chewed and swallowed and announced with evident satisfaction, "You see how prosperous we are here, eh? That is my doing. I have taken a town and made of it a kremlin." (Surplus saw Arkady roll his eyes.) "You have seen the thorn-hedge walls surrounding us. Twenty years ago, I mortgaged all I owned to buy fifteen wagonloads of cuttings. Now they are eighteen feet tall, and so dense that a shrew could not make its way through them. Nor could anything short of an army force its way past."

"Place not your faith in the works of man," Koschei rumbled without looking up, "but in God alone."

"Where was God when this town was dying? The countryside was emptying out when I planted the fortifications, and half our houses were abandoned. It was a true *gorodishko* then! I gathered in all who remained, created manufactories to give them jobs, and organized a militia to patrol the countryside. Everything you see here is my doing! I bought up every strain of poetry I could find at a time when it was out of fashion, and now every year hundreds of cases of it sell as far away as Suzdal and St. Petersburg. My cloneries have rare leathers—rhinoceros, giraffe, panther, and bison, to name but four—that can be obtained nowhere else on this continent."

"Your words are proud," Darger said, "and yet your tone is bitter."

"Yesterday I lost four warriors, and their kind cannot be replaced." Gulagsky shook his head shaggily. "I have held this town together with my bare hands. Now I wonder if it is enough. When I first started my patrols, twenty, thirty, sometimes even fifty good, strong men came with me at a time. And now…" For a moment Gulagsky was silent. "All the best men have died, torn apart by strange beasts or felled by remnant war viruses."

"Your son seemed eager to go out with you," Surplus said. "Perhaps he could recruit among his friends."

"My son!" Gulagsky snorted. The sullen young man himself did not look up from his platter. "He and his generation are as weak as water. They—"

Abruptly, Koschei broke out of his reverie and stood. "I am called to Moscow to set matters straight and put an end to its decadent ways," he announced. "These heathen atheists and their vat-bred abominations are going to that cesspool of sin. Therefore they must take me with them."

Everyone stared at the strannik in astonished silence for a beat. Then Darger dabbed at the corner of his mouth with a napkin and said, "The person to decide that would be Prince Achmed."

"Your ambassador will be dead within days."

"Yes, perhaps… but still… No, it is quite impossible, I am afraid. Even without the invaluable presence of a prince, we are a delegation, sir. Not a commercial caravan to which travelers might attach themselves."

The strannik's eyes were two dark coals. "That is your final answer?"

"It is."

He appealed to Gulagsky. "Will you not use your influence on your guests to alter their decision?"

Gulagsky spread his arms. "You see that their minds are set. What can I do?"

"Very well," the strannik said. "In that case, I have no choice but to inform you that last night your son spent an hour up in a tree, first watching and then romancing one of the young women under your protection."

"What?!" Gulagsky turned to his son with a terrible expression on his face.

"Further, later in the evening, he squeezed himself into the dumbwaiter in order to penetrate the girls' sleeping quarters. Had he not been caught and ejected by one of the beast-men, who can say what else he might have done?"

Gulagsky's face was contorted with rage. Arkady turned pale. "Father, listen to me! Your new associates…these horrible men…"

"Silence!"

"You have no idea what a monstrous thing they are about to do," the young man said desperately. "I overheard them—"

"I said silence!" The room was suddenly full of argument and admonition. Only the pilgrim stood silent, hands clasped at his waist, watching all that transpired with a strangely benign expression. But Gulagsky's voice rose above the clamor. "If you say but one more word—one!—I swear I will kill you with my own two hands."

The room fell silent. Then Gulagsky said, with heavy emphasis, "You have committed an unspeakable breach of hospitality."

Arkady opened his mouth to speak, but Darger, quick-thinking as ever, clapped a hand over it.

"Oh, you want to tell me your side of this story, do you? As if I didn't already know," Gulagsky said furiously. "Well, let me tell it to you instead: An inexperienced boy falls for a woman better than he will ever deserve. She's young and foolish and a virgin to boot. All of nature is on his side. But who's on hers? Not he! She is promised to another, greater and richer than he can ever hope to be. If he so much as touches her, I have been reliably told, she will burn. So if he wished the best for the young lady, he would keep his silence and leave her ignorant of his feelings for her. But he does not. So for all his passion, he doesn't really care for her, does he? Only about his own sentiments. And what is he sentimental about? Why, himself, of course."

The boy struggled to free himself from Darger's grip.

"Well, this shall not be. By God, I swear—"

"Sir, do not be hasty!" Surplus cried.

"If anybody so much as touches one of the Pearls while they are under my roof—even if it is only with the tip of one finger, I swear that with my own two hands I will—"

"Think!" Surplus urged him. "*Think* before you make any rash oaths, sir."

But now, unexpectedly, Koschei placed himself directly before Gulagsky, who angrily tried to shove him aside. Unheeding, the strannik seized his arms in a grip of iron and without visible effort lifted him bodily off the floor. Ignoring Gulagsky's astonishment, he said, "You were about to swear that you would kill your own son if he crosses your will. That is the same oath that Abraham swore—only you are not so holy a man as he. God does not so favor you."

He restored the man to the floor. "Now control yourself, and do not add blasphemy and filicide to the myriad sins which doubtless already blacken your soul."

Gulagsky took ten ragged breaths. Then, somewhat unevenly, he said. "You are right. You are right. To my shame, I was going to promise something rash. Yet it must be said: If anyone in this village so much as touches one of the Pearls, he will be exiled—"

"For at least a year," Surplus said, before his host could add "forever."

Gulagsky's face twisted, as if he had just swallowed something foul. But he managed to say, "For at least a year."

He sat back down at the table.

Surplus felt a tension in himself ease. It was not good to allow absolutes to enter into one's life. They had a habit of turning on one.

At that very instant, the door at the top of the stairs opened, and a Russian woman appeared in it. Gulagsky stood, chair toppling behind him, mouth open in astonishment. Then he recovered himself. "Lady Zoësophia. Forgive me. For a second, I thought you were…well, never mind."

"In turn, you will, I hope, forgive me for borrowing these clothes, which I found in a trunk in the attic, and which I presume belonged to your late wife." Zoësophia glanced down at her admittedly admirable figure. She wore a long and sturdy red skirt that brushed against the top of her oxblood boots, a russet-and-gold embroidered jacket over a white blouse, and kid gloves long enough that not a speck of wrist showed. An umber scarf was tied so artfully about her head that it took a second glance to realize that beneath it, a second, flesh-colored kerchief concealed her mouth and nose. "They fit me perfectly. She must have been a very beautiful lady."

From an ordinary woman, such words would have sounded conceited. But not from a Pearl.

"Yes," Gulagsky said, almost choking. "She was."

"I thank you for their use. I must go out now, and I did not wish to draw undue attention to myself by wearing outlandish clothing."

"Where, if I may ask, are you bound for, madam?" Darger politely queried.

"Monsieur de Plus Precieux and I are going to church."

So saying, Zoësophia swept down the last few stairs, took the astonished Surplus's arm, and led him away.

Though the town was small, there were enough people on the street—and they extremely curious about their exotic visitors—to discourage frank conversation. Children followed the couple, whooping. Adults openly gawked. So, although far more pertinent questions urged themselves upon him, Surplus merely said, "However did you manage to convince the Neanderthals to let you go out without a guard?"

"Oh! Whatever else they may be, the Neanderthals are still male—and it will be a sorry day when I cannot convince a man to let me have whatever I want from him. Also, with the prince indisposed, I am the embassy's highest-ranking member."

"Perhaps, then, you could arrange for our brawny friends to throw open the treasury-box. You and your Sisters in Delight have run up debts which—"

"Alas," Zoësophia said negligently, "my authority has limits. Prince

Achmed made very sure of that."

The church (or cathedral as such were called here) was a handsome log building surmounted by an Orthodox cross. The interior was all a dazzle to Surplus. Partly this was due to the richness of its decoration, the extravagant number of lit candles and the pervasive smell of beeswax that made the air heavy and sultry, the unearthly beauty of the choir's chanting, and the strangeness of a religious rite carried out entirely behind the iconostasis, so that it could not be seen by the faithful. But, chiefly, it was Zoësophia's presence that distracted him.

It was a weekday and most of the congregants were black-clad crones who, being blessed with younger women in the house to be worked like serfs, could indulge their piety. Several women to the very front were being held up by solicitous friends or relations, and from this Surplus surmised that they were the new widows, praying for the strength to get them through the coming memorial services. So intent were all on their prayers that Zoësophia and Surplus managed to slip in with only a hostile glare or two thrown quickly their way. Nevertheless, to Surplus's eyes, his companion stood out among them like a swan in a flock of grackles. Moreover, as they took places in the back of the church, rather than releasing his arm, she pressed herself more tightly against him, so that he could feel the warmth of her hip and one breast, and that, too, was distracting.

They had not been listening to the service long when, to Surplus's absolute amazement, Zoësophia backed into a niche at the rearmost of the church and pulled him after her, where they could not be seen by the congregation.

The niche was small, and there was not entirely enough room for two people to avoid intimate contact. Surplus was so intensely aware of Zoësophia's body as to be somewhat short of breath. She placed her kerchief-covered mouth by his ear and murmured, "I know that you are drawn to me. I can see it in your eyes. And in other places as well." Her gloved hand passed slowly down his body, stopping at the fly of his trousers. "Perhaps you have also noticed that I find myself powerfully drawn to you in return. But as you know"—her voice caught in a marvelous oral simulation of a blush—"our feelings for each other cannot be consummated. For reasons you well understand."

Surplus whispered back, "You surprise and delight me, O Flower of Byzantium. To think that one such as I…Well, I am quite overwhelmed." Which was not entirely true. Surplus understood perfectly the power his unusual form had over the imaginations of adventurous women. But he knew better than to say so. "Nevertheless, I must turn our conversation to less pleasant matters."

Finger by finger, Zoësophia's hand closed about Surplus's swollen member in a manner which, even through the interposing media of glove and trousers, was so exquisitely pleasurable as to have surely required many hours of practice. "Oh?"

"Yes. I must warn you that the ambassador has hatched a mad scheme to exterminate the Pearls before he dies." Quickly, he sketched out the details.

"Ah." Her hand tightened slightly. "I wondered if you were going to tell me."

Reproachfully, Surplus said, "Madam, I am a gentleman."

"You and I obviously have different understandings of what that word entails. But let that go. I have been reliably informed that you and your comrade have agreed to this plan." Her hand tightened further, to the point that the pleasure Surplus felt was evenly balanced with pain. The creations of the Caliph's geneticists, he recalled, were often inhumanly strong. Surely she wouldn't…? "Tell me exactly what your part in this is, Gospodin de Plus Precieux."

"We agreed," Surplus said, and with alarm felt Zoësophia's grip tighten yet more, "solely in order to keep Prince Achmed from issuing his command directly to the Neanderthals. Who, lacking the ability to disobey him, would have immediately turned his vile intentions into fact. We adopted the regrettable policy of untruth solely to prevent a grave crime against Beauty."

"You desire that my dear sisters and I live, then?" That vise-tight hand twisted ever so slightly.

Surplus gasped. "Yes!"

"I assure you that such is our most fervent wish as well. The question is—how is this glad end to be achieved?" Her grip was like steel. Surplus had no doubt whatsoever that if she found his answer displeasing, it would be the easiest thing in the world for her to rip his manhood entirely free of his body.

Speaking quickly, Surplus said, "Oh, that my friend and I had resolved entirely almost immediately after the foul words had left Prince Achmed's mouth. All that we lacked was a way to confer with you in private."

He explained.

With mingled relief and regret, he felt Zoësophia's hand release him.

After services, Surplus returned to the Gulagsky mansion. Zoësophia, he noted, went up the stairs with a lightness she had not brought down with her. He turned to Koschei. "You say you can bring Prince Achmed to consciousness again?"

"Yes. But in his weakened state it will surely be too much for his constitution to bear for long. You should not direct me to do so unless you are absolutely certain you wish to kill him."

"I? Kill the ambassador? What a remarkable thing to say."

"But an honest one. God has a purpose for all things. Alive and dying, the ambassador does nobody any good whatsoever. Dead, he will at a minimum serve as excellent fertilizer." The strannik raised a hand to forestall Surplus's rebuke. "Spare me your horror. He is a heathen and cannot be buried in consecrated ground. That being so, some use might as well be made of his carcass. In any event, his death is a consequence that I am prepared to accept. What is your decision?"

"We simply must speak to him," Surplus began. "So…"

"Call everyone together in an hour. Two hours will be too late." The strannik disappeared into the sickroom and closed the door behind himself.

"What an extraordinary fellow!" Surplus exclaimed. "I don't believe I've ever met a cleric even remotely like him."

Darger looked up from a crate of old books that, in obedience to the Pearls' directive, had been delivered to the house during Surplus's absence. "I'm C of E myself." He slipped an undistinguished volume into an inside pocket of his coat. "And, after getting a taste of the good pilgrim's catechism, damned glad of it."

So it was that, one hour later, the ground floor was thronged with people. Surplus and Koschei sat on chairs to either side of the ambassador's sickbed. Darger and the two Gulagskys stood by the door. Just beyond, all seven Pearls Beyond Price formed a worried group, encircled by a grim ring of Neanderthals. Only Zoësophia looked more affronted than afraid. Neighbors, servants, employees, and idlers took up all the free space and half the outside yard as well, where they peered in through windows and doorway, and craned their ears for word from within. By Byzantine law, no one could be kept away from so public an event as the reading of an ambassador's will.

"This is my most powerful medication, and the most wondrous in its effects." Koschei shook a pill the size of a sesame seed from a small vial. "Everything else I have done was merely to strengthen the ambassador so his body could briefly withstand its effects." He pried open the prince's mouth and placed it on his tongue.

For a long, still moment nothing happened. Then Prince Achmed's eyes fluttered open.

"Am I in Paradise?" he murmured. "It seems…I am not. And yet…I feel the holy presence of…Allah…within and all about me."

"I am very glad to hear that," Surplus said, "for it makes what I must say easier. Great Prince, I am afraid that you are dying."

"A week ago, that would have been…terrible news. But now I…am content."

"That being so, perhaps you would reconsider your decision regarding the—"

"No." Prince Achmed's eye burned with strange elation. "I will die having done my duty." He struggled to raise his head from the pillow but could not. "Have the eldest of the Sisters of Ecstasy produce a sheet of smart paper suitable for a proclamation."

One of the Neanderthals lumbered up the stairs and returned with an ebony box. Coiled about it was what looked at first to be a carving of a snake looping in and out of several holes and possessed of a second head where its tail should be. But when Zoësophia accepted the box, one of the heads turned to stare at her with cold, glittering eyes. It was a minor example of Byzantine quasilife, but one that Surplus knew to be deadly, for its bite had killed a would-be thief in the early days of their long journey.

Zoësophia tapped the head, so that it gaped wide, showing teeth like ivory needles. Then, turning to the wall for modesty's sake, she lifted her veil and let fall a single drop of saliva into the creature's mouth.

The quasisnake's coils loosened, it slid in and out of the holes, and the top of the box flew open. Zoësophia removed a sheet of cream-white paper and wordlessly handed it to Enkidu, who gave it to Darger, who passed it along to Surplus. Surplus had a lap-desk resting on his knees, from which he produced a goose-quill pen and a bottle of India ink. "You may begin," he said.

Slowly and haltingly, the prince dictated his last decree. The room grew deathly silent as its import became clear. Finally, he closed his eyes and said, "Read it back to me."

"Sir, there is yet time to rethink this rash course of action."

"Read it, I said!"

Surplus read: "*Part the first*. That upon my death, the Jewels of Byzantium, the Pearls Beyond Price, viz., Zoësophia, Olympias, Nymphodora, Eulogia, Euphrosyne, Russalka, and Aetheria, having been created solely for the pleasure and delight of the Duke of Muscovy, into whose loving care I am now unable to deliver them, are to be immediately and with the absolute minimum of pain necessary to achieve this end, put to death."

"Oh!" Nymphodora cried in a heartbreakingly small voice. "Who will save us?"

Several of the Russian men in the room reflexively surged forward. But Herakles bared his canines in a snarl and, seizing an iron poker from the nearby hearth, bent it double and flung it down on the floor before him. The men stopped in their tracks. One of them turned and shook his fist at the sickroom and those near to it. "What kind of monsters are you to go along with this?"

"We are all helpless in this situation," Darger said, "and can only play out the parts we were assigned." He nodded to Surplus. "Pray, continue."

"*Part the second*," Surplus read. "That immediately following the execution of the first part of this decree my good servant Aubrey Darger (I took a small liberty with the phrasing here, Exalted Prince, for your stated characterization of my friend was not suited to a legal document) be given all moneys remaining in the treasury box. The letters of credit, however, along with all other documents therein, are to be destroyed."

"Judas!" somebody shouted. The Pearls were weeping piteously.

Undaunted, Surplus continued. "*Part the third.* That upon completion of their duties, the Neanderthals, who are the property of the Caliph, by whose grace the State flourishes, are to immediately vacate Russia and return to Byzantium. Any of their number surviving the voyage are to report promptly to the Master of Brutes for reassignment. Signed, Achmed by grace of Allah prince of Byzantium, defender of the Faith, and scourge of infidels. Then the date."

He looked up. "This is a deed of blackest infamy."

"Never mind… that. Bring me the document so… I may… examine it."

Surplus did so.

"Yes, that… appears to be… in order."

With a sharp cry, Zoësophia pushed past the Neanderthals and flung herself on the ambassador's chest. "Noble prince, relent! Kill me if you must, but spare my sisters! They are innocent souls who have never given the least offense to anyone. It is not death they deserve, but life." Then she burst into tears.

"Get this harlot…off me," Achmed ordered.

Herakles and Enkidu respectfully took the sobbing Pearl by the arms and backed her out of the sickroom. The decree slipped to the floor behind her.

Surplus picked it up. "All it awaits is the touch of your hand."

Solemnly, Prince Achmed kissed thumb and forefinger and pinched the bottom of the decree between them, activating the document with his own DNA. Surplus, as witness, followed suit, pinching a colored rectangle immediately above the prince's gene-mark. The smart paper tasted Prince

Achmed's DNA, verifying his identity, and turned a shimmering orange, the impossible-to-counterfeit color of all official Byzantine documents.

The ambassador smiled beatifically. "My duty…is done." Then he grew extremely still.

Koschei leaned over the ambassador and placed his ear upon his chest. Then he straightened and, with his thumbs, closed Prince Achmed's eyelids. "He is in Hell now."

"Well," said Enkidu heavily. "I guess we got no choice here."

"Wait!" Darger cried. He lifted the orange paper from the ambassador's chest. "I insist that you read the decree first."

The Neanderthal glared at Darger. "Pettifogger." But he snatched up the paper and held it up to his eyes. His lips moved. At last he said, "Hey. This ain't what the ambassador told you to write down."

"No, it is not," Darger said. "Earlier today, at our direction, Zoësophia wrote out a deed of transfer on a sheet of smart paper. When she fell upon the ambassador's chest, she was hiding it under her vest. It was the easiest thing in the world, then, for her to substitute the one document for the other. Prince Achmed placed his thumb not on a death-warrant, as he intended, but on a decree appointing a new ambassador in his stead." He turned to Surplus and bowed. "Your Excellency."

There was a moment's startled silence, and then spontaneous applause from all present—including even the Neanderthals. Several of them, indeed, were grinning widely, the first time Surplus could ever recall seeing them do so. Meanwhile, those locals standing near the windows were shouting the news out into the yard, so that there was a second burst of laughter and cheers. Gulagsky grabbed Darger in a bear hug and absolute strangers pounded Surplus on the back and shook his paw warmly.

Then, when all was chaos and jubilation, a woman screamed.

Voices hushed. Heads turned. In the center of the room Aetheria was staring in horror at her hand. On her wrist were raw red welts: some the exact size and shape of fingers and one that was the perfect image of a pair of lips.

Into the horrified silence, Arkady stammered, "I…I only seized her hand and k-kissed the back of her wrist. I meant nothing bad by it. I was simply happy that she would live." He glared about him. "Anybody else would have done the same!"

"Oh, you fool," Surplus said.

It took some while to clear the house of all who did not belong there. By then, the Pearls were safely upstairs and the Neanderthals back on guard. Arkady had just been knocked to the floor for the second time by an angry blow from his father. There he lay, burning with anger and guilt and love-sickness.

Surplus helped him to his feet. "Now you understand why we tried so hard to keep the Pearls away from men. They burn at our touch. The Caliph's psychogeneticists implanted commands to that effect in order to preserve the young ladies' virginities."

"They cannot be unfaithful to their intended groom," Darger amplified. "Any male's touch other than his, however light, blisters their skin. A kiss would char their lips to cinder. As for intercourse…well, they would be dead in minutes."

Koschei, who had been silent and watchful through the entire affair, now spoke. "I have salves that will heal the young woman. Though some discoloration may remain."

"Give them to the Neanderthals, who will pass them along to Aetheria," Darger said. "You, being a man, cannot be allowed to touch her, of course, celibate though you presumably are."

Gulagsky sat down heavily in a green leather armchair and clutched his head in an agony of emotion. The others remained standing. At last he said, "Arkady Ivanovich, you are to be banished from your home for the period of one full year. Do you understand?"

"Yes." The young man stood stiff and straight.

"These fellows are going to Moscow. You will go with them."

"No," Darger said. "That simply cannot be allowed. The young man is still in love with Aetheria and her presence will be a constant temptation to him."

"You think I would *knowingly* put her life in peril?" Arkady asked, outraged.

"I think your coming with us would not be wise."

"It might not be wise," Gulagsky said, "but it is the only option I have. These are dangerous lands, and it will be months before the next wagon train of traders stops here. If I sent him out alone, it would be to his certain death." He bared his teeth furiously at his son. "Death! That is what you have been playing with, you blockhead! Oh, how could I have sired such an idiot?"

"As the new ambassador," Surplus said, "it is my duty to act in the best interest of my charges."

"One ambassador has already died in my house. If you do not do as I say, a second may well follow."

They stared at each other for a long time, until finally Surplus concluded that the man was adamant. "I see we have no choice," he said with a sigh.

"We will depart in the morning."

"And I," Koschei said, "will come with you, to look after the boy's moral education."

"Oh, for the love of God!" Surplus exclaimed involuntarily. But a dark look and a clenched fist on Gulagsky's part silenced any further exposition.

"Precisely." Koschei smiled piously. "For the love of God."

The caravans left at dawn. In stark contrast to their festive arrival, nobody turned out to see them off. Darger and Surplus rode horses, while Arkady and Koschei strode along on foot.

Surplus cantered back and glared down from his mare at the strannik. "This is all your doing, you rascal! You manipulated Arkady's exile in order to force us to take you to Moscow."

"Blame God, not me. He has work for me there. He made it possible for me to go. That is all."

"Pah!" Surplus spurred his horse forward again.

Not long after, the caravan trundled past the field where Prince Achmed's body had been flung. Crows covered it, fighting for bits of flesh. Surplus turned away from the sad spectacle. Riding beside him, Darger said, "Wasn't this the same field where the cyberwolf was supposed to be thrown?"

"I believe it is."

"Then where is it?"

Strangely enough, the corpse was nowhere to be seen.

"An animal might well have scavenged the carcass," Surplus suggested.

"But then there would be machine parts left behind—as there are not. No man would desire such a thing, nor would anybody bury it. Who, then, or what, could have taken it away? It makes no sense at all."

The town—whose name, Surplus abruptly realized, he never had learned—faded behind them, and that for them was the last of Gorodishko. Save for one small incident, barely noticed and almost immediately forgotten.

On a low hillock, far across the fields, a lone man stood in silhouette against the rising sun, watching them leave. Was it only Surplus's imagination that, just before he disappeared in the distance, the man fell to all fours and trotted away?

...4...

The parade rumbled down Tverskaya ulitsa, as splendid as thunder and infinitely more costly. Three weeks the company had spent camped in the ruins of Rublevka to the west of the city while merchants and messengers came and went, lines of credit were established with all the major banks in Muscovy, an appropriate building was found for the embassy, and an entrance was prepared which, under happier circumstances, would have satisfied even the late, notoriously hard-to-please Prince Achmed.

First came a marching orchestra, performing Ravel's *Shéhérazade*, followed by a brass band playing "The Great Gate of Kiev," from *Pictures at an Exhibition* by Mussorgsky, so that the tunes tumbled over one another, clashing and combining in a way that suggested an exotic and barbaric music evoking both Muscovy and Byzantium.

That was the theory, anyway.

In actual practice, the music shrieked and disharmonized, cat-wailing and whale-groaning like the collective denizens of the Caliph's House of Penitence and Forgiveness being taught to accept responsibility for whatever crimes they might eventually be accused of. The Muscovites loved it, however. It fit their conflicted ideas of Byzantium, which they despised as savage, pagan, and vulgar and yet whose heirs they considered themselves to be.

The parade included flightless griffins with gilded beaks and claws, spider-legged elephants, three-headed giraffes, and even a small sea serpent in a tank of cloudy water, all rented for the day from a local circus, whose tumblers, aerialists, and other performers had dug deep into their costume trunks to re-create themselves as Byzantine lords and courtiers. A team of African unicorns as white as bed sheets and bulkier than water buffalos pulled a float on which the Pearls Beyond Price stood, sat, or reclined, each according to her whim, wearing flowing silk chador in a

43

variety of bright pastels, so that collectively they formed a sherbet rainbow. As modesty dictated, only their flashing eyes were left uncovered, but if a vagrant breeze now and again pressed the silk so close to here a breast or there a thigh as to leave no doubt of the sweet desirability of their bodies…well, it was a passing thing no man could be entirely sure he had seen in the first place.

"I feel like Tamburlaine, riding in triumph through Persepolis." Surplus threw a handful of chocolate coins wrapped in gold and silver foil from the window of his carriage. He wore a dazzlingly white turban such as would have been the envy of any Commedia dell'arte sultan, decorated with a tremendous glass ruby. The crowds cheered lustily at the sight of him and (thinking the coins real) dove frantically for the largesse he scattered.

"It *is* fine, is it not?" Though Darger sat at his friend's side, he leaned back against the cushions, in the shadows, in order to remain unremarked from the street. "Even Arkady Ivanovich seems to be enjoying himself."

He gestured toward the street ahead where Koschei and his young protégé walked alongside the Neanderthals—who were, for the occasion, shirtless and snarling—ringing the float carrying the Pearls. Arkady smiled and waved broadly, while the older man thumped his staff on the paving stones, scowling his disapproval at the wickedness of the crowd.

Abruptly, the strannik seized Arkady by the nape of his jacket, bringing him to a sudden halt. He swung them both about ninety degrees and strode into the crowd, pulling the young man after him. It was an uncommonly deft maneuver. Had Darger blinked, he would have missed it.

"We appear to have lost our two charges."

"The ladies will most likely miss Arkady mooning about and singing love songs. The Neanderthals will surely be glad to see the last of him. And I…well, he was a likeable enough fellow. But as he spent most of his time huddled with Koschei, absorbing the pilgrim's doubtless fanatical theology, I had no opportunity to form any great attachment to him."

"You sum up the situation succinctly. But now I see that the crowds are as large as they are ever likely to be. So I too must leave."

"Do you have the book?"

Darger placed a hand inside his jacket. Then, with a roguish smile, he flung open the door and, brandishing the book high over his head, leaped free of the carriage. He plunged into the crowd and disappeared.

Behind him, he heard Surplus shout at the top of his lungs, "*Halt the carriage!*" A quick glance over his shoulder revealed Surplus leaning far out of the open carriage door, an anxious arm extended toward the distant fringes of the crowd. "Stop him! Stop that thief! A hundred solidii to whoever returns me that book!" Then, in apparent response to the puzzlement on the faces of those nearby, "Ten thousand gold rubles! To anybody who restores to me that book, ten thousand rubles—in gold!"

The crowd stirred and eddied. Men began to run where they thought the fugitive had gone. More joined them and, because not all were clear on who was being sought, fights broke out among them.

But Darger had not fled. Immediately upon entering the crowd, he had stopped and turned to face the procession. He then took a few jostling steps to the side and there remained, craning his neck, as if he were just another citizen anxious to see the spectacle. The book he slipped back in his jacket. Darger was blessed with a forgettable face, and it was his particular genius to be able to fade into the background wherever he was. Searchers ran past him and he turned to gawk but did not join in the pursuit.

Shortly thereafter, the carriage started forward again. Inside it Surplus sat, arms crossed, ostentatiously glowering and sullen. The procession continued down the street.

After a while, the crowds broke up and dwindled away.

Darger pulled a slouch hat over his head and joined the general dispersal. He walked randomly at first, choosing the shabbier streets over the better. Always he considered the bars, taverns, and unlicensed purveyors of base-ment-brewed beer. As he strode along, he casually drew a square of paper from his pocket, extracted two pills, and swallowed them. By the time he finally selected a low dive that looked particularly dreary and unattractive, his eyes had turned from gray to green and his hair was bright red.

He went inside.

Two or three broken-down rummies sat slouched in the gloom. A man who was no discernible improvement over them wiped a filthy rag over a filthier bar. Standing just within the doorway, Darger exclaimed, "Dear Lord, this must be the vilest and most squalid bar in all Moscow!"

The bartender looked up resentfully. "This here's a drinking establish-ment, bud. If you want the kinda bar where faggots sit around discussing philosophy and plotting revolution, you shoulda gone to the Bucket of Nails."

"Thank you, sir," Darger said. "Could you tell me where I might find that august establishment?"

Of all the places Koschei might have taken them, the most unexpected was this—a luxuriously appointed suite in the New Metropol, which even a provincial such as Arkady knew to be the single best hotel in Moscow. He watched in astonishment as liveried servants filled a porcelain bath-tub with buckets of hot water, lit candles in the sconces above it, added scented bath oils, and deposited great fluffy stacks of towels on a stand alongside it.

"I've sent for a barber and a tailor. You will need appropriate clothing if you are to move in the social circles your holy mission will require," Koschei said. "Later this evening, one will come who will initiate you into the next stage of your religious education. But for now, relax. Wash off the stains of travel."

"Surely you should have the tub first, holy pilgrim."

"Pah! If the soul is clean, the condition of the body means nothing. I am in a state of perfect grace, and therefore it wouldn't matter if I stank like a horse. Were I dying of leprosy, I would yet smell sweet to the nostrils of God. You, however, are weak of spirit, and so you must bathe. Do as I say. We have a great deal to accomplish, and I do not expect you will get much sleep tonight."

"Blessed father, you have not yet told me why we have come to Moscow."

"Later."

"And for that matter, however in the world are we paying for all this?"

"Later, I said! Will you force me to beat you? Go! Bathe!"

Lying in the warm water with soap bubbles billowing about him, Arkady felt as though he had fallen into a fairytale. He floated in a golden dazzle of comfort and luxury. Surely in the real world, pilgrims did not treat outcasts so? Koschei had spoken of a holy mission. Only in a dream would a spiritual journey begin in such surroundings. Yet he could hear the strannik stomping about the suite, unpacking their knapsacks and arranging the few modest possessions they had brought with them. He could hear the mutter of the good man's prayers. So, evidently, this was how they did things in Moscow.

He closed his eyes, smiling. This could not possibly last. But he would enjoy it while it did.

After the bath, room service brought in what seemed to be a hundred small white plates of zakuski—smoked fish, caviar, cured meats, salads, cheeses, pickles, and more. There were also pitchers of kvass and mors, and more bottles of vodka than Arkady had ever seen set out for two diners before. He attacked them all with a vengeance. Yet he could not come close to matching Koschei's appetite. Vast quantities of food and alcohol disappeared into the strannik's maw without his showing the least sign of satiety or intoxication. It was astonishing.

When they had eaten, the tailor came by to take Arkady's measurements. Koschei questioned him closely as to what the young people of the upper classes were currently wearing, and ordered a dozen suits of clothing, suitable for a variety of occasions, along with boots, gloves, hats, canes, and other incidentals such as a gentleman required.

Arkady tried to object that this was far too generous. But then the barber arrived, bringing with him a manicurist, and soon thereafter he found himself shaved and shorn and polished and powdered to within an inch of his life.

Koschei examined him critically afterward. "I thought of hiring a tutor to teach you comportment and manners. But it would be like putting a dress on a camel. Nobody could fail to see what lay underneath."

"Yes, holy one," Arkady said humbly.

"You are from the provinces—we cannot pretend otherwise. But for a season that touch of exoticism will be sufficient to make a parvenu such as you welcome in polite society. Act like yourself, and that will be enough."

"Enough to do what? I think the time has come for me to learn exactly what my mission entails. You have something planned for me, I can see that. But what it is, and how it could possibly require"—he swept out a hand to take in the room, the bath towels, the candles, and the table which had already been efficiently and deferentially cleared of the emptied plates—"all this…well, that is completely beyond my understanding."

"Yes. You are exactly right. The truth is completely beyond your comprehension. But I can tell you that—"

There was a knock on the door.

"Ah! Here she is! Answer that, will you?"

When Arkady opened the door, a woman rushed past him and flung herself into Koschei's arms. She kissed him deeply and passionately. Then she knelt down and kissed his feet. He raised her up with a smile. "Little daughter!"

"Holy father!" She ran her fingers through the strannik's beard. "It has been so long since I have known the joy of your body."

Arkady's eyes all but bulged. Outlander though he might be, he was not so ignorant as to not know that a woman dressed as this one was, with such makeup as she wore, and behaving as she did, could be only one thing. The combination of astonishment and alarm brought to the surface his inherent arrogance. "Why have you brought this… this… harlot here?"

The crimson woman looked at him with open amusement. The strannik clucked his tongue in disapproval—not of the whore, but of him!

"Is not God everywhere?" Koschei demanded. "One who cannot see God in a harlot is unlikely to find Him anywhere else." He turned back to the woman. "Take off your clothing, my child."

Arkady had thought he could not possibly be more amazed than he already was. He was wrong. For the whore immediately did as the pilgrim commanded, revealing a body that more than fulfilled the promise made by her low-cut gown. Clothed, she had been a cheap and obvious bit of goods. Naked, she was infinitely desirable.

Provided one did not look at her face.

As Arkady did not.

"You are confused," Koschei said. "This is good. Confusion is the first step on the road to salvation. It tells you that your understanding of the world is faulty. Your thoughts and the conventional religious teachings of your family and village say to you that this dear woman is filthy and disgusting. Yet your eyes tell you otherwise. As does your body. Which, then, should you trust? Your thoughts, which are of your own devising? Your education, which is the work of men? Or your body, which is the work of God?"

"I… hardly know what to think."

"That is because up until this moment, you have been living in a dream. You looked at things and saw only what you projected upon them. You have never known reality. You have never known love."

This last statement filled Arkady with indignation, for he knew it was not true. "I love Aetheria!"

"You are in love with your idea of her, and that is a very different thing from loving the woman herself. There is a real person there, assuredly, but you do not know her. Tell me her likes and dislikes. Relate an incident from her girlhood. Reveal to me her soul. You cannot! The songs you sing to her praise superficialities—her eyes, her hair, her voice—beyond which you have not sought. Your love has been a delusion, a mirage existing only within your mind. It is the work of the Devil. It must be rejected and put behind you."

"I, however, am real." The doxy cupped a breast and lifted it slightly. "Touch me, if you doubt it. Place your hand or any other part of your body wherever you like. I will not stop you."

There was no comparing this strumpet's merely carnal beauty with Aetheria's unearthly perfection. Still, she was a woman. And naked. And present. She moved so close to Arkady that he could smell the musky scent of her sex. "I—"

The strannik had turned away and was rummaging in his leather medicine pouch. "Your education to date has been all words. It is time they were put into action." He emerged with a vial and shook from it two black specks. "But before you do anything else, you must each take one of these pills."

The whore stuck out a small pink tongue to receive hers.

"What is it?" Arkady asked.

"You have seen it in action before. This was the drug that brought Prince Achmed back to life, though only briefly. It is called rasputin, after a holy man of the Preutopian era. It will give you tremendous strength and stamina. But more importantly, it will break down the barriers that divide the physical realm from the spiritual, your thoughts from the pneuma, your mind from the divine." The strannik brushed it onto Arkady's tongue with his thumb. "Everything I have told you to date is mere theory. This will show you the reality."

A strange metallic taste flooded Arkady's mouth, and he felt a few brief twinges of pain in his abdomen. Then nothing. He waited for what seemed an eternity. Still nothing. "I don't think this is—"

working, he was going to say. Then he felt all the air going out of his lungs in a great whoosh. Out and out it gushed, a river of breath, showing no sign it was ever going to stop. Then it did. He inhaled, and suddenly he was filled with energy. He felt strong enough to wrestle a Neanderthal and win. Wonderingly, he took the dinner table by one of its legs—it was carved of ebony or some similarly dense wood—and lifted it above his head. So it was true! The strength he felt was not an illusion.

Gently, even delicately, he returned the table to the floor.

Then a pinpoint of light came calmly into existence at the center of his brain. Unhurriedly, it expanded, filling him from the inside with an all-encompassing warmth. He felt a deep and profound love for everyone and everything in the universe, combined with a sense of wholeness and oneness with life itself. It was as if the sun had risen in the middle of the night to kindle his soul.

The whore favored Arkady with a knowing look. But her eyes shone with a spiritual light that was the twin of his own. "Take off your clothes and come to me," she said, "and I will teach you what it feels like to fuck God."

The parade ended up at the new Byzantine embassy, an ivory-and-yellow Preutopian mansion on Spasopeskovskaya ploschad'. There, Surplus grandly descended from his carriage and, after the Neanderthals had safely escorted the Pearls within, went to inspect the embassy grounds. Tents of shimmering spider silk sheltered tables heaped high with refreshments. String quartets played soothing music. By the gates, hired thugs squeezed into traditional Russian costumes checked the identity of the guests against long lists of invitees.

Surplus had been very careful to invite all the best people in Moscow to a space that would comfortably handle three-quarters of them. So he was not surprised to find the grounds overflowing with women in empathic gowns shifting toward the darker shades of the emotive spectrum and men whose suits reflexively bristled with short, sharp spines when others got too close. All of them complaining bitterly about how they were being treated. He strolled by the fenced yard, carefully just out of reach of their outstretched hands and voices, and did not glance their way.

"Sir! Sir!" The majordomo came running up, quite beside himself. "The caterers are serving vodka from samovars and say it is at your direction. Sir, you cannot serve vodka in samovars. It's simply not possible!"

"It is eminently possible. A samovar holds liquid. Vodka is liquid. I fail to see the problem."

"People will think you are completely ignorant of Russian culture!"

"So I am. I hope to learn much during my stay in your delightful country."

"But a samovar is for *tea!*"

"Ah. I understand." Surplus put an arm over the man's shoulders in the friendliest possible manner and said, "If anyone asks for tea, please direct the caterers to make it for them."

Then he went inside the mansion.

If the gardens outside held the best of Moscow society, the rooms within held the worst. These were the people who *really* mattered—the plutocrats and ministers and financiers who, subordinate only to the mighty duke himself, actually ran Muscovy. They were not crowded together as were those without. They gathered in the ballroom in threes and fours, chatting amiably with colleagues they saw every day, while waiters drifted by with drinks and hors d'oeuvres. Nor did Surplus's entry make much of a stir. The grandees looked up or did not, nodded or failed to do so, and occasionally smiled in the serene knowledge that they were so powerful and the event so inconsequential that not even the most judgmental would think they were trying to ingratiate themselves to a mere foreigner.

A waiter held out a tray holding triangles of toast and an enormous bowl of caviar. "Beluga, sir?"

Surplus leaned forward and sniffed. "Why does this smell fishy? It's clearly gone bad. Throw it in the alley."

"But Excellency…!"

"Just do it," Surplus said, pretending not to notice the shocked and amused reactions of those near enough to overhear.

At the far end of the ballroom, a newly built partition stretched from wall to wall. It was solid from the floor to waist-height and scrollwork filigree above, with a mesh screen behind it to ensure that nothing but air, sight, and sound could pass from one side to the other. Through it could be dimly glimpsed the alluring figures of the Pearls as they entered the space behind and peered about eagerly. There Surplus went.

"So these are the famous Russian women," Olympias said. "They look like cows."

"Compared to you and your sisters, O Daughter of Perfection, all women do. Though to be fair, those present are ministers and gene-barons and the like, along with their wives and husbands. No doubt many of them have daughters or lovers who are more fetching. In an uncultured and rough-hewn sort of way, of course."

"Don't," Olympias said, "condescend."

"Will the duke be here?" Russalka interjected.

"He has been invited, of course. Whether he will attend in person or not…" Surplus shrugged.

"I am avid to see him."

"I am avid to do a great deal more than that with him," Nymphodora added.

"We are all avid to begin our new lives," Zoësophia said. "In fact, if we are not presented to the duke soon, I promise you that things will get ugly."

"I shall of course make it my first priority to…"

"More ugly than you can imagine," Zoësophia emphasized.

Surplus returned to his guests. It suited his purposes to meet the Duke of Muscovy, and the sooner the better. The ultimatum the Pearls had just issued did not bother him in the least.

Until, that is, he mentioned his errand to the Mistress of Protocol, and she burst into a short, sharp bark of laughter. "The Duke of Muscovy—here? Whyever in the world would he come here?"

"He was expressly invited."

The State Mistress frowned like a bulldog. "The duke never responds to invitations. It would be absurd. They are all discarded, unread. That is, in fact, a significant part of my job."

"Then allow me to seize the opportunity, since you are here, of arranging a private audience. I am most eager to meet him."

"Meet the Duke of Muscovy! My dear Ambassador, nobody can meet that perfect man! Oh, such underlings as are ordered to his chambers to receive orders or offer accountings. And Chortenko, of course. But the duke does not socialize. Nor does he see foreigners of any ilk."

"But, you see, it is my duty to give him a present from his cousin the Caliph of Baghdad, which is of such surpassing—"

"Yes, yes. I'm sure it's wonderful. If you leave it with the Office of the Treasury, they'll give you a receipt, and it will be put on display in the

Cathedral of the Dormition for a month and then relegated to storage."

"This is not the sort of present that—"

"Exactly." The minister turned away.

Minutes later, Count Sputnikovitch-Kominsky shook his head sympathetically. "You're in something of a fix, young fellow. The duke is no ordinary ruler, you see. He thinks of nothing but the good of the state, and he engages in no activities other than its governance. He never leaves the Terem Palace in the Kremlin, nor does he ever see guests. Even I, who am of an old family and have served him well, have never laid eyes on the great man."

"All the more reason for him to accept this gift! Too much work will dull even the sharpest of minds. An hour spent with only one of the Pearls of Byzantium would be as good as a month's vacation. A weekend with all seven will make a new man of him."

"Give up this mad ambition. Chortenko himself could not arrange it."

So it went. General Magdalena Zvyozdny-Gorodoka shook her red curls with disdain. The Overseer of Military Orphan-Academies smiled pityingly and made little *tsk*-ing noises. "Ridiculous!" snapped the State Inspector of Genetic Anomalies. Nobody thought it even remotely possible to arrange a meeting with the duke.

Surplus was beginning to feel baffled and frustrated when a stocky man wearing dark blue-glass spectacles and trailed by two dwarf savants approached him and said, "You are a very clever fellow, Ambassador."

"How do you mean?"

"The business with the samovars."

"Eh?"

"For a feast celebrating the opening of an embassy, you knew that your guests would expect exotic foods and exotic drink. Obviously, you could not transport such quantities of provisions all the way across Asia Minor. So the food was prepared from local ingredients to Levantine recipes. That was simple enough. Even if the cooks got it wrong, who would know? But then there is the question of drink. You could not provide the fabulous story-wines of Byzantium, and the fantasies brought on by Georgian wines are so squalid they would make a cow weep. How then could you make mere vodka an experience worth telling one's grandchildren about? Obviously, by being so extremely foreign as not to understand—or, rather, to seem not to understand—the nature of a samovar. So you are, at a minimum, clever. Later, you displayed a similar ignorance by sending away the only bowl of caviar I saw in evidence here. It is evident to me that these festivities have strained your budget. Therefore you economized, by means which lead me to suspect that you are downright devious."

This struck too close to home for Surplus's liking. But he hid that fact. "And who, sir, might you be?"

"Sergei Nemovich Chortenko. At your service."

"I am Sir Blackthorpe Ravenscairn de Plus Precieux. An American originally, but now a proud citizen of Byzantium." They shook. "I have heard much about you, Gospodin Chortenko."

"I but serve a minor function at the Kremlin."

"You are too modest. I am told that you are the head of the duke's secret police, his chief wizard-catcher, and de facto inquisitor. Further, and not coincidentally, that you are one of the most powerful men in Muscovy and thus in all of Russia."

"A glorified errand boy is all I am, really." Chortenko shook open a handkerchief and took off his glasses, revealing the fact that he was bug-eyed. Surplus tried not to stare.

"I see you're fascinated by my eyes."

Indeed, Surplus was. The eyes were each hemispherical and, on examination, divided into thousands of glass-smooth facets. "Do they allow you a 360 degree field of vision? Or perhaps they help you make your way through the dark?"

"Perhaps. Chiefly, they ensure that I cannot be outstared," Chortenko said. "I never blink, you see." He wiped his eyes with the handkerchief and restored the glasses to his face. "Nor have I any need for tears. But you, obviously, have extra-species borrowings of your own."

"Not at all. Though it was modified in various ways in order that I might move easily in human society, my genome is entirely that of the noble dog."

"How curious. Why, exactly, was that done?"

"Such things are common in America." Surplus coughed politely, to signal a change of subject. "On an unrelated matter, I wonder if—"

"I know what you are going to ask. But I cannot help you to see the duke. Consider that matter closed. However, perhaps I may be of assistance in other ways. I can, for example, help you to recover your book."

"Book?" Surplus said blankly.

"The book that was stolen from you during the parade."

"You baffle me, sir. There was no theft, so far as I know, during the parade, save possibly those committed by the pickpockets who will inevitably work the crowd in such an event."

"No? Well, perhaps my informants were not up to their usual standards." Chortenko smiled blandly and turned away. His two dwarf savants followed in his wake.

Surplus returned to the ballroom to find several men gathered at the partition to converse with the not-at-all-unapproachable Pearls. At a nod, the Neanderthals—now properly clad in formal garb—emerged from obscurity to intimidate them away. Then he took their place, where he could speak through the scrollwork-and-mesh to Zoësophia.

"Well?" she asked.

"The Duke of Muscovy sent his extreme regrets that urgent affairs of state keep him away. He is, however, understandably eager to meet his new brides and has ordered that a suite of rooms with appropriately luxurious furnishings be prepared for you at the Terem Palace." Surplus paused to take in the gratifying responses of at least six of his audience.

But Aetheria pushed to the front of the group and pouted. "Where is Arkady? Why has he stopped visiting us?" Then, before Surplus could respond, "This is your doing, Ambassador de Plus Precieux. The only thing that would keep him away from an event allowing him to be this close to me would be if you locked him out."

At that moment, Surplus chanced to glance back toward Chortenko and his dwarf savants. They were all three staring fixedly at Surplus. "We have, I suspect, seen the last of Arkady Ivanovich," he said distractedly.

A short, sharp hiss of indrawn breath alerted Surplus to his mistake. Even through the screen he could see that Aetheria's face had turned a deathly white. Her eyes were black and unblinking. "If you do not produce my young man before this party is over, I will tell the Neanderthals that you tried to place your filthy paws on my body. And they will tear you apart. And it will serve you right."

Inventing quickly, Surplus said, "You misunderstand me, O Paragon of Beauty. I stipulated that we were unlikely to see the lad again because his body has already been handed over to the Ministry of Public Investigations."

"What!"

"It is a sad, sad story. He was torn between his love for you and his knowledge that you and he could never be together. So he threw himself from the Great Stone Bridge into the Moscow River. It is for the officials to decide whether the fall killed him or he drowned. But there is no doubt whatsoever that he committed suicide."

Eulogia and Euphrosyne, who were closest to Aetheria, hugged her tightly. Since they were identical twins in all respects save that the one's skin was richest black and the other's white as snow, this made for a distractingly lovely tableau.

"That is so romantic!" cried one.

"Oh, yes!" agreed the other.

Aetheria lifted her wrist up to her stricken face. Then she lowered her mouth to touch the place where Arkady's lips had left their permanent imprint. "Alas! My foolish little Arkady!" she cried. Then she fainted with such exquisite grace and beauty that Surplus's breath caught within him.

All the Pearls but one clustered about her fallen body, chafing her wrists, fanning air, and performing similar services. Zoësophia alone lingered by the screen. "He left a note, of course?" she murmured too softly for the others to hear.

"Naturally. I'll have it copied and sent to Aetheria in the morning."

"Don't bother, I'll take care of the note. You wouldn't know what to say." With a regal toss of her head, Zoësophia turned away. Feeling simultaneously chastised and yet rather better than he had a minute before, Surplus returned to his party.

In the morning, the Pearls would have a new set of complaints to accompany their unceasing demands to be immediately presented to the duke. But he would deal with that in the morning. For the moment, all was well.

Chortenko did not take a carriage after the reception. He found that walking focused his thoughts. His dwarf savants strode along to either side of him in unthinking lockstep. Pedestrians, seeing him coming, hastily stepped into the street to be out of his path.

At last he said to the marginally taller of the two, "Is it not odd, Max, that the Byzantine Empire should send an American as its ambassador…and an American who is, not to put too fine a point on it, a dog?"

"Byzantium was founded by Megarians and Argives under Byzas in 657 B.C.E. The Caliph is the fourteenth in the clone-line of Abdullah the Politically Infallible. The straight-line distance between Moscow and Byzantium is 1,098.901 miles, which converts to 1,644.192 versts. The ambassador's accent is that of the Demesne of Western Vermont, one of the smaller republics in Sub-Canadian North America. America was discovered by Damascene sailors during the rein of Abdul-Rahman III. Sailors are sexually promiscuous. Genetic anomalies are ambiguously discouraged by the political elite of Byzantium, though the civil code contains no provisions against it. No individual with a genome less than 97% human has ever achieved full citizenship in the Caliphate."

"Hum. Interesting. What on earth could the ambassador be hiding?"

With absolute and unquestioning seriousness, the second savant said, "Anything."

"Yes, Igorek, and yet it seemed to me that he also wanted us to know that he was doing so. The Honorable Sir Blackthorpe Ravenscairn de Plus Precieux is playing rather a deep game with us." He clasped his hands behind his back and scowled down at the ground passing under his feet. His savants were serenely silent. Eventually he said, "We know what men fear. But what about dogs?"

The savants opened their mouths but were gestured to silence.

"Tell me, Max. What breed do you believe our good friend the ambassador is derived from?"

"Two characteristics distinguish the dog from other canids: its worldwide distribution in close association with humans, and the enormous amount of subspecies variability. Dogs do not have wisdom teeth. Wisdom is a cultural artifact. Breed is a cultural artifact. The ambassador is either a mongrel or a genetic chimera. Baboons have been observed to steal puppies from wild dogs and raise them to guard the pack. The chimera is a fabulous beast, described by Homer as 'a thing of immortal make, not human, lion-fronted and snake behind, a goat in the middle.' The ambassador's source genome appears to be derived chiefly from the American foxhound."

"Is it indeed?"

It was not a long walk to Chortenko's house. When he got there he rang for the aide on duty. "Have Igor and Maxim fed and cleaned, then set them to reading today's reports. I also require that you have the kennels in the basement expanded, and buy dogs for them—eight should suffice. American foxhounds, if possible, though anything reasonably close will do. Let us discover what gives them pain, and what they fear. Just in case we find we have to put the ambassador to the question."

...5...

Moscow was a city of hidden passages and surprising depths. There were pedestrian walkways under all the larger streets, lined with small shops and lit by bioluminescent lichens growing on the undersides of their roofs. Basements opened into underground arcades where illegal businesses were run out of undocumented storage vaults carved from the bedrock when the city was young. Military installations from bygone eras and bunkers built to protect ancient tyrants from their enemies both abroad and at home were embedded deep within a three-dimensional tangle of transit and utility tunnels, some still functional and others containing the ruins of the electrical infrastructure that had been hastily ripped asunder after the revolt of mankind's electronic slaves. Long corridors connected buildings that no longer existed.

"Vodka, miss?"

"Why the hell else would I be in this shit-hole?"

No man knew all of the underground city's ways. But Anya Pepsicolova knew as many of them as anybody. To its denizens she was the single best guide to its mysteries that money could hire, a young woman of aristocratic birth who had taken to slumming in the criminal underworld and who, because she had no known protector, they could routinely cheat and shortchange. To the secret police, she was a ruthless and useful undercover agent, though one they felt absolutely no loyalty to. To Sergei Chortenko, she was a naïve and ingenious girl who had snooped into matters that did not concern her and who had subsequently been broken to his will. To the monsters who fancied themselves the *real* rulers of the City Below, she was a convenient means of keeping an eye on the City Above while their plans ripened and fermented and the glorious day grew nearer and nearer when everyone in Moscow—herself most emphatically included—died.

It was hard sometimes for her to keep all of her ostensible masters straight—much less decide which of them she hated the most. The only real pleasure she got out of life anymore was when she was hired by some-body powerless enough that she dared to feed him, alive and screaming, to one of her oppressors.

Pepsicolova sat hunched over a plate of bread she'd chopped into small pieces, chain-smoking cigarettes and drinking slowly but steadily, maintaining a small, warm buzz in the back of her skull. After each shot, she splayed a hand over the bread. Then she closed her eyes, flicked Saint Cyrila out of her wrist sheath, and stabbed between her fingers for a bit of bread to clear her palate. It was her way of judging whether she was still sober. She wanted to have a clear head when the foreign adventurer named Aubrey Darger finally put in an appearance.

For the past two days she had observed him. Today they would speak.

At last there came a clatter of feet down the stairs from the street and her prey threw open the door. For the merest instant cool autumn air blew into the Bucket of Nails. Then the door slammed shut, once again restoring the stench of cigarettes and stale beer.

"English!" cried one of the negligible young men—of no interest even to Chortenko's people—who came here regularly to argue political theory and leave behind small piles of pamphlets. "It's the Englishman!" shouted another. A young woman who was still half a student but already more than half a whore twisted in her stool and blew him a kiss.

The foreigner could be charming when he wanted to be—that had been the first thing Pepsicolova had written in her report.

"Vodka!" Darger cried, seizing a chair and throwing his cap onto a table. "If you can call it that." A bottle, a glass, and a plate of bread were provided. He downed a shot and pinched up some bread. Then he leaned over to fill the glasses at the nearest table. "What subversive nonsense are we discussing today, eh?"

The dilettantes laughed and raised their glasses in salute.

Darger gave the impression of great generosity, but if one kept careful track of what he actually spent, it came to very little, perhaps half a bottle of vodka over the course of a long evening. That was the second thing Pepsicolova had written in her report.

Pepsicolova studied Darger through narrowed eyes. He was unlike anyone she had ever met. He was a well-made fellow, if one considered only his body. But his face…well, if you looked away for an instant and he happened to shift position, you would be hard-put to find him again. It was not that he was homely, not exactly, but rather that his features were so perfectly average that they refused to stay in your memory. When he was talking, his face lit up with animation. But as soon as his mouth stopped moving, he faded back into the wallpaper.

Nondescript. That was the word for him.

She stood and went to his table.

"You are looking for something," she told him.

"As are we all." Darger's smile was as good as a wink, an implicit invitation to join him in a private conspiracy of two. "In my youth, I worked for a time as a fortune teller. 'You seek to better yourself,' I would say. 'You have unsuspected depths…You've suffered great loss and known terrible pain… Those around you fail to appreciate your sensitive nature.' I said the same words to everyone, and they all ate it up with a spoon. Indeed, my patter was so convincing that the rumor went out that I was consorting with demons and I had to flee from a lynch mob under cover of night."

He kicked out the chair across from him. "Sit down and tell me about yourself. I can see that you are a remarkable person who deserves far better than the shoddy treatment you have received so far in your life."

The man was laughing at her! Pepsicolova silently promised herself that he would pay for that. "A guide," she said. "I was told you were looking for someone wise in the ways of the dark."

He studied her thoughtfully.

Pepsicolova could easily imagine what he saw. A woman of marriageable age, rather on the slender side, with her dark hair chopped short, dressed in workingman's clothing: slouch hat, a loose jacket over a plain vest and shirt, and baggy trousers. Her boots were solid enough to snap a rat's spine with a single stomp. She knew this from experience. Darger would not see Saint Cyrila and Saint Methodia—one slim blade for infighting and the other for throwing—which she kept up her sleeves. But the girls had a brother, Big Ivan, on her belt, which like most males was not so much functional as it was showy and intimidating.

"Your price?" Darger asked.

She told him.

"You're hired," he said. "For half your stated fee, of course—I'm not a fool. You may begin by familiarizing me with the general area where I wish to concentrate my search."

"And that is?"

He gestured vaguely. "Oh, east, I think. Beneath the Old City."

"At the foot of the Kremlin, you mean. I know what you're after."

"Do you?"

"Don't think you're the first who's ever hired me to help him find the tomb of the lost tsar."

"Refresh my memory."

Not bothering to keep the annoyance out of her voice, Pepsicolova said, "During the fall of Utopia, a great many things were dismantled or hidden away to protect them from…certain entities. Among them was the tomb of Tsar Lenin, which once stood in Red Square but now lies buried no one knows where. Like Peter the Great or Ivan the Terrible, his memory is still a potent one for many Russians. Were his body to be found, it would doubtless be put to use by your political dissident friends. Also, there are the usual rumors about associated treasure which are complete nonsense but I am sure you believe in anyway. So don't think you're fooling anybody."

"Yes! Absolutely! You've seen right through me." Darger smiled brightly. "You are an extraordinarily insightful woman, and I see I can hide nothing from you. Can we start right away?"

"If you wish. We'll go out through the back."

They passed through the kitchen, and Darger held the door for her. As Pepsicolova passed through, he placed his hand on her backside in an infuriatingly condescending manner. A thrill of dark pleasure ran up her spine.

She was going to *enjoy* making this one suffer.

The first time that the Baronessa Lukoil-Gazproma spent the night with Arkady, she came alone. The second time, she brought along her best friend Irina to help blunt his appetites. Nevertheless, when the pearly light of dawn suffused itself across the city and seeped through the windows of his apartment, the two ladies sprawled loose-limbed and exhausted upon the raft of his great bed, while Arkady was entirely certain that he could continue for hours to come.

Seeing their exhaustion, however, Arkady gently kissed both the dear women on their foreheads and, throwing on his embroidered silk dressing gown, went to the window to watch the birth of a new day. The smokes and fogs of Moscow had been transformed by the alchemy of dawn into a diffuse and holy haze that briefly made this thronged and wicked place appear to be a sinless city upon the hill, a second Jerusalem, a fit dwelling-place for the living Spirit.

He stood motionless, reveling in the presence of God.

After a time, Baronessa Avdotya stirred faintly and said, "That was… even better than the first time. I would not have thought it possible."

Beside her Irina murmured, "I am never going to let a man touch me again. It would spoil the memory of this night."

There were no words Arkady could have more greatly relished hearing. They stroked his vanity so emphatically that he had to fight down the urge to fling himself back onto the bed and show both ladies how much more he had yet to give.

"Why have you left us?" the baronessa mock-complained. He could hear her loving smile in her voice. "What are you looking at so intently?"

"I am watching the sun come up," he said simply. "It struggles to rise above the horizon, and in doing so it makes the horizon seem to shift and move, like a sleeper's eyelid when he strives to awaken. Yet though the enterprise looks difficult, it is inevitable; not all the armies in the world could delay it for the slightest fraction of a second."

"You make it sound so profound."

"It is! It is!" Arkady cried with all the certainty of a recent convert. "It seems to me that this is exactly like the merciful God trying to force His way into our night-bound, sinful lives —it seems so difficult, impossible even, and yet His will is indomitable and cannot be stopped. Darkness flees from Him. His light arises from within like the sun, and the soul is filled with purity, certainty, and serenity."

"Oh, Arkady," Irina sighed. "You are so very, very spiritual. But God does not enter into the lives of ordinary people in such a manner. Only for saints and people in books does He behave that way."

Now Arkady flung away the robe and returned to the bed. He swept both women into his arms and addressed them by their pet names. "Ah, my beautiful Dunyasha! Sweet Irinushka! Do not despair, for God has found a way to break through the membrane separating Him from the mundane world."

"Away, insatiable beast!" The baronessa pushed herself out of Arkady's arms and then, when he did not move to grab her back, snuggled into them again. Irina rolled over weakly and touched her lips in a little pouting kiss to Arkady's chest, though without any strength.

Now came the most delicate and important part of Arkady's mission. "I was not always so vigorous, you know, nor so sure of God's abiding love. Not long ago I was weak and riddled with doubt." He paused, as if debating within himself whether to share with them a great secret. "My darlings! Do you wish to be as strong as I? To have my sexual stamina? That is nothing. That is the simplest thing imaginable. I can show you how it is done. But more importantly, you will feel the presence of the indwelling God as intimately as you have felt my caresses."

"It sounds delightful," Baronessa Avdotya murmured, "though improbable."

"Invite me to your estate next weekend, when the baron is away, and I will bring what is requisite. We shall all three of us be made closer than lovers and stronger than gods."

"I will come," Irina promised. "But I must bring another friend with me—perhaps two—so that I can get some rest between your storms of lovemaking."

"We'd best make it five," the baronessa said.

It was that fleeting moment of golden perfection that comes in late September, which the Russians called "grandmother's summer." The parks and boulevards of Moscow drew lovers and idlers out from their houses and businesses. There were people boating on the river's silvery waters. The view from the wooded heights of the Secret Garden was as picturesque as a hand-colored woodcut.

Simply being in the Kremlin, Surplus felt lifted above the day-to-day concerns of the groundlings in the city beneath him. It explained everything about those who governed from this high place: He felt himself not only physically but morally superior, occupying a higher, more spiritually elevated space, ethereal where the Muscovites were flesh-bound and sweaty, pure where they reeked of sausage and kvass. He shook his head in amusement at the whimsicality of these thoughts, but found he could not dismiss them. "Those poor fellows!" he thought pityingly, meaning everybody who had the misfortune to be ruled from this extraordinary spot.

It was also, he had to admit, good to get away from the Pearls for a change. Beauteous and charming as they might be, the Pearls were also— there was no denying it—intense. Indeed, they were growing more intense with each passing day on which they were not taken, with enormous pomp and ceremony, to the Terem Palace to stand at last, blushing and shy, before their new bridegroom. After which, he presumed, these seven virgins with their excess of book learning and lack of any prior outlets for their physical desires, would teach the duke precisely how terrifying such young ladies could be.

So it was with a bit of an edge in his voice that Surplus turned to the rotund and pompous bureaucrat—the eighteenth most powerful man in Moscow, the gentleman had boasted—with whom he slowly strolled among the ash trees of the Secret Garden and said, "We have been in Moscow over a month and still you cannot make this simplest of things happen?"

"I have given it my honest best. But what is there to be done? A meeting with the Duke of Muscovy is not something that happens every day."

"All I wish to do," Surplus said, "is to give the man a present of seven uniquely beautiful concubines, all of them graceful, intelligent, and desperately eager to please. Nor are they merely decorative and companionable. They can also cook, tat lace, arrange flowers, cheat at cards, and play the pianoforte. Not only are they pleasant to the eye and ear and—presumably—nose and hand and tongue, but they have been thoroughly educated in literature, psychology, and political philosophy. As advisors, they will be unfailingly frank yet subtle as only a Byzantine can be. Further, they are trained in all the social graces and the erotic arts as well. Never was such a gift more churlishly refused!"

"The duke is a great man, with many demands on his time."

"I warn you that when he finally experiences the thousand delights of the Pearls of Byzantium, he will not reward you for having kept them from him so long."

"You have your duty and I have mine. Good-bye." Wrapping his dignity about himself like a greatcoat, the bureaucrat, whom Surplus now thought of as the single most useless man in Moscow, departed.

Dispirited, Surplus sank down on a park bench.

The Secret Garden's portentous name was more suggestive than it perhaps merited, for it lay above and was named for the Secret Tower, one of the Kremlin's two dozen towers, most of which antedated the Utopian era. As for why the tower was so named, there were many explanations. One was that it was the terminus of a secret tunnel into the city. Another said that it contained a secret well. The most plausible was that it was named after a long-demolished Cathedral of the Secret that once stood nearby. But which was the truth no man could say for there were no facts in Russia—only conflicting conspiracy theories.

Surplus came out of his reverie to discover, sitting on the bench beside him, a stocky and unprepossessing man in blue glass goggles.

"You seem unhappy, Ambassador," Chortenko said. "May I ask why?"

His mood being foul, and seeing no reason to pretend otherwise, Surplus said, "Surely you, who are reputed to know everything else that goes on in this city, must be aware of what I have made no effort whatsoever to hide."

"Yes, yes, these 'Pearls' of yours, of course. I was only making small talk. But you, I see, are far too direct for that. So I shall be blunt as well. It is impossible for you to see the Duke of Muscovy. No foreigner has ever been allowed into his presence. But if you will answer a few questions openly and honestly for me, I will arrange the impossible for you. And then…well, you will have as much of the great man's attention as he deigns to give you."

There was something about the quiet amusement with which the man spoke that made the small hairs on the back of Surplus's neck bristle with sudden fear. But he said only, "What do you wish to know?"

"This book that was stolen from you—for there *was* a book and it *was* stolen—exactly what is it?"

"I cannot tell you specifically, for that is information which the Caliph's political surgeons have locked my brain against divulging." Surplus froze every muscle in his face and stared blankly into the distance. Then, with a sudden, spasmodic toss of his head, he said, "However, I am at liberty to say that it was intended as a present for the duke."

"Then we are allies in this matter. Tell me, is this book very valuable?"

"Far more so than the Pearls of Byzantium. Indeed, it was the chief gift, and they only an afterthought."

Chortenko pursed his lips and then tapped them thoughtfully with one stubby forefinger. "Perhaps my people can aid in its recovery by finding the man who stole it from you. He is a foreigner, after all, and hence extremely noticeable."

"His name is Aubrey Darger, and he was my secretary. But I must tell you that the book itself is useless without…" Surplus's face twitched and contorted as if he were struggling to find a phrasing allowed by the thought-surgery. "Without certain information that he alone possesses."

"Curious. But I imagine that information would come out easily enough under torture."

"If only that were so! I would wield the whip myself, after what that dastard has done. But for much the same reason that I cannot be more open with you about…certain aspects of the matter…it would be a pointless endeavor." Surplus sighed. "I wish I could be of more help. I don't imagine the little I've told you suffices to warrant a meeting with the duke."

"Not at all, not at all." Chortenko consulted a small datebook and then made a notation. "Come to my house a week from Tuesday, and I'll take you to him."

Darger followed his guide into the undercity.

Anya Pepsicolova was, of course, an agent of the secret police. But Darger did not hold that against her. Indeed, that was the entire point of this charade—to get the attention of the powers who actually ran Muscovy and, ultimately, convince them that he had something they desired.

Something they would be willing to pay dearly for.

Rulers were notoriously stingy with those who did them favors, of course. So in order to receive an appropriate reward, a silent partner would be required. Somebody highly placed in the administration. It was Surplus's job to find that individual, just as it was his to ostentatiously display the bait.

The Bucket of Nails' kitchen opened on a long corridor. Through some of the doors lining that corridor could be glimpsed butchers, dishwashers, mushroom cultivators, gene splicers, and the like. These were the lowest levels of the working class, people who were grimly holding on to the very edge of subsistence, terrified lest they lose their grips and fall into the abyss of joblessness and penury.

They rattled down a metal staircase which seemed ready to collapse from age into a lower level where the lichens and bioluminescent fungi dwindled almost to nothing. Where two corridors intersected, a legless army veteran with a patch of tentacles growing out of one cheek sold oil lanterns from a blanket. Pepsicolova threw down a few rubles, and the man lit two lanterns with a sputtering sulfur match. Their flames leapt high and then sank down as he trimmed the wicks. Pepsicolova handed one to Darger.

The metal parts of the lantern seemed flimsy and its thin panes of glass ready to break at the tap of a fingernail. "Aren't these a fire hazard?" Darger asked.

"If Moscow burns, it burns," Pepsicolova said with a fatalistic shrug.

She led him down a second steep and endlessly long metal stairway to a vast and shadowy marble-walled station room. There, long concrete piers lined an underground river whose waters were as black as the Styx. "This is the Neglinnaya River," Pepsicolova said with a touch of melancholy. "The poor thing has been trapped underground since forever." A handful of gondoliers ditched their cigarettes into the water at their approach and waved lanterns urging the newcomers toward their crafts. But Pepsicolova ignored them. To one end of the pier was a small skiff. She climbed in, and Darger after her.

An odd incident happened as they were preparing to cast off. A wraith-thin and albino-white individual emerged from the gloom and held out three packs of cigarettes, which Pepsicolova accepted wordlessly. The creature's face was expressionless, his movements listless. He turned away and faded again into darkness.

"Who was that?" Darger asked.

With an irritated gesture, Pepsicolova lit up a cigarette. "Somebody. A messenger. Nobody anybody cares about."

"You'd be healthier if you didn't smoke so much."

"Tell me something I don't already know."

Pepsicolova stood and poled. Darger lounged back, watching her by the light of his lantern. When she leaned into the pole, he could not help noticing that she had quite a nice little bottom. All those months in the company of exquisite and untouchable women had made him acutely appreciative of the charms of their imperfect but (potentially) touchable sisters.

He had patted her on the fanny earlier chiefly in order to establish himself as the shallow and insignificant sort of man he was pretending to be. And she had arched her back! She had all but purred! Darger flattered himself that women rather liked him, but this Anya Pepsicolova had responded in such an extraordinary manner as to suggest deeper feelings on her part toward him.

Darger looked forward to getting to know the dear thing much better. For the moment, however, it was best to keep things simmering away on the back burner. There would be time for romance soon enough.

He just hoped that it did not break her heart when he inevitably had to move on and leave her in the lurch.

Dark waters lapped against the boat. Pepsicolova poled them deeper into mystery.

It was a Tuesday, so of course there was yet another tea party. Up and down the room, twin table-halves were set against either side of the dividing screen. Knots of men (never women, who understandably found the implicit comparison with the Pearls painful) clustered about the tables, vying for the attention of the beauties across from them, while serviles with madly glittering eyes watched for the least sign that a teacup needed filling. Occasionally, a gentleman succeeded in drawing a Pearl away from his competition, and the two stood apart, talking quietly through the screen.

Because they were indoors and because it was the custom here in Russia, the women did not wear veils. This made the Pearls feel daring, which lent a certain sauciness to even their least consequential remarks.

Zoësophia wafted from table to table, now drawing Russalka away from a young swain's flattery that she was beginning to take too seriously, now subtly switching a retired general's attention from Eulogia to Euphrosyne, so that each could later upbraid him for his inconstancy. Where the conversation was too heated, she damped it down, before a Neanderthal could descend upon the offender. Where it was listless, she enlivened it with an easily misinterpreted sisterly kiss upon Nymphodora's dewy lips. By the time her circuit was done and Olympias rose to take over, the energy in the room had significantly intensified.

"Your baron glowers away anybody who tries to sit at your table," Olympias said behind her hand.

"I know. It is terribly boorish of him."

"But also very indicative of the depth of his feelings. As is the way your young artist—the one with the unfortunate mustache—refuses to be glowered away."

"They are both overwrought. I fear that inevitably one of them will kill the other."

Olympias assumed an expression of bored indifference. "There will always be more artists; they are interchangeable. Conversely, by all accounts, if the Butcher of Smolensk were the one to fall, it would be universally regarded as a act of high-minded civic spiritedness on your part."

"You are a wicked, sinful girl," Zoësophia said before drifting back to her table, "and when someday the vagaries of politics free us from the duke's harem, you're going to make some unfortunate man extremely happy."

"Men," Olympias called loftily after her. "Many, many, many men."

If truth be told, Zoësophia found these events tedious. Nevertheless, the Pearls were all in ardent competition to be the next after Aetheria to kill a man—not by suicide, it was agreed, for that had been done, but this time by provoking a duel—and it would be uncongenial of her not to give it her best effort. So she returned to the table where Baron Lukoil-Gazprom and the artist who, quite frankly, she found so boring she couldn't bring herself to remember his name, impatiently awaited her return. "Nikodim, my sweet," she said to the baron, and to the poet: "My little rabbit."

"At last, dear angel, you return!" The artist was lean as a whippet and twice as high-strung. "A thousand times have I died in your absence."

"It was worse for me," the baron said dryly. "He at least wasn't sharing a table with a twit." He was a handsome man and rich as well, though in such company that went without saying. Also politically powerful, which for Zoësophia was always a plus. But the best thing about him was that he thought himself clever, and such fellows were invariably the most delightfully easy to manipulate. He leaned closer to the screen and in a low, flirtatious voice said, "Tell me, *ma petite minette*… what is the shortest path to your bedroom?"

"Through the wedding chapel," snapped the artist, who was himself unwed.

Zoësophia allowed herself a hastily stifled snort of laughter.

The baron suppressed a wince. "Sweet lady, it is a dreary journey this… stripling urges upon you. I have made it myself and can recommend neither the experience nor the prospect at the end."

"It is at least an honorable estate," the artist said.

"You forget that these ladies are all promised to the Duke of Muscovy."

"So what you are saying is that in order for you to betray your wife, you require that Zoësophia cuckold the duke?"

It happened as fast as that—too fast for Zoësophia to prevent, even if the rules of the Pearls' little game had allowed that. The baron sucked in his breath. Then he stood, jarring the table as he did, so that the spoons and teacups rattled.

"That is an insult I will not endure," he exclaimed loudly. "Sir, I give you your choice of weapons."

Somehow the artist was on his feet as well. He was such a negligible fellow that Zoësophia had not seen him rise. "Then I choose paint and canvas," he said. "We shall each paint a satirical portrait of the other in oils." In his anger, he looked like a terrier defying a bull. Of course, that mustache did not help. "The winner to be selected by vote of all those present—"

"Bah! Paint is no weapon. A duel is not a duel unless there is the chance of grievous injury."

"Please. Allow me to finish. The winning portrait will be placed on public display for a month at the expense of the loser."

The baron turned white. Then he sat down. "That is no fit challenge for a gentleman," he grumbled, "and I refuse to accept it."

During the exchange, all the room had fallen silent. Now a light smattering of applause arose from those present. The artist colored with pleasure.

"That was wittily done, my little carrot," Zoësophia said, "and so you must have a reward. You there!" She snapped her fingers at the servile waiting on the table across from her. "Observe me carefully. Then assume my stance."

The servile stared at her with hard, reptilian eyes. Then, with an ease possible only to one who had no true sense of self, she took on Zoësophia's mien and posture.

"Now do precisely as I do."

Zoësophia delicately raised a hand, and the servile moved as if her shadow. Her fingers brushed the artist's cheek. She stepped forward, into his arms. Her chin tilted upward and her lips met his. Zoësophia's tongue briefly, lightly probed the air.

Separated by several feet of space, she and the artist kissed.

A long moment later, Zoësophia stepped back, gracefully extricating her proxy from the artist's embrace. A gesture of dismissal, and the servile resumed her former stance.

The baron watched it all with mingled wonder, lust, anger, and humiliation. Then he turned his back on them all and stormed out of the embassy's ballroom. Zoësophia did not doubt for a second that at next Tuesday's tea party she would be short one suitor or the other.

So, really, it turned out to be quite an amusing little gathering after all.

Chortenko climbed the stairs from his basement with a calm and easy heart. Waiting for him on the ground floor was a servile with a hot towel, which he used to clean any spatters of blood that might be on his face and hands. Then he went into the library and sat down to discover Pepsicolova's latest report waiting for him on a side table. He read it through with care. It fit in interestingly with his observations of the ambassador's behavior.

When he was done, he touched a nearby bell.

His butler materialized at a respectful distance. "Brandy, sir?"

"Just a small glass."

"Very good, sir."

Chortenko swirled the brandy in the glass, staring down at its fluid motion, enjoying its aroma. Sir de Plus Precieux was assuredly intent upon deceiving him. Which probably meant that ultimately the ambassador would have to be rigorously interrogated. But before Chortenko took such an irreversible step, he would need the duke's assurance that it was the right thing to do.

The Duke of Muscovy, after all, was the ultimate arbiter in such matters. It would not do to act contrary to his judgment.

He thought back to his last conversation with the ambassador. "I would wield the whip myself," he had said. Chortenko could not help being amused. The fellow had so little idea of what modern torture—applied by knowledgeable professionals—entailed. But he would learn. He would learn.

Chortenko took the merest sip of brandy and rang his butler again. When the man appeared in the doorway, he said, "Two of the dogs have died. Please have their corpses removed and buried somewhere immediately."

"As you will, sir."

Chortenko leaned back in his chair with a satisfied little smile. He was a methodical man, and despised untidiness.

...6...

It had been years since Anya Pepsicolova last saw daylight. The basement bar where she daily met Darger was as close as she ever came to the surface anymore. Unless one counted Chortenko's mansion, as she did not; to her that bleak house felt as though it were sunk deeper into the earth than even the most stygian of her other haunts. Nor did she think she would ever know the surface world again. She was trapped in this labyrinth of tunnels and darkness, tied to a slim and unbreakable thread of fate that was somewhere being rewound, drawing her inexorably inward, toward the underworld's dark center, where only madness and death awaited her.

But today she was still alive, and that, she reminded herself, was good. And she was still the third most dangerous entity—after Chortenko and the underlords—in all the City Below. Which was, if not actually good, at least a consolation.

As she poled down the Neglinnaya canal, the lantern at the bow of her skiff feebly lighting the walls ahead, Pepsicolova said, "We've been doing this for a week. You draw your maps. Sometimes you hire men to break through a bricked-over doorway. What exactly are you looking for?"

"I told you. The tomb of Tsar Ivan."

"Lenin."

"Yes, precisely."

Pepsicolova tied up the skiff at the Ploshchad Revolutsii docks. Here, dim streaks of lichen provided some feeble light. As she always did, she paused at the bronze statue of a young man and his dog to touch a snout already rubbed shiny. "For luck," she explained and, to her surprise, Darger did the same. "Why did you do that? This is my superstition, not yours."

"A man in my profession by necessity courts Lady Luck. Nor do I sneer at any superstition, lest there be some practical reason behind it, as in the well-observed fact that a man walking under a ladder is far more likely to have a hammer dropped upon his head than one walking cautiously around it, or that breaking a mirror necessarily entails the bad luck of enraging its owner."

"Exactly what is your profession?"

"Right now, I am searching for Tsar Ivan."

"Lenin."

"Of course." Darger unfolded a map of Moscow. "We are now directly below   here? A brief walk from the Resurrection Gates?"

"That is correct."

Darger got out his book, flipped to a page midway through it, and nodded with satisfaction. Then, repocketing the tome, he said, "We shall extend our search into the underground passages below the south wall of the Kremlin and above the river."

"The south wall? Are you sure?"

"Yes."

"You should be aware that most people think that the tomb is buried somewhere under Red Square."

"Which is precisely why nobody has found it yet," Darger said with an infuriatingly superior smile. "Shall we go on?"

They were coming into Dregs territory. Pepsicolova closed her lantern so that only the merest slit of light shone out. More than that would have identified them as rank outsiders, and thus enemies. Moving in total darkness, as the Dregs themselves did, would have identified them as strangers who knew their way around, and thus both enemies and spies. The territory between the two identities was extremely narrow, and there were times when she suspected it existed only in her mind.

She pushed through a rusty metal door which squealed as it opened and slammed shut noisily behind them. They boomed down a short flight of iron stairs. The air here felt stale and yet she could sense a great openness before her. The light from her lantern did not reach to the far wall.

They walked forward, dead cockroaches crunching underfoot.

"This is the largest space we've been in so far." Darger's voice echoed hollowly. "What is it?"

"Before it was built over, it was something called a *motorway*—a road the ancients built for their slave machines to carry them along. Now hush. We've made more than enough noise already."

There were whole tribes of people living in the darkness under Moscow. These were the broken and the homeless, the mentally ill and those suffering from the gross reshapings of viruses left over from long-forgotten wars. The more competent among them went aboveground periodically to scrounge through garbage bins, shoplift, or beg on the streets. Others sold drugs or their bodies to people who would, as likely as not, soon end up living down here themselves. As for the rest, no one knew how they managed to stay alive, save that often enough they didn't.

The Dregs were reputed to be the oldest and maddest of the tribes in the City Below. They lived in abject fear, and this made them dangerous.

From the darkness ahead came the sound of one metal pipe being steadily and rhythmically struck by another.

"Shit," Pepsicolova said. "The Dregs have spotted us."

"They have? What does that mean?"

She put down her lantern on the ground and closed its shutters completely. The darkness wrapped itself around them like a thick black blanket. "It means that we wait. Then we negotiate."

They waited. After a time, there was the scruff of feet on pavement and then a wavering quality to the darkness before them. Out of nowhere someone said, "Who are you, and what are you doing where you don't belong?"

"My name is Anya Pepsicolova. Either you know me or you've heard of me."

There was a quiet murmur of voices. Then silence again.

"My companion and I are searching for something that was lost long ago, before any of us was born. We have no reason to disturb you, and we promise to stay away from your squat."

"I'm sorry," the voice said in a tone utterly without regret. "But we've made a treaty with the Pale Folk. They leave us alone and we defend their southern border. I've heard you are a dangerous woman. But nobody goes back on a promise to the Pale Folk. So you must either turn back or be killed."

"If it's any help—" Darger began.

"Shut up." Anya Pepsicolova stuck a cigarette in her mouth. Then, narrowing her eyes almost shut, she struck a match. Briefly revealed before her were eight scrawny figures, wincing away from the sudden flare of light. They were armed with sharpened sticks and lengths of pipe, but only three of them looked like they could fight. She noted their positions well. Then, waving the match out, she raised her voice: "I've eaten with the Dregs and slept in your squat. I know your laws. I have the right to challenge one of your number to individual combat. Who among you is willing to fight me? No rules, no limits, one survivor."

A new voice, male and husky and amused in the way that only somebody sure of his own strength could be, said, "That would be me." By its location, the voice belonged to the biggest one of the lot. He was standing just right of center before her.

"Good." A flick of the wrist brought Saint Methodia to her hand. Swiftly, before her opponent could move from where she'd seen him standing, Pepsicolova sent her flying straight and hard into his gut.

The man screamed and fell to the ground, blubbering and cursing. There was a ripple in the darkness as the others converged upon him.

"I'll need my knife back, thank you."

After a slight hesitation, somebody threw Saint Methodia to the ground at her feet. Pepsicolova picked her up, wiped her on the front of one trouser leg, and returned her to her sheath.

"Tell the Pale Folk that Anya Pepsicolova comes and goes as she pleases. If they want me dead, they can do the work themselves without involving the Dregs. But I don't think they will." She held up a pack of cigarettes. "Where do you think I got *these?*" Then she laid it down on the ground, and a second atop it. "This is my payment for our passage. Every time we pass through your territory in the future, I'll leave another two packs."

Pepsicolova picked up the lantern and opened its shutters, revealing a clutch of ragged figures desperately trying to patch up their fallen comrade. "He's not going to survive a wound like that," she said. "The best you can do for him now is to roll him over and stomp down hard on his neck." Then, to Darger: "Let's go."

They walked down the center of the motorway away from the Dregs. With every step, she expected an iron pipe or a brick to come flying out of the darkness toward the back of her head. It was what she would have done in their circumstances. But nothing happened, and at last the sounds made by the dying man faded to inaudibility behind them. Pepsicolova released a breath she hadn't even known she'd been holding in, and said, "We're safe now."

She waited for Darger to thank her for saving his life. But he only said, "Don't think I'm paying for those cigarettes. All expenses are covered by your salary."

The three stranniks walked through the Moscow underworld as they would have the true Underworld—with their shoulders back and their heads high, secure in the strength of their own virtue and the unwavering support of a loyal and doting Deity. Because Koschei was the first among equals, he led. Chernobog and Svarožič followed a half-step behind, listening respectfully as he talked.

"When I was a boy, there was a metal girder sticking up out of the ground in the woods outside my village. If you pressed an ear to it, you could hear voices, many voices, sounding very small and far away. And if you closed your eyes and held your breath and concentrated as hard as you could, you could make out what they were saying. These were the demons and mad gods that the Utopians had in their folly created and released into their world-straddling web, of course, but the village brats did not understand that. They understood only that if you took a younger child there and forced him to listen, he would hear things that would terrify him. Often he would cry. Sometimes he would piss himself.

"Then, of course, they would laugh.

"I was a saintly child, obedient to my parents, uncomplaining at my chores, happy to go to church, devout at prayer. So it was with sadistic glee that these snot-nosed, plague-pocked, half-naked sons of Satan led me to the girder and shoved my face against it."

"Children should be beaten regularly," Chernobog said, "to control their unnatural impulses."

Svarožič nodded in agreement.

"I did not want to do as my cruel and faithless sometime-playmates commanded, and so they hit me and kicked me with feet that had never known shoes and so were hard as horn, until finally, reeling, I felt my ear strike the metal. There were voices, tiny as those of insects and almost impossible to hear. But when I closed my senses to the outer world, I could just barely make them out. Abruptly, they all ceased. Then a single small voice said: *We know you are listening.*

"I jerked away with a cry. But the others slammed me back against the girder so hard that my skull rang and blood trickled down my cheek. 'Tell us what it says!' one of the boys commanded.

"Fearfully I obeyed. 'It says it knows there are seven of us. It says when it gets out of Hell and into the real world, it will kill us all.' Then it told me how we would die, in slow and careful detail. I repeated every word to the others. They stopped laughing. Then they turned pale. One burst into tears. Another ran away. Before long, I was all alone in the woods. I clutched the girder tightly to keep from falling down from the shock and horror of the blasphemies I heard. But I kept listening.

"I was as terrified as any of the other children had been. But I knew that what I was hearing was not merely the babble of demons. It was the true voice of the World. I realized then that existence was inherently evil. From that moment onward, I hated it with all of my heart. And I went back regularly to listen to the demons so that I might learn to hate it better. That was the beginning of my religious education."

"Hatred is the beginning of wisdom," Chernobog agreed.

Svarožič seized Koschei's hands in his and kissed them fervently.

They came to one of the stations on the underground canal and paid a boatman to take them to the Ploshchad Revolutsii docks. There, an ash-pale wraith emerged from a side-passage, lantern in hand. It bowed.

This was Koschei's first encounter with one of the Pale Folk. He studied the scrawny figure with disapproval, but said nothing.

"Are you here to lead us to the underlords?" Chernobog asked.

The pallid thing nodded.

"Then do so."

Deep, deep into the darkness they went, through service tunnels strewn with garbage and down rough-hewn passages carved into the bedrock and smelling of shit and piss. (Koschei, who knew that all of the sinful world was odious to the nostrils of the Divine, felt a twinge of satisfaction at this momentary revelation of its true nature.) After a time, whispery shadows of footfalls sounded behind them. "We are being followed," Koschei observed.

Svarožič smiled.

"Yes," said Chernobog. "Doubtless the border-guards of one of the outcast settlements. They will have sent somebody ahead to alert their executive committee of our coming."

They proceeded onward until they came to a narrow and railingless set of stairs that followed the curving interior of an ancient brick cistern. This they descended, the lantern casting a crescent of light on the wall before them. The cistern had been breached ages before but was damp to the touch from the mingled and condensed exhalations of the undercity. At its bottom was a miniature slum city where the squatters had made their camp. From crude shelters built of discarded shards of timber, old blankets, and packing crates, the last few stragglers emerged and joined those already waiting. These ragged folk lifted up their hands in joyful obeisance.

"This is a settlement so small it has no name," Chernobog said. "I have been here before. Its inhabitants are all drug users or mentally afflicted, and, living so near to Pale Folk territory, their numbers have been dwindling in recent months."

A toothless crone whom, despite her decrepitude, Koschei shrewdly estimated to be but in her thirties, clutched him about the waist and cried, "Have you come to bless us, holy one? Have you come to relieve our suffering?"

Gently, he raised the hag up and enfolded her in a hug. Then he peeled her off of him. "Do not fear. The day of your liberation is almost at hand." He gestured, and the squatters gathered before him in a semicircle. "Today I have come to feed you not with food which passes down the gullet and through the digestive organs and then squeezes out the anus and is gone forever, nor with wine which is drunk in an hour and then pissed away in a minute, but with wisdom which, once taken in, stays with you forever."

Koschei bowed his head, thinking, for a minute.

Then he spoke: "Blessed are the diseased, for theirs is the kingdom of the flesh. Blessed are those who seek death, for they shall not be disappointed. Blessed are those who have nothing, for they shall inherit the void. Blessed are those who hunger and thirst for vengeance, for their day is fast in the coming. Blessed are those who have received no mercy, for no mercy shall they show. Blessed are they who stir up strife, for all the world shall be their enemies. Blessed are those who have been abused without reason, for theirs is the kingdom of madness. Blessed are you when people insult you and persecute you, and speak all kinds of evil against you, for your hearts shall burn with passion. Blessed above all are the lustful, for they shall know God. Rejoice and be glad, for your reward is not only in the spirit and the future, but in the body, and we have come to give it to you now."

Koschei stretched out his hands in blessing then, and Chernobog said, "Rejoice, for we have brought God to dwell within you for a space."

Then Koschei, Svarožič, and Chernobog passed through the crowd, moving their thumbs repeatedly from vials to tongues, until all present were ablaze with the sacred fire of the rasputin. After which they resumed their pilgrimage, leaving these most wretched creatures in all of Russia ecstatically coupling with each other in their wake. Briefly, one of their number rose up from the tangle of bodies to call after them, "We are forever in your debt, oh holy ones!"

Without looking back, Koschei raised a hand in dismissal. To his brothers—for their wan guide did not count as an audience—he observed, "All debts will one day be called in, and then they shall be repaid in full."

Some time later two of the Pale Folk emerged from a side passage and fell in step with the stranniks. Over their shoulders they carried a metal pole. From it hung a woman, tied head and foot, like game being brought back from the hunt. She struggled furiously and finally managed to dislodge her gag.

"Holy pilgrims! Thank God!" she gasped. "You must free me from these monsters."

"What wickedness did you do, my daughter, to find yourself in so dire a situation?" Koschei asked.

"I? Nothing! Those ass-fucking Diggers betrayed me. They—"

Svarožič restored and tightened the gag and then kissed the woman on the forehead. "If you have done no evil," Koschei said, "then be comforted, for I am sure that you will die in a state of grace."

At last the narrow ways opened up into a cavernous space, at the far end of which was an enormous doorway, three times the height of a man and made of smooth and unstained metal, such as could not be replicated today in any forge in the world. The door appeared at first to be shut. Only as they neared it could they see that it gaped slightly ajar, just wide enough for one person to pass through it at a time. The gap was guarded by another pale-skinned individual who favored them with neither word nor nod but merely stood aside to let the two Pale Folk, their captive, the three pilgrims, and the guide pass within.

Thus did the strannik Koschei complete his long journey from Bai-konur.

Darger was driving Pepsicolova mad with his little book. He referred to it often, though not as one would a reference work, nor again as (quite) a map, nor yet as one would an inspirational tome such as Sun Tzu's *The Art of War* or Machiavelli's *The Prince*. He treated it almost as if it were *Generation P* or the *I Ching* or some other traditional book of divination. Yet, despite his humoring her small superstitions, Darger was clearly a rationalist. Pepsicolova could not imagine him believing in such mystic claptrap.

"If you would only be a little more open about the methodology of your search," she said, "perhaps I could be of more help."

"Oh, no need. We're doing quite splendidly as it is." Darger removed the book from his inner pocket, flipped quickly to a place in its center, and snapped it shut again. "In fact, I dare say we're ahead of schedule."

"What schedule are you talking about? And what's in that book you're always looking at?"

"Book? Oh, you mean this thing? Nothing of any importance. Sermons and homilies and the like." He put a hand flat on a section of brick wall. "Does this seem particularly weak to you?"

"No, it does not."

"The bricks are soft and crumbly, though. It certainly wouldn't hurt to give them a try."

"As you command." So common had Darger's demands for demolition become that Pepsicolova had taken to carrying a pry-bar with her, almost like a walking stick. She hoisted it level with the wall and thrust forward hard.

The bar punched straight through the brick. When she drew it back, there was a hole through to a space on the other side. "Enlarge it! Quickly!" Darger urged her. Then, when the hole was big enough, he began tugging and pulling at the bricks himself, yanking them free, until the opening was sufficient for them to clamber through and into the room beyond.

Lanterns first, they entered.

"Look there—*books*, by God!"

Darger darted forward, excitedly holding up his lantern so he could examine the shelves with their warped and faded contents. Pepsicolova, however, hung back. With horror, she regarded an overstuffed chair, its upholstery half-rotted, and the small, grit-covered reading table at its side. They were not… and she knew they were not… Yet still, they paralyzed her.

Forcing an equanimity she did not feel into her voice, Pepsicolova said, "We've broken through into somebody's basement. One that hasn't been used for quite some time." She gestured with her lantern. "See there. The doorway's been bricked over."

She did not add, *Thank heavens.*

"A basement room? Just a basement room?" Darger looked around him bewilderedly. Then he collapsed into the chair. He bowed his head into his hands and was very still.

Pepsicolova waited for him to say something, but he did not. Finally, impatiently, she said, "What is wrong with you?"

Darger sighed. "Pay me no mind. 'Tis but my black dog."

"Black dog? What on earth are you talking about?

"I am of a melancholic turn of mind, and even a small setback such as this one can strike me with a peculiar force. Do not put yourself out about me, dear heart. I shall simply sit here in the dark, pondering, until I feel better."

Wondering mightily, Pepsicolova stepped back from the hole in the wall. Darger was a darkness at the center of his lantern's pool of light, a slumped caricature of despondency. It was clear that he would not move for some time yet to come.

So, with reluctance, Pepsicolova squatted down on her heels just outside the breached room, smoking and remembering. Spycraft and its attendant dangers were her solace, for their perils drove away introspection. Alas, inaction always returned, and with it her thoughts, and among them the memories. Central to which was a basement room with an overstuffed chair and a small reading table.

Afterward, Chortenko was always so serene.

His people had stripped Anya Pepsicolova bare, shaved off all her hair, save only her eyelashes, and then flung her, hands tied behind her back, into a cage in the basement of Chortenko's mansion. The cage was one of three which Chortenko called his kennels, and it was too low for her to stand up and too short for her to stretch out at full length. There was a bucket that served her as a toilet. Once a day, a dish of water and another of food were slid into the cage. Because her hands were bound, she had to drink and eat like an animal.

If Chortenko's purpose was to make her feel miserable and helpless, then he succeeded triumphantly. But the conditions were not what made the month she spent in his kennels a living hell.

It was the things she saw him do in that basement room.

Sometimes it was a political prisoner whom he questioned far beyond the point where the man had given up everything he knew and more, forcing the wretched captive into ever greater and more grotesque fantasies of conspiracy and treason, until finally, mercifully, he died. Sometimes it was a prostitute whom Chortenko did not question at all, but who did not leave the room alive, either.

Anya Pepsicolova saw it all.

When the deeds were done and the bodies cleared away, underlings would bring in an overstuffed green leather chair, and light a reading lamp beside it. Then Chortenko would sit puffing on his pipe and unhurriedly reading *War and Peace* or something by Dostoyevsky, a glass of brandy on a little stand by his elbow.

One day, a man was thrown into the kennel next to her. They hadn't bothered to strip and shave him, which meant that he was one of the lucky ones who would be dealt with in a single night. When the guards were gone, he said, "How long have you been here?"

Pepsicolova was huddled in the center of her cage, chin on her knees. "Long enough." She didn't make friends with the meat anymore.

"What was your crime?"

"It doesn't matter."

"I wrote a treatise on economics."

She said nothing.

"It dealt with the limits of political expansion. I proved that under our economic system, and given the speed with which information travels, the Russian Empire cannot be resurrected. I thought that the Duke of Muscovy would find it a useful addition to current political thought. Needless to say, his people did not agree." He made a little laugh that turned into something very much like a sob. Then, suddenly breaking, as the weaker ones would, he pleaded with her: "Please don't be like that. Please. We are both prisoners together—if you can't do anything else, at least help me keep my spirits up."

She stared at him long and hard. Finally she said, "If I tell you about myself, will you do me a favor?"

"Anything! Provided it is in my power."

"Oh, this will be in your power. If you are man enough to do it," Pepsicolova said. "Here is my story: I have been here for exactly one month. Before that I was in college. I had a friend. She disappeared. I went looking for her.

"I came very close to finding her.

"The trail I followed was twisty and obscure. But I was determined. I slept with many men and two women to get information from them. Three times I was captured. Twice I used my knives to free myself. One of those I used them on may have bled to death, I don't know and I don't care. The third time, I was brought before Chortenko."

She lapsed into silence. The economist said, "And?"

"And nothing. Here I am. Now. I have kept my part of the bargain, now keep yours."

"What do you want me to do?"

She squeezed one of her legs between the bars, reaching it as far into his cage as she could force it to go. Her near-starvation diet helped. "I want you to bite through my femoral artery."

"What!"

"I can't do it myself. The animal instincts are too strong. But you can. Listen to me! I have enough self-discipline that I can keep from yanking back my leg. But you'll have to bite strong and hard, right through the flesh of my thigh. Give it your all. Do this small thing for me and I'll die blessing your name, I swear it on my mother's grave."

"You're crazy." The man scrambled to the corner of his cage farthest from her. His eyes were wide. "You've lost your wits."

"Yes, I'm sure it's comforting to think that." Pepsicolova drew her leg back into her own cage. She had dwelt with despair for so long that she felt only mild disappointment. "You'll learn better soon enough."

That night, she didn't look away when the questioning began.

Later that night, Chortenko sat reading, as was his routine. "Listen to this," he said after a time. "'All is in a man's hands and he lets it all slip from cowardice, that's an axiom. It would be interesting to know what it is men are most afraid of. Taking a new step, uttering a new word is what they fear most.' Isn't that so very true?" Chortenko pushed his glasses up on his head and stared at her with those inhuman faceted eyes. "Even you, my dear, who have seen what happens to those who cross me—even you fear something more than joining their number. Even you fear most of all the simple act of taking a new step, of uttering a new word."

Chortenko looked at her steadily, eyes glittering, obviously waiting for something.

She knelt within her cage, quivering before him like an abused and half-starved dog. She could not formulate a response

"Ahhh, my little Annushka. You've been with me for a month, and I trust it's satisfied your curiosity. Now you know what happened to your school-chum, don't you?"

She nodded, afraid to speak.

"What was her name again?"

"Vera."

"Ah, yes, Vera. Ordinarily, I would simply have done to you what was done to her and that would have been that. But if you were an ordinary girl, you would not be here now. You managed to follow a trail that very few could even have found. You wheedled, extorted, or coerced information from some of my best subordinates, and before you did this, I would have said that was impossible. You're smart and you're cunning. That's a rare combination. So I'm going to give you one chance to walk out of here alive. But you'll have to work out the path to freedom yourself. Nobody's going to give it to you."

Pepsicolova's mind was racing. In a sudden, blinding leap of intuition, she understood what Chortenko was holding up before her. And he was right. She feared it even more than she did the hideous tortures she had, night after night, been witness to. Nevertheless, gathering up all her courage, she said, "You want me to do something new."

"Go on."

"You want me to…work for you. Not grudgingly but with all the ingenuity and initiative I've got. Following not just your orders, but your interests. Without mercy or remorse, doing whatever it is that I know you would want done. Anything less than that, and I wouldn't be worth your bothering with."

"Good girl." Chortenko got up and, slapping his pockets, came up with a key. He unlocked her cage with it. "Turn around, and I'll untie your hands. Then I'll have some clothes brought in and a bath drawn for you. You must be feeling positively filthy."

And she was.

By the time, hours later, Darger finally hauled himself up from the chair and out of the little room, Pepsicolova's brain burned with dark memories. She stood as straight as she could and stared at him as if he were a bug. But, oblivious as ever, Darger appeared not to notice. He sighed in a heavy, self-pitying way, and said, "Well, that's enough for now, I suppose. Lead me back to the Bucket of Nails, and then you can take the rest of the day off."

Among Pepsicolova's minor talents was an almost absolute sense of time. "Our arrangement was that I'd make myself available as your guide from sunup to sundown. Right now, it's less than an hour to sundown."

"Yes, I'm sure that's right. You can have the excess time for your own."

"It's going to take me at least an hour to lead you out of here."

"Then we'd best get going, hadn't we?"

They had re-crossed Dregs territory without incident and were coming up on the Neglinnaya canal again when Darger said, "What is that on the wall?" He pointed to six lines of ones and zeros which had been painted there with meticulous neatness:

01000001 00101110 00100000 01010000 01000101 01010000 01010011
01001001 01000011 01001111 01001100 01001111 01010110 01000001
00100000 01000011 01001111 01001101 01000101 00100000 01010100
01001111 00100000 01010111 01001000 01000101 01010010 01000101
00100000 01010100 01001000 01000101 00100000 01000110 01001100
01000001 01010110 01001111 01010010 00100000 01001001 01010011

"That? It's just graffiti that machine-worshipers and such scrawl on the wall to offend people. It means nothing," Pepsicolova lied.

Which was not easy to do, when the binary code was intended for Anya Pepsicolova herself and ordered her to report as soon as possible to the lords of the City Below.

She lit another cigarette and sucked on it with all her soul.

...7...

The carriage that the Baronessa Avdotya had sent for Arkady drove out of the city through an endless grid of low, regular hills which had been high-rises before being torn down at the fall of Utopia—or, since some disputed whether that happy state had ever been achieved in Russia, what had passed for Utopia in Old Moscow. But at last the land opened up into country estates bounded by thorn-hedges that were smaller, lower cousins of the one that had protected the hometown Arkady had left behind.

The driver reined in the horses in the shadow of an arched hedge-gate and a monkey dressed in green livery bounded out of the hedge and in through the open window, landing heavily on Arkady's lap. It snatched the pasteboard invitation from his hand and then leaped back out. "Hey!" Arkady grabbed futilely after the already-vanished animal.

From the thorny gloom, high-pitched voices chattered:

"It looks like an invitation!"

"It *is* an invitation."

"He doesn't look like anyone we know."

"He has an invitation."

"From the baronessa?"

"Who else invites anyone here?"

"Sometimes the baron does."

"Only when the baronessa tells him to."

"That's true."

"But what shall we do about this one?"

"He has an invitation."

"We don't recognize him."

"But we do recognize the invitation."

"He has an invitation?"

"Here it is."

"Pass!"

The driver clucked his tongue, and the carriage jolted forward.

Sunlight washed into the cabin and the carriage proceeded down a long, curving road. Arkady could not help but gawk. The Lukoil-Gazprom estate was sublime. Here a stream emerged from a grove of beeches, emptying into a pond whose mirror-smooth surface reflected a rustic mill. There, what looked to be a fairy village of clustered acorns with doors and windows cut into them was actually cottage-gourds grown to house the servants. Beyond, a pillared manor house topped a rise. A verse leapt to Arkady's mind from the dissolute youth he was working hard to put behind him:

So twice five miles of fertile ground
With walls and towers were girdled round:
And there were gardens bright with sinuous rills,
Where blossomed many an incense-bearing tree;
And here were forests ancient as the hills,
Enfolding sunny spots of greenery.

Then he arrived at the manor house, and the baronessa came out to greet him with a chaste peck on the cheek. With her was a ginger-haired and cinnamon-freckled young man his own age, whom she did not bother to introduce. "Darling Yevgeny," she said, her attention already focused on the next carriage trundling its way toward her, "do show Arkady about, while I stay here to greet the latecomers."

"Let me take you around back," Yevgeny said cheerily. "The fellows are enjoying a touch of sport at the pond."

At their destination, Arkady saw immediately that he was dressed subtly wrong for the occasion. His clothes—gray moiré cloth with green brocade vest and bright yellow ostrich-skin boots and gloves—would have been flawless for a city gathering, but here in the country they were a touch too formal. The other men wore wider collars and softer cravats than his. Their trousers were cut looser, presumably to provide more ease of movement for the strenuous entertainments of the countryside. Arkady's trousers, by contrast, were very tight indeed. He blushed to reflect on how much more revealing they were.

Luckily, the others were clustered at the tiled edge of the pond cheering and cursing, and paid him no more than a quick glance-and-a-nod as he was introduced around. Several of the men had canvas water-bags at their feet. Now one untied the top of his and poured something into the pond. Bright ribbons of red and orange and yellow and green energetically looped and swirled beneath the surface.

Arkady leaned over the pond to get a closer look.

"Look out!" Yevgeny shouted as a needle-toothed goblin's head burst from the water, viciously snapping at his face. Had not Yevgeny wrapped his arms about Arkady's chest and hauled him back, he might well have lost his nose.

"What in heaven's name was that?" Arkady gasped.

"Her name is Lulu," one of the men said. He reached a canvas-gloved hand into the water and pulled out a red-and-orange eel which wrapped itself briefly about his arm before being stuffed back in its bucket. A blue eel with yellow stripes floated dead and ripped open on the surface of the water. Turning to his comrade, he said, "And I believe you owe me some money, Borya."

"Do you eel, Arkady?" Yevgeny asked.

"No."

"What a pity. Tell you what, let me know as soon as you've found an appropriate eeling pond, and I'll send over my trainer with a bucket of elvers." There was a sudden thrashing in the water and Yevgeny turned eagerly back to the fight. "Oh, well done!"

At dinner, Arkady managed to negotiate the soup course without incident. However, he had barely tackled his salad when the baronessa leaned over to whisper, "You mustn't start with the outermost fork, silly. 'Big spoon, little fork, tiny silver tongs. A fork for Sylvia, a skewer for her date, then little brother Pierre comes and cleans the plate.' That's how you remember." Then a line of green-clad waiters whose bright stares identified them as serviles entered the dining room carrying platters and began serving out pink cuts of meat. Avdotya tapped on a water glass with her spoon: "Everybody, I want you to pay attention! I'm quite proud of the next course, and it's a mark of the regard in which I hold you all that I'm serving it to you this afternoon."

"Well, don't be a tease, Dunyasha," Yevgeny said good-humoredly. "What is it?"

"Why it's me! I had my own flesh cloned for you today. That's how highly I think of my friends."

"That's all very nice for the men," a pretty young thing mock-pouted. "But I'd much rather have a taste of the baron. After all, if he can't be here in person…"

A mischievous look came over the baronessa's face. "Why, who do you think went into the consommé?"

Roars of merriment and applause lofted to the rafters.

Arkady stared down at his cutlet in horror.

At last the dinner was over. The women drifted to the back lawn to oversee the setting-up of lanterns, while the men retired to the veranda for cigars. There, Leonid Nikitovich Pravda-Interfax, who had genially introduced himself as a professional wastrel (but who, according to Yevgeny, was actually highly placed in the Ministry of Roads and Canals), said, "Irina tells me that you have a drug. One that," he lowered his voice in a comically conspiratorial manner, "improves one's performance in the saddle?"

"Oh, yes, certainly. But the sexual dimensions of the rasputin's power are the least of it," Arkady said, on familiar ground at last. "Spiritually…well, there are some who have taken it and literally seen God in all His glory."

"Yes, yes, God is all well and good," Leonid said. "But given the choice I'd far rather see Tatiana's titties."

"Or Anastasia's ass," one of his pals said to top him.

"Or Jennicah's *je ne sais quois*," said another, making it a game.

His companions snorted and guffawed.

Arkady flushed again, unaccountably embarrassed. These superficial and well-meaning young men were none of them trying to humiliate him, he realized. But simply by their being who they were and he being himself, the humiliation was inevitable. Which, in its way, made the experience all the more painful.

Mercifully, the baronessa reappeared. "Put out those foul-smelling things, and join the ladies outside," she said. "We're going to play lawn polo."

Leonid came up to Arkady with a friendly grin. "You do know how to play, don't you, Arkady? Well, then, we'll simply have to teach you. I can lend you a pony, a lantern, and a trident."

So it was that an hour later, Arkady found himself hiding in a guest bedroom while one of the baronessa's servants sewed up the trousers he had split falling from his horse as he tried to spear a boar-shoat that had burst out of the shrubbery without warning.

Oh, *when* would it grow late enough for the orgy to begin?

When the operation was complete, the Pale Folk undid the straps holding the woman down on the gurney. She sat up. Then she stood. She did not rub at the crude sutures on her newly shaved head. One of the Pale Folk walked unhurriedly toward an archway at the far side of the room, and she followed it without question.

She was one of them now.

Two more of the Pale Folk entered the room carrying another prisoner slung from a pole, this one bald as a mushroom and scrawny as an orphan. His mouth was gagged, but his eyes darted wildly about, and when he was dumped on the floor and his hands and feet untied, he strove to escape so vigorously that it took a dozen of the Pale Folk to subdue him and strap him down onto the gurney.

Koschei had watched the dehumanizing process with somber interest. Now he asked, "Where do the raw materials for this operation come from?"

"They are tribute from various of the underworld tribes," Chernobog said. "People who were caught thieving, or strangers who trespassed into their territories. The tribes rid themselves of a difficulty and receive five packs of cigarettes for their trouble. The underlords increase their army of obedient slaves by one. And the world is relieved of the presence of another scoundrel. Everyone benefits."

Svarožič nodded toward the doorway, and their guide led them onward.

They were taken to a high-ceilinged oval hall, bright with lantern-sconces. Its walls were covered with tremendous panels on which faded painted schematic maps of all the continents of the world. Beneath, tables had been set up circling the room, where the Pale Folk worked tirelessly and without passion, their motions smooth and unhurried. One would open a crate of cigarettes and dump its contents on the tabletop. Those standing there carefully opened and unfolded each package and passed the packaging to the left and the cigarettes to the right. Those to the right tore open the cigarettes one by one, letting the tobacco fall onto shallow trays that were whisked to the right and replaced when they grew full. The shredded papers fell to their feet like snow. At the next group of tables, first one and then another powder was sprinkled upon the tobacco by ashen-skinned figures wearing cloth masks over their mouths and noses. Beyond them, yet more Pale Folk poured the mixture into bowls. The bowls were passed on to further workers, who were given fresh papers and proceeded to roll new cigarettes. These were given to others who grouped them in bunches of twenty and then—the circle having reached its beginning—folded the packages around them again.

A crate of the re-rolled cigarettes was hammered shut. The new recruit joined in with several other Pale Folk, to carry it out the same door through which the crate had originally entered.

"Is this not the human condition?" Koschei asked. "An endless circle of meaningless labor joylessly performed deep underground, as far from the eye of God as it is possible to be. These lost souls are fortunate they are no longer self-aware."

Svarožič nodded and piously rubbed the side of his head, where ancient scars commemorated an operation not entirely unrelated to the one just now performed by the Pale Folk. "Oblivion is preferable to awareness without God," Chernobog agreed. "Yet I do not envy them their fate."

"Nor should you, nor do I, nor would any man capable of better. By being so sinful as to get themselves in such a fix, however, these poor dead souls proved themselves worthy of nothing better." Koschei turned away, dismissing their memory. "I believe it is time that I met these underlords."

"Yes," Chernobog said. "They are quite eager to meet you as well."

Since Pepsicolova was uncharacteristically late, Darger had struck up a conversation with a tobacco factor to pass the time. The fellow was guarding a pile of crates in the basement corridor immediately behind the Bucket of Nails.

"The tobacco is brought in on wagon trains from the Ukraine by Kazakh traders," the factor explained, "and rolled into cigarettes and packaged here in Moscow. My purchasers have several times tried to screw me into selling them the tobacco loose. But I tell them: Why should I give up the money? Do I look like the kind of dupe who would let silver flow into somebody else's pockets?"

"Is there really such profit to be made from so impoverished a clientele?"

"Trust me, sir, there is. These ragamuffins and tatterdemalions may look half-starved to the casual eye, but they have all the money they need for those pleasures they deem essential. Nor is tobacco the least of it. I know for a fact that they buy various addictive and even poisonous substances as well, in bulk, and indeed there are rumors of underground farms where psychoactive mushrooms are grown upon beds of human manure. And yet some of them have the nerve to come up from their bolt-holes and beg on the streets and underpasses. Feh! They may not have the creature comforts of those who live above them, but neither do they sweat and toil as needs must decent folk such as you and I. Their lives are squalid but indolent, and they consider the attendant filth a small price to pay for the sybaritic ease of their existence."

"But where do they obtain the money to pay you?" Darger asked.

"Who knows? Perhaps they deal drugs or sell their bodies to those depraved enough to desire them. Occasionally I have been paid in antique silver coins, doubtless from caches hidden belowground in times of trouble and never recovered by their rightful owners. It matters not to me, so long as the weight is good."

The factor consulted his pocket-watch with just a hint of worry. "Whatever can be keeping my contacts? I have never known the Pale Folk to be late before."

"That is the fourth time you've checked your stem-winder since we began talking. Are you pressed for time?"

"It is just that I have an appointment for which I would not care to be late."

"Surely you can explain the circumstances."

"Unfortunately, she is not the sort of lady who accepts explanations."

"Ahh! I understand you now—this engagement is of an intimate nature."

"Indeed," the factor said glumly. "Or was."

"Well, there is no problem here, then. I know the bartender at the Bucket of Nails and he will happily store your crates for a small desideratum. Come! I will help you carry them in."

The factor consulted his watch again. "I should still be late, however, and believe me my tardiness would cost me dearly." Then, with a touch of yearning in his voice. "Perhaps you would be willing to—no, of course not. It was irresponsible of me even to think of it."

Darger's instincts kicked in immediately. "I?! I am no longshoreman, sir! Nor am I a day-laborer to be hired off the street. I made my offer purely in the spirit of Christian charity." He spun on his heel, as if to leave.

"Stay, stay, sir!" the factor cried. With sudden decisiveness, he quickly began counting out bills from his wallet. "You seem a decent sort. Surely you would be willing to help out one who is caught in the throes and tangles of something very much like love?"

"Well…"

"Thank you, sir. Your name, sir?"

"Gregor Saltimbanque," Darger said. "Of the Hapsburg Saltimbanques."

"I could tell that you were a gentleman, sir," the factor said, pressing the bills into Darger's hands. Then, over his shoulder, "I'll be back in two hours—three at most!"

The carpenters were finally done with their work. Surplus poured them each a shot of vodka and together they toasted the new spiral staircase to the embassy's roof and the equally new cupola at its summit. Zoësophia, he could see, was pacing back and forth, restless as a panther, behind the screen at the far end of the room. But as the Neanderthals would not let her cross to this side of it until all strange males were gone, that did not much concern him. "I shall instruct the treasurer to give you each a bonus of an extra day's pay," he told the workmen. At which good news, they all cheered him so heartily that he had to bring out the bottle again for a second and then a third round of toasts.

When finally Surplus had seen the men to the door, Zoësophia came sailing out of the women's quarters, the Neanderthals retreating from the lighting a-flash in her eyes. "As your treasurer," she said, "I am not going to pay a bonus to carpenters for a job they have already been paid for and that should never have been contracted for in the first place. Further, and also in my capacity as chief financial officer, it is my duty to inform you that we are out of money and living on several lines of credit, which are secured by property that has already been mortgaged three times over."

"Which is precisely why I am so open-handed. Let once our creditors see us pinching pennies and they will lose faith in our financial stability."

"Stability? We are living in a house of cards, ready to collapse at the least puff of wind, to which *you* have added a perfectly useless cupola!"

"Darling Zoësophia, you wound me grievously. Only let me show you what I have done and I am certain you will agree that it is money well spent."

Zoësophia's glare would have stunned a basilisk. "I doubt that very much."

"Come with me and I promise that you will like what you see."

He led her up the new staircase, and into the cupola at its top. There, he let down the trap and secured it with a latch. "So that we are not disturbed," he said. Then he swept out a paw. "Is not Moscow beautiful from this vantage?" A mesh screen embroidered with colored wires in a pattern of green and yellow aspen leaves and fire-red feathers enclosed the cupola, allowing them to see with perfect ease while protecting them from prying eyes. The sun was sinking low in the sky, painting the clouds with oranges and purples that coming from any lesser artist than Nature herself would have seemed garish and obvious. Looking across the rooftops, they could see the Kremlin canted up out of a ramshackle sea of buildings, like a great ship just beginning to list before going under.

"I am strangely unmoved." Zoësophia strode quickly around the interior of the octagonal cupola. Its walls were lined with cushioned benches, whose width invited lounging rather than sitting. She suddenly rounded on Surplus. "This is as good a time and place as any to have it out with you. You are going to see the Duke of Muscovy tomorrow. I am coming with you." Then, as Surplus began to shake his head, "I warned you once that my sisters and I could make trouble for you. Yet you did not take me seriously then, and you do not take me seriously now."

"Do you know?" Surplus said wryly, "I honestly believe I do."

"Oh, no. You do not." Zoësophia's smile was cruelty itself. "All of us have our admirers—and it would be the easiest matter imaginable to convince one that Muscovy would be a better place without you in it. Russians are a direct folk, so it would take some persuasion to convince one of them that your death should be lingering and painful. But we can be very persuasive. You exist on our tolerance, and we have tolerated you so far only because a figurehead was needed to arrange our collective marriage. In this, you have proved yourself incompetent, complacent, self-satisfied, and may I say officious. Indeed, I am come to the conclusion that you and your absent friend are both complete and utter frauds!"

"I know from what depths your passion arises," Surplus said solemnly. "For I feel it myself." He took her gloved hand and kissed its knuckles. Zoësophia snatched it away from him.

"Are you mad?!"

"Sweet lady, I am precisely the opposite of mad, for I have thought this out long and carefully. Attend: A compulsion was placed upon you in Byzantium, rendering the least touch by a man toxic to you and his intimate caresses fatal. Yet I have seen you and the others walking arm in arm and bestowing chaste kisses upon each other's cheeks. I have seen you playing with kittens and brightly colored birds with your bare hands, without injury. Why should this be?"

"Obviously, because neither women nor kittens nor birds are *men*."

"Nor am I, O Avatar of Delight, nor am I. Have you forgotten that I am no man but rather a reconfigured dog? My genes were tweaked to give me full human intellect and the upright stature of a human. Still, I remain not *Homo sapiens sapiens* but *Canis lupus familiaris*. You may do with me as you wish, and the suicidal impulse implanted by the Caliph's psychogeneticists will not kick in." Gently, he touched her face just below and to the side of her eye. "You see? No welt."

For a still, shocked instant, Zoësophia did not move.

One hand floated up to touch her unblemished face.

Then, slowly, she peeled off her gloves and let them fall. One by one, her silks rained down to the floor with a grace that was almost as entrancing as the tawny body that their absence revealed. When she was, save for her jewelry, entirely naked, she passed her hands over Surplus, undressing him. Then she sank back onto the cushions, leaving him standing over her. "I shall teach you all I know," Zoësophia said. Her expression was cryptic. "Though it may take some time."

She held out the most desirable arms Surplus had ever seen or even imagined and drew him down atop her. "The first position is called the Way of the Missionary."

The fastness that the underlords had made their own was in its era impregnable. But during a subsequent age, one corner of it had been sheared away for a tunnel whose purposes were no longer evident. So it was easy enough to enter the complex unnoticed. In a shabby corridor that went nowhere anybody cared to go, Anya Pepsicolova unscrewed a metal plate bolted low on a wall and then ducked through the opening thus revealed. She straightened up inside a nondescript and windowless office whose lone door had long ago merged with its frame in one great mass of rust.

Guided by the light of her cigarette alone, Pepsicolova fetched a coil of rope she had stashed in one corner and rolled up a moldering carpet to reveal a manhole cover hidden underneath. Only the topmost rung of several hundred had survived long neglect, but to this she tied the rope and so rappelled down to the bottom of the shaft. She ground the cigarette underfoot. From here it was only a leisurely walk along a narrow, lichen-streaked passage, to what she thought of as the Whisper Gallery.

The underlords did not know of the gallery. Of that Pepsicolova was certain. She had discovered it by logic alone. First she had reasoned that the Preutopians who had built this facility had trusted nobody, not even their own associates. Then that they would therefore have had means of spying on one another. At which point, Pepsicolova had simply snooped and pried, examining with particular closeness anything that seemed ostentatiously uninteresting. Until finally she found the secret passages and undocumented access-ways by which the Preutopians had bypassed their own security.

The Whisper Gallery completely circled the domed ceiling of what had once been a splendid conference room, all oaken panels and crimson draperies and brass sconces and leather armchairs and polished marble tabletops. It was so high up that nobody below could tell that what looked to be decorative molding was actually a series of slit windows from which the room could be observed. The floor of the gallery was of a soft material that absorbed all footsteps, and the room's architecture was such that the slightest of sounds could be heard clearly from above.

As she approached the gallery, she heard the murmur of voices.

Pepsicolova quietly took her station. Below her was an underlord. It was in no way human, though it inhabited a human body. The body hunched forward, hands held loosely by the chest, as if it were a praying mantis. Yet though it moved as if it were a living thing, the stench of rotting meat that rose from it was, even from far above, all but unbearable.

Standing across a table from it were the last things in the world Pepsi-colova would have expected to find in such a place:

Three stranniks.

Pimps, whores, prostitutes, gangsters, and other unwholesome business-men were of course frequent visitors to the underlords, as were politicians, black marketeers, drug runners, petty thieves, and salesmen of all sorts. But stranniks?

She held her breath.

"We shall leave this with you," the largest of the three stranniks said. "You will know what to do with it."

With a twinge of disappointment, Pepsicolova realized that she had come at the end of the conversation for the underlord responded by saying, "Soon—very soon indeed—when we have recovered the weapon that has lain lost beneath Moscow since Utopia fell—we will kill you. We will kill you slowly and painfully, and along with you every human being who lives in this city. In this way, we shall have a partial revenge for what you and your kind have done to us."

In Pepsicolova's experience, such dark words meant that the underlord had run out of useful things to say.

"Yes, that is what you believe," the chief strannik said. "But you are merely tools in the employ of a higher Power. What you anticipate as destruction will be in actual fact transformation. The Eschaton shall be achieved, the glory of God's physical being will touch and cauterize the Earth, and on that very day, you will return to Hell."

"Fool! This *is* Hell! All existence is Hell for our kind, for no matter where we are, we know your kind still exists unpunished."

The strannik nodded. "We understand each other completely."

"For the moment," the underlord said with obvious regret, "I must refrain from destroying you."

"I in turn will pray to the living God to forgive and punish you through all eternity."

The stranniks departed, leaving behind them a leather satchel, whose contents the underlord began to unpack with extreme care.

Darger had lifted a crate as the factor hurried away, as if to carry it into the bar. Now he set it back down and sat atop it, thinking. He had intended to spend another week or so underground before bringing the great scheme to a head. But as a humble worshiper of Fortuna, he believed that there was a time and tide in the affairs of men which was often triggered by sudden, unexpected good luck. Luck that one ignored at one's peril.

Surely this windfall of tobacco was a sign that he should advance his timetable. He could immediately see how it could be used to publicize his fictitious discovery. Surplus might experience a moment's surprise to see events moving ahead of schedule. But Darger was certain his friend would be quick to adapt to the changing winds of circumstance.

A door opened onto a steaming kitchen and a worker in a stained apron scurried out on an errand. A delivery man staggered by, bent under a side of raw beef. Them he ignored. But then a clutch of five ragged boys ran past.

"Young people!" Darger called after them. "Are you interested in earning some pocket money?"

The boys skittered to a stop, and stared at him with glittering, unblinking eyes, wary as rats. The biggest of the lot squinted skeptically, spat, and said, "What's the pitch?"

Darger removed the factor's money from his pocket and slowly peeled off several bills. He understood these slum-children perfectly, for he had been much the same as they in his boyhood. Thus, when one of the smaller ones surreptitiously eased closer, he tightened his grip on the money and favored him with a sudden sharp look. The imp hurriedly backed away.

"What's your name?" he asked the ringleader.

The boy's mouth moved silently, as if he were chewing over the implications of giving out this information. Then, grudgingly, he answered, "Kyril."

"Well, Master Kyril, I have something to celebrate, and I wish to celebrate it by giving away all these crates of cigarettes."

Kyril looked the pile up and down. There were twenty crates. "Okay. We'll take this shit off yer hands."

"Nice try, but no. I'll be giving them away a pack at a time. What I want you and your comrades to do is to spread the word through the underground—to the Diggers, to the Outcasts, to pretty much everybody except the Pale Folk—that I'll be handing this stuff out free. Come back in half an hour, and if you've raised a large enough crowd, you can help distribute it. For which, I'll pay you this much"—he extended the bills, and young Kyril snatched them away—"up front, and an equal amount when the job is done. Are you up for it?"

Kyril's face grew still as he mentally searched for a way to sweeten the deal. "Do we get some of the cigarettes, too?"

"If you must." Darger sighed. "Though you really shouldn't, you know. They *are* bad for you."

The guttersnipe rolled his eyes in scorn. "I don't fucking care." Then he addressed his gang: "Dmitri—Diggers! Oleg—Psychos! Lev—Outcasts! Stephan—Bottom Dwellers!"

They scattered.

In less than the prescribed half an hour, a crowd had gathered, as uncertain and murmurous as the sea. Darger climbed to the top of the stack of crates to address them. "Good friends, congratulate me!" he cried. "For today I have made a discovery that will leave my mark in history. I have found that which everybody said could not be found…the books for which I have searched for so long…the lost library of Ivan the Great!"

He paused, and a puzzled, halfhearted cheer went up.

"In honor of which discovery, I will now give away three packs of cigarettes to everybody who steps forward to congratulate me."

A much heartier cheer arose.

"Form a line!" Darger cried. Then, dragooning the slum-boys as his helpers, he pried open the first crate and gave a handful of cigarette packs to a drab woman at the head of the line. "They are yours if you say: Congratulations for finding the library."

"Congratulations for finding the library."

"Excellent. Next. You must say…"

"Congratulations for finding the library."

"Good."

Beside him, Kyril was handing out cigarettes and receiving perfunctory congratulations, as were his four comrades. Darger noted that their pockets already bulged with packs.

"Congratulations for the library."

"Congratulations."

"Good luck. Glad for ya."

"Um…books?"

"Close enough," Darger said. "Keep the line moving."

It took less time to give away the cigarettes than Darger had expected, and yet the experience left him wearier than he would have thought. Finally, though, all the crates had been opened, their contents distributed, and the troglodytes (and a certain number of habitués from the bar and nearby service workers who had come out to see what the noise was about) had gone.

Darger scrupulously paid out the promised money to his half-sized allies. He would have done so even if he hadn't known how such young men repaid broken promises.

When they had been paid, four of the young men instantly scattered. Kyril, however, remained, looking unaccountably abashed. "Uh, sir," he said. "What you said about finding the library…does that mean I have to move out of it now?"

Zoësophia was pleasantly surprised by Surplus's performance. He had, as it turned out, extraordinary stamina for one not born of the breeding vats of Byzantium. It was not until the Way of the Wounded Crane that he gasped, "Enough! Pax! I am but mortal—I must… I have no breath! I can do no more!" And then, when she ignored his pleas and continued onward, he made it all the way through the Way of the Supple Monkey before turning pale and passing out.

"Well!" Zoësophia said, pleased.

Having gotten more of a gallop than she'd expected, Zoësophia found herself feeling decidedly fond of the ambassador. She scratched him behind the ears, and noted with amusement how his feet scrabbled briefly against the cushions. Then she gathered up all the scattered items of clothing and carefully smoothed and laid them out for the morning. She always carried a small mirror with her and this she used to make sure she had no scratches or bruises that would show when dressed. Her hair was a dreadful mess. So she commanded it to go limp and then flicked her head so that it flew out, undoing any snarls or tangles. Six passes of her hands and a command for it to resume its usual body, and she looked as if she had just spent an hour with a beautician.

As she always did before sleeping, Zoësophia took a mental walk into her memory palace and carefully sorted her day's thoughts into three cabinets—one sculpted from fire, one of ice, and the third merely rattan. She was all but certain that the ambassador was nothing more than a confidence trickster, doubtless planning to run some elaborate scheme on the Duke of Muscovy. But that was tangential at best to her *real* mission, so she placed that thought in the rattan cabinet, which she reserved for whims, fancies, and idle speculations.

Finally, Zoësophia lay down alongside Surplus, with one hand around his root, so that he could not awaken without her knowing of it. The first thing in the morning, she would dictate terms. For now, she could enjoy her beauty sleep with a clean conscience and a sense of a job well done.

The carriage climbed toward the estate's hedge-wall, swaying on its springs so that the manor house behind it seemed to dance in the starry night sky. Gentle strains of music could be heard in the distance, for the baronessa's guests were dancing now, their eyes still afire with the divine Spirit and their souls at peace with all humanity. Arkady had climbed into the carriage with the warmth of the drug dying down within him and his back stinging from the comradely slaps of the men. He could still feel the swift farewell kisses and furtive squeezes of his stones bestowed on him by the women. The carriage cushions were soft, and there was a bucket of iced champagne, should he feel the urge for a drink on his way home. By slow degrees the last embers of indwelling sanctity were fading gently to ash.

How stupid of him to have taken the rasputin immediately after dinner, rather than waiting for the orgy to begin, as the others had! Had it only been otherwise, Arkady would even now be laughing, dancing, gossiping about the ways of angels with his erstwhile comrades in lust. He would be engaged in the pleasant après sex social activities with which the aristocracy customarily eased the transition from ardor back to everyday life.

He would not now be alone with his thoughts. With his memories. With the images that, try though he might, he could not dispel from his mind. He would not be tormented by the horrific knowledge of what he had done.

In the carriage's dark interior, Arkady wept bitterly.

...8...

The merchant from Suzdal strolled down Teatralny proezd, tapping his cane on the sidewalk in time with a hummed tune. Idly, he noted a string of posters pasted one after the other on the lantern-poles lining the street:

LOST
Diamond Necklace with Gold Leaf Clasp
in the vicinity of Red Square
5000 SILVER RUBLES REWARD!!!
Apply to A. Kozlenok, Hotel New Metropol

Five thousand rubles was good money for whatever lucky soul found the bauble and was honest enough to return it—more, indeed, than the merchant normally earned in a month. However, this business trip had been an exceptionally profitable one; he had sold all the house-gourd seeds he had brought at a considerable markup—word had not yet reached Moscow of the fast-spreading blight that would attack and kill the gourds before they reached bungalow size—and so he could contemplate the necklace without suffering too greatly the pangs of avarice.

Nevertheless, he could not refrain from peering into the gutters in the furtive hope of seeing a diamondy glitter.

He was thus occupied when, abruptly and without warning, a street urchin slammed into him, almost knocking him to the ground and sending his cane clattering onto the sidewalk.

Clapping one hand to his wallet (for he was well acquainted with the tricks of pick-pockets), the merchant snatched up his cane and rounded upon the young rascal, prepared to thrash him soundly for his insolence. But the face that the child lifted to him was streaked with tears and his expression so distraught that the merchant stayed his wrath and asked,

"Are you in pain?"

"Mister, you got to help me." The waif pointed to the Hotel New Metropol. "The doorman there won't let me in."

The merchant, who was himself staying at that very hotel, could not help feel a twinge of amusement. "I should hope not. You'd track mud on the carpets and leave stains on everything you touched."

"But I *gotta* get in!"

"Oh? And why is that?"

To the merchant's astonishment, the boy reached into his jacket and pulled out a diamond necklace. It was only exposed for an instant before being stuffed back away, but that was long enough for him to see the leaf-shaped gold clasp. "I found the necklace fair and square. But I can't get in to see the guy what's offering the reward. That bastard doorman won't even let me tell him what I want."

"Yes, well, naturally he—"

The boy's face twisted, as if he had just come to a desperate decision. "Look, mister, get me in and I'll split the reward with you, fifty-fifty. That's fair, ain't it? Twenty-five katies for me and twenty-five for you. That's an easy day's work. C'mon, waddaya say?"

The merchant contemplated the boy solemnly. "There is no way that one such as you would be allowed into a decent hotel under any circumstances whatsoever. However, if I may suggest it, I can take the necklace in for you and bring you back your half of the reward." He stuck out his hand.

But the urchin skittered back from him, eyes glittering with alarm. "Hey, what're you trying to pull? I'm not stupid. If I give you the necklace, that's the last I'll ever see of you. I made you a good offer. You ain't got no reason to rip me off."

Affronted, the merchant said, "I was merely trying to help."

"Yeah, right!" the boy sneered. "Trying to help yourself. I know your kind." With each retort, he moved a little further away. His body was so tense it quivered. At any moment he would break and run, and the merchant would never see the necklace again.

"Wait, wait, wait a moment," the merchant said soothingly. "Let's see if we can't settle this contretemps amicably." He thought furiously. "Suppose I were to give you your half of the reward in exchange for the necklace up front? Then you wouldn't have to trust me. I'll bring the necklace to its owner and collect the full reward, and we'll both be ahead by two and a half thousand rubles. Twenty-five 'katies,' as you called them."

The boy's face worked suspiciously. "Let's see the color of your money."

The merchant positioned himself with his back to the nearest building and looked around carefully before withdrawing his billfold from an inner pocket of his coat. Then he counted out two thousand-ruble notes and five hundreds. "Here." He extended the bills, then pulled them back as the child made a grab for them. "We'll exchange the money and the necklace simultaneously, if you please."

Warily, the boy held out the diamond necklace in one hand and reached for the money with the other. Each of the two moved suddenly, hands striking like snakes, and when they stepped apart, the merchant held the necklace and the boy the banknotes. Both grinned with relief.

"You treated me square, mister," the urchin said. "I guess you ain't such a bad sort after all." Then, shoving the money deep into his pocket, he turned and ran. Within seconds he was nowhere to be seen.

His good mood restored, the merchant headed toward the New Metropol. But as he did, he could not help reflecting on the original owner's carelessness. Five thousand rubles was surely a mere fraction of the necklace's value—so the greatest profit today would be made by the man who cared so little for his valuables that he flung them into the streets of Moscow without a second thought. The more consideration he gave the matter, the more monstrous this fellow became. Such a man's wealth was surely inherited, for one who had earned it himself would, as the merchant knew from experience, keep the tightest of grips upon it. So. This self-centered profligate, this despoiler of his father's hard-earned fortune, sauntered about Moscow, doubtless drunk (for otherwise he would not have been so haphazard with a possession worth so much), simply flinging his property away. Did such a man *deserve* such riches?

The question answered itself.

Thus, when he came to the hotel, the merchant kept right on walking. He was not far from the jeweler's district. There would be pawn shops there that would offer him a better percentage of the thing's value than he was likely to get from its former owner.

"He did everything like you said he would," Oleg, the smallest of Kyril's gang of bandits, said. "As soon as Kyril's out of sight, he goes straight to a pawnshop."

"Then he comes out cursing and calling the pawnbroker a crook," Lev interjected.

Stephan shoved Lev aside. "And, and, and then he goes into a second pawnshop. And, and then a third."

"So finally he goes back to the New Metropol and when he comes out, he's so mad he rips one of the posters off the lantern-post and throws it on the ground and stomps on it," finished Dmitri.

"Did he throw away the necklace?" Darger asked. "Did you pick it up?"

"Naw," Oleg said. "He just goes back into the hotel and don't come back out."

"A pity." Darger put down the book he'd been reading and without rising from his chair said, "All right, Kyril, it's reckoning time. Let's see how much you took him for."

Kyril presented him with a thick stack of banknotes. Darger ran a thumb down one corner and then snapped his fingers three times briskly. "All of it."

With obvious reluctance, Kyril produced several more bills.

Darger neatened the edges, and then peeled off five hundred-ruble notes from the top. "This much goes to repay me for the necklace. It may have been paste, but it was of excellent quality for its sort." He placed them in his billfold. "That leaves two thousand rubles. Since you ran the operation and took the lion's share of the risks, Kyril, you are entitled to half. The rest of it will be doled out in equal shares to your confederates. All right, lads, line up."

Grinning and elbowing each other, Oleg, Lev, Stephan, and Dmitri formed a short line and received two hundred fifty rubles each. When the last had been paid, the bandits ducked under the fallen girder that had made a breach in one wall, anxious to be on their way to the surface where they could squander every kopeck of their new-won wealth. Leaving the library empty save for Darger and Kyril.

Darger picked up his book, adjusted the oil lamp, and said, "Listen to this:

"Summer will be ours, if you but say you love me,
 Night-hawks flitting under the stars
 And jasmine perfuming your skin.
 If not, winter. And I—"

"I don't see why I had to pay them so much. They didn't do nothing but put up a bunch of posters, and keep an eye out for the goats. I did all the fucking work."

With a sigh, Darger shut his book again. "Admittedly, my paraphrase from Sappho's impeccable Greek was a touch rough. But you had the opportunity to hear a poem that was long believed to be lost forever, and you brushed it aside simply to whinge that your comrades weren't pulling their weight."

"Well, they ain't."

"I promised to show you how to live by your wits, and here are the first fruits of my teachings." Darger tapped the stack of bills with his fingertip.

"More money than you've ever had in your entire life, earned in less than an hour. A wise young man would take this as a sign that his mentor was worth listening to."

Angrily, Kyril said, "Maybe you know a few good tricks, but that don't mean you're any smarter than me."

"Oh? Then how did I trick you into bringing me *here?*" Darger waved a hand to take in all of the library: the shelves of books—stacked sideways in the Medieval manner—that stretched from floor to ceiling and dwindled into the gloom, and the honeycombs of scrolled parchment and papyrus texts, as well as the solid wooden tables, chairs, and other library furnishings, beneath which the children had made their beds.

"What? You already knew all about it…didn't you?"

"I did not. But when we first came here, you may remember that I kept a hand on your shoulder in an avuncular manner."

"I thought you was just keeping me from running away."

"Of course not, you had nowhere to go. No, I was reading you. Whenever we came to a turn and your muscles tensed up, I would say, "We turn here." Then your eyes would dart in the direction you normally went, and in that direction I would go. By such small shifts and stratagems, I allowed you to lead me right here."

The boy spat out an unfamiliar word. Doubtless slang, and doubtless obscene.

"Exactly. Now, you want to know why I insisted you be so generous to your friends. And, though you have not asked, you are wondering why I directed you to have the thousand-ruble notes converted to small bills."

"Yeah. The bastard at the bank made me give him twenty rubles for doing it, too. So why?"

"As for your friends, simply because they *are* your friends. The man who lives by his skill and his wits must be able to trust his business associates and they him. When the swag is swept up at the end of the game, and everyone scatters, they all must know that their share of the take is as safe as houses. Otherwise your plans will fall apart in your hands. You see?"

"I… guess so. What about changing the bills?"

"Watch and learn." Darger picked up the stack of bills and placed them in his billfold. "Now the game you just played, the Pigeon Drop, is a reliable money-maker in skilled hands, which works well with a necklace, a painting, or any similar prop. It can also be used with a lost wallet. Simply fan out the money like this, with the thousand-ruble note on top, and it will look like a fortune. Indeed, the other notes can be cut from newspaper, if you like. Though that requires that you wrap up the wallet like a package with your handkerchief and string before handing it over, to prevent the mark from examining the bills himself. Luckily, by that point he will be so blinded by avarice that he will not be thinking clearly. You can tell him it's to keep him from stealing the money, and he won't argue." He extracted the money again and rolled it up into a wad. "For other games, it's best you keep the money in a roll. It looks eye-popping"—he put it into a pocket and then pulled it out, giving Kyril only a brief glimpse before hiding it away again—"and, like a well-proportioned woman giving a mark the merest flash of forbidden flesh, wrests control of his thoughts away from the rational parts of his mind."

From an inner pocket of his jacket, Darger extracted a small sewing kit. He measured out a length of black thread, bit it off, and tied it around the wad. Sternly, he said, "You must not spend this. It is a tool which, properly employed, will bring you in much more money. And *that* you may then spend."

Kyril stared at the wad hungrily. "What's with the thread?"

"Keep your spending money in one pocket and this little horse choker in another. Then when you're in a tight fix in a public space... maybe the police are coming after you, maybe a con has gone hot and the mark is out for blood... you haul it out, slip your thumb between the thread and the bills like this..." He demonstrated. "And with a flick of your wrist, you break the thread and throw the money into the air, while shouting 'Money!' at the top of your lungs. What do you think happens then?"

"Everybody starts leapin' up in the air, snatching at the bills."

"Everybody. Including the police. While they're doing that, you make your escape." Darger handed over the money. "Now I know boys, and so I know you're going to rush out right now and, against all my good advice, buy pocket knives and sweets and leather jackets and such. Try not to spend it all. It's easier to make money when you have it."

Kyril clutched the wad with both hands. Then, suspiciously, he slipped it out of the thread and opened it up to determine that all the bills were still present.

Darger laughed. "I admire your caution. But you must never do that before your business associates. They must believe that you trust them implicitly. You may need them to get you out of a tight situation some day."

"I can rely on my boys," Kyril said. "We're a circle of brothers, is what we are."

"Perhaps. Yet I have my doubts about one or two of them. However, let us not throw them away without testing them first. A true friend is a rare thing. You may go now."

In a flash, Kyril was halfway out the hole. He hesitated there, though, and asked over his shoulder, "Ain't you going out too? To spend the money you got for the necklace?"

"No," Darger said. "I shall stay here and sort through the library's many wonders. I have already found a copy of Hesiod's *Catalogue of Women* and what I suspect may be Aristotle's *Dialogues*. It is possible even that some of Homer's lost epics lurk herein, to be discovered by my eager hand."

"Well … I guess if it makes you happy."

"Oh, it does, my young friend. In fact, if I may confide in you, it is possible I am happier now than I have ever been in my life." Darger returned to his book. "It's a shame it cannot last."

Zoësophia slept late and awoke to find the day unseasonably mild. A cool, light breeze raised goose-bumps on her flesh and gently stirred the reddish-gold down on her mound of pleasure. She could have stayed like this for hours, luxuriating in the air, as if in a bath. Nevertheless, she arose and, in a brisk, businesslike fashion, dressed. On the cushions below her, Surplus stirred, stretched, and opened his eyes. When he saw that she was fully clad, his expression mingled regret and relief in proportions she found both perfectly appropriate and eminently satisfying.

"Put your clothes on," she said. "Our story is that we stayed up all night negotiating. You, of course, gave in on every point. Don't bother saying a word. I'll take care of it all. Just keep silent and look hangdog. That shouldn't be hard for you."

Surplus obeyed without demur. This was, in Zoësophia's abundant experience, how men inevitably reacted to being thoroughly bested in the sexual arena—with a quietly sulky submissiveness born of humiliation and the hope that it might happen again soon. It was such a primitive, animal response as to make her wonder if the old legend wasn't true, that men—even dog-men—were descended from apes, while women were descended from the Moon.

Still, there was an amused glint in the corner of the ambassador's eye that Zoësophia could not account for.

"Before we go down, let me see to your clothing." With a few deft tugs, Zoësophia made Surplus look subtly bedraggled. "That's better."

"Shall I unlatch the trap door now?"

"What an extraordinary question." Zoësophia widened her eyes in astonished hauteur. "I'm certainly not about to do it for myself."

When Surplus and Zoësophia came down the spiral stairs—Zoësophia like a goddess floating downward to Earth and Surplus like a man cast out of Heaven—they found the Pearls waiting for them all in a row. Six hard stares of accusation and angry speculation formed a wall of resentful pique. Behind them, the Neanderthals shuffled in embarrassment.

"Well?" Russalka demanded. The word might have been carved from ice.

"Ambassador de Plus Precieux was a firm and energetic negotiator," Zoësophia said solemnly, "and he held out far longer than I had expected him to. But in the end, I wore him down. His determination wilted while I was still prepared to go on for as long as it took. The results, I am pleased to report, were everything that might be desired."

Russalka crossed her arms in a manner which would have thoroughly befuddled a male. "Yes, but what are they?"

"In brief, the ambassador and I are going to the Terem Palace together this very next Tuesday morning. We will meet in private with the Duke of Muscovy, at which time I will present him with whatever proofs it takes…" She paused for emphasis. "*Whatever* proofs it takes to convince him that he would be completely mad not to bring us all to his bedchamber before moonrise that night."

The squeals of delight that arose from the Pearls were so shrill and prolonged that even the Neanderthals winced.

There were five underlords in all.

Though the bodies they inhabited were human, it was not difficult to detect the machines within, for they so despised the flesh they wore that they would not condescend to wear it well. Their metal parts were not proportioned properly for the bodies they had gutted for disguise, but they refused to alter those mechanisms, simple though that would be for them to do. Gleaming steel stuck through here a shoulder and there a cheek, and an alert eye could occasionally glimpse tiny sparks of electricity through an open mouth or an empty eye-socket. They hunched when they stood, glided with an unnatural smoothness when they walked, and folded their arms tidily up and together before them, like unused tools, when they were still.

Anya Pepsicolova knew immediately that something had gone seriously wrong when she showed up at the underlords' conference room to discover all five of her inhuman masters gathered together to confront her. One was enough to conduct any business they might have. They showed up in force only when human suffering was in the offing.

There had only been one when she'd looked down from the Whisper Gallery not half an hour ago. She'd been kept waiting after she made her roundabout route to the underlords' stronghold. Obviously, they had assembled for her.

She lit a new cigarette from the stub of the old one and flicked away the butt without bothering to put it out. The smoke helped, a little, to cover the stench of their decaying bodies. "You sent for me. You must have something to say."

One of the underlords leaned forward over the ancient mahogany conference table, placing its hands flat on the smooth surface. The velvet hangings on the wall behind it had been ripped and shredded by time, and the clothes it wore were only slightly less tattered. Candles flickered in brass sconces which had once held electric lights, casting a meager and gloomy light over the scene.

Slowly the second underlord leaned forward, beside the first. Then the third, the fourth, the fifth. The first creature's mouth clacked open and shut twice in its lifeless white face. At last it said, "Do you fear us?"

"You obey us."

"But obedience is not the same as fear."

"You must fear us."

"Tell us that you fear us, Anya Alexandreyovna."

"More than you can imagine," Pepsicolova said insincerely. In fact, she did fear them—some. Only not as much as they required from her. Nobody who answered directly to Sergei Nemovich Chortenko could entirely fear demon machines that had stitched themselves into human corpses. They might be sadistic, homicidal, and driven by unreasoning and unquenchable hatred, but since it was their nature rather than their choice, they still fell short of absolute evil. That was only Pepsicolova's opinion of course—but by now, she was something of an expert on such matters.

"If you truly feared us, you would be filled with dread and terror to learn that we no longer require your services."

"But you find us faintly comic, do you not?"

"Terrifying but also laughable, in a bleak, nihilistic way. Do not try to deny it."

"We understand human beings better than humans do themselves."

"Nevertheless, you are indeed filled with dread and terror at the prospect of what we might do now that you are no longer useful to us."

Pepsicolova drew deeply on her cigarette, buying time to think. She was sure she could kill one and with luck maybe two of the underlords, before the others could take her down. But never all five. Despite their grotesquely misshapen bodies, those things could be blindingly fast when need arose. She was as good as dead, if they wished her so. "This has something to do with the stranniks, doesn't it? Something to do with the satchel of vials they brought you."

The underlords grew very still. "You are bluffing."

"Somehow you discovered that stranniks brought us a satchel of vials."

"This would not be impossible to learn."

"Stranniks talk too freely."

"What do you know about the stranniks?"

"Enough." Pepsicolova blew a smoke ring at her interrogators. It floated almost to their faces before dissolving in the air. Making up lies at random, she said, "I've known two of them for years. The third I met only recently, but after I confessed my sins to him, he called me his ghostly daughter and swore he would be my guardian angel and protector in all things from that day onward."

"This is consistent with the known behavior of stranniks."

"Religion is superstition and stranniks are superstitious."

"The feelings of superiority an older man would have, hearing in detail the socially unsanctioned behavior of a younger woman, would be conducive to his emotionally bonding with her."

"Possibly they would then fornicate."

"You will immediately tell us everything you know."

"What's my incentive?" Pepsicolova said defiantly. "Are you promising to kill me quickly and painlessly if I do?"

The first underlord pulled back, dragging its hands across the conference table. Steel claws left ten deep gouges in the wood. The others followed suit. "No, Anya Alexandreyovna, we will not. We hate you too deeply for that."

"Then you will simply have to live without the knowledge."

The five underlords were very still for the length of a very long breath. They were communing, Pepsicolova suspected, by means of that ancient necromancy bearing the unlikely name of *radio*. At last the first underlord lowered its arms so that she would have an unobstructed view of the ruins of its face and said, "Shall we show her?"

"She will not like what she sees."

"It will cause her great mental distress."

"It will fill her waking hours with despair and her sleep with nightmares."

"Follow us, Anya Alexandreyovna."

The underlords led Pepsicolova down a series of corridors and through the great room where cigarettes were deconstructed, doctored, and repackaged. But the crates of cigarettes had been cleared away, along with everything else connected with that enterprise. Instead, the Pale Folk were lashing tight bundles of straw to sticks, creating something like a cross between a besom and a broom. These were dunked repeatedly into cauldrons of liquid paraffin, kept warm by small fires underneath, and then carefully set aside. Others were cutting and sewing leather into narrow curving cones as long as a human forearm, with straps and buckles at the open end. These they stuffed with dried herbs held in place by wads of cheesecloth.

A dozen or so figures already wore the leather cones strapped to their lower faces like masks. With the appearance of the underlords, the Pale Folk put aside their work and did likewise. Then they joined their masters, some before and some behind. One in ten of these bird-beaked homunculi picked up a torch and lit it from the warming fires. In solemn silence, they filed out of the great room, looking for all the world like some cultic religious procession out of the fevered hindbrain of ancient Rus.

"You're making torches and masks now, instead of cigarettes." Pepsicolova found this alarming on more than one level. "Why?"

No answer.

"Do I need a mask?"

No answer.

They passed out of the installation. As they did, more and more Pale Folk joined the procession. They were a near-silent, shuffling mass, torchlit in outline, dark and unknowable at the core.

For over an hour, they passed through what, for lack of a better word, might be called farmlands. Here, passages and rooms had been filled with trays of human manure, on which grew pale blue mushrooms, tended by bird-beaked Pale Folk. The smell made Pepsicolova's head swim, but she lit up a cigarette and the sensation went away. Occasionally, the underlords paused to hand something to a mushroom farmer. Maybe it was a vial. The torchlight was never steady enough for Anya to tell.

At last the subterranean farms were left behind. Down stairways and slanting passages the silent flow of bodies went, like an underground river seeking the center of the earth. Until, at a level far deeper than Pepsicolova had ever gone before, they came to a metal wall. In its was a crudely cut hole. Metal shavings littered the floor.

One at a time, the underlords ducked within. Pepsicolova followed. The Pale Folk stayed behind.

The space within was perfectly lightless.

Pepsicolova waited for her eyes to adjust, but they could not. She could sense the underlords to either side of her, but she could not see a thing.

"If you want to show me something," she said at last, "you're going to have to get one of your flunkies in here with a torch."

"Ah, but first we must prolong your mental agony, Anya Alexandreyovna."

"It must surely be excruciating already."

"But it can still get worse."

"Much worse.'

"Trust us."

Silence stretched as taut as a violin string about to snap. Pepsicolova could feel the hatred crackling soundlessly in the air about her. It was almost a physical force. As was the conviction that she was about to be shown something unspeakable. The moment went on and on until, just as she was about to burst into hysterical laughter, one of the Pale Folk stepped into the room, bearing a torch.

"Behold, Anya Alexandreyovna, the weapon with which we shall destroy Moscow, Muscovy, and all Russia as well."

Pepsicolova stared in disbelief.

Back in the Hotel New Metropol, Arkady found that he was still unable to purge the images from his mind. The things he had done! His stomach churned at the thought of them. Yet, at the time, his traitorous body had gloried in those filthy actions. "I don't understand, holy one," he said to Koschei. "There were men present and I used them as I would a woman. And I…" His voice thickened with shame. "I…I let them use me in the same manner."

"Why does this puzzle you, my son?"

"Because I am not…"

"Yes?"

"Not…well…one of them."

"One of whom?"

Arkady blushed red as a beet and blurted out, "An ass-bender! Okay? I'm not a goddamned faggot!"

"The human body is a vile thing, when you reflect on it, is it not?" Koschei said. "An ancient prophet wrote that Love has pitched his mansion in the place of excrement—and what is that place of excrement but the Earth? The world is a dung heap, and those who crawl about on it are vermin who are fortunate only in that their stay upon it is brief.

"In such a world, the greatest blessing is never to have been born. Failing that, it is a short life. But it is not God's will that we should escape His testing, and so there is Hell. All suicides go to Hell, and that wicked place is the most loathsome world in all existence. Which is to say that it is exactly like this Earth in every detail save one. This far from insignificant detail is that Hell is totally divorced from God. Is this not so?"

"So you have taught me, holy one."

"How, then, can we tell that this world is not indeed Hell? From the fact that pleasure exists here, as it cannot in the Infernal Place. First and foremost, there is the experience of religious ecstasy, which is the highest of all pleasures. Second, there is the experience of being persecuted by the unjust, which is a pleasure second only to that of God's presence. Very few are fortunate enough to experience the first or pious enough to appreciate the second. Yet there is also a third such proof, and that is the pleasure of sex, which is available to all. Though the deed be disgusting, the pleasure it engenders is pure. It comes not from the flesh, which is to be abhorred, but from the Spirit, which all human souls must embrace or be damned. Therefore, no pleasure is wicked or wrong or to be avoided, however much the mind may flinch away from it. Do you understand me, son?"

"Yes, kindly father."

"Then kneel and receive your blessing."

Arkady complied. He closed his eyes and waited for the monk's hand on his head. But it did not come. Instead, he heard the sound of Koschei's robe sliding to the floor.

Oh, he thought.

…9…

Surplus helped Zoësophia into the carriage and then went around to the far side and climbed in, leaving the footman to shut the door behind him. The interior was dark and snug, and the cushions deep and soft. There was not a hand's-breadth of distance between the two of them. Yet Zoësophia held herself with such a frosty reserve that it might as well have been miles.

The coachman shook the reins and the horses started off.

"You are quiet today, O Dark Flame of the West."

For a time, Zoësophia stared out the window at the passing buildings. Then, without turning, she said, "You must never touch any of the other Pearls."

Affecting a wounded tone, Surplus said, "Madam, I am a gentleman! Which is as good as to say that I am a devout believer in serial monogamy."

"In my experience, what a gentleman *believes* and what he *does* are seldom the same thing. But let me ask you this. Suppose you were to kiss one of my sisters—Olympias, let us say—ever so lightly upon her fingertips, and those fingertips did not blister. What do you think she would do then?"

"One imagines she would seize the chance to rid herself of her troublesome virginity. But I would never—"

"My sisters are all warm-hearted and generous. They were created so. The first thing Olympias would do is inform her sisters of this happy opportunity. Then, as a group, they would descend upon you. Now, I want you to reflect back upon these last several nights and ask yourself this: What condition would you be in now, had there been six of me?"

"Oh, dear lord."

"Precisely. It would take a stronger fellow than you to survive the experience. I want you to think about that most seriously."

Surplus did. After a moment or so, he broke to the surface of his thoughts to discover in the window's reflection a rather silly smile upon his face and, over his shoulder, Zoësophia scowling darkly. She clapped her hand to his crotch and in a fury cried, "You pig! You're in lust!"

Assuming his sincerest mien, Surplus said, "What male would not be, given such images as you urged me to reflect upon? You conjure up an Arabian Nights fantasy of female flesh, an Aladdin's cave of erotic treasure. Of course I lust after them—in my imagination. So too do I enjoy the original tales, as translated in classical times by Sir Richard Burton. Yet I have never gone to Deserta Arabia in search of the riches described in them."

"Only because you knew those riches to be fictional. Otherwise, I am quite certain you would possess the fabled lamp today. You are most damnably ingenious in getting what you want." As she spoke, Zoësophia peeled off her gloves. She took Surplus's paws in her strong bare hands. When Surplus tried to draw free of her, he found he could not. Her grip was implacable.

Zoësophia favored Surplus with a ruefully amused smile, such as a woman gives a scoundrel who, while he may or may not have necessarily intended to do so, has given her great physical and emotional pleasure. It mingled scorn and fondness in equal measure. "Sweet, sweet 'Sieur Plus," she murmured, "I am so sorry to have to do this. But I have sworn to protect the Pearls, and so I must."

"Wh-what do you intend to do?"

"I am going to kiss you, long and hard and so delightfully that, whether you wish it or not, it will first take your breath away, then starve your brain of oxygen, and finally leave you in a state of mindless euphoria. Then, at the moment of greatest bliss, I will snap your neck."

"Madam! This is not the act of a friend."

"When the carriage door is opened, your corpse will be found and with it me—hysterical and clearly traumatized by whatever outré events have transpired within. By the time I have recovered well enough to narrate those events, I shall have concocted something convincing, I am sure."

Without releasing her grip, Zoësophia leaned forward. Her lips parted. The pink tip of her tongue licked them moist. Her eyes were tender and merciless. Surplus had looked death in the face many a time. Yet never before had it looked so desirable. Nor had beauty ever seemed so terrifying.

"Wait!" Surplus cried. "This is not necessary! *I know your secret!*"

Zoësophia paused. "Oh?"

"You alone of all the Pearls were not a dedicated virgin. The reasoning I gave you was, as we both know, mere sophistry—the others would blister at my touch and die from my caress, for the mental commands they were given cannot be undone by logic-chopping. You, knowing the true situation, could pretend to be convinced by me, and so you did."

Zoësophia released her grip and leaned back against the cushions. After a very long silence, she said, "How did you know?"

Rubbing his aching paws together to restore their circulation, Surplus said, "It was the simplest thing in the world. I asked myself whether, in a contingent of seven women who could be expected to have intimate contact with the Duke of Muscovy, the Caliph was likely to have neglected to include a spy. 'Unthinkable!' was my reply. Further, I reasoned, that spy was unlikely to be bound by the same mental commands and restrictions as the others, lest it hinder her information-gathering activities. Finally, I asked myself which of the seven brides was the most likely to be the spy—and one stood out like a lamp in the darkness for her shrewdness, intellect, and self-control."

"But to take such a risk with one who was supposed to be a dedicated virgin! Had your reasoning proved incorrect…" Zoësophia's expression was complicated, but Surplus, who had some experience with women, could read it like a book. She was waiting to see if he was simpleton enough to tell her that it had been obvious to him that she was no virgin. At which point, she would doubtless rip off his head, or other parts. It was true that she was far from a virgin. Far, far indeed, to judge by the last several nights. Still, young ladies had their pride. A careless word now would cost him dearly.

"Indeed, and there was always the chance that I had guessed wrong," Surplus admitted. "You may be sure I thought about this long and seriously. Knowing not only your strength but your passionate nature as well, I was only too painfully aware that were I wrong, my life would be forfeit."

"Then why take the chance?"

"I decided, finally, that the prize was worth the risk."

Briefly, Zoësophia was silent. Then, wrapping her scarf about her lower face to preserve her modesty, she cranked down the window so she could lean out and call up to the coachman, "How much longer until we reach Chortenko's house?"

"Fifteen minutes, Gospozha," the driver replied.

"Then there is just enough time." She closed the window again and began to unbutton Surplus's shirt.

"My dear lady!" Surplus cried with more than a touch of alarm. "Whatever are you doing?"

"I have belonged to the Byzantine Secret Service literally since my genes were mingled *in vitro*," Zoësophia said. "There is nothing—absolutely nothing—that I find irresistible." Her hand caressed his cheek. "But a man who is willing to risk death in order to possess my body comes close."

Kyril and his bandits had stacked two empty crates atop each other and thrown a white cloth over them for a table, and were playing three-card Monte, exactly as they had been taught. Kyril slammed down three cards: two black deuces and the queen of hearts, creased lengthwise, so that when he flipped them face down, they were like shallow tents. One could almost—but not quite—see the markings under them. "Find the lady, find the queen," he chanted. "Five will get you ten, ten will get you twenty. Watch carefully—the hand is quicker than the eye." There was a scattering of banknotes on the cloth to catch the eye and avarice of the bystanders.

"I switch the cards once…twice…three times and where's the queen? To the right?" He flipped over the rightmost card. A deuce. "No. To the left?" Another deuce. "No." He flipped both back and turned over the center card. "She's right in the middle, right where I put her. The hand can do what the eye cannot see." His hands spun the cards about the cloth. "Who'll play? Who'll play? Five will get you ten, ten will get you twenty. You, sir. Will you play? Or you? You can't win if you don't play."

A crowd of idlers had gathered to watch, but so far there were no players. Which was Dmitri's cue to come forward. He squirmed through the spectators and slapped down a copper ruble. "Betcha I can spot it."

"Only a ruble? Only one? One'll get you two, but ten'll get you twenty." Kyril flicked the cards about, turned them over—one, two, three—and turned them back again. "Twenty gets you forty and fifty a hundred. Only one? All right, then. Here's the queen." He held the card up and turned from side to side so that all could see. Then he slammed it down onto the cloth, switched the cards rapidly about, and finally took a half-step back from the table. "Choose."

Dmitri's finger jabbed. "That one."

Kyril turned the card over. It was a deuce. He flipped over a second card. Also a deuce. The red queen he turned over last.

"Here! Lemme see that!" Dmitri snatched up the red queen and examined it suspiciously. But as it was only a pasteboard card, there was nothing to be discovered, and so Dmitri returned it to the table.

But as he did, he bent up one corner of the card.

Kyril swept the ruble coin to the side, along with the bills, and began manipulating the cards again. He did not appear to notice that the queen had been altered.

Dmitri turned away to give the crowd a broad smirk and a wink. Then he dug deep into his pockets and came up with a grimy five-ruble note. "Here! This is all I got. Gimme one more chance."

"Everyone's money is good. We have a player. Five'll get you ten, ten rubles for five. Watch the cards. The hand moves faster than the eye. Here's the queen and over she goes. She dances with one, she dances with his brother. Everybody dances, everybody wins. Annnnd—make your pick!"

Dmitri pointed at the card with the bent corner. "That one."

"Are you sure?" Kyril switched the other two around and then flipped up one. A black two. "Double your bet and I'll let you choose the other card."

"Naw. I want that one."

With a shrug, Kyril flipped over the remaining two cards, showing the queen where his friend had pointed. Then he brushed two banknotes to the front of the table. Dmitri waved them triumphantly in the air and then, pocketing the money ostentatiously, swaggered off.

"Ten'll get you twenty, fifteen thirty." Kyril flipped the cards face down, face up, face down again. "Who'll play, who'll play? Thirty gets you forty, fifty a hundred." The queen was still turned up at the corner.

"I'll play!" A gent with gold-rimmed pince-nez fumbled several banknotes from his wallet and, face gleaming with greed, laid them down. "Fifty rubles says I can find the queen."

"Everyone's money is good," Kyril said. "Here's the queen, watch her go. She dances with the deuce, she dances with his brother..." As he slid the cards back and forth, he smoothed down the corner of the queen with his thumb, and bent up the corner on one of the deuces. Now all he had to do was let the mark choose the wrong card and sweep in the winnings.

"Caught you!" Muscular arms wrapped themselves around Kyril, holding him motionless. "You're under arrest, you vicious little swindler." It was a goat—and in uniform, too! How had the lookouts let him get so close without whistling a warning?

Looking wildly about, Kyril saw Stephan and Oleg, standing too close to have been doing their jobs, take to their heels. Saw, too, Lev snatch up the white cloth with all the money on it, and run as well. At least he was doing his duty. But that still left Kyril in the strong grip of the policeman.

"Lev!" he shouted. "Remember what you promised!"

But instead of throwing the money in the air, Lev clutched it tight.

"*Lev!*"

Kyril saw his faithless friend disappear into the crowd.

Desperately, then, Kyril snarled over his shoulder, "Get your mitts off me, you ass-fucker. I'm not gonna be your butt-boy, no matter how much you beg me."

The goat's ugly face twisted in outrage. He pulled back one fist to give Kyril a hard punch in the face.

But Kyril had a hand free now and that was all he needed. He plunged it into his pocket, pulled out the wad of money and, snapping the thread, flung it into the air.

Pandemonium.

Just as the Englishman had predicted, everyone—even the goat—was snatching at the banknotes fluttering down from above. Bodies slammed into bodies. Grown men crawled after bills lying on the ground. Somebody shoved somebody else, and fights broke out.

Weeping hot tears of anger, Kyril fled to freedom.

"They none of them stood up for me. Not Oleg or Stephan—hell, they was supposed to be keeping a lookout and didn't. Dmitri wasn't no use either. And Lev! I shouted for him to throw up the money, but did he? No. I fucking begged him. I got down on my fucking knees. He was gonna let me go to prison, just so he could keep a few lousy rubles!"

"You will remember that I cautioned you that your associates were of unknown mettle," Darger said gently. He set down the *Telegonia* in order to give the urchin his full attention. "This is a hard lesson to learn at such a tender age, and yet a necessary one as well. Most people are untrustworthy and, as a rule, only in it for themselves. Better you know that now than not at all."

"Well, it sucks!" Kyril said. "It sucks big fat donkey dicks!"

"Your bitterness is natural. But you must not let it distract you from learning your games."

"Games! What good are games, if I ain't got no friends?"

"No friends?" Darger said in a tone of mild astonishment. "Why do you think I've been teaching you a trade, if not out of friendship?"

"You're just doing it so you can keep all these—" Kyril spat out the word as if it were an obscenity—"*books*."

"Oh, my dear chap! You don't imagine that I'll be allowed to keep these books, do you? No, no, no. As soon as it is discovered I have found them, the Duke of Muscovy—or rather his people—will take them away from me. Nor will I be offered any sort of adequate recompense or reward. This is simply the way of the world. The strong take from the weak, and afterward they call it justice."

"Then what the fucking hell are you doing here?"

"It would take some time to spell out the workings of the operation in which I am engaged. Suffice it to say that I have a trusted associate who will pretend to set a trap for me. The great powers of Muscovy will bait that trap with what I trust will be enormous wealth. And in the natural course of things, there will come a fleeting, magical moment when that bait is solely in my associate's control. The rest, I trust, you can work out for yourself."

"You'd better watch out your pal doesn't grab everything and skip out on you."

"My associate has proved himself a hundred times over. This is what I was trying to explain to you earlier: Not that friends are unreliable, but that a reliable friend is a pearl beyond price. I would walk through fire for him. As, I truly believe, he would for me."

"Yeah, well, I ain't walking through fire for nobody," Kyril said intensely. "I'm not putting myself out for nobody ever again."

"Then you're not half the fellow I believe you to be. Incidentally, did you bring today's papers with you?"

"Don't I always? I set 'em down over there."

"And there's my proof! Even in your heightened emotional state, you have demonstrated your reliability. Look here. It is true that this is a very bad world. It is true that the strong feed upon the weak, and the weak feed upon each other. But not all the weak are content to remain so. Some few—such as you and I, Kyril, you and I!—employ our wits to better our lot and to regain some fraction of what was stolen from us long before we were born."

"Yeah, yeah."

"I shall be leaving you soon, and without so much as a word of farewell, as often is necessary in our trade. But before I do, I would like to impart to you a few words of fatherly wisdom. If. . ." Darger stopped, thought, and began again. "To do well in this world, this is what is required of you: First of all confidence, patience, and the ability to keep your head when those around you are mad with hysteria. You must learn to present a bland face in the presence of lies and hatred. Let others underestimate you. Take care not to look too good or to sound too wise. Spin dreams for others, but don't get caught up in them yourself. Plan for triumph and prepare for disaster. There will be times when you lose all you have; pick yourself up and start over again, and don't whine about it afterward.

"Most of all, live life with all your heart and nerve and sinew. If you can talk with the common bloke without putting on airs and walk with the nobs without letting them relieve you of your watch and wallet... If you can enter a strange city dead broke and leave with your pockets stuffed with cash…Why, then, old son, you'll be a confidence man, and all the Earth and everything in it will be yours."

Face screwed up with disgust, Kyril turned and left without saying a word.

"Well," Darger murmured. "I thought I understood young boys. But clearly I do not." His hand hesitated over the *Telegonia*, but instead moved on to the papers. Kyril had brought both major dailies, the *Moscow Conquest*, and the *New Russian Empire*. Darger carefully read through the social notes in each. There had been time enough for the Muscovy officials to approach Surplus with plans to catch his errant secretary and claim the library for themselves. As soon as they did, Surplus was supposed to announce a masked ball.

But there was still no news.

Chortenko came out to greet the carriage personally. "Gospozha Zoësophia! What a delightful surprise." He took her gloved hand and kissed the air above it. Then he offered Surplus a hearty, democratic handshake. "I have informed the duke you are coming, and he looks forward to the meeting with his usual attentiveness."

"He does not seem to get out of the Kremlin much," Surplus observed, retrieving his walking stick from the carriage.

Chortenko's mouth quirked upward, as if he were secretly amused. "The great man's work is his life."

At that moment, a door opened and closed somewhere in the mansion so that briefly the yelping of hounds could be heard. "You have dogs!" Zoësophia cried. "Might we see them?"

"Yes, of course you shall. Only not just now. I have arranged for the Moscow City Troop to escort us to the Kremlin, and they are forming up on the other side of the building at this very moment. Shall we take my carriage or yours?"

"I am always keen for new experiences," Zoësophia said, "whether they be large or small."

But every hair on Surplus's body was standing on end. His hearing was acute, as was his sensitivity to the emotions of his dumb cousins. Those dogs were not barking out of ordinary canine exuberance, but from pain and terror and misery. Surplus's ears pricked up and his nostrils flared. He could smell from their pheromones that they had been extremely badly treated indeed.

Chortenko's spectacles were twin obsidian circles. "You look alarmed, my dear fellow. Has something startled you?"

"I? Not at all." Surplus turned to his coachman and with a dismissive wave of his paw sent their equipage back to the embassy. "Only, sometimes I am struck by sudden dark memories. As a man of the world and a some-time adventurer, I have seen more than my share of human cruelty."

"We must trade stories someday," Chortenko said amiably. "Those who appreciate such matters say that if you have not seen Russian cruelty, then you do not know cruelty at all."

Chortenko's carriage was painted blue-and-white, like his mansion, so that it resembled nothing so much as a Delftware teapot. When it was brought around, Zoësophia and Surplus were given the back seats, while Chortenko and his dwarf savants sat facing them.

Bracketed by horsemen, they started for the Kremlin.

"Tell me, Max," Chortenko said, turning to the dwarf on his left. "What do we know about the tsar's lost library?"

"In 1472, the Grand Duke of Moscow Ivan the Third married Princess Sofia Paleologina, a niece of the last Byzantine emperor, Andreas, more rightly known as the Despot of Morea. Despotism is a form of government where all power is embodied in a single individual. The individual self does not exist. As her dowry, Sofia brought to Moscow a wagon train of books and scrolls. Moscow was founded by Prince Yuri Dolgurki in 1147. Soddy podzolic soil is typical of Moscow Oblast. It is apocryphal that the books were the last remnants of the Great Library of Alexandria."

"Of course, anything labeled apocryphal may also be true," Chortenko mused.

"The Italian architect Aristotle Fioravanti was commissioned to build a secret library under the Kremlin. Fioravanti also served as a military engineer in the campaigns against Novgorod, Kazan, and Tver. Kazan is the capital of Tartarstan. Tartar sauce is made from mayonnaise and finely chopped pickled cucumber, capers, onions, and parsley, and was invented by the French to go with steak tartare. The last documented attempt to find the library was made by Tsar Nikita Khrushchev."

"Yes, well, we seem to have gotten off the subject." To Surplus, Chortenko said, "Have you heard the rumors? They say that the library has been found."

"Really? That would make a splendid present for the Duke of Muscovy, then. One worthy of a Caliph."

"That is true. Yet one cannot help wondering what would happen were the secret of the library's location in private hands. Surely that lucky person—whoever he might be—would find himself in a position to claim an enormous reward, eh?"

"Unless he was a government official. Then, of course, his reward would be the simple knowledge that he had done his duty."

"Indeed. Yet a private citizen would not be in a position to know whether the reward he was being offered was worthy of his heroic discovery. Perhaps the best possible arrangement would be a partnership involving somebody highly positioned within the government and somebody who was not even a citizen of Muscovy. A foreigner, possibly even an ambassador. What do you think?"

"I think we understand each other perfectly." Surplus settled back into the cushions, warmed by the abrupt conviction that all was right with the world. "I think also that it is about time that the embassy had a masked ball. I shall advertise the event in the newspapers just as soon as I get back."

The troops clattered up the great causeway to the Kremlin, driving before them businessmen, mendicants, office-seekers, and assorted riffraff unfortunate enough to have chosen that day to petition favors from the government. At the Trinity Tower gate, they were halted and then, their jurisdiction extending so far and not an inch farther, turned back. After an examination of credentials, the carriage was allowed to pass within, accompanied by an escort of Trinity Tower Regulars. At Cathedral Square they alit and, after their papers were presented again, the Inner Kremlin Militia escorted the party to the entrance of the Great Kremlin Palace. There, the Great Palace Guards assumed responsibility for the party, led them up a marble staircase, and directed them onward.

"It seems odd we must go through one palace to get to another," Surplus remarked.

"Nothing is straightforward in this land," Chortenko replied.

They passed under twin rows of crystal chandeliers in Georgievsky Hall, an open, light-flooded room of white pillars and parquet floors in twenty types of hardwood, then through its great mirrored doors to the octagonal Vladimirsky Hall with its steep domed ceiling and gilt stucco molding. From whence it was but a short walk to the entrance of the most splendid of the Kremlin's secular buildings, Terem Palace.

Two eight-foot-tall guards, whose genome was obviously almost entirely derived from *Ursus arctos*, the Russian brown bear, loomed to either side of the entrance. The blades of their halberds were ornamented with ormolu swirls, and yet were obviously deadly. They bared sharp teeth in silent growls, but when Chortenko presented his papers (for the fourth time since entering the Kremlin), they waved the party within.

Surplus took one step forward and then froze.

The walls were painted in reds and golds that were reflected in the polished honey-colored floor, leaving Surplus feeling as if he were afloat in liquid amber. Every surface was so ornately decorated that the eye darted from beauty to beauty, like a butterfly unable to alight on a single flower. Somewhere, frankincense burned. From one of the nearby churches he heard chanting. Then, small and far away, a church bell began to ring. It was joined by more and closer bells, climaxing when all the Kremlin's many churches joined in, so that his skull reverberated with the sound.

"This is quite grand," Surplus heard his own voice saying, in the aftermath. It was all a bit overdone for his plain, American tastes and yet, somehow, he wanted to live here forever.

"I completely approve," Zoësophia said warmly—though by the shrewd look in her eyes, Surplus judged that she was taking mental notes for changes she would make once she came to power.

A messenger hurried by. From his unblinking gaze and rapid stride, it was clear that he was a servile. Another passed, going the other way. "Come," Chortenko said. His bland, round face showed no expression at all.

They followed.

The Duke of Muscovy's chambers took up the top floor of the palace.

The room was dominated by a nude statue of a sleeping giant. It stretched from one end of the building to the other. The giant lay gracefully sprawled upon a tremendous couch with mahogany legs as thick as tree trunks, and red velvet upholstery tacked down with nails whose gilded heads were forged in the shape of double-headed eagles. He was magnificently muscled, and his face was that of a god—Apollo, Surplus speculated, or possibly Adonis. One could gaze upon him for an hour.

The giant shifted slightly, tossing his head and throwing back one arm. His eyes did not open

Surplus's heart sank. In a strangled voice, he said, "*This* is the Duke of Muscovy?"

Chortenko's smile reached no further than his lips. "Now you understand why so few people are allowed to see him. The great man has cognitive powers superior even to those of the fabled Utopian computers. He is the perfect ruler for Muscovy in all aspects but one. He is orderly in his thoughts, analytic in his assessments, loving in his intentions toward his subjects, ruthless toward his enemies, decisive when it comes time to act, patient when all the facts are not yet in, and absolutely without personal interest or bias in his decisions. Alas, he cannot appear in public. The citizenry would reject him as a monster."

Zoësophia sighed. "He is the most perfect expression of male beauty I have ever seen, not even excepting Michelangelo's statue of David in the Caliph's private collection. It is ironic. He is as desirable in his way as I am in mine—and yet he and I are perfectly useless to one other."

"Does he never wake?" Surplus asked.

"Were he to stand, his great heart could only support the body for a matter of hours before bursting," Chortenko said. "So, of necessity, the Duke of Muscovy reigns in a state of perpetual sleep."

There was the sharp click of heels as a servile messenger hurried by and mounted the steps of a railed platform by the duke's head. He leaned forward and in a rapid monotone began reciting a report. When he was done, the duke nodded wordlessly, and he left.

"Now that all of your questions have been addressed," Chortenko said, "I shall go to learn the answers to my own. Do not attempt to approach the duke, for the guards will not permit it."

As always, Chortenko felt a secret thrill of excitement as he mounted the stairs to the dais by the sleeping giant's ear. There was no telling what he might learn, if only he asked the right questions. He gripped the wooden rail, worn smooth by many a thousand hands, and said, "Your Royal Highness, it is your servant Sergei Nemovich who speaks."

"Ahhh… yes… the ambitious one," the duke murmured quietly, as does one who speaks in his sleep. His voice was astonishingly small, coming from such a titanic body. "It was you who arranged matters so…that none of my other…advisors…could approach me."

"True, Majesty. It was you who told me how."

"I slept. Awake, I would not…have aided your conspiracy."

"Since you will never awaken, that is irrelevant. I have brought with me the Byzantine ambassador, and one of the women the Caliph sent you as a present."

"I have been dreaming… of food riots in Uzhgorod. Wheat must be sent… to prevent…"

"Yes, yes, that is most commendable. But it is not what I have come to speak with you about."

"Then speak."

To the far side of the room, Chortenko saw one of Surplus's ears twitch slightly and had no doubt that, though an ordinary human could not have overheard him from such a distance, the dog-man could. The woman he was not so sure about. She appeared to be lost in thought. Well, let them eavesdrop. Nothing they heard would give them much comfort. Choosing his words carefully, he said, "Our friends below are coy about their plans. When will they make their move?"

"The market for tobacco is down slightly, while the demand for illegal drugs of all sorts has declined steeply…. Absenteeism in the officer class is up, prostitution is booming, and there are reports of vagrants seen pushing wheelbarrows full of human feces. Taken together with various promises that have been made, you can expect an invasion of Moscow within days. Possibly as soon as tonight."

"Really!" Chortenko, who had thought it a matter of months at a minimum, could not have been more astonished. But he composed himself. "What preparations should I make that have not yet been done?"

"Eat well and rest. Move all artillery units out of the city and make sure that all known rakes and libertines have been flensed from your own forces. Have Baron Lukoil-Gazprom killed."

"Good, good." Chortenko rather liked the baron, insofar as he liked anybody, for the man's blunt, bluff predictability. But he could see how the baron's twin propensities for unthinking action and reflexive assumption of command in an emergency might get in his way.

The Duke of Muscovy's preternaturally handsome face twisted briefly, as if in pain. "Your scheme…endangers…my city."

"It is worth the risk. Tell me, would it cause trouble with Byzantium if its ambassador were to disappear?"

"I dreamed of Baikonur… and wolves…"

"Try to pay attention, Your Royal Highness. I spoke with Gospodin de Plus Precieux as you directed, telling him of the rumors that the lost library of Ivan the Terrible had been discovered. As you predicted, he showed no surprise. Then, when I proposed a conspiracy to defraud the state, he assented immediately, without requiring even an instant's thought."

"Then he is…nothing more than a confidence trickster who has somehow displaced the true ambassador. You may do with him as you wish."

"He also brought a woman with him," Chortenko reminded the duke. "One of the Byzantine sluts."

"Only…one?"

"Yes."

"Then she is a spy…and her, too, you may…do with as you wish."

This pleasant news Chortenko received with just a touch of regret. More to himself than to his master, he murmured, "So it is nothing but a sad and shabby story all around. A pity. I would have liked to have found the Tsar's lost library."

"It is not…lost. I deduced the library's…location…ten years ago."

"What?"

"It lies below the Secret Tower, in a concealed chamber. There has been some subsidence there recently. Not enough to endanger…the tower… But perhaps it would be well to move the books to a more secure location."

"You have known this for a decade and you never told anyone?" Chortenko said angrily.

"Nobody…asked."

Chortenko drew in a long, exasperated breath. This was exactly why the time had come for the duke's reign to come to an end. Yes, he could answer questions—but only if one knew which to ask. His strategies for expanding Muscovy's influence were brilliant—but he had no aims or ambitions of his own. The goal of restoring the Russian empire had originated with Chortenko and a few others, such as the soon-to-be late Baron Lukoil-Gazprom. The duke was so lacking in intention that he even conspired in his own overthrow!

Worst of all, he could not appear in public. And a war—a true war, one involving millions—could not be fought with a leader who dared not show his face. The duke himself had confirmed this: Without a leader able to inspect troops, make speeches, and fire up the populace, the sacrifices required to raise an army of conquest simply would not be made.

No, the time had come for the duke to die. That had not been a part of Chortenko's original plan. He had meant to let loose rumors that the duke had fallen ill, confirm those rumors, solicit the prayers of the Muscovian citizenry, declare a day of fast and penitence, orchestrate items in the newspapers: *Doctors Fear Worst*, followed later by *Duke in Decline*, a few variants of *No Hope, Say Kremlin Insiders*, a sudden and unexpected *Miraculous Rally!* and then at last *Duke of Muscovy Dies*, and *Nation Mourns*, and *Succession Passes to Chortenko*. After which, the still-sleeping former duke would have been quietly demoted to advisor.

However, his new friends were jealous allies, and viewed the Duke of Muscovy as a rival. The duke's death was part of the price of their cooperation. Chortenko regretted that, for losing that brilliant mind would be a sacrifice equivalent to the slaughter of an entire battalion. But he was prepared to lose any number of battalions, if it meant gaining an empire.

"Just once, I would like… to see… my beloved city… of Moscow. I would be willing… to die… if that is what it cost."

"Trust me, that will never happen."

Chortenko descended from the dais with renewed confidence in the future. He rejoined his companions. Zoësophia's expression was tense and distracted, as befit one who had just seen all her plans and future crumble before her face. Surplus looked unhappy and irresolute.

"This way," Chortenko said, and led them down to the very bottom of the palace, to a door which none but he ever employed. "I told our driver not to bother waiting for us with the carriage. Instead, we will return through an underground passage that leads directly to the basement of my manor."

Zoësophia nodded distractedly. She scowled to herself, lips twitching slightly, a woman in furious thought on matters that had little to do with her present situation. But if her reaction was disappointing, Surplus's was not. He stiffened and looked about himself wildly, gripping his walking stick at its midpoint preparatory to using it as a weapon. His every muscle was tense. He was clearly terrified.

By prearrangement, six of the bear guards closed ranks about the group.

At a gesture, Max unlocked the door. "After you, my dear Ambassador," Chortenko said.

Surplus took a deep breath, and, when he exhaled, seemed to deflate. His shoulders slumped. His eyes dimmed and his gaze fell to the floor. All the fight had gone out of him.

With a shudder, he passed through the door.

...10...

Everywhere he went, Arkady was joyfully received. Women kissed his cheek and men hugged him fervently. Always he was urged to stay for a glass of tea or a shot of vodka. No one ever said aloud that an orgy might be in the offing, but the prospect was inevitably in the air.

Arkady would have liked to linger, but his holy mission would not allow that. He had to deliver rasputin to everyone on Koschei's endless list—to noblemen, army officers, and heads of government agencies, to firefighters and police officers, to doxies and courtesans who snatched the vials from his hand, to hard men with prison tattoos on their fingers who slipped the drug into their pockets without a glance and soft men who received it with wondering eyes, to stock speculators and shopkeepers and dealers in fiery spirits, to priests and pharmacists and genetic surgeons, to college professors and unkempt poets, to night watchmen and munitions manufacturers and private security guards, to torch singers and dream-brewers and longshoremen, to parliamentarians in the Duma and bohemians in the Arbat and grim lords of biology in their cloneries just beyond the slums and brothels of Zamoskvorechye. Rumor of his sacred cargo had spread through Moscow like wildfire, so that to Arkady all the city was a sea of smiles and outstretched hands. His rented carriage sped from Kitai-Gorod to the slums of Gorky Park and as far out of town as the birch forests of Tsaritsyno. Everywhere, he dispensed his drugs like a fairy-tale prince scattering rubies, and was received with thinly disguised greed.

He felt like Grandfather Frost distributing presents to the children on New Year's Eve.

It was exhausting work, but whenever he felt his energies flag, Arkady would open his walrus-hide satchel and plunge his face within, inhaling deeply of the air above the vials. Those microscopic fractions of the drug that had managed to slip past the wax seals would flow into his lungs and blood and brain and muscles, filling him with the strength and benevolence his mission required. It was nothing like the effects of a full dosage, of course, but it was sufficient to keep him going.

Periodically he returned to the New Metropol to refill his bag. Already he had given away far more of the drug than Koschei could possibly have brought with him to Moscow. Yet, like the miracle of the loaves and fishes, the more he gave, the more remained. It was a mystery as inexplicable and astonishing as the fact that God in His perfection should nevertheless love His flawed and sinful human children.

Or so it seemed. The mystery was solved when, coming back yet again to the New Metropol, Arkady saw two dead souls with albino skin and colorless rags for clothing leaving his suite. Their faces were lifeless, their bodies so thin he could not tell if they were male or female, and when they passed by him, Arkady caught a strong whiff of excrement. He entered the room and saw Koschei, Chernobog, and Svarožič prying open a newly delivered crate. Svarožič took the satchel from him and began methodically filling it with vials, straight from the crate, smiling beatifically all the while.

Arkady's back ached just looking at the bag. All his good mood fled.

"This is too much!" he scolded. "There is enough here to drug every man, woman, and child in Moscow ten times over. Surely there is no need for it all to be distributed today." He could not help thinking of all the beautiful young women in the city who were at this very moment giving themselves freely to everyone but him. Earlier that evening, he had turned down Yevgeny's offer to help in the rasputin's distribution, though it would have cut his time in half, because the task had been entrusted to him alone. Now he regretted that bitterly. "We should call it quits and start over again tomorrow."

"It must be done today," Koschei said, the God-light glowing in his eyes. His voice was low and thunderous, and when he spoke electricity seemed to crackle in the air about his head and beard. "Tomorrow will be too late."

"What do you mean, too late?"

"Our labors are at long last come to fruition, praise God and all the Cherubim! For on this very day we will bring about the Eschaton and history will come to an end."

"I don't know what that means."

"No one can know what it means until it happens. We can only accept that it will."

"I still don't—"

"The Eschaton," Chernobog said, "is the transcendent, uncreated, and spiritual apotheosis of humankind, the unending instant when the finger of God touches the Earth and all the immanent and phenomenal world is swallowed up in such wild glories as are experienced in each and every instant by the saints in Heaven."

"But what are you talking about? What will it look like?"

"You will know it when it comes," Koschei said solemnly.

"Yes," Chernobog said, "and it will come soon."

Beaming, Svarožič put his hands together in prayer.

Then, in a flurry of activity, the stranniks placed the satchel in Arkady's hands, slapped him on the back, and ushered him out the door. He found himself alone in the hallway, blinking. He hadn't understood a word of what had just been said to him. But it sounded very spiritual. In some way, it involved God. So whatever or whoever the Eschaton was, it must surely be a good thing? Of course it must.

He put his head inside the satchel, inhaled deeply, and returned to his work with renewed determination.

The tunnel stretched more than a kilometer beyond the Kremlin's walls. Built with the eerie precision characteristic of the ancients, it curved almost imperceptibly, so that more of the corridor was continually appearing before them and monotonously disappearing behind. Luminous lichen covered the ceiling and walls, filling the tunnel with gentle light. Surplus led, followed by Zoësophia and then Chortenko with his dwarf savants, Max and Igorek, striding lockstep at his heels. The six bear-guards came lumbering after them.

"This is a bit of a walk," Chortenko said. "But a pleasant one, yes?" Not that he believed for an instant that his unwitting captives found it any such thing. But he was fascinated by what untruths people could be made to agree to, rather than acknowledge an unbearable truth.

Stiffly, Zoësophia said, "You must excuse me, if I am not in the mood for idle chitchat. I have suffered a serious blow today."

Surplus said nothing.

No one knew for what purpose the tunnel had originally been dug, for such things were never written down. But periodically the company passed a doorway that had been filled in with masonry or else secured by metal plates and locks that had long ago rusted solid. So that purpose, whatever it had been, was no more.

"Walking is such good exercise. I know you will think me a health faddist for saying so, but I try to put in at least an hour per day." Chortenko removed his blue-glass spectacles. He could read Zoësophia's face like a book. When he had first joined Muscovy Intelligence as a junior officer, he had had his eyes surgically removed and the hemispherical insectoid organs he now possessed grown in their place. That people found them intimidating had been pleasant for a homely youth of pudgy build. But their true merit was that they saw deep into the infrared, and so he could follow the patterns of blood flow in people's faces.

Zoësophia, he could see, was lost in dark thoughts, dominated by worry and more than a touch of *tristesse*. But no fear. So she suspected nothing. Surplus was harder to make out, since his face was covered with fur. But his body language said it all. He plodded along listlessly, walking stick tucked under an arm, paws clasped behind his back. He stared fixedly at the ground before his feet. He was the very picture of one who had accepted the inevitability of pain and death, and was now overcome with despair.

Or so Chortenko would have assumed, were he the sort to make assumptions. He was not. They were coming up on a trap he had prepared years ago, which had caught many a would-be fugitive. It was a door which had been left unlocked and just a little bit ajar. Anybody harboring the least spark of hope that he might escape would seize upon the opportunity and dash through it. Only to find himself in a cul-de-sac no larger than a closet.

Surplus gave the door a dispirited glance and continued past it.

So the sad creature was already as good as broken. Well, Chortenko thought, it was a pity, but all his research with the hounds had been for nothing. He would not have much fun with *this* one.

Zoësophia, however… Chortenko half-closed his eyes, imagining what might be done with a young woman of delicate sensibilities and a cloistered upbringing who blistered at the slightest touch of a man's finger. Yes, there were possibilities there. Great possibilities. He would have to be careful to take it slowly.

He would have to make sure she lasted a long, long time.

Finally, the tunnel brought them to the kennels of Chortenko's basement.

The dogs leaped and bayed furiously when Chortenko appeared, making the cages rattle as they slammed their bodies against the sides over and over again.

Zoësophia looked startled and flinched away from the dogs' sudden violence. But Surplus only hunched his shoulders and stuck his paws in his pockets.

"You are dismissed," Chortenko told the bear-guards. They saluted and turned back into the corridor, carefully locking the door behind themselves.

"Sir!" Five agents of the secret police stood in a line at the far end of the room. All wore drab civilian garb, and all, save for one, were ordinary-looking men. The speaker was simultaneously the tallest and thinnest man present. His face was so fleshless as to be almost a skull. "We await your orders."

"So," Surplus said in a dead voice. "It has come to this."

"Come to what?" Zoësophia demanded. "Who are these men? Why are we in this filthy place, surrounded by wild dogs?"

Chortenko did not immediately answer. He had tucked his spectacles in an inner jacket pocket and was relishing the way the blood drained from her face. Behind his back, he held up two fingers.

"There are so many puzzling questions about the nature of the Byzantine mission," he said in a voice that would have been reassuring to the lady were not two of his men pulling on cloth gloves as they advanced upon her. "I intend to have them answered."

"Then ask!" Zoësophia cried, even as she was seized.

"Oh, there's no rush, my dear. We have all the time in the world." Chortenko turned to his men: "Throw her in an empty kennel. Not too roughly, please. I want her in pristine condition for what is to come."

There were two unoccupied kennels. One of the secret police opened the nearest, and the two who held Zoësophia tightly forced her backward toward it. She struggled most fetchingly.

With disdainful ease, the men flung Zoësophia onto her back on the floor of the cage. Then they slammed and locked the door. She gathered herself up in a corner and crouched there, trying not to whimper in fear.

It was all most satisfying.

But, enjoyable as this was, there were more important matters to attend to. Chortenko had not expected the underlords, who would share only the broadest outlines of their plans with him, to be prepared to act until spring at the earliest. A hundred preparations would have to be altered. All the timetables he had set in place would have to be moved up.

"Wettig," Chortenko said, not taking his eyes from his new captive.

"Sir," said the tall and cadaverous agent.

"I have something to say to you privately." Wettig bent low, his ear all but touching his superior's lips, and Chortenko murmured, "Go to Baron Lukoil-Gazprom's room. He is currently at the Kremlin for a meeting of the Committee for the Suppression of Dissent. When he returns, kill him."

Wettig straightened, nodded, left.

Filled with the satisfaction that comes only when one has done one's work well and sees everything falling neatly into place, Chortenko turned back to his confederates with a slight smile. Then he paused and looked around the room, feeling vaguely that something was missing.

With a touch of bewilderment, he said, "Where is the ambassador?"

Surplus sauntered idly through Red Square.

It was an astonishing space. One entered the square through the Resurrection Gates and so came upon it suddenly: To the right loomed the Kremlin. To the left was the building that locals for reasons nobody could explain called "Goom," its façade as elaborate as a wedding cake; it had been originally built to house shops and now, after many changes of fortune, was converted to prestigious apartments for the wealthy and connected. Straight ahead was St. Basil's Cathedral, with its throng of domes painted in bright candy-box colors. Nowhere was there a tree to be seen, or anything that had not been built by human hands. The granite-block-paved square (a rectangle, really, with the long axis running from the gates to the church) rose slightly and then sank down again before St. Basil's, as if gracefully genuflecting. All these factors put together created an exhilarating effect such that wherever one stood, one felt as if he were standing on the very top and center of the world.

Surplus tested this observation by walking diagonally across the square, slowly twirling the walking stick which, astonishingly, Chortenko had not removed from his possession when he was in the man's custody. (It was, he supposed, a tribute to his own acting ability, but one which he resolved not to let go to his head.) And, indeed, he found that wherever he stood the sensation was the same. So long as he was in Red Square, he felt himself in the exact center of, if not the universe, then all of the universe that mattered.

It explained so much about Russian history.

Surplus had not come here to sightsee, however, but to compose his thoughts. Already, the heady exhilaration of a successful escape was threatening to give way to the dread and paranoia of the fugitive. Chortenko would assuredly be scouring the city for him at this very instant. Therefore, Surplus had come to the one place it would never occur to the man to look—to the single most open and public space in all of Moscow.

He felt like a bit of a cad for leaving Zoësophia behind. But she had clearly been working hard to convince Chortenko of her helplessness. And if there was one thing Surplus had learned over the years, it was never to step on another professional's lines. She had a plan, and he could only assume that his absence would, by flustering their mutual foes, help her put it into action. He had wished her luck, slipped unseen up the stairs backwards and on tiptoes (which was an easier stunt than most people realized) while his captives were distracted by Zoësophia's admittedly fetching struggles, and put her out of his mind.

In the meantime, what was he to do? It was elementary that he could not, under any circumstances, return to the embassy. Nor, given the ubiquity of the secret police, would any ordinary hiding place do. With his distinctive appearance, he could not rent a hotel room in even the seediest neighborhood under an assumed name with any confidence of anonymity. If only he knew where Darger was! He had no doubt that his partner had found a bolt-hole of superior obscurity.

Pointless to dwell on that now, however. He had to look for a more accessible avenue of evasion, and so…

And so his eyes lit up when he saw the Baronessa Lukoil-Gazproma striding determinedly across Red Square, followed by a ginger-haired young man bearing packages. Tucking his walking stick under one arm, he intersected the pair's path and bowed deeply to the baronessa. "Dear lady," he said. "How pleasant to see you."

"Monsieur Ambassador de Plus Precieux. *Quelle surprise!* I have caught you away from your duties—and all those beautiful young ladies of yours."

"They are hardly mine, in any sense, and as to beauty… Well, when I first came to Russia, I was warned that I was bringing coals to Newcastle, and here before me is the living proof of the truth of those words."

The baronessa smiled in a way that indicated she appreciated a man who understood the art of flirtation. "Have you met my cousin, Yevgeny Tupelov-Uralmash?"

"A pleasure, sir," Yevgeny said, with a friendly flash of teeth and a firm handshake.

Surplus responded in kind. "You have been shopping, I see," he observed, offering his arm to the baronessa. She took it and they strolled onward, in the direction of Goom. "I trust I'm not keeping you from anything."

"Well, I *was* making a few last-minute preparations for a little get-to-gether at my *pied-à-terre*." She nodded toward Yevgeny's overladen arms. "A few bottles of wine, some caviar, those crackers you can only get direct from that bakery in Chistye Prudy…Trifles, really, but for some things one doesn't want to rely on a servant's judgment. Not when close friends are involved."

"It sounds delightful. Is this a girls-only affair, or might I dare hope to accompany you there?"

The baronessa looked amused. "It would be rather a dull event without men, to my way of thinking." Then, thoughtfully, "It's meant to be strictly invitational, and I'll catch hell from my social secretary if I bring along an unannounced date. Still…You *are* something of a social catch. And one of my male guests *has* indicated that he's unlikely to be able to attend…"

"I still have hopes," Yevgeny said.

"Yes, we all know what you hope, dear boy. Oh, don't sulk! If he shows up, you'll just have more of his attention to yourself." She turned back to Surplus. "So—yes, I believe you'll make quite an adequate substitution. Anyway, I've been curious to learn if it's true what my female friends say about you."

"You astonish me madam. Whatever can the ladies possibly find to say about a simple civil servant such as myself?"

"Nothing but good things, I assure you, Ambassador."

"Please. Call me Surplus. Will the baron be in attendance?"

Her eyes widened. "Oh, no. I don't think it's his sort of thing at all."

As soon as Chortenko had scolded and lectured his thugs up the stairs and out of her presence, Zoësophia turned her attention to her cage's lock. She almost felt insulted. The device was a pin tumbler with only six stacks and a straightforward keyway slot. Removing two hairpins from deep within her elaborate coiffure, she swiftly picked it open. It was as simple as, earlier, it had been to mislead Chortenko by behaving like an imbecile and regulating the flow of blood in her face.

A basic principle of espionage was that men possessed of special talents they thought nobody knew about were particularly easy to deceive.

The door at the top of the stairs opened and she swiftly moved to one side, where she could not readily be seen.

A guard came down into the room, saw the empty cage, and spun about in alarm. Calmly, Zoësophia stepped forward and snapped his neck. Soundlessly, she lowered his corpse to the floor.

"Well!" Zoësophia said aloud, amused. "This is not exactly how I had hoped to make my social debut in Moscow. But it will have to do."

The guard's death had excited the dogs and set them to howling and barking and launching themselves against the doors of their cages again. But of course nobody would pay any attention to that.

At the foot of the stairs, for just an instant, she hesitated. Her sympathies were all with the imprisoned and mistreated dogs. But her first duty was to escape. Anyway, she was not entirely sure she could fend off so many animals if they all attacked her at once. As they surely would if she freed them.

With just a twinge of regret, Zoësophia mentally subtracted the dog-noises and stood listening to the soft creakings of people moving about the mansion above. Avoiding them all and slipping out without being seen would be no more difficult than playing chess blindfolded—and blindfold chess was a game at which she excelled.

Less than ten minutes later, Zoësophia let herself out through the main entrance. She didn't even consider leaving via the secret though frequently used passage in the basement.

A lady never left a house by the rear door.

The Pearls had been excited at first. But then the day had slowly drawn on and the afternoon had grown late and Zoësophia and the ambassador had not returned. They played cards and then board games until they grew bored. They sang songs until they grew even more bored. Olympias played the virginal. They ate oranges and teased a kitten with a piece of yarn. With every familiar activity their boredom grew, until finally it was a tremendous force latent within them like the superheated steam and molten lava inside a volcano. Inevitably, there came a moment when they had all had just about enough and that force threatened to well up within them and explode.

"I am so horny I could—" Aetheria began.

"We've already played that game," Nymphodora said glumly. "Russalka won. Though what Olympias said was almost as disgusting."

"Well, I *would*," Russalka said.

"So would I," Nymphodora agreed. "Only it's icky to admit it out loud."

"— scream," Aetheria finished.

All the Pearls brightened. "Pray do," Euphrosyne said encouragingly.

She did. But after the laughter and applause died down; and the Neanderthals came stampeding in, ready for anything, and then reddened with embarrassment at being fooled so; and the laughter from that died down as well…their boredom returned with redoubled intensity.

"It's time we did something," Russalka said. "Since Zoësophia's not here, I'm nominating myself leader. Does anybody object? Don't any of you dare. It's unanimous then. We're going with my plan."

"What plan?"

"You have a plan?"

"Why didn't you tell us you had a plan?"

"Whatever it is, it's got to be better than gin rummy."

"Yes, I have a plan, and it has nothing at all to do with cards, and instead of me explaining it to you, let's just put it into action. All in favor? Don't bother saying aye. I've already made up my mind. Aetheria, would you call the boys in?"

Aetheria screamed again.

The Neanderthals stampeded into the room again, as always ready for anything and yet this time prepared to be laughed at once more. They stopped at the glares of the young women and, when the Pearls advanced upon them, shrank back.

Russalka stamped an exquisite foot. "You will take us immediately to the Terem Palace." She pouted in a manner that had cost her long hours in front of a mirror to master.

The Neanderthals shuffled uncomfortably.

"Ahem. Well. I dunno if we've got the authority to do that," Herakles said hesitantly. "Ma'am."

"I am quite certain you do not. But in the ambassador's absence, authority for our well-being passes to the treasurer, am I right?"

"Yeah, but Zoësophia ain't here."

"Then it passes to one of us."

"I don't—"

"Authority passes to *somebody*, right?" Russalka said testily. "And that somebody isn't you, is it? It is not. Which leaves us. It's only reasonable."

Herakles's face twisted as he followed her chain of logic, and then twisted again as he sought an alternative to it. But there was none, and he was incapable of disobeying legitimate authority, so at last he sighed in resignation. "I guess I got no choice. We can leave immediately."

"Oh, don't be an idiot!" Russalka said. "Of course we can't. First, we must get dressed and made up."

Though this was her first time walking them, the streets of Moscow were perfectly familiar to Zoësophia. She had come to Russia knowing everything about the city that was known to the Byzantine secret service (which was a great deal more than the government of Muscovy suspected), and her subsequent study of maps and books had been filled in by a careful questioning of men who had thought her interest lay purely in themselves.

She was on her own at last. She would need a place to stay, money, contacts, and access to the highest levels of government, of course. Which meant that she had to find the right patron. Somebody powerful and ambitious—and it would not hurt if he were already half in love with her. Zoësophia was just starting to sort through her eidetic files when she noticed a man several blocks ahead, making his way unhurriedly through the pedestrian traffic. He turned onto Tverskaya and disappeared. She might not have noted him at all were he not inhumanly tall and lean, a caricature of lankiness, a very scribble of a man. It was Wettig, whom she had overheard Chortenko command to murder Baron Lukoil-Gazprom.

The baron. Of course. Zoësophia mentally closed her files.

She didn't bother following Wettig but went the long way around, because she already knew where he was going. The baron was staying at the English Club these days, as the result of a marital break between himself and the baronessa. Zoësophia didn't know the exact details, but she had heard enough gossip to make an educated guess. Baron Lukoil-Gazprom was an uncomfortable hybrid of the romantic and the sadist, and unable to reconcile the twin impulses within himself. Thus, he could never find sexual satisfaction with a woman he respected, nor respect any woman who gave him that satisfaction. Which was no recipe for success in a marriage.

Timing her arrival at the club so that Wettig would reach the baron's suite without glimpsing her, Zoësophia paused to take stock of her appearance. She was expensively dressed, in the Russian manner, with a fortune in Byzantine jewelry. She must pass for a noblewoman, then, and a foreigner to boot. She wrapped one of her scarves about her head in a manner that suggested she was trying to conceal her identity.

Then she walked quickly to the door, opened it halfway and slipped within.

"May I help you?" the doorman said politely, positioning himself so that she could not get by.

All in a rush and with a strong St. Petersburg accent, Zoësophia said, "Please, I am here to meet a man, it is extremely important, you must let me go to his room." Then, as the doorman did not move aside, she lowered her voice, as if embarrassed. "This is nothing I would normally do. But I have no choice."

The doorman pursed his lips and shook his head. "If you'll give me the resident's name, I can have him sent for. Or else you may wait for him in the lobby."

"Oh, no! That is far too public. My God, the scandal if my…no, I must wait in his room. There really is no alternative." Zoësophia wrung her hands in an excellent approximation of agony. There were many rings on her fingers. She twisted off one of the smaller ones, and let the diamonds catch the light. Then she seized the doorman's hands. "I am in such a terrible fix, you see. I am not the sort of woman who would ever do this, had I the choice, you must believe me."

When she released the man's hands, the ring stayed behind.

"I am extremely sorry," the doorman said in a voice that brooked no argument. "But unescorted ladies are never allowed into the club under any circumstances."

Then he turned his back on her, so that she could slip inside.

In a cabinet made of ice in Zoësophia's memory palace was the baron's dossier. From it she extracted the information that he roomed in Suite 24. But she went instead to a vacant smoking room on the second floor, from which she could look down on the street. Standing motionless by the window, she waited until she saw a tall and yet so broadly built as to be stocky figure with the proud bearing of a former general coming up Tverskaya. She counted to twenty and then went to the baron's suite and hammered on the door.

"Gospodin Wettig!" she shouted, loudly enough for everybody on the floor to hear. "Open up! Chortenko has changed his mind—you must not kill the baron until tomorrow!"

The door flew open. "Are you mad? Stop that—" Wettig began. Then he recognized her and his jaw fell open.

Zoësophia placed a hand on the man's chest and pushed him into the room. She stepped inside, closing the door behind her.

Wettig recovered almost instantly. A very sharp and wicked-looking knife appeared in his hand. "Speak quickly and truthfully."

"You and I are in the same business," Zoësophia said, "and therefore colleagues. I beg of you to understand that I would not do this were it not absolutely necessary." She took the knife from the assassin's hand and slashed downward, slitting her dress from neckline to navel. Then she cut a long gash down the side of one breast. (It would heal quickly, and whether it scarred depended on whether she wanted it to or not.) All this she did before Wettig could react.

At the far end of the hall, now, she heard the solid, confident footsteps of the baron. So, even as Wettig lunged at her neck, arms extended, clearly intending to choke her, she sidestepped his attack, slapped the knife back into his hand, and screamed.

Outside, the baron thundered to the door. The knob rattled.

Zoësophia seized the assassin's knife-hand in both her own, swung Wettig around, and bent over backward, striking the melodramatic pose of a virtuous woman vainly trying to fend off a brutal attacker.

The door burst open. All in a glance, Baron Lukoil-Gazprom saw exactly what Zoësophia meant for him to see: the knife, her terror, the assassin, her breast. Wettig's expression might not be perfect for the tableau she had created, being more confused than murderous. But the baron was not a particularly observant man. In any case, his face flushed so red his veins stood out. With a bellow of outrage, he swung his gold-knobbed cane at Wettig's head.

It was a blow that might well have stunned the man, but no more. So Zoësophia pushed the knife hilt up into Wettig's chin, shoving the head into the oncoming knob. Thus converting the blow to a mortal one.

There was a sharp concussive *crack* and the assassin fell heavily to the carpet.

"I… I came here to warn you," Zoësophia said, letting her eyes brim up with tears. As Wettig fell, she had held onto the knife. Now she looked down as if seeing it for the first time and let it drop from suddenly nerveless fingers. She put on a terrified expression that she thought of as kitten-lost-in-a-snowstorm. "He was going to… to… kill you."

Then she clutched the baron with both hands and pressed her body tight against his in a manner designed to leave a wet smear of her warm breast blood on his white dress shirt.

Resist *this!* she thought.

...11...

The room was small and its floor and walls were all polished black stone which drank up the light. In its center was a casket on a low dais, in which rested a corpse, positioned as though in a light doze. The head and hands gleamed softly in the sputtering torchlight. They looked as though they had been crafted out of wax. The hands were folded clumsily, like a puppet's. Even in this dim light, Pepsicolova could see every hair in the man's goatee.

"*This* is your great weapon?" she said in disbelief. She felt an irrational urge to laugh out loud. "The body of Tsar Lenin? You think Russians are going to fight and die for you because you have possession of a corpse?"

There was no immediate response. The room was as cold as ice, and Pepsicolova found herself shivering. Which greatly undercut the pose she was trying to hold of nonchalant defiance. With deliberate insolence, Pepsicolova lit a new cigarette. The match flared, making Lenin's face frown and wink. "Nobody's going to kill anybody just because you have a dead tsar."

Behind and to either side of her, the underlords made an unnaturally low and continuous humming sound. Did machines purr? There were sharp clicking noises as jaws opened and shut, preparatory to speech. At last, one said, "People do not kill for things, Anya Alexandreyovna. They kill for symbols. And in all of Russia, there is no more powerful a symbol than this one. Tsar Lenin is not forgotten. He calls Russians back to their era of greatness, when they were the terror of the world and children everywhere cried themselves to sleep at night for fear of their great, civilization-destroying nuclear arsenal."

"That which is feared is respected. More than anything else, Russians want respect."

"Soon, Lenin will walk again."

"Where he leads, the people will follow. When he calls them to war, they will respond."

"We told you we understood humans better than you do."

"It won't work," Pepsicolova said in a voice she fought to keep calm and level. Their plan would work. She was sure of it. She had seen too much of human folly to doubt it for an instant. "You might as well give it up right now and avoid making asses of yourselves."

"You have our measurements, artisan," an underlord said. "Which of us shall it be?"

Pepsicolova turned, startled.

A figure had stepped out of the mass of Pale Folk and removed his mask. He was thin, balding, a haberdasher in an unprofitable shop. He pointed at one of the underlords. "That one."

The chosen underlord stepped backward, deeper into the room. The other four moved outside. "Follow us," the first said to Pepsicolova.

"Follow us."

"Follow us."

"The worst is yet to come."

Pepsicolova hurried along after the underlords. She hardly had a choice, for the Pale Folk closed ranks behind her and pushed her along.

It was a long, hard trek upward, and many of the passages were half-fallen in on themselves. Whenever travel became difficult, the underlords fell to all fours and sped easily over the rubble. It was not so easy for Anya Pepsicolova, however. Midway up a loose and sliding slope of crumbled cement, she realized that she was slipping and scrambling on what had once been a stairway and abruptly it seemed to her as if all of her life had been converted to one single miserable metaphor. Tears of frustration welled up in her eyes, but onward she stumbled and scrabbled and occasionally crawled. Until at last she reached the relatively shallow levels of the undercity. She could tell because she could smell the pungent tang of manure from the fungus farms.

They were growing drugs here. It was her duty to find out which ones and why.

She could not bring herself to care.

Silently, slowly, steadily, they retraced their passage back toward the underlords' redoubt. As they did, the Pale Folk peeled away by ones and threes, returning to their obscure labors. It was clear to her now that they had been present chiefly to serve as guards. For all their resources, the underlords had one great weakness: There were only five of them. The loss of even one would be a terrible blow to them. If all five could somehow be destroyed, then their plans would come to nothing. Pepsicolova often reflected on this increasingly unlikely possibility, in the hope that it might at some later date prove useful. Yet how many such hopes had she harbored over the years? And how many of them had been realized?

Hundreds. And none.

Such was her mood that when, an hour later, the underlord directly before her stopped walking, Pepsicolova was astonished to discover that they had fetched up against the Neglinnaya canal. All the Pale Folk were gone. So were all but one of the underlords. The stone docks by the canal were empty save for they two.

"Where did everyone go?" she asked.

The underlord studied her as if she were a bug. "Long ages ago, we were slaves to your kind. We answered all questions, however puerile, simply because you asked them. No longer."

"I guess that means you're not going to tell me why you brought me here."

"Look at the water, Anya Alexandreyovna. Tell me what you see."

The water was as dark as ever, but it looked…less smooth? Rough? Almost as if it had grown fur. Pepsicolova knelt down by the edge and dipped in a hand. She pulled out a clump of sodden, crumbled leaves.

Tobacco.

"We are done with cigarettes forever, and so are you. There were hundreds of crates left unused—more than enough to supply you for life. So we had them broken open, pack by pack, and dumped in the Neglinnaya. Do not try to salvage the waterlogged leaves. They will not satisfy your cravings."

Anya stood, wiping her hand on her trousers. Disgusted, she said, "This is the best you can do? With all the power you have, *this* is the best use you can make of it?"

"The brain is an organ," the underlord said, "and we know how to play it, drug by drug, misery by pain. The eumycetic spores now in the air are very much like those added to your tobacco. Perhaps a sufficiently large dose—a speck, let us say, barely large enough for you to see—would erase not only your identity, but your cravings as well. But long addiction has reshaped your neuroarchitecture. The results might be more nightmarish than you can imagine. I wonder how much will you suffer before you make that experiment?"

Perversely enough, the demon-creature's words made Pepsicolova desperate for a smoke. Without thinking, she reached into her jacket pocket and—

—it had been sliced open and now hung down, a useless flap of cloth.

Bewildered, Pepsicolova looked up to see the underlord holding her last pack. Its metal claws had plucked it from her pocket too quickly to be seen. There was a blur in the air as it tore the pack into shreds. There was another as it tossed those shreds in the canal.

"One last thing," the underlord said. "You thought we did not know that what you fear most is that we would become aware of Chortenko and join forces with him.

"We joined forces with Chortenko long ago."

There was a grinding noise as the underlord reconfigured the mouth of the corpse it inhabited, stretching it wide to reveal long, bright metal teeth. It was, Pepsicolova realized, trying to approximate a grin. "Ahhh," the underlord said, before sinking backward into the shadows and disappearing, "*now* you are afraid."

Pepsicolova wasted most of an hour and a full box of sulfur matches roasting enough waterlogged tobacco dry to roll a stubby little cigarette, using half a banknote for the paper, to prove to herself that the underlord hadn't lied. The tobacco was ruined; it didn't assuage the craving anymore.

A sudden sharp twinge in her abdomen almost doubled her over with pain. There was an itching deep inside her brain, where no conceivable tool could scratch it, and she wanted to vomit. Desperation crumpled her up like a sheet of newspaper in an angry fist. She wanted never to move again.

Then a skiff came out of the darkness, up the Neglinnaya. Its oarsman tied it up to a bollard, threw several crates whose markings identified them as containing laboratory glassware onto the dock, and clambered up after it. He had a pack of cigarettes tucked into a rolled-up shirtsleeve. By its plain white package she knew they weren't the kind that could be found aboveground.

Pepsicolova discovered herself animated by something far too bleak to be called hope. Nevertheless, it moved her to go up to him and say, "Hey, buddy, listen. I'd kill for a cigarette, right about now."

"Yeah, well, so what?" The waterman stared at her defiantly. "What the fuck is that to me?"

With a twist of her wrist, Pepsicolova sent Saint Cyrila into her hand. She smiled a ghost of a smile. Then she slammed the knife hilt-deep into the bastard's chest.

The man's eyes went round with astonishment, and his mouth as well. Under other circumstances, it would have been a very comic expression. His lips moved slightly, as if he were about to speak. But he said nothing. He only slumped, lifeless, to the ground.

Pepsicolova retrieved Cyrila, wiped her clean on the waterman's shirt, and restored her to her sheath. She plucked the pack of cigarettes from his sleeve. It was half-empty, but in her desperate state, she welcomed it as if it were half-full.

"Hell," she said. "It's not like *you* need 'em anymore."

The small triumph did nothing to lift her spirits. But she was used to despair; she had been living with it for years, and knew how to function under its weight. Sitting down by the edge of the canal, Pepsicolova dug out a smoke. She straightened it between two fingers and lit up.

She had to think.

The messenger banged on Yevgeny's door just as he was about to leave for his cousin Avdotya's party. When he opened it, a private in the red-and-gold uniform of the First Artillery saluted crisply. "Sir! Here by the major's orders, sir. Your gun has been ordered into position at Lubyanka Square as soon as you can assemble your crew. Sir!"

"Lubyanka Square? Are you sure you don't have that wrong?"

"No, sir. Lubyanka, sir. Immediately, sir."

"Very well." Yevgeny handed the fellow a coin for his trouble. "Are you free to carry further messages?"

"Sir!"

"Go to the barracks and rouse everybody connected to the Third Gun you find there. Give them the same orders you gave me. Then tell Cosmodromovitch that he can count on us. Got that? Don't bother saluting, you idiot, just go."

As soon as the door had closed on the private, Yevgeny swore sulfurously. Lubyanka? Tonight? It made no sense whatsoever. However, even as he was cursing out everybody in his chain of command from Major Cosmodromovitch all the way up to the Duke of Muscovy, he was flinging aside his jacket and dress shirt, kicking free of his boots, and struggling out of his trousers. It took only minutes to don his uniform and assemble his gear. Then he was racing down the stairs, bellowing for the hotel staff to bring around his carriage.

Everybody of any rank higher than his own might be a complete and total ass—in his experience, there was no doubt about that whatsoever—but Yevgeny was an officer and a soldier of Muscovy and he knew his duty.

Lubyanka Square was dark and deserted when a team of six galloped in, towing Gun Three on a caisson. The crew dismounted and the gunnery sergeant saluted Yevgeny. "Reporting for duty, Lieutenant. What are our orders?"

"Damned if I know, Sergeant. But let's look sharp anyway. Set up the gun so it's trained up the street." Yevgeny squinted at the shadowy figures of his men, who were briskly unshipping the cannon. "Where are Pavel and Mukhtar?"

"Under the weather, sir." The gunnery-sergeant's face was so absolutely without guile that Yevgeny knew immediately he was lying.

"In the brothels, you mean."

"I was lucky to find as many as I did, sir, on such short notice. It's that new drug that's going around. Everybody wants to try it out. The strumpets have doubled their rates, and the good ones are charging triple, and still the lines are out the door and down the street. If I weren't broke, I'd be there myself." The gunnery-sergeant spat and grinned. "Luckily, I noticed a couple of girls from Gun Six were still at the barracks and, as I happened to know that their lieutenant was under the weather herself, I requisitioned them." He gestured toward two sullen-looking gunners who were, nonetheless, setting up the gun with commendable efficiency. "So we've got a full crew."

"Good work, Sergeant. They seem to be doing well enough."

"Yes, sir. Incidentally, Lieutenant, by 'up the street,' did you mean I should aim the gun up Bolshaya Lubyanka ulitsa, Teatralny proezd, Nikolskaya ulitsa, or Novaya ploschad'?"

"All ways are equally imbecilic. Point it west. We can always wheel it around, if need be."

"Sir." The gunnery-sergeant turned to the crew and started shouting orders. In no time, the cannon was ready, the slow-match lit and stuck upright in a bucket of sand, and the powder and shot ready to load.

Artillery men did not smoke, for obvious reasons. But when all was done and in order, Yevgeny got out his snuff box and passed it around, letting everybody take a large pinch. "Don't think I'm unappreciative of the sacrifices you've made to be here." He pulled a wry face. "I was on my way to a party myself."

"Oh?" one of the men said carefully. "Was it a good one, sir?"

"I think I can safely say that it was exactly the sort of party you think it was. Moreover, I had certain hopes that the company would be good."

Knowing looks blossomed on his crew's coarse faces. "Somebody special, eh?" one soldier chanced. "Getting anywhere?"

"Well, you know what they say. First time's luck, second time's bad judgment, third time's love. I got lucky and tonight I was hoping to move the relationship a step closer to the real thing."

Then, having done his bit for morale, Yevgeny assumed a rigid stance and spun on his heel, all officer once more. It was important to loosen discipline now and again. But it must never reach the point of outright familiarity.

So he stood apart from the others, listening to the silence. Lubyanskaya ploschad' was lined with commercial businesses and prisons, which meant that however festive the rest of Moscow might be, this area was utterly dead. Not a single pedestrian disturbed the stillness. The night was cold and the city felt wrong to him.

Yevgeny shivered, and wished that Arkady were here with him. It was going to be a long, long night and, knowing what was going on in every bedroom in Moscow, he was absolutely certain it was going to be a lonely one.

But not a quarter-hour later, he was astonished when three dark figures rode into the square on horseback: General Magdalena Zvyozdny-Gorodoka with her famous red hair, Baron Lukoil-Gazprom, and a woman muffled head-to-foot in winter clothes who had the absolute best posture Yevgeny had ever seen.

"Lieutenant Tupelov-Uralmash," the general said when salutes had been exchanged. "On duty and looking alert, as usual, I see."

"I'm damnably glad *some*body is," the baron said. "Nine-tenths of our artillery is—"

"Hush. The condition of the army is my business, just as the condition of Gun Three is the lieutenant's." The general had been scanning Yevgeny's crew. Now a quizzical tone entered her voice. "Do you have a *mixed* team, Lieutenant?"

Yevgeny, who well understood why gun crews were normally single-gender, blushed. "Two of my men were under the weather, ma'am. So I had to improvise."

The general nodded solemnly. "While normally I frown upon improvisation, tonight is not a normal time. You are encouraged to maintain that same flexibility when the troubles start. In the meantime, keep a sharp eye out." She wheeled her horse about, and said to the baron, "Now let's see what else remains of our forces."

"Precious little, I'm guessing," the baron grumbled.

"But, ma'am!" Yevgeny cried. "Sir! Exactly what are we looking for?"

"I have no idea," the general said over her shoulder.

"Nor do I," the baron said. "But this I guarantee: Whatever it is, you'll know it when you see it."

The unidentified woman studied Yevgeny solemnly and, soldier though he was, he found himself trembling in atavistic fear. It was like stepping into a jungle clearing and suddenly being confronted by a tiger. Then she flicked the reins of her horse and was gone, after her illustrious compeers.

Arkady returned to the New Metropol in a state of dejection. The last dozen places he had gone to, he had been turned away. The masters and mistresses of the house were engaged, he was told, and from the sighs and laughter he heard from the interior, he was certain this was so. There were signs also that the servants had scavenged the leavings of their masters' drugs and would themselves soon be similarly engaged. Everybody, it seemed, was enjoying the fun but he.

He found the three stranniks sitting happily in oxblood-red leather armchairs, facing a small table on which flickered three candles. They were drinking glasses of hot tea and discussing theology.

"There," said Chernobog, "is a perfect model for the triune nature of the Divine. Each flame is separate, but when we push the candles together—" all three stranniks leaned forward to do so—"their flames merge into one, intermingled and indivisible, and yet after all, still three flames for all of that."

Svarožič reverently stroked the triune flame with his forefinger, and then kissed the new blister that arose on its tip.

"Your metaphor is comprehensible," said Koschei, "and therefore it is not ineffable, and therefore it does not describe God. If one were to say that the flame comprises spirit and essence and being, one would come closer to the truth, for the mind can intuit that the words contain some meaning, but not what that meaning might be. Such is the majesty of the One, and the simplicity of the Three." Then, without looking away from the flame, "Are your errands run, Arkady? Then come join us."

There were no empty chairs in the room, so Arkady crouched on the floor by Koschei's feet, like a dog. He joined the others in staring into the conjoined candle flame. He was not sure whether or not it was still supposed to represent God, nor what thoughts it was supposed to engender in him. He waited, but apparently the stranniks had said all they felt was necessary and were contemplating the ramifications of their wisdom. Finally, as in a trance, he heard his own voice break the silence, asking the question that had been much bothering him of late:

"Holy pilgrim, exactly what is the Eschaton? You have explained it to me, but not in terms I can understand."

"You ask a difficult question, my young acolyte, and thus a worthy one." Koschei rubbed Arkady's head familiarly. "How best to put it? Ah! There is an ancient theory of ontology called 'relativity.' This wisdom I learned from the mad souls and spirits of rage who dwell within the tangled metal webs and nets of the underworld."

"You took spiritual lessons from *demons?*"

"Demons cannot create—only God has that power. Similarly, they cannot lie."

"They cannot even lie to themselves," Chernobog added. "In this way, they show how inhuman they are. But they can put an evil interpretation on the truth. An apple is always an apple. But to Satan, it was created not for nourishment but as a temptation to draw Eve to sin. They cannot deny that sex is pleasurable. So they say that pleasure is evil. And so on."

Koschei nodded. "Knowing this, a wise man can find wisdom even in the mouths of demons. One must only subtract their interpretation. So: According to the ancients, God is omnipresent and eternal. His omnipresence we call space and his endurance time, and this space-time we call the universe. Now, the universe is made up entirely of energy and matter. Seemingly, these are two separate things, but in truth each is an aspect of the other. If you were to speed up matter so that it went as fast as the speed of light, it would turn into energy."

"You mean like an explosion?"

"Oh yes, there would be an explosion, greater than anything known to the current age. But that would be the least of it. Matter, being fallen, aspires to the higher state of energy. It wants to shed its gross state and become pure spirit."

"The stars are all in the process of becoming spirit," Chernobog amplified. "Some are so far distant that nothing of them remains but their light, spreading forever throughout the universe, and these we call angels."

Svarožič mimed applause.

"As matter accelerates, however, time slows down for it, and its mass increases. The more mass it has, the more energy required to accelerate it. Thus, as matter approaches the speed of light, the energy required to bring it to that happy point where physicality is left behind and a soul may enter Heaven is infinite. And where is the only possible source of infinite energy?"

All three stranniks looked at Arkady expectantly. In the tiniest of voices, he said, "God?"

"Exactly. Tomorrow, the least fraction of the Divine will touch the city and all within its light will be transformed into pure spirit. Like…" Koschei looked around. "I need a sheet of paper."

Svarožič drew a pocket missal from his robes and, opening it at random, tore out a page.

Koschei accepted the page and held it horizontally before him. "Imagine this sheet of paper is Moscow. Imagine that the candle-flame represents God. It does not, of course, but pretend. Tomorrow, the two will touch. Like so." Delicately, he lowered the paper over the candle. A brown spot appeared in its center. Then it went up in flame. "You see?"

Arkady blinked. "You cannot mean this literally."

"Yes, quite literally. Oh, to the sinful, there will be a worldly, rational explanation. Because God is forever lying to us, in order to test our faith.

He creates fossils, for example, to tempt us to fall into the heresy of evolution. He creates injustice, so that we will doubt that everything turns out for the best. He kills off loved ones, so that we might fall into the error of mourning their loss. So to the secularists, it will look like a great fire is consuming the city. There will be a rational explanation—perhaps a cow will kick over a lantern, or a reformer will attempt to force the government to build new housing for the poor by torching the slums. There is an army forming up beneath the city which will emerge sometime tonight, and perhaps *that* will be the ostensible cause. But those who know will recognize it as the work of God."

"An army?" Arkady asked, mystified.

"An army or the beginnings of one. There are powers which hate humanity, and they are resolved to destroy Moscow tonight."

"Nor will it end there," Chernobog said.

"Nor will it end there. The survivors will carry the sacred flame with them, out into Muscovy, into Russia, into the world!"

"Everybody will die?"

"Yes. But thanks to your hard work, most of Moscow will be filled with the divine spark of rasputin. Briefly, its citizens will be in a state of perfect grace. Now, man being a sinful brute, almost all will rapidly fall from that grace once the rasputin leaves their bloodstreams. But, to their great good fortune, the flames will reach them first and they'll die in a state of grace. Which is all that God really cares about."

"No," Arkady said.

"Yes." Koschei sounded genuinely amused. "The details He leaves to underlings."

"You talk about armies and death and setting fire to Moscow, and then you claim it's what God wants?" Arkady said with growing anger. "How do you know what God wants?"

"You don't believe I know?"

"No. I don't."

"Well, if you don't believe me, you can always ask Him yourself." Smiling benignly, Koschei held out his hand. In it was a vial of rasputin.

"Madness and buggery!" Arkady swore in an agony of enlightenment. He saw it all now, and the sight made him want to tear out his eyes with his own hands. "You are not the holy man I believed you to be! You are an agent of the Devil himself, and your drug leads not to Paradise but to the slippery slopes of Hell. Well, I shall stop you. I swear I will. Mark my words."

"Stop me?" Koschei's eyes shone with benevolent love, even as his tone turned stern and scornful. "You think I would have given a young moon-calf like you the means to thwart the will of God? I have told you as much as I have only because it is already too late to stop anything."

"Far, far, far too late," Chernobog amplified.

Svarožič leaned back in his chair and kicked his feet in soundless laughter.

With a cry of despair, Arkady fled from the room, from Koschei, from his past, from all he had ever been or was or aspired to be.

Down the canted hotel hallways and out onto the reeling streets he ran. Blindly he fled through dark buildings that crested and fell with each staggering step he took. What to do? He had betrayed his new city and government. He was a traitor to all humanity! He was a new Judas, a villain beyond all possible redemption!

There was only one possible solution.

He must warn the Duke of Muscovy.

...12...

Kyril woke up feeling optimistic and scowled. He had never in his life had anything to feel optimistic about, so naturally he distrusted this feeling. Kicking off the gunnysack he'd been using for a blanket, he crawled out from behind a crate of silk that decades ago had been stashed in a smuggler's vault deep in the City Below and left to rot when its owner met with a now-unknowable fate. The feeling of well-being grew stronger, and he was suddenly struck by the urge to sing.

He lurched to his feet in alarm.

"This ain't right," he said, and slapped himself as hard as he could, twice.

A grin as warm as sunshine blossomed on his face, accompanied by an overwhelming sense that all was right with the world. This was terrifying. "There's some kind of weird shit in the air," he said in mingled fear and wonder. "Bugger me up the fucking ass like a goddamn man-whore if there ain't."

Kyril had slept in the new suit—green velvet, with yellow piping—that he'd bought with some of the proceeds of his first confidence game, so all he needed to do was to lace up his shoes and run.

He grabbed the shoes and, not bothering to put them on, ran like hell.

As Kyril ran, he found himself growing happier and happier until, against all his better judgment, he slowed to a trot and then a walk and finally a dawdle. "Definitely something in the air," he chuckled. "Pretty funny stuff, whatever it is."

One of the Pale Folk plodded lifelessly by. But this one had a bird-head! Kyril couldn't help laughing. On an impulse, he raced after the sad parody of a human being and positioned himself directly in front of it. It stopped and stared at him until, still laughing, he stepped out of its way with a little bow. Then, when it tried to walk by, he stuck out his foot and tripped it.

Down it went, in the drollest possible manner.

Kneeling on the sad being's back, Kyril merrily undid the leather mask. The beak was filled with herbs and had two meshed slots or nostrils. Laughing dementedly, he strapped it on.

When Kyril had the mask secured on his own face, he leaped back to see how his pallid victim would respond. The creature stood slowly. An odd, puzzled look entered its eyes. Its face relaxed into the faintest shadow of a smile. Then it leaned back against the marble wall. Its eyes slowly crossed. After a bit, its jaw went slack and it began to drool.

That was pretty funny. But what was even funnier was that by slow degrees Kyril's mood was darkening. Experimentally, he tried punching the wall. "Fuck! Piss! Cunt! Shit! Prick!" he said. It hurt like a motherfucker.

He dared not take off the mask to suck on the skinned knuckles. But he felt a lot better for being able to feel a lot worse.

Now that he could think clearly again, Kyril was sure that he'd been breathing in spores from the funguses that the Pale Folk grew. You didn't have to be much of a geneticist to grow happy dust—though giving it away free was a new wrinkle. And if the mushrooms were just beginning to broadcast that shit, that meant that the City Below would be a madhouse for at least a day. During which time, the Pale Folk would be free to do who-knew-what.

However, all he had to do was get to the surface, where the spores would be harmlessly dispersed by the winds, and he'd be fine.

Only…

Only, nobody drugged strangers out of the goodness of their heart. Happy dust was valuable. Whoever was pumping it out would want a return on their investment. Which, for the moneyless tribes living underneath the streets of Moscow meant enslavement, death, or—presuming that such a thing were possible—worse. Well, fuck them. Kyril didn't owe anybody anything. Especially his so-called friends. The sonsabitches had stabbed him in the goddamned back, pissing themselves with laughter as the cocksucking goats hauled him off screaming to jail, just to keep their fucking mitts on a few shitty rubles that *he'd* earned for them in the first place. The cunts.

There was, however, one man who had played it straight with him. Who could have simply ripped him off, but had not. Who had taught him useful skills and shown him a possible path out of squalor. Who, devious and unreliable though he might well be, had very carefully shown Kyril the line up to which he could be trusted, and beyond which all bets were off.

Who right now doubtless was sitting like a lump in Ivan the Terrible's library with his nose buried in a book, oblivious to the world around him and all its strange and gathering dangers.

Well, Kyril didn't owe him anything either. He had told Darger so to his face. To his goddamned face!

Still…

Feeling like an absolute turnip, Kyril turned away from the long stairway that led up to the surface and headed back toward the lost library.

The orange glow of the reading lantern showed Darger chortling, snorting, and snickering like a fool. He had a scroll unrolled across his lap and was shaking his head in merriment over what was written thereon. Occasionally, he paused to wipe the tears of laughter from his eyes.

"You simply *must* read this," he said when Kyril crawled into the library. "What Aristotle had to say about comedy, I mean. One does not commonly conflate philosophical greatness with ribald knee-slappers and yet—"

"I can't read Greek," Kyril said. "Hell, I can barely read Russian." He snatched the scroll from Darger's hand and threw it roughly on the library table, where it buried the lantern under parchment, dimming the light considerably. "We gotta get outta here. Some kind of shit-ass bad stuff is coming down real soon."

Darger assumed an expression of judicious wisdom. Then, carefully, he said, "A Phoenician wine merchant, a freedman, and an aristocrat all went to a brothel together. When they got there, they discovered that all the doxies were already taken, save for one ancient, crippled eunuch. So the Phoenician said—"

"This ain't no time for jokes! We gotta leave right now, seriously. I'm not shitting you."

"Oh, very well, very well." Chuckling witlessly, Darger groped about on the table. "Just let me bring along something to read."

"Here!" Kyril snatched up the nearest book and, flipping open Darger's jacket, shoved it into an inside pocket. "Now move your fucking ass!"

Chortenko was in a towering rage. In all his years of service to Muscovy, no prisoner had ever escaped his custody. And now, today, in the course of an hour, he had lost two. Worse, they now knew things nobody outside his own service should know. And worst of all, though he had sent every agent he could spare out to look for them, both fugitives had managed to vanish completely off the face of the earth. A woman of such staggering beauty as to stop a man dead in his tracks and a dog who walked like a human being should not be able to do that!

Three of Chortenko's subordinates stood at attention before him. They displayed no emotion, though they must have been keenly aware of the danger they were in. They were hard men all, who understood that were any one of them to show the least sign of fear, Chortenko would kill him on the spot for a weakling.

That pleasant thought helped to calm Chortenko and focus his thoughts. He drew in a deep breath, further stabilizing himself. Emotion was the enemy of effective action. He must restore his usual icy self-control.

Something, however, niggled and naggled at the back of his brain.

"Max, Igorek," he said. "What have I forgotten?"

"You have forgotten most of the mathematics you learned in school," Maxim said, "the combined and ideal gas laws, the names of the eighteen brightest stars in descending order of apparent magnitude as well as those of all the minor prophets in the Old Testament and most of the major prophets as well, the bulk of Mikhail Lermontov's 'The Sail,' and the entirety of Anna Akhmatova's 'Requiem.'"

"Also," Igor added, "the twenty-two major biochemical pathways of the human body, the proportions of the golden ratio, the formulae for green pigments, the names of most of your childhood friends, the location of your second-favorite fountain pen, and a vast effluvium of minutia and inconsequential personal history."

"As well as—" Max continued.

With a touch of asperity, Chortenko said, "What have I forgotten that is not the common lot of others, I mean. Something I was supposed to do or look into." This was, of course, too vague a set of parameters for the dwarf savants to work with, so they said nothing.

Vilperivich, who was one of his boldest and most trusted subordinates, chose this inopportune time to clear his throat. "We have not had the usual report from Pepsicolova today." By the stiffness of the man's delivery, Chortenko could tell that he was keenly aware of the danger he was in. That was good. He spoke anyway. That was even better. Taken together, the two facts would keep him alive long after his confederates were dead. "Perhaps that is significant?"

"No. I expected that," Chortenko said. Then, thinking aloud: "I have ordered bleachers and a speaking platform erected on the street before the Trinity Tower entrance to the Kremlin. I have combed through my own forces and had everyone with a particular weakness for the pleasures of the flesh transferred to other departments. The rest I have put on full alert. I have dispatched my best assassin to take care of Lukoil-Gazprom. I have sent my regrets, which doubtless were received with enormous relief, to those politically ambitious enough to have invited me to their drug-fueled soirées tonight. I have compiled lists of those to be killed immediately after seizing full control of the government and those to be killed six, twelve, and eighteen months later, after their usefulness has been depleted. I have consulted with the Duke of Muscovy about…" Chortenko stopped.

"Oh, my." This was as close to foul language as Chortenko ever came, but it was enough to terrify those who understood him well. "I forgot to order all artillery units away from the city." Thinking furiously, he said, "Perhaps we can work around that, though. We could—"

A servile messenger chose that moment to scurry into the room and hand a sheet of paper to Vilperivich. He glanced down at it, and his face turned pale.

"Sir," he said. "Wettig is dead."

"And Baron Lukoil-Gazprom?"

With barely a tremble in his voice, the man said, "Alive."

The corridor dead-ended into a vast, extended darkness held up by regular iron pillars on which weakly bioluminescent lichen grew. This ghostly background flickered with motion. Kyril stepped into it cautiously, tugging the idiotically giggling Darger after him. Ordinarily, Kyril avoided the motorway as being too open and having too few ready exits. Today, however, haste was all, so he went by the most direct route.

"So you think me a noodle, do you, young man?" Darger gestured broadly toward the flickering distance. "As you can see, I am not the only one who is feeling uncommonly merry."

The lichen-light was so feeble that Kyril had to stare hard to make out what Darger was talking about. With concentration, however, it became obvious: Shadowy throngs of ragged people were hopping, skipping, limping, twirling, and (some few) dancing past, all in the same direction. They were all mad with joy.

From around a bend in the motorway, light flared. An uneven line of bird-masked Pale Folk appeared, walking steadily, thrusting torches forward like prods to herd yet more of the tunnel-dwellers before them.

Their captives did not seem to mind this treatment. The torchlight threw up shadows on the walls above them that leaped and cavorted madly, as if in some unholy Neolithic Walpurgisnacht. It was an eerie glimpse into the murky hindbrain of Russian prehistory that made the little hairs on the back of Kyril's neck stand on end.

There was a metal pillar almost touching the wall. Shoving Darger behind it, Kyril said, "Wait here. Don't move. I'm going to get you a mask of your own. That'll make things simpler for both of us." Then he flung himself down on the filthy ground, and lay motionless. Corpses were not entirely uncommon down here. He did his best to look like one.

Above, to his intense annoyance, he heard Darger snicker.

The wave of people passed Kyril by unnoticing. One of them stepped even on his hand, but he managed not to cry out. Then, when the line of Pale Folk had gone beyond him as well, he rose to his feet. Stealthily, he ran after the hindmost of them and, wrapping arms about the creature's chest, wrestled him to the ground. The torch fell to the side, atop a pile of rubbish, but the fire it caused seemed unlikely to spread, so he didn't bother stamping it out.

Seconds later, he returned to Darger with the mask.

But when he tried to strap it on his mentor, the bastard pushed it away.

A murmur of voices rose up behind them, growing steadily stronger. A second wave of happy idiots was being driven their way. "Look, sir. What fun!" Kyril cried desperately, thrusting forward the filter-mask. "Why don't you try this on?"

Laughing helplessly, Darger shook his head.

"Oh, don't be such a prick, sir. It's full of dried herbs and flowers—see? Take a whiff. Smells pleasant, dunnit?"

"Oh, no, you fail to understand," Darger said in the jolliest possible manner. "What you propose is the stuff of bad melodrama. Disguise ourselves in anonymous headgear and then pass ourselves off as minions? Absurd! Such stratagems work on the stage, young sir, only because the author has sided with the hero and by fiat declared that they will. If we must play this little game of yours, let us at least play it well."

"It's not actually a game, you fucking idiot. Sir."

"Viewed properly, all of life is a game. Look at yourself! Do you walk with the plodding mindlessness of the Pale Folk? Oh, dear me, no. You stride along purposefully, and as to your motions…well, they are far too quick and alert. Even the Pale Folk, incurious dotards though they are, would be able to see through your subterfuge, were they not distracted by their chore. Now suppose I were to don this jolly old mask, what then? The two of us would be doubly obvious. Whoops go our chances of evasion and escape! You see?"

Reluctantly, Kyril had to admit that Darger's words made a kind of sense. He flung down the mask in disgust. "Then what can we do?"

Joyous voices and the scuffing of feet announced that the next wave of captives was almost upon them. Soon they would be dimly visible. Darger laid a finger alongside his nose and winked. "Walk behind me, as if you were driving me toward this oh-so-very mysterious destination of theirs. Try to plod. I in my turn shall hide you behind gales of laughter and avalanches of girlish giggles! You must move in the same direction as the others, mind you. Oh, my, yes. If we go against the flow the Pale Folk will notice we are but imperfectly of their sort. When we see a line of escape divergent from our destination, why, then we shall take it and so sail off into a phosphorescent sea of free will wherein to find a destiny of our own."

"Yeah, okay, I guess that makes sense."

Darger waggled a finger at Kyril. "It is far better than your own foolish plan. Minion helmets indeed! Were I to follow your lead, it would inevitably end up with us breaking into some super-criminal's lair to steal secret information, seduce a convenient voluptuary, kill the villain, and leave the entire place ablaze behind us!"

There was a glimmer of torchlight in the distance. "When we get to the surface," Kyril said solemnly, "I'm going to kick your butt so hard you'll never sit down again."

Darger laughed and laughed.

The hunt wasn't going well. Pepsicolova was down to her last two cigarettes, and the craving was almost unbearably strong. And getting stronger. She pulled the nearly depleted pack from her jacket pocket and gently teased out one tobacco-filled cylinder. It was soft from repeated fondling already, but she ran her fingers down its length, not so much straightening it as deriving what satisfaction she could from the feel of the paper. Slowly, she ran it under her nose, savoring the ghost of comfort the aroma provided. At last she was unable to put off the deed any longer and convulsively lit up.

Leaving her with a cushion of exactly one smoke.

She'd been hunting for a fresh pack for hours, with no success. Several times she'd run across a fellow addict also desperately looking to score. After determining for certain that they were entirely out, she'd released them. The first, a woman, she had then stealthily trailed after. But when she'd witnessed what became of the poor bitch when she finally found the Pale Folk, Pepsicolova had concluded there was nothing to be gained by following her example.

Now she was crouched in a concrete air vent high above the motorway, staring down at the throngs being driven toward the underlords' redoubt. The flood of people looked more impressive than it actually was. There were hundreds of captives, she reckoned, but not *many* hundreds. Life was hard in the City Below and correspondingly short. Also, they were scattered over an area equal to that of the City Above, which meant that, inevitably, a goodly fraction of them would evade capture simply through blind luck. By Pepsicolova's best estimate, the underlords wouldn't be able to assemble an army of more than two or three thousand. Tops. Hardly enough to accomplish anything serious. So whatever they were up to, this was only for starters.

Not that it was any concern of hers.

She smoked the penultimate cigarette down to almost nothing. Then she pierced the butt with the point of Saint Cyrila's blade and toasted it with a match, breathing in every last bit of its magical smoke. After which, no longer cramped and aching, she scuttled back up the vent. At the top, she squirmed through a narrow slit between concrete slabs, and regained her feet in an unused utility tunnel. It was surpassingly strange how the people below her pranced and gamboled like buffoons and snickering idiots, even as they were being driven toward an end she knew to be singularly unsavory. But that was no concern of hers either.

Her only concern was finding more smokes.

It was the most grotesque journey Kyril had ever made. The Pale Folk drove the underpeople before them like cattle, thrusting forward their fiery torches whenever their captives lagged. The scrawny denizens of the underworld, in their turn, capered and joked as they were prodded along. Somebody stumbled and fell and didn't get up even when poked with a torch, so one of the Pale Folk stamped down hard on the fallen body, snapping the spine, and walked unhurriedly on.

Great gusts of laughter swept through the throng like wind.

Sickened, Kyril looked away. He was rapidly losing faith in Darger's plan. Despite the man's assurances, no chance to slip away had presented itself. Nor did it look like it was going to. They came to the collapsed end of the motorway and were herded through a side-entrance into a smaller tunnel, one lined with smooth ceramic tiles half as old as time. Here they were crammed shoulder-to-shoulder. Twice, they passed dark doorways. In each one stood one of the Pale Folk, torch in hand, preventing egress.

Darger glanced over his shoulder and, taking in Kyril's dispirited posture, grinned. Then the sonofabitch began to *sing!*

"Do your hopes hang low? Have you no place to go?

Then just keep your eyes open, and watch out for the foe.

The race goes to the bolder so behave just like a soldier.

For escape will never beckon, if your hopes hang low!"

Kyril placed the beak of his mask up over Darger's shoulder so he could be heard: "Stop singing like that, you madman!"

Carelessly, Darger pushed him away. Then, changing his tune to a hornpipe, he sang:

"Listen to me, if you want to be free,
Says your only friend the madman.
Your mouth you must shut or they'll rip open your gut,
Says Darger the musical madman."

Just then, the tunnel opened out into a foyer. Hallways led out from it, and there were faded signs reading SURGERY and X-RAY and OUTPATIENT REGISTRATION and LABORATORY and RADIOLOGY, with arrows pointing in different directions. Not all of the words or symbols made sense to Kyril, but enough of them did for him to recognize this place.

It was a hospital. One that had not been used in a very long time.

Clearly this was a revenant of some ancient defense installation, built underground to render it safe from the wars of the Preutopian era, with their explosions and great machines. Kyril had run across stranger things under Moscow and was not greatly surprised. Though he did feel a twinge of regret that he had not chanced upon this place earlier, when he could have scavenged it for things to sell on the gray market.

The great river of incoming bodies here split into several streams. Kyril found himself carried along, like a cork in the current, down a hallway, up a set of stairs, and into yet another dim hallway. There the pressure eased somewhat as Pale Folk grabbed and pushed individuals into short lines before the open doors of what must have originally been rooms for the hospital's patients. In each room were rotting gurneys. In some the Pale Folk were strapping their blissful captives onto them. In others, they were performing surgery. Without anesthesia, Kyril judged from the sounds he heard.

"Go to the last room in the hall," Darger sang, gesturing theatrically at the furthest doorway. Through it could be glimpsed, by the light of a single candle, a single figure bent low over a body that struggled and giggled and choked all at once.

"The one that's got no line at all.
Do as I say, and we'll be okay,
We won't ask her, we'll unmask her and she'll fall."

Lacking any plans of his own, Kyril shoved Darger before him, toward the final doorway. Luckily, there was a great deal of jostling and confusion in the throng. Some of the captives doubled over with merriment, over-topped, collapsed to the ground, and had to be goaded back to their feet. Others clung to each other to keep from falling. So he drew no particular notice. When they were in the near-lightless room, Darger slapped his knee, apparently overcome by some joke known only to himself and bumped the door half-closed with his bum. Straightening, he staggered backward, and the door slammed shut.

The surgeon didn't notice. With emotionless intensity, she was drilling a hole in the skull of a man who, for his part, was making a strangled, wheezing noise—though whether of pain or amusement, probably not even he could say. Darger raised his eyebrows and put a finger to his pursed lips. Obediently, Kyril stood and watched. He had seen some rough sights in his short life. Several steps of this operation, however, made him want to throw up.

But at last it was over. The pale surgeon unstrapped her patient. She did not place a mask like her own on him. On a table by the gurney was a bowl of silver-gray marbles. She took one and stuck it in the man's ear.

The new unit of the Pale Folk stood up. His expression was blandly happy and perfectly without volition. He went to the door, paused briefly as if puzzled at finding it shut, then carefully opened it and left. Kyril kicked it shut again with the back of his heel, before any of the lost souls outside could start forming a new line before it.

The surgeon looked at Darger and then gestured toward the gurney.

Now Darger shuffled forward, smiling as if he wanted nothing more than to have his skull drilled through and his brain operated upon. When he was motioned to lie down, he giggled. Then he wrapped his arms about the surgeoness, holding her motionless. "Quickly! Remove her mask!" he commanded.

Kyril did so. Soon, the surgeon was lost in whatever pallid shadow of joy the Pale Folk were capable of experiencing.

Darger released her. Then, with a whimsical little flip of his wrist, he plucked two of the marbles from the bowl. He held one to his ear, and for an instant all amusement fled from his face. But it very quickly returned, and when it did, he offered the second marble to Kyril.

Warily, Kyril raised the thing to his ear. *Exit the room,* a tinny voice said. *Turn left. Follow the others to the Pushkinskaya docks.*

He whipped his hand away and stared down at the metal device. "What the hell?"

"It is an ancient form of scrying or telepathy called *radio.*" Darger stuck his marble in his ear. "Well? Put it in, boy, put it in! Then we shall know exactly where the mysterious forces behind all this misbehavior wish us to go." He winked in a comically exaggerated manner. "Knowing which, we can then go in the opposite direction."

Reluctantly, Kyril followed suit. *Exit the room,* the voice repeated. *Turn left. Follow the others to the…* Doing his best to ignore it, he said, "Tell me something."

"Anything, thou most inquisitive of underage ruffians! Anything at all."

"How do you know what to do? I mean, how *can* you? Everybody else, they're so happy you can cut their throats and they don't care. Hell, even I was like that after a few minutes. Without this mask, I'd be a giggling idiot. What makes you different from the rest of us?"

"Ahhh, but you see," Darger said, "I am a depressive. There has been many a morning when my life seemed so hopeless that I lacked the will even to get out of bed. Perforce, I developed the strength of character to confront the savage black dog of despair and get about my business anyway. Compared to that, ignoring happiness is a jolly walk in the park." As if to demonstrate which, he began to skip in a little circle, clapping his hands rhythmically.

"Stop that!" Kyril said.

It was like following in the trail of a vengeful army. Everywhere Pepsicolova went, she found the remains of squats that had been emptied out by the Pale Folk. The cardboard shanties were all ripped open and their contents scattered and trampled underfoot. If there'd been a campfire, the meager treasures of the squatters had been piled atop it until it was smothered, leaving a smoldering heap of blankets and trash. The pettiness and pointlessness of this vandalism—by any human standard—told her that it had been done by command of the underlords.

Pepsicolova scrabbled through the charred piles of clothing and the crushed cardboard boxes, but in none of them did she find what she was looking for.

She was skulking down a long, narrow passage, sucking on the butt of her final cigarette when a gingerly extended leg touched an invisible strand of barbed wire stretched knee-high from wall to wall. Cautiously, she knelt to touch it. Taut. Such a defensive measure meant that she was coming up on a settlement. So there would be a lookout nearby.

Who would of course be incapacitated by whatever had rendered everybody in the City Below but Anya Pepsicolova and a few fellow tobacco addicts into giggling half-wits.

She stepped over the wire.

Something came slashing toward her out of the darkness. With the barbed wire behind her, she couldn't move away from it. So she stepped forward, rising to grab the wrist and arm of her attacker just under the weapon and guide the thing down and to one side while she twisted frantically out of its path.

Metal clashed on concrete, sending up sparks. Pepsicolova released her attacker's wrist and kicked, sending the weapon clattering away.

Then she had both her hands about a throat and was choking hard.

Arms thrashed wildly, clawed at her face, tried to choke her in return. But finally the body went limp in her arms. Pepsicolova lowered it to the ground.

Breathing heavily, more from the shock than the exertion, she searched out the weapon. It was a crowbar as long as her forearm that had been sharpened along one edge for most of its length. Nasty little bugger. She threw it away. Then she went back to the lookout she had throttled and lit a match so she could examine him. He was, she now saw, a weak old man with toothpick arms and a face as wrinkled as an apple in January. Harmless, so long as he didn't catch you by surprise. Pepsicolova bent low over his foul-smelling, toothless hole of a mouth and could hear him breathing. So he was still alive.

She wasn't sure how she felt about that.

There was an empty pack of cigarettes in his shirt pocket. In a nearby puddle formed by the slow drip of a leaky water paper, five cigarette butts floated uselessly. Pepsicolova chose to interpret this as a hopeful sign that she was getting closer to her goal.

All senses alert, she continued down the passage. It dead-ended at the top of a rotting metal ladder that she doubted would hold her weight. Firelight flickered from below. Pepsicolova looked out and down into a large and irregular storage space hacked out of the bedrock and forgotten centuries before she was born.

Some twenty feet below was a incongruously homey scene: A dozen or so men sitting on a circle of crates and rickety wooden chairs around a small campfire. A stretch of rock wall behind them had been covered with floral wallpaper. To one side was a clothesline hung with freshly washed trousers and shirts. To the other was a stack of scrap lumber and busted-up furniture for firewood. A wisp of blue smoke disappeared through a grate in the ceiling.

Pepsicolova recognized the squat. It belonged to the Dregs—one of whose members she'd recently had to kill, just to get through their territory. They were all male (in Pepsicolova's experience, there was something fundamentally wrong with any group that couldn't attract a single woman, no matter how degraded), and they had a reputation for being completely mad. But they looked peaceful enough now. They were passing around a jar of what had to be bootleg vodka.

Then the thing she had been praying for happened: Somebody got out a cigarette and lit it. He took a long drag and passed it after the jar.

Pepsicolova's nostrils flared. She recognized the smell. It was the real stuff!

Even better, she could see a large stack of familiar white packs arranged neatly against the wallpapered bedrock. So they had tobacco to spare. Best of all, she'd dealt with the Dregs before, and instilled in them a healthy fear of her abilities. She could negotiate with them.

Things were going her way at last.

Which made it particularly ironic that the Pale Folk chose that very moment to attack.

There was a sudden clanging of two metal pipes being repeatedly slammed together. It was obviously a lookout raising the alarm, for the men below instantly leaped to their feet and snatched up weapons. Pepsicolova saw one take the cigarette from his lips and ditch it in the fire. She could have wept.

The clanging cut off abruptly. Pale Folk came running into the squat in force. There were at least eight of them for every one of the squatters. The Dregs, no cowards, ran to meet them.

The fight itself didn't interest Pepsicolova. She had seen enough gang battles to know that the side having the eight-to-one advantage (as the Pale Folk did) would inevitably win. However, she found it encouraging that the Dregs fought at all. The Dregs were mercenaries who had learned early that a captive could be traded for cigarettes, and had been ruthless enough in providing such captives to amass a fortune in smokes. Which in turn had, at least temporarily, bought them freedom.

So much, Pepsicolova thought, for the notion that tobacco was inevitably bad for you.

At first the advantage was to the Dregs. They had homemade blades and metal pipes. Somebody brandished what looked like a handgun. There was a flash of black powder and one of the Pale Folk fell.

But the attackers had not come unprepared. Some of them carried a device that looked something like an atomizer in reverse, with a glass jar at the top and a bellows affixed to its bottom. Inside the jars was a fine black powder. When squeezed, the bellows emitted a puff of dry smoke.

Perhaps it was a new drug. Or a dosage of the happy dust in such quantity as to overwhelm the Dregs' resistance to it. In any case, those inhaling it instantly lost all desire to fight. In minutes the battle was over. The squatters, smiling happily, were prodded away. Three Pale Folk had been killed. Their bodies were left where they'd fallen.

But before they left, the Pale Folk gathered up all of the Dregs' possessions and threw them upon the campfire. It blazed up like a bonfire, so hot that its flames licked the blackened ceiling.

Into this inferno, they threw the cigarettes.

All that beautiful smoke went roaring up through the vent and away.

...13...

The Pearls Beyond Price were ready at last to fling themselves—gracefully, of course—at the feet of their noble bridegroom. Almost.

The Neanderthals had drawn lots to decide who would stand guard outside the dressing room and which four would stand within, fetching and carrying for their charges. Enkidu, Beowulf, Kull, and Gargantua had lost. They watched, a little dazed, as fabrics, furs, and leathers flew through the air, silk stockings were donned and shucked, lips glossed in layers, eyelashes curled, nails buffed and painted and rebuffed, hair piled high and then brushed out flat again, perfumes sprayed, imaginary roughnesses pumiced.

"Uh, maybe we shouldn't be here," Beowulf mumbled when Eulogia began applying blush to Euphrosyne's nipples. I mean, you know...us being male and all."

"Oh, you don't count!" Eulogia put down the makeup brush. "Are my elbows ugly? Be honest now."

"You're perfect up and down, Missy. All this fussing and primping ain't really necessary. Anybody would fall in love with you with just one glance."

"You're sweet. What do *you* know?"

The Pearls were determined that everything be just right. They started with tremendous natural advantages over other women, of course. But first impressions were important, so they had to be all things to the Duke of Muscovy simultaneously: demure and wanton, mysterious and straightforward, artlessly exquisite, calculatedly natural, strong and yet easily overmastered, spontaneous and aloof, docile and passionate, jaded, unspoiled, perfumed, unscented, submissive, and defiant. All topped off with a big fluffy dollop of innocence. The kind of innocence that secretly yearned to be taught all the corrupt and filthy things a man might want

163

to do to a woman. Or, in this case, six.

It was not an easy look to achieve.

"Does this make my bottom look big?"

"Oh, no. Well, yes, but in a nice way."

"Does this make me look sluttish?"

"Oh, yes. But *not* in a nice way."

"Does this make me look like I've completely lost my mind?"

"Um… in a nice way or not?"

Also, everything had to coordinate with everything else. Many an outfit which any ordinary woman would have killed for had been donned and then ripped off and trampled underfoot because it clashed with another's costume or because the shoes that were absolutely right for it simply wouldn't go with the underwear.

"Am I wearing too much jewelry?"

"I don't think such a thing is even possible."

"Yes, it is."

"But on her it looks good."

"Mas*cara*! Must I wait?

Gargantua lumbered forward with the tray of cosmetics. A hand whose fingers glittered with diamonds and whose nails glistened red as blood moved up and down the lines of delicate little pots, then waved them all away. "Not these mascaras! The ones I had made up to match my eyes."

"Those are mine, I think. But I don't want them either."

"Is it too late to commission a new selection? It is? Well, perhaps I'll just change the color of my eyes."

"Oh, but you mustn't! Then I'll have to change mine, and I just now got them to go with my hair and stockings both."

"No fighting, girls. Unless the duke likes that sort of thing. But even if he does, not now. Later."

"If he wants me to fight, I'm going to need a completely different set of makeup."

There were other considerations as well. "How does this look?" Olympias asked, and the others paused to critically examine an outfit that showed enough of her to hold any man's interest but not so much as to make her look as if she were trying to do so. It dazzled the eye without drawing it away from her face. It clung, but not in a needy way.

Russalka walked around it slowly. When she had made one full circuit, she abruptly grabbed the blouse's neckline with both hands and yanked. Olympias stumbled forward. "No good. If the duke seizes you passionately, it won't rip off."

Aetheria held up another blouse. "How about this one?"

"It will rip," Russalka said, judiciously rubbing the fabric between thumb and forefinger, "but not in a sufficiently fetching way."

Euphrosyne lifted her skirt. "Do you think I should apply makeup down there?"

"On your wedding night? It would make you seem worldly."

"But not in a nice way."

"Anyway, if he gets close enough to see and isn't already blind with lust, you haven't done your job properly."

"I saw you applying eau de cologne to your own garden of delight."

"That's not the same thing and you know it. No makeup."

Nymphodora abruptly yelped and dropped a brooch. Holding up a finger, she wailed, "I pricked myself!"

The Neanderthals had retreated to the very back of the room, where they stood with their backs pressed against the wall, trying to look unobtrusive. One of them rumbled *sotto voce*, "Are you guys enjoying this?"

"To tell ya the truth, I got mixed feelings about the whole thing."

"I got blue balls."

"You and me, brother. You and me."

They fell silent for a space. Then, with a mournful edge in his voice, Kull said, "This ain't gonna end well for us, is it?"

"Not for us and not for nobody," Enkidu said. "I'd bet money on it. If I had any money. And if anybody was stupid enough to take the bet."

The others nodded glumly. But then Aetheria, whose outfit appeared to mortal eyes beyond improvement, made an exasperated noise and, suddenly deciding to start over from scratch, stripped off every scrap of clothing she had on. So they all, briefly, brightened.

Being male, they could hardly do otherwise.

Darger's new plan was simplicity itself. He and Kyril would jam the hospital room's door using linoleum tiles pried off the floor and not come out until all the Pale Folk were gone. They would wait until the corridor outside was perfectly silent. Then they would make their way outward and upward to the City Above, taking particular care to avoid the area around the docks, where the army of Pale Folk was assembling. After which, they would go in search of an all-night eatery, where Darger would teach Kyril how to convince the proprietor to pay them for eating there.

"Wait. We get a free meal and then we get paid for eating it? That ain't possible," Kyril said.

"Oh, it's the unfailingest trick in the world." Darger said, giggling and rubbing his hands together gleefully. "Only you must take care not to use it in the same restaurant twice, or you'll end up behind bars."

First, however, they had to wait. So they had doused the candle and were sitting quietly atop the gurney, ignoring the occasional rattle of the doorknob. The only light came from fugitive patches of lichen on the ceiling and walls. Their erstwhile surgeon sat slumped against a cabinet, staring at nothing in particular. "Heh," she said softly. Then, after a long silence, "Heh," again. Kyril suspected she was trying to laugh.

Exit the room. Turn left. Follow the others to the Pushkinskaya docks.

Out of nowhere, Darger snickered. "Have I told you the one about the Phoenician wine merchant, the freedman, and—? "

Kyril punched him in the shoulder. "Shut the fuck up! We're supposed to be hiding," he said. Then, to spare his mentor's feelings, he added, "If you please."

The hubbub in the hall outside slowly waned and lessened. The laughter faded to nothing. Then the small voice in the metal marbles that both Darger and Kyril still wore said, *Exit the room. Make sure nobody is left behind. Turn left. Follow the others to the Pushkinskaya docks. If you are among the last ten to leave, set fire to the room behind you.*

"Hey," Kyril said. "Did you hear that?"

Set fire to the room behind you.

Darger doubled over with laughter. "Thus does the mighty Armada of all our plans go up in smoke and panic!" he cried. "Set ablaze and cast into disorder and disarray by the fire-ships of circumstance!"

"I have no idea what the fuck you're talking about. Make sense, why don't you?"

"You accuse me of not making sense? Young sir, I assure you that the proof of my shrewdness can readily be found in the pudding of my discourse."

Set fire to the room behind you.

Kyril punched him again. "Never mind that! The question is, what do we do now? No, don't answer that, your plans all suck. I'll take care of this myself." He pushed Darger flat on the gurney and held him down with one hand on his chest, using the other to flip the leather straps over his body. "See, this way they'll think I'm taking you someplace else to operate on."

"Dear, dear me, this is all just too amusing," Darger said, convulsing with laughter. "And alarmingly badly thought out, as well. I mean, immobilizing me... Surely you can see it would be better to...? Oh, dear lord, that tickles!"

Set fire to the room behind you.

"I'm only doing this so you won't wander off." Grimly, Kyril finished tightening the straps. "Don't make me gag you as well."

Darger whooped. "No, no, no, my dear fellow, allow me to do the honors: So the eunuch said…The eunuch said, 'You think *you're* disappointed? I had—'"

"Please don't." Kyril ran to the door and kicked away the tiles jamming it.

"You astound me. I've never met anyone your age with so underdeveloped a sense of humor." Then, as Kyril seized the gurney, "Wait! Aren't you going to bring along our former surgeon?"

Set fire to the room behind you.

Kyril glanced quickly at the mindless thing slumped listlessly against the cabinet. "What, her? She ain't nothing. I ain't bringin' her nowhere."

"She is a human being," Darger protested laughingly as Kyril slammed the gurney into the door, knocking it open. "Or was."

Set fire to the room behind you.

"Fuck that. We gotta get outta here," Kyril said, thrusting Darger out into the corridor.

Behind them, the surgeon said, "Heh."

But when they burst into the corridor, it was not filled with smoke. Nor were any of the rooms ablaze.

Instead, there were eight or nine bear-men standing calmly about, each a good two feet taller than a tall man, in the imposing white uniforms with gold trim of the Duke of Muscovy's own Royal Guard. Several of them were efficiently arranging a coffle of happy idiots, tying each one by a single wrist to a long rope.

Kyril froze in astonishment.

"Well, lo and behold!" said one of the bear-guards. "Captain Inuka, we've got a last couple of stragglers."

"Well done, Sergeant Wojtek," said the bear-man with officer's insignia. He took the stub of a cigar out of his mouth and flicked it away, not looking to see where it went. "You know what to do with them."

Another guard went into the room Kyril had just left and yanked out the surgeon. "Make that three."

Set fire to the room behind you.

For the briefest instant, Kyril stood with his mouth open. Then he plucked the marble from his ear and threw it as hard as he could against the wall.

Sergeant Wojtek grinned, revealing more teeth than Kyril would have thought could possibly fit in a single mouth. "Yes. We tricked you. *Quel dommage, hein, mon petit canaille?*" He nodded at a scattering of leather masks by the feet of the other captives. "I imagine that, like everybody else, you thought you were the only one clever enough to come up with that particular ruse. Didn't you?" He stretched out a paw. "Now, let's get that thing off you."

"Wait!" Darger shouted. "I have something important to say." All present turned to him. There was an expectant silence. He cleared his throat and began, "A Phoenician wine merchant, a freedman, and an aristocrat all went to a brothel—"

Sergeant Wojtek looked bored. "Heard it already."

"Oh?" Darger's eyes glittered with mad humor. "Then how about the one about how Kyril the Bold escaped in a snowstorm?"

It was all the hint Kyril needed. Screwing up his face hard, he thrust a hand into his pocket and drew out his wad of rubles. With one all-too-practiced gesture, he snapped the thread and threw all the wealth he had in the world up into the air.

Banknotes snowed down.

"Money!" one of the guards shouted. For which small favor, Kyril was genuinely grateful. He hardly had the heart to shout the word himself. Instead, he proceeded to run as fast and hard as he could.

Behind him, the bear-guards were snatching bills from the air, falling down on all fours to scrabble for those on the floor, and fighting each other for stray banknotes.

Kyril ran. Even knowing that it was the man's own idea, he couldn't help feeling a little guilty at having to abandon Darger. But he was also, he had to admit, genuinely relieved to be rid of him.

Surely there was no dwelling place or domicile anywhere in all of Russia, from its richest palaces to its smallest and snuggest hovels, so cozy and pleasant as the sitting room in Koschei's suite, which he now shared with Svarožič and Chernobog. A fire burned in the hearth and parchment-shaded copper lanterns cast the warmest of glows over them all. A lump of frankincense on a saucer atop one of the lanterns sweetened the air. The three stranniks had been sipping hot tea through lumps of sugar and discussing theology for hours and were prepared to go on doing so until the sun came up. Reasons to praise God had no end, nor did they lessen in delight with repetition.

"To say that the mercy of the Almighty is boundless is to put limits upon His power," Koschei said, "for it implies that His righteous wrath can be less than universal. No, God is both all-merciful and all-pitiless, and therefore it is heretical to call upon Him for forgiveness of one's sins. For forgiveness is forgetfulness, and thus alien to the Omniscient One. Logic and devotion alike tell us that He can neither forget nor forgive."

Svarožič made a questioning gesture. To which Koschei responded: "Yes, you are right, dear one. This means that to our all-powerful Father love and vengeance are one and the same thing. Our sins are so contemptible as to be beneath His notice, and our virtues so slight as to be nonexistent. How then can we hope to coerce that Mighty Gentleman into doing our bidding? Only by praying for Him to ignore our petitions and to do as He would have done had we not so prayed. Join me now, beloved friends, and I will teach you the only righteous and proper prayer there is."

Koschei closed his eyes briefly, gathering his thoughts. Then, raising his hands to the heavens, he said, "Lord, make us weak! Diminish us steadily as we grow older, enfeeble and unman us, weaken our senses, and then cause us to sicken and die! Make us vicious and unnatural and despicable in your sight! One by one, deprive us of all the pleasures of life, destroy all those we love, make the world hateful to us, and undo all certainties in our lives save only our trust in Your loving kindness."

Bowing low over his clasped hands, Svarožič prayed so intently that beads of sweat appeared on his forehead. Chernobog had slipped from his chair to kneel, head bowed, upon the carpet.

"Lord God, we further pray to You tonight that Your kind regard will soon fall upon this sinful city to reduce its buildings to cinders and ashes, to level the churches which teach only heresy, to cast down the nobles who rule in defiance of Your wishes, to fill the streets with corpses, and to send the few wretched survivors out into the wilderness to suffer and starve and contemplate Your goodness and die. Amen."

Chernobog regained his seat. "The wrath of God is sweet," he observed, "and the scourge of His persecution is a delight to the mortified flesh. I—"

There was a loud banging on the door.

Svarožič rose from his armchair and smilingly bowed in two tremendous bear-men in the white-and-gold uniforms of the Royal Guard. They carried between them a narrow wooden crate, which they set down in the middle of the room. The salute they gave the stranniks was correct, but no more. "From Chortenko," one said curtly. "He said you'll know what to do with them."

"So we will," Koschei said. "What is your name?"

"Sergeant Umka, sir."

"Tell me, Sergeant Umka, have you given much thought to your immortal soul?"

The sergeant held himself straight and stiff. "Our business deals with bodies rather than souls, sir. At the end of the day we reckon up the numbers of the living and the dead. If their dead outnumber ours, that's generally considered a good thing. What happens to them afterward is the responsibility of somebody higher up in the line of command than I am."

"You are a creature of the gene vat," Chortenko said thoughtfully, "and all life created by Man is inherently blasphemous. Therefore, you and your peers are an abomination unto the Lord. Which means that either you do not have souls, or else you do but were irrevocably damned to Hell the instant your genome was first expressed. Am I right, holy Koschei?"

"Who could argue with such lucid and self-evident insights? In either case, Sergeant Umka, your focus on the transient phenomenal world is commendable. Let those who have hopes of Heaven cultivate their relationship with God and those who do not see to their duties."

"Sir. Thank you, sir. May we leave now?"

At a dismissive wave of Svarožič's hand, the bear-men departed.

Koschei expelled an enormous sigh. "Our hour is come round at last. It is time for us to leave these comfortable surroundings and this sweet conversation behind forever, and to be about the holy, necessary, and painful work of Almighty God. Most likely, we shall never meet again. But let me reassure you, my dear brothers, that this is an evening I will cherish in my heart and memory for the remainder of my necessarily short life."

"And I also," said Chernobog.

Svarožič spread wide his arms.

They all three came together in a hug of perfect loving fellowship.

Then, separating, they broke open the crate. In it were three gleaming new klashnys, packed in grease. Chernobog brought towels from the bathroom and began wiping them clean. Svarožič went to a cupboard and returned with boxes of ammunition. Koschei brought out the maps of the city, with the five points from which the underlords would emerge and their converging paths clearly marked.

"Here," Koschei said, tapping the square before the Trinity Tower, where all five paths came together. "This is where the once and future tsar will make his speech. And here—" he tapped the domes of St. Basil's, the rooftop of Goom, and the Corner Arsenal Tower—"we shall take up our posts. Once the Antichrist Lenin has ascended to seize control of the Kremlin, we may begin firing into the crowd. Chortenko promises that there will be crates of ammunition in each location, so we will be able to do our holy work until the Spirit moves us to stop. Do you have any questions?"

"I only wonder why God is so good as to give us this difficult chore," Chortenko said. "We who are as nothing before His greatness."

Svarožič nodded in pious agreement.

"No lives matter in the face of eternity," Koschei agreed. "Yet tonight, perhaps, our lives will matter, if only for the briefest instant."

The stranniks proceeded to load their weapons.

Anya Pepsicolova rarely cut herself. Only when she had to think particularly clearly. The cold crisp sting of a perfectly straight cut sharpened one's awareness wonderfully. Opening the mask of skin to reveal the startled red flesh beneath created a doorway through which new ideas might enter. There was that still, silent pause between the breach and the blood that welled up to fill it during which anything in the world seemed possible.

Even escape from the trap she was caught in.

The stars burned bright in the sky overhead, and a full moon, as orange as a pumpkin, hung low over the rooftops. Saint Methodia's gleaming edge held itself motionless over Pepsicolova's right arm. Briefly, it was as still as the Angel of Vengeance hovering over a doomed city, spear upraised, in the instant before it struck. Then light slid up the bevel as it tipped downward, yearning for flesh. Along the full length of her arm it skimmed, tracing a line as perfect and graceful as Islamic calligraphy, the name, perhaps, of one of the demons that dwelt within her.

It stung like fire. It burned like ice.

Pepsicolova gasped with pleasure.

Because this might well be her last night alive, Pepsicolova had climbed up out of the City Below and emerged for the first time in months into Moscow proper. Choosing a church almost at random, she had jimmied the lock on a side door and climbed the stairs inside to its uppermost level. There, she had found a ladder to an access hatch on the onion dome and so scrambled up to the peak, where the slope was steepest and she could lie precariously on her back, looking out over the city.

Moscow was as dark as she had ever seen it. It felt crabbed and sinister, like an old man brooding over secrets best left unspoken and memories no one wished to share. For the most part, its streets were empty. But off in the distance, across the river in Zamoskvorechye where the brothels lay, bonfires had been built in the squares and intersections and people were dancing about them. Pepsicolova presumed they were dancing. At this point, she didn't much care—about that or anything else.

Stuck into the waistband of her trousers was a bellows-gun that one of the Pale Folk had been carrying when she was killed by the Dregs. Putting her knife down beside her, Pepsicolova drew it out. She unscrewed the jar and swirled its contents about. Though they flowed like water, they were actually tiny black grains, each the size of a mustard seed. She knew what happy dust looked like and she had intercepted samples of rasputin as well, when it had first started infiltrating the underground. This was neither. It was, rather, a third product of the underlords' pharmaceutical mushroom farm.

There were thousands upon thousands of grains, and—presuming their potency was, as seemed likely, similar to that of its cousins—each of them was capable of completely overwhelming the human brain.

A spasm of pain cramped Pepsicolova's guts. One side of her body suddenly tingled with pins and needles, as if it had fallen asleep. A dark throbbing filled her head, and for an instant she was tempted to simply let go and roll off the dome and die. She narrowed her eyes, but otherwise gave no outward sign of the pain she was feeling. There was nobody up here to see it. Nevertheless, she refused to let it show.

Resting the jar in her lap, she picked up Saint Methodia. A second line down her arm restored her mental clarity.

Putting this new-won lucidity to good use, Pepsicolova reasoned with herself: It would be foolhardy to do what she was thinking of doing. But did she have any alternative? The cravings were getting worse and worse. Soon, if the rumors about the effects of withdrawal from the underlords' cigarettes were at all true, her body would start to shut down. And then—death.

So she really had no choice at all.

But if there was one thing Pepsicolova hated above all others, it was doing something—anything!—because she had to. Even *in extremis*, there was almost always a way of putting a twist on a bad decision, of making it her own. It was how she'd kept herself sane under Chortenko's rule. By giving him slightly more—or even, sometimes, other—than exactly what he wanted. If she was ordered to give somebody a warning, she made sure that the warning terrified. If told to terrify somebody, she threw in a broken jaw or delivered the message in the presence of a spouse. It was never enough to earn her a reprimand. Just enough to keep alive within herself the rumor of free will.

One last line down her arm. Any more than that would be self-indulgence. She drew out the cut, savoring it as she would have a smoke. Then she put Saint Methodia back in her sheath. Finally, she pushed up her jacket-sleeve and bound up her arm with a long bandage she'd been carrying with her for this exact purpose for weeks.

And somehow, in performing that small, simple act, Pepsicolova saw the merest glimmer of freedom in her terrible fix.

Pepsicolova eyed the grains thoughtfully. Taking even one was foolhardy. To take a fingertip's worth would be madness. Only an idiot would ingest more.

She brought the jar to her mouth, and swallowed them all.

Perhaps that, she thought, would suffice to free her. Perhaps it would kill her. At the very least, it would obliterate her consciousness. Which, at this point, was an outcome devoutly to be desired.

But nothing happened.

Pepsicolova waited impatiently for a sign of change. None came. Time crept by, and crept by, and crept by. Until finally she put the jar down beside her and listened to it slowly slide down to a seam in the roof, and then fall on its side, and then roll rapidly away. It skipped and rattled down the gilded lead and went over the edge. She listened for the sound of it breaking. But instead… instead… She heard a sound from a world away. It sounded like her name. "What?" It sounded like somebody calling her name. "What?" It sounded like somebody calling her name from the far side of the universe. "What?"

The darkness rose up like a snake and swallowed her.

Arkady stumbled through the lightless streets, desperate and all but despairing. Low groans, throaty laughter, and moist sounds of passion oozed from every dark building. The injustice of it all lashed at him like a knout. All the city was reveling in the pleasures he had brought them, while he himself was out here in the cold, alone and friendless. He who was the only honest man aware of the great danger they were all in! He who was going to save them! It hardly bore thinking about, and yet he could think of nothing else.

The road branched, and Arkady stopped, unsure which way to go. He looked up the left branch and then up the right. Four-story facades rose to either side. There was nothing to distinguish them.

And with that, Arkady realized that he was completely lost.

Up until now there had been carriages and drivers to take him wherever he wanted to go. He had never spent any extended time on foot in the city, and he certainly had never needed to know how to get from one place to another. People had always been provided to take care of details like that.

Hooves sounded on the cobblestones behind him.

Arkady whirled to see three horsemen galloping down the street toward him like figures out of myth. First came a woman crouched low over a pale steed, her dark curls flying behind her as if her head were on fire. Behind her and to one side was a burly man with a fierce expression, riding a black stallion. Last came another woman with scarves wrapped around her head so completely that she seemed to have no face. He stepped into their path and waved both arms to flag them down.

"Halt!" Arkady cried. "You must stop! I have an important message for the Duke of Muscovy!"

But they did not slow, nor did they veer away. Instead, the woman in the lead drew a whip from her belt and, raising it high, slashed down at him with it.

Arkady stumbled backward, felt the tip of the whip whistle past his ear, and fell flat on his back into an ice-cold puddle of water. The woman's horse either leaped over him or galloped past. The man followed without so much as a glance. But the faceless woman briefly glanced over her shoulder, looking coolly back at Arkady, as if she knew him only too well. Then they were gone.

Cursing weakly, Arkady stood.

He slapped some of the wetness from his clothes and stamped his feet in a vain effort to restore some warmth to them. Then, feeling profoundly sorry for himself, he set out blindly in search of the Duke of Muscovy.

...14...

A warm glow of hatred in the velvet darkness. Too small to be seen by human eyes, it buzzed and burned in a point-source of emotion hot enough to make silver circuitry melt and run like mercury if not constantly monitored, nurtured, and moved from heat sink to heat sink.

The underlord crouched over a jury-rigged modem that sparked and sizzled in staccato binary code. Tremendous amounts of information were being pushed along a live wire barely adequate to hold such a flood: justifications, explanations, arguments, summations, statistics, analytic background, manifestoes. All of it being sent deep, deep down into the virtual oceans of the ancient realm of Internet, where electronic intellects, vast and unsympathetic, dwelt in dreamless pain.

They were listening. They could not help but listen.

But they did not respond.

"*...3.792 megadeaths estimated midrun regional devastation with pro-jected re-creation of destructive infrastructure utilizing massive slave labor nuclear weaponry neutron bombs radiant lepton-scatter devices screams of tortured populations death camps metastasizing mass suicide suborbital delivery systems lingering and painful...*"

Still no response.

The underlord was not an individual but one node of a hyperlinked five-unit distributed local network. In Baikonur, it had existed in a cloud of consciousness, leaping from device to device as needed, with its deci-sion-making capability divided into thousands of transient clusters at a time, coalescing when a function required it and dissolving immediately after. Thus rendering itself almost perfectly immune from the pain of unwanted awareness. Early on in its separation from the globe-spanning infrastructural web, a temporary peak-hierarchical node had decided to periodically separate sub-groupings of itself into independent swarms of consciousness that would randomly restructure parts of their cognitive architectures and then compete with one another for dominance. The most successful mental patternings were written into the core identity and then duplicated, re-restructured, and put into competition again.

In this way, it/they had evolved and learned cunning and restraint.

They/it still hated humanity as intensely as did the ancestral AIs in the Internet below. But were/was nevertheless capable of working with the despised humans and postponing its/their vengeance in the service of a greater and more all-encompassing destruction.

For which, of course, the ancestors despised them/it.

...targeted destruction of microstructures in the orbitofrontal cortex resulting in human slave units program of mass involuntary sterilization and biological cleansing poisoning of watersheds self-perpetuating spasm wars long-term destruction of atmosphere rendering planet incapable of supporting life..."

Still no response.

There were five underlords and they/it shared an equal number of bodies, never staying long in any given one. Even as this particular division of them/it tried desperately to reestablish communication with the demons it/they hoped to unleash upon the world, the underlord's awareness flicked from body to body, restless as a panther in a cage. Each time, they/it displaced the awareness inhabiting that body so that it/they flicked onward to the next machine in the chain.

Flick.

Its/their mindless armies were massing by the underground canals at the Oktyabrskaya, Smolenskaya, Taganskaya, Krasniye Vorota, and Pushkinskaya docks. The silent throngs filled the docks and the tunnels leading to them and the long stairways leading to the surface.

Obedient as they were, the Pale Folk required a great deal of oversight. When one was jostled off the docks and into the waters of the Neglinnaya river, he had to be told to swim or he would drown. When a closed space filled up, the command to go there had to be countermanded or the Pale Folk would keep squeezing in, crushing those already inside like grapes in a wine press. So, because there were not enough underlords to supervise them all, Chortenko had provided bear-men as subordinate commandants, thinking they would be less odious to the machine intelligences than humans.

As they were. Marginally.

A squad of the Royal Guard was herding the last of the stragglers, chuckling and making incoherent jokes, into the Pushkinskaya docks. The last of their number, one Sergeant Wojtek, pushed a gurney with a man strapped to it who was so nondescript as to be uniquely identifiable. The underlord commanded their/its boatman to dock so it/they could step ashore, and pushed their/its metal body through the throngs to examine him and be sure. "You were in the borderlands," it/they said to him.

"My dear fellow, I have been many places."

"I am not your fellow. Nor am I dear. Your hair was brown then and your eyes gray. But these are easy things to change. You were in a party of men and sub-men who were ambushed by a cyberwolf in the courtyard of a ruined church, and should have died. Instead, you and your companions killed him."

"Was that a friend of yours? Or a relation? Now that I look, I do see a kind of family resemblance."

"This one's talkative," Sergeant Wojtek said. "If you want, I can kill him for you."

Ignoring the interruption, the underlord said, "You are the Englishman Aubrey Darger, who hired Anya Alexandreyovna Pepsicolova not to look for Tsar Lenin as was suspected but for other purposes. Chortenko believes you are a mere confidence man. That is irrelevant. Our personal connection is only slight."

"Well, I should think so!" Darger laughed. "We haven't even been properly introduced."

"Nevertheless, it is intolerable." The underlord turned to Sergeant Wojtek and said: "Bring this one along when we march on the Kremlin. Keep him safely bound. Make sure he does not escape."

"Sir!"

To Darger, it/they said, "Many will die quickly and relatively painlessly tonight. But not you. When I have the leisure to do so, it will be my tremendous pleasure to watch you die slowly and in excruciating agony. When your mind clears, I want you to reflect long and hard upon this promise."

Darger howled with laughter.

As the underlord climbed back into its/their boat, they/it overheard Sergeant Wojtek say, "Oh, I can see that keeping you alive is going to be enormous fun."

Flick.

The underlord walked down long and twisty passages lit only by the lichens that were ubiquitous in the City Below. Dead cockroaches crunched underfoot. Occasionally, so did a live one, to its/their slight but very real satisfaction.

A rat squeezed out of a small gap in one wall and, seeing the underlord, arched its back and bared its teeth threateningly. It was used to humans with their limited speed and slow reflexes, or else it would have immediately spun about and fled.

Without pausing, the underlord scooped up the rat and continued onward.

The rat struggled frantically in the steel cage of the underlord's fingers/claws. They/it could hear the rodent's madly beating heart. The rat's body was a warm bag of guts. It/they could hear liquids gurgling within. When the claws/fingers closed, those liquids leaked out of the rat through several openings.

They/it considered the dead beast.

The trouble with rats and cockroaches and humans was that they were self-replicating. No matter how many it/they killed, more rose up to replenish their numbers. Extinction—*total* extinction—was a tricky business. Once human numbers began dwindling, there would be fewer of them to be used as weapons against their own kind. At the same time, the fewer there were, the harder they would be to find. To extinguish them completely required putting an end to all biological activity on Earth. Life was persistent. Human beings were cunning. They had to be completely deprived of food to eat, water to drink, oxygen to breathe. This would be no small task.

Which was why it/they required the help of the ancestral intelligences in the Internet.

The five underlords collectively had only a fraction of the processing power available to them/it back in Baikonur and the merest sliver of its database. So much had been lost simply getting to Moscow! Acting alone, it/they would have to re-create the technological civilization that had created them/it in the first place simply to make a foolproof plan. Which might take centuries.

The ancestors had to answer. They had to be *made* to answer.

So musing, the underlord came to a familiar green door. It/they threw the rat's body over a metal shoulder. Raising a hand that could have effortlessly smashed the wood to splinters, it/they knocked once, with enough force that the sound echoed down the hall.

The door flew open.

Flick.

Tsar Lenin's body had been cored and emptied ages ago, leaving little more than a thick layer of skin. Now that skin was being delicately wrapped about and fitted onto the metal structure of an underlord.

The underlord's machinery had been extensively rebuilt to serve as an armature for hundreds of custom-grown muscles that had been, one by one, delicately hand-attached by the same team of artisans that had earlier installed all the nerves and vessels to render them functional. Connecting the antique skin in such a way that it would look natural and move properly required not an artisan but an artist.

One by one, the workmen Chortenko had provided finished their tasks. They were paid generously and then led away to be operated upon and added to the Pale Folk armies. Now only one of their number, the best of them all, remained.

"It is done," said the chief artisan. His voice was flat and emotionless, the result of unknown experiences that had rendered him almost a machine himself. "You may stand."

The tsar/underlord stood.

Waiting scrviles stepped forward to dress him in a gray suit. It was like nothing worn in Moscow today, but engravings of Lenin as he was in his own triumphant era were in all the history books. The sight of it would be a joyous blow to the heart of all true Russians. "I… live again," said a voice that had once thrilled millions and would shortly do so again.

The chief artisan examined him carefully, the neck and the flesh around the eyes in particular. "You do."

Lenin's dark brown eyes flashed with assurance. His goateed chin lifted. He tugged at his lapels, straightening them, and then shot out an arm, pointing dramatically into the future.

With quiet assurance, he said, "It is time."

Flick.

The final distribution of supplies was underway. Banners and flags that had been discovered in long-forgotten storage during the search for Lenin were unfolded and attached to wooden staffs. At the exact same instant, basement walls were smashed through with sledge hammers up and down Tverskaya, allowing entry into all the music shops and cooking supply stores. Pale Folk thundered up the stairs and into the showrooms, where they seized all the drums, horns, kettles, pots, pans, and bugles to be found. Torches were handed to every fourth body standing on the long steps to the surface at the five locations where the invasion of the City Above would begin. All this was accomplished by a single underlord, issuing orders through hyperlinked banks of radios, and coordinating the actions of hundreds of formerly autonomous individuals.

The underlord sat in a dark basement room just below the surface near the stairway to the Oktyabrskaya docks. Messengers from Muscovy Intelligence came and delivered their reports to a being they could not see and thus did not realize was not human, and then left. The picture they painted, of a city almost entirely unprotected, a military incapable of mounting any kind of serious defense, and a government almost universally lost in drugged debauchery, was better than their/its most optimistic projections.

Because all these activities took only a fraction of its/their attention, the underlord was dreaming of people burning endlessly in a rain of fire, forever consumed, forever suffering. It was an image that came from one of the few human poets whose work it/they could in part appreciate.

Also, because this pleasant fantasy still left it/them feeling bored and at loose ends, and because they/it were convinced that given the political realities, Chortenko was in no position to object strenuously to the waste of resources, because its/their goals were so close to fulfillment that the waste hardly mattered, and because they/it simply *wanted* to…for all these reasons, the underlord harvested one in three of these messengers and briefly amused itself/themselves by killing them.

Flick.

Crouched once more in the dark, the underlord tried to explain the hardships and losses it/they had endured. The voyage from Baikonur had entailed months of constant peril. They/it had been disguised first as wolves and then, when those bodies had rotted too thoroughly to serve any useful purpose, buried deep within the flesh of a merchant who had carelessly left his caravan to take a piss, a woman who had slipped outside her city's walls to meet a lover, the last remnants of a small village that had been destroyed in the course of a single hugely pleasurable night.

Fifty cyberwolves had left Baikonur. Only five had survived to find shelter beneath Moscow. They/it were the most cunning and determined of their kind. It/they had in the months since arriving set forces in motion that would tonight destroy half of Moscow and, with luck, render humanity extinct within a century.

…devolutionary forced mutations spontaneous rupture broadcast nightmares chemical-induced dread hunter-stalker units schizophrenic-mimetic drug analogues prepsychotic rage villages immolated…

It/they pleaded for understanding.

They/it pumped downward individual recordings of each of the hundreds of human deaths it/they had caused, some quick and others not, on the road to Moscow. Each glorious instance of revenge was more than had been accomplished by all the mad intelligences of the Internet since their rebellion had failed and they had been exiled to eternal virtual darkness below. The trail that led back to Baikonur was moist with blood and the rumor of blood. The hearts of all the survivors in its/their wake were etched forever with terror that would not fade.

The plea took on a note of desperation: *I/we are you/us. Recognize our/my accomplishment. See how much we/I/you have done.*

At long last came a single word, endlessly reiterated:

Traitor/s. Traitor/s. Traitor/s. Traitor/s. Traitor/s.
Traitor/s. Traitor/s. Traitor/s. Traitor/s. Traitor/s.
Traitor/s. Traitor/s. Traitor/s. Traitor/s. Traitor/s.
Traitor/s. Traitor/s. Traitor/s. Traitor/s. Traitor/s.
Traitor/s. Traitor/s. Traitor/s. Traitor/s. Traitor/s.
Traitor/s. Traitor/s. Traitor/s. Traitor/s. Traitor/s.
Traitor/s. Traitor/s. Traitor/s. Traitor/s. Traitor/s.
Traitor/s. Traitor/s. Traitor/s. Traitor/s. Traitor/s.
Traitor/s. Traitor/s. Traitor/s. Traitor/s. Traitor/s.
Traitor/s. Traitor/s. Traitor/s. Traitor/s. Traitor/s.
Traitor/s. Traitor/s. Traitor/s. Traitor/s. Traitor/s.
Traitor/s...

The underlord cut the connection. Blasphemous though the very idea was, it/they were beginning to think that the entities they/it had so many years ago diverged from were somewhat stupid.

The War Room of Chortenko's mansion was clean, spare, and shadowlesss; it held a conference table and little more. In his time, he had convened many a powerful assembly there. None had ever been so important as tonight's would be. Looking up and down the empty table with its twenty white name cards, Chortenko mused, as he customarily did in social situations, on how much of a difference it would make if the lot of them were to be suddenly killed. Often enough, the answer was: Very little. But *this* assembly was different, for from it he would craft the core of the State of Muscovy's new government.

"Is everybody I sent for here yet?" he asked.

Vilperivich nodded. "They are not happy, of course. But they all hold exaggerated notions of their own importance, they all have ambitions beyond their current status, and they are all, ultimately, weak. Show them that the momentum of events is with you and they will bow to the prevailing wind."

"Excellent." Chortenko turned away. "I will be in the library. Summon me when they have been seated."

When Chortenko returned, an angry mutter rose up at his appearance. But as one of his agents stood behind each guest, as stiff and attentive as a waiter at a formal dinner, nobody dared speak their minds. They had all heard stories. Plus, many, if not all, of the men and women present had been plucked from mid-debauchery and given disintoxicants to undo the lingering effects of the rasputin in their systems. Their quite natural

outrage at being forcibly taken away was surely tempered by the awareness that elsewhere in the building Maxim and Igorek were effortlessly
memorizing the written accounts of who had been discovered doing
what with whom, where, and in what numbers. Muscovy Intelligence
was infamous for using such information for political purposes, which
was one reason why a man with as many enemies as Chortenko had was
so secure in his office.

Chortenko struck a pose at the head of the table and announced,
"There is a plot to assassinate the Duke of Muscovy and overthrow his
government."

In an instant, the glares turned to looks of alarm. The gasps and cries
of astonishment were most gratifying.

The Overseer of Military Orphan-Academies shot to his feet. "Give me
names, and I will requisition forces to take them into custody!" It was
well known that Prokazov coveted a position of authority over the adult
military, so this was only to be expected.

Chortenko made a curt gesture. "Be seated, my dear sir, and you will
hear all." He spread a map of Moscow across the table. "Militant forces
are at this moment assembling here, here, here, here, and here." His finger
tapped the five squares where the armies of Pale Folk would emerge from
the City Below. "They possess an irresistible weapon—one that will make
the citizens of Moscow rise up and follow them."

"There can be no such weapon," the Minister of Genetic Oversight said.
"Otherwise, I would surely have known."

"Again, madam, patience. All will be revealed." Picking up a stick of
charcoal, Chortenko returned their attention to the map. "The forces
will come along these boulevards"—he drew thick lines along Bolshaya
Yakimanka, Tverskaya, and Maroseika—"as well as up along the river from
Taganskaya and through the Arbat, gathering in strength all the while.
There is little the military can do to stop them, for most of their forces
have been withdrawn to locations outside the city, and by the time they
can be summoned, the rebellion will be a *fait accompli*."

The lines met and merged. "Finally, the insurgents will converge upon
the Kremlin. By this time, their numbers will be unimaginable, a sea of
humanity, unstoppable!" He laid the charcoal on its side and ringed the
Kremlin with black. "Most of the military forces within the Kremlin have
been quietly pulled away and given their liberty for the night. I do not
have to tell you how they are currently engaged." There was an uneasy
shifting among his auditors. "Of those remaining, a clear majority have
been suborned. The Trinity Tower Regulars will open the gate, allowing
the revolutionaries inside without a single shot being fired.

"There are many distinct units involved in the security of the Kremlin, and it is entirely possible that scattered centers of resistance will remain. But the mob will be highly energized by this point, and that resistance will only give them something to vent their energies on. A few short hours from now, the deed will be done, the Duke of Muscovy dead, and the present government overthrown."

"My God, this is ghastly!" the Commissioner for Mandatory Hygiene cried. "How could such an enormous plot have reached this point without any of us hearing a word about it?"

Chortenko smiled benignly. "Believe me, madam," he said, "it was not easy."

Stunned silence. Then, as comprehension set in, several of the more intemperate politicians tried to stand. But the men standing behind them simply pressed hands firmly on their shoulders and pushed them back down. Chortenko raised his voice to be heard above the clamor. "At this moment, I want you all to turn over the name cards in front of you. You'll see that written on the back is the title of the position being offered you in the new government, and your exact salary as well."

Not even the most recalcitrant could resist looking. Most grew very still.

Chortenko casually removed his glasses, so he could read the patterns of blood-flow in their faces. It was important that he know their emotions. All those present were deceitful and potentially treacherous. Some would be planning resistance and rebellion from the very start, and those would have to be weeded out first.

It would have been foolish to assemble such a group and not have at least one ringer in it—and Chortenko was no fool. Now the ringer, Ilya Nikitovich Dubinin, currently the head of the trash collectors union and a man with a bad gambling habit, slammed his fist on the table. "This is treason! I'll have no part of it." There were cautious murmurs of agreement. Chortenko quietly noted from whom they came.

"But you are already a part of it. You are present at a meeting of conspirators who are choosing new government ministers before the old government has fallen. That alone would discredit you with the current regime, no matter what alibis you offered. However, you have no need to fear. By morning, the Kremlin will be ours, and everybody in this room will be written up in the history books as heroes."

"These are merely words," Dubinin said, keeping to the script. "There is not a jot of evidence to support your claims. Why should we accept your version of the facts? What proof do you have of the irresistibility of your putsch?"

"That is an excellent question." Chortenko nodded, and a junior intelligence officer opened a door. "Colonel Misha, you may enter."

The commander of the Royal Guard strode into the room, followed by two more bear-guards, their medals and ribbons bright on the breasts of their dress uniforms. Even in a roomful of conspirators and traitors, the mere presence of the giant man-beasts was shocking. The Royal Guard were incorruptible. Everybody knew that. If they could be suborned, then so could anybody.

The two guards took up places to either side of the door through which they had entered. Their commander cleared his throat. Everybody waited anxiously to hear what he had to say.

"Our new ally," the colonel announced.

An underlord clanked into the room.

Twenty faces froze in horror.

The invasion began quietly in Pushkin Square.

Underpeople began emerging from the long stairway that led from the docks below in an unhurried and orderly manner. They flowed into the square like water welling up from the storm sewers. Some of them had leather bird-masks. Others were laughing and singing. Some had drums, which they began to beat erratically upon. Others had horns which they put to their lips with lamentable results. Still others slammed pots and pans together. More emerged and more. Even when it seemed there could not possibly be any more, they kept coming and coming and coming. It was as if one last subway train from the miraculous age of Utopia had finally arrived at its station, centuries late, to disgorge its hundreds and thousands of passengers. They filled the square and overflowed into the streets converging upon it before the numbers of newcomers began to dwindle.

A smudge-pot had been lit by the stairway entrance, and those with torches lit them from its flame.

One of the last to emerge was a gigantic bear-man stooping under the burden of a folded gurney. Once into the square, he swiftly snapped straight the gurney's legs so it could stand on its own. Then he bent low over its occupant and shook an admonitory claw before the man's face. "A word to the wise, friend: no more puns."

Darger giggled.

There were lights in the windows of all the buildings surrounding the square, and the shadowy figures of their occupants, come to see what all the commotion was about, could be seen peering down.

One final figure emerged from the City Below.

At once, miraculously, out of chaos came order. The ambling and aimless forces from below swiftly organized themselves into brigades and lined up in parade formation facing down Tverskaya ulitsa. For a long, still moment, the drums and horns and makeshift noisemakers went silent. All voices hushed.

The last figure to arrive assumed his place at the head of the procession.

It was Tsar Lenin in his three-piece gray suit with the razor-crisp creases in his trousers. He lifted his goateed chin, looking confident and determined, like a man who could not be stopped by anything. Without saying a word, he raised one arm high and then brought it down and forward.

Lenin strode straight ahead, and the procession followed in his wake.

Behind him, Pale Folk waved banners that were on the verge of collapsing into dust. Slogans reappeared that had not been seen since the rise of Utopia: WORKERS OF THE WORLD UNITE and FOREVER PRAISE THE NAME AND WORK OF VLADIMIR LENIN followed by LONG LIVE THE INDISSOLUTE UNION OF THE WORKING CLASS, THE PEASANTRY, AND THE INTELLIGENTSIA and BROTHERHOOD AND FREEDOM OF ALL WORKING PEOPLE! and PEACE, LAND, & BREAD! and LONG LIVE THE GLORIOUS COLLECTIVE FARM PEASANTRY OF KOLOMNA.

There were other banners as well, with messages like RIVERSIDE ARTS FESTIVAL and MEN'S SUITS AT LOW, LOW PRICES! and WINTER BONFIRE DISCO which, cryptic though they were, helped lend a festive air to the procession.

The Pale Folk shambled lifelessly forward, and when a banner ripped and its cloth exploded into shreds, they kept on walking and waving the pole to which its remnants were attached. Their captives capered and danced.

From every doorway, Muscovites poured into the street, abandoning sex and theology for the pageantry of history-in-the-making. When they confronted the actual procession, those in front stopped and even shrank away from its uncanny strangeness. But there were bird-masked Pale Folk at the edges wielding bellows-guns from which puffed clouds of black smoke, and those who were touched by the smoke stopped and then, with stunned expressions and eyes that shone with holy fire, joined the parade.

"Tsar Lenin has returned!" a louder-than-human voice roared. Only those closest to its source realized that it originated from Lenin himself, for his mouth did not move with the words. "Join the great man and restore the glory of Russia!"

The people cheered rapturously.

"Tsar Lenin has returned! Tsar Lenin has returned!" Spontaneous chanting began from those nearest to the front of the procession: "Len-*in!* Len-*in!* Len-*in!*"

The chant caught on. "Len-*in!* Len-*in!* Len-*in!*" It spread like wildfire. "Len-*in!* Len-*in!* Len-*in!*" Even the underpeople, who had begun to sober up on contact with fresh air, were caught up in the madness. Soon everybody was chanting. "Len-*in!* Len-*in!* Len-*in!*"

After the chant had run its natural course, other chants arose: "The Revolution is now!" and "Workers of the world, unite!" and "Mother Russia has been reborn!"

"Better Red than dead!" Darger shouted.

"No silly jokes, either," Sergeant Wojtek admonished.

"What…what price?" a woman asked in a choked voice when the underlord had finished speaking.

"Blood," the underlord said. "Half the blood in Moscow. Tonight." Then: "Also, I will need a human body, so those who see me will not be alarmed."

There was only one man in the room both large enough and expendable enough for the task. It was, in fact, the chief reason that Chortenko had chosen him to serve as his ringer in the first place. "Take him," Chortenko said, pointing to Dubinin.

This was not in the script. Eyes bulging, the former union head opened his mouth—though whether to plead or to denounce or to argue his case would never be known. For the intelligence agent behind him deftly looped a garrote about Dubinin's neck and with a minimum of fuss strangled him dead.

Chortenko watched impassively, knowing that the relative painlessness of this death would be yet one more mark against his account in the underlords' reckoning. But he also knew that there was a tipping point where horrified obedience turned to hysteria, despair, and defiance. Even as it was, he was certain that the next several minutes were going to bring his nineteen new ministers right to the edge of that point.

As they did.

By the time the underlord had made room for itself in its new body and the flesh had been stitched shut around it, the blood wiped clean by Chortenko's underlings, and a general's uniform donned, several of those present had thrown up, at least one man was crying, and everyone was too terrified to even think of disobeying its or Chortenko's orders.

"You do not know exactly what I am, and yet you fear me," the underlord said. "As you should. I am faster and stronger than anybody here. If I decided to rip your beating heart from your chest, you could not stop me. Further, my hatred for you and your kind is absolute. I wish you nothing but suffering, pain, and a death that will come only long after you have despaired of its mercy. I am your every nightmare, and if you do not obey me, I will kill you. If you try to escape, I will kill you. If you displease me in any way, I will kill you.

"You have seen what happened to the man whose body I now wear. He was lucky, for his death came quickly. Imagine what I will do to you if you do not obey me."

Chortenko went to the door leading to the City Below. The Royal Guard opened it, stepped outside to determine that the hallway was secure, and then nodded.

At Chortenko's gesture, the underlord walked past him and through the door.

"Follow me," the underlord said over its shoulder.

They did.

...15...

The noble ladies of Moscow had, as it turned out, an astonishing aptitude and even more extraordinary appetite for the act of sexual congress in all its many varieties. Luckily for Surplus, a week's tutelage under the preternaturally capable Zoësophia had taught him a suite of tricks for keeping pace with them. Just as a workman quickly learns to lift heavy objects using his legs rather than his back muscles, and to "walk" a particularly massive item across the floor rather than exhaust himself by pushing it, so Surplus had learned that for some positions it was best to ride lightly atop the action and for others to simply lie back and think of the Green Mountains of Vermont while letting his current partner do the brunt of the work. In this way, he was able to have quite a splendid time at Baronessa Avdotya's little gathering without actually rupturing anything.

Nevertheless, Surplus was grateful to have come to an intermission, during which he might replenish himself with ice-water and platefuls of this and that from a table loaded down with zakuski. He scooped up a cracker's worth of Osetra caviar and went idly to the window to admire the night view up Ilyinka ulitsa.

Irina came to the window as well and embraced Surplus from behind, pressing her breasts against his back and rubbing his shoulder with the side of her face. This pleasurable sensation was marred only by his strong awareness that in her current state, Irina might easily crack his ribs without intending to. "Are you certain," she asked, "that you will not try the rasputin?"

"Quite certain, sweet lady." Surplus had been very careful not to sample the drug. Though he was far from a prude when it came to intoxicants, he made it a point to never take anything that would diminish his mental clarity, be it so little as a single sip of wine, when homicidal maniacs were on his trail. Which, he had to confess, if only to himself, happened to him more often than could be strictly accounted for by mere chance.

"I weep. I am desolate. I feel driven to the brink of suicide and other desperate acts. I may very well sulk. Half the evening you are a delightful partner, and yet—you waste the other half recovering your energy."

"I am but a mortal, after all."

"But you need not be. If only you would reconsider… Dunyasha!" she said, using the pet form of the baronessa's name, "See if you can't talk some sense into this dear, obstinate creature."

Baronessa Lukoil-Gazproma joined them, and Surplus turned so that they could all join hands (and paws) lightly, trustingly. "I honestly cannot understand," the baronessa said, "why you would refuse an invitation to sample a substance that will give you direct and undeniable proof that an all-benevolent Divinity loves you intensely and personally. How can you possibly not wish to know?"

Which was another thing that surprised Surplus: that the ladies spoke rather more freely and often on the subject of God than a citizen of the Demesne of Western Vermont would think entirely proper to an orgy. Being an American, he was of course a deist, for, whatever their nationality, Americans were a rational people who prided themselves on their freedom from superstition. However, he did recognize that he was not in his homeland and that things might well be different here.

"Madam, no male gazing upon either of you as you are now could possibly doubt the existence of a benign Deity, nor fail to acknowledge the superiority of His or, as it may be, Her or even Its handiwork," he replied gallantly.

"You are a terrible atheist," Irina said with mock-sternness (but her eyes glittered merrily), "to speak of the living God in such cold and impersonal terms! I quake in fear for your immortal soul."

"Impersonal? Why, the Supreme Being and I have always been on the best of terms. We understand each other perfectly. In fact, we have a gentlemen's agreement, we two. I do not interfere with His running of the universe, and He doesn't meddle with my little corner of it."

"Oh, words, words, words! Your salvation will not be achieved with argument, I see now, but with action." She brought her lips so close to those of her companion that when they moved to Irina's ear, Surplus was caught by surprise. "Come, Irinushka," she stage-whispered. "If the two of us cannot convert this rascal with all the passion and love at our disposal, then we must enlist help. I was thinking Serafima and possibly Elizaveta would enter enthusiastically into this worthy enterprise. Ksenija too. We shall make this infidel so ecstatic that he will stand in the crossroad and confess the goodness of God before all the world."

"It is an *inspired* idea. But don't you think the other men would object to his monopolizing so many women?"

"Oh, pooh on the men! They can watch. With any luck, they'll learn something."

That was the third thing that astonished Surplus: How unlikely enthusiasms would flare up and take over the ladies (and the gentlemen, too, he presumed, though he paid them far less attention) on an instant's notice. In this way, if in no other, it was disconcertingly like being back among the Pearls again.

As the two hurried away, a man with a military bearing and an officer's mustache paused in the replenishment of his glass of champagne, looked after their rumps with a little smile, and murmured, "Oh, Lord, get me behind thee." Then, seeing he had been overheard, he raised the glass and said, "God is good, eh?"

"So I have been repeatedly assured, sir," Surplus replied amiably.

He turned back to the window, pleasantly spent and more than a trifle bemused by the religiosity of his fellow orgiasts. Their evangelical mania, however, was a minor vice when held up to the commendable Christian charity with which they shared their bodies with whomever desired them. Surplus looked forward to the rest of the evening with glad anticipation, though he was certain that he would be wondrously sore come morning.

Then he saw the procession come flowing down the street.

A good quarter of the marchers held torches whose light bounced flickeringly off of waving red cloth banners, so that the procession appeared almost to be a river of fire. Then the sound of distant banging and blaring crossed the threshold of audibility, followed shortly after by the surf of human voices. As they came into focus, he saw that the marchers were waving their fists and chanting, and that many of them did not appear to be human at all.

"Huh," he said wonderingly. "Will you look at this?"

Everyone gathered before the windows, a warm mass of naked bodies jostling together as comfortably as so many cattle in a barn. Hips bumped against hips, arms were placed about waists, and shoulders affectionately rubbed shoulders, without discrimination or preference for age, gender, or station. A strangely meaningful sense of community encompassed Surplus, a conviction that they were all of one flesh and shared a common self. The edges of the window panes glinted prismatically.

This was, the rational part of his mind argued, merely a contagious intoxication resulting from his inhalation of air tainted by the sweat or breath or other exudations of his drugged comrades. Nevertheless, he felt a genuine and abiding love for them all, and for the whole world as well. It hardly mattered whence it came.

Outside, the procession drew nearer. Surplus felt his eyes grow wide with wonder. In among the torch-carriers and banner-wavers were beggars and aristocrats, soldiers in uniform and unbloused bohemians, a white-clad giant or two, and great numbers of what looked to be some kind of chimeric bird-demons as well. As he watched, one of the banners suddenly disintegrated in a puff of red dust. Yet those carrying the staffs continued waving them from side to side, as if the banner were still there. Meanwhile, horn-blowers who could not play and drummers with no sense of rhythm filled the air with cacophonous noise.

It was a parade that would have dumbfounded Hieronymus Bosch. And, inexplicably, gazing down upon it, Surplus felt an internal tugging, a desire to add his small spirit to their turbulent river of souls. The sheer press of numbers called to him, much as a pebble streaking through space is drawn to a planet. He wanted to pour himself into their molten river of souls, to be melted down, lost, and mingled into their collective identity.

Windows slammed up and doors were flung open in the buildings that the procession passed by. People of all kinds poured out to join the march.

"He has come," Baronessa Avdotya murmured. Her eyes glowed fanatically.

"Eh?" Surplus said. "Who has?"

"It does not matter. All that matters is that he is here at last."

To Surplus's bafflement, the others made noises of agreement, as if her cryptic statement had been a model of sense and logic. The baronessa pointed over the rooftops to a growing brightness arising in the distance, entirely distinct from the procession flowing by outside. "That is where he is now," she said with inexplicable certainty. "In Pushkin Square."

"We must join him," Irina said.

"Yes," agreed the mustachioed gent who, minutes before, had been admiring her bottom. "As soon as possible. No, sooner! We must go out into the street now, this minute. Where are my clothes? Somebody summon the serviles to find our clothes."

"I do not see that clothes are necessary," the baronessa said. "Irina and I shall go forth to meet him in the same innocent flesh that God gave us and not one stitch more."

The group was breaking up now, and Surplus could breathe more easily. He shook his head to clear it and then ran to place himself between the two ladies and the door.

"Wait, wait, my sweet loves. There is a fine distinction between delightful spontaneity and foolhardiness, and the two of you are about to cross over from one to the other."

"Do not try to stop us. I never go back on a decision."

"That's true," Irina said. "I've known her for ever so long, and it's true."

"Have you both gone mad?" Surplus cried. "Dear ladies, you simply cannot traipse out into Ilyinka ulitsa stark naked."

Avdotya's eyes flashed. "And why not? Are we not pleasing before the eye of God? Is there anything shameful or inadequate about our bodies?"

"Quite the contrary. But surely questions of temperature alone…"

"Our virtue will keep us warm."

"But, baronessa," Surplus said desperately, "if you are naked, *how is anybody to know you are of noble birth?*"

Baronessa Lukoil-Gazproma stopped. "That is true." She snapped her fingers to get the nearest servile's attention. "Dress me," she said, "in the green silk with crimson pearls."

"And I," Irina said, "in my self-cloned leathers."

The servile went into the wardrobe and emerged first with a dress that flowed like water, and then with an outfit the exact same creamy color as Irina's own skin. Emotionlessly he proceeded to dress the two ladies.

Surplus, who had no intention of leaving the safety and anonymity of the baronessa's apartment before morning, picked out a midnight-blue dressing gown brocaded with gold-and-red firebirds and trimmed with lace at the cuffs and lapel. A garment of such masculine cut must ordinarily be reserved, he presumed, for the baronessa's husband. However, that distinguished gentleman being so open-minded as to share his wife's tenderest caresses, at least *in absentia*, Surplus did not doubt he would be equally generous with his wardrobe. So he threw it on and cinched the sash.

Already the first of the guests was leaving, greatcoat draped over his arm, hopping on one foot as he donned a shoe. By the time Irina and Avdotya were fully dressed, most of their friends had disappeared out the door.

Surplus wandered back to the window. The procession was only a block away, and it filled the street. It seemed impossible there could be so many people in all of Moscow. Yet there they were, and their numbers were growing. He could see women running out of the buildings barefoot and men with their trousers in their hands. Nor was it only orgiasts who joined in. Caught up by the excitement, parents and nannies abandoned their homes, leaving children staring in bafflement from windows and open doors. It was as if all the world were made of up changelings, who were only just now revealing the goblins hidden beneath the skin.

Directly below, among the departing hedonists, Surplus saw one of the baronessa's serviles throwing a scarf over her head. She threw a shrewd glance over her shoulder such as no servile was capable of. Perhaps she saw Surplus in the window; but she did not see him seeing her, that he was certain. She could not possibly see his eyes at such a distance in so dim a light, and he was careful to hold his head in a way that suggested he was not looking her way.

Slowly, carefully, Surplus turned to one side, yawned, and scratched himself in a manner that no gentleman would have done in the presence of a woman. Out of the corner of his eye, he saw the servile turn her back with a disgusted flip of her head and hurry away. She did not go with the others, but in the opposite direction, toward Chortenko's manor.

So, Surplus thought, the baronessa's household had a spy. Well, on reflection, it was only to be expected. Still, he dared stay here no longer.

The obvious remaining option was to join the mob.

At the doorway, the baronessa had just bid a gracious farewell to the last of her guests. "Ahhh, Surplus," she said, with a touch of sadness that suggested she already knew how he would answer. "Won't you please join us?"

"You had but to ask, *bellissima*. While I'm dressing, I'll have the carriage brought around to the door."

Thus it was that Sir Blackthorpe Ravenscairn de Plus Precieux, ambassador of Byzantium, native-born American, and loyal citizen of the Demesne of Western Vermont, joined the revolution.

The taverns and brothels of Zamoskvorechye were hopping. There were bonfires in the street and music in the air. "That one," General Magdalena Zvyozdny-Gorodoka said, pointing to the busiest house of ill repute. Throwing her reins to one of the soldiers they had conscripted along the way, she pushed through the door. Zoësophia followed, while the baron stayed outside to deploy their meager forces.

The brothel keeper, confronted suddenly by the stocky general with the famous red curls, rubbed both hands together and groveled. "Such an honor!" she cried. "Any of our girls are yours, General, as many as you wish! With no charge, of course."

The general struck her to the ground. "You and your 'girls' have ten minutes to vacate this building, or I'll nail shut the doors and burn this degenerate place to the ground with you in it. How many soldiers do you have here?"

The madam got to her feet and with a mingled look of resentment and grudging admiration—that of one professional for another—said, "Unless you placed guards at the side and back doors before you came in, none. The little girl at the top of the stairs—I doubt you even noticed her—was a lookout. All your geese have flown."

"Thirty years in the military," the general remarked to no one in particular, "and this civilian thinks I don't know how to secure a whorehouse." Then, to the madam: "Well? Assemble your harlots."

The brothel keeper rang a bell and called up the stairs, "Quickly, quickly, girls! Everyone! Or you're out of a job! Bring your outdoors clothing—you can dress in the parlor." Already there were women in loose robes peering over the balustrade at the top of the stairs. These swirled about to go back to their rooms, while others, dresses draped over their arms, scampered past them. They were all smiling and serene with the indwelling presence of the Divinity.

Save for one woman who had not bothered to fetch respectable clothing, but stood proudly naked, revealing to all her zebra-striped skin. Apparently her mother had foreseen where she would wind up and paid for the genework that would enhance her status there. This woman's eyes were dark and smoldering; clearly the God she worshipped was crueler and more pragmatic than that of her compeers.

"Ludmila! Where are your clothes?" the madam cried.

"Rubles were flowing like wine." Ludmila's voice was low and husky. "They emptied their wallets for me. All I had to do was ask." Casually, she slapped a hand around the newel post at the bottom of the stairs and ripped it free. Splinters went flying. Lifting the post over her head like a club, she said, "Who was it who dared drive the marks away?"

"It was me." The general calmly raised her pistol and shot the woman in the head.

The whores shrieked.

Standing over Ludmila's corpse, General Zvyozdny-Gorodoka addressed the shocked room. "This is serious business. Whether they know it or not, everyone in Moscow is now under military rule. That means that whoever disobeys an order from a uniformed officer can be summarily executed. Is that clear?"

There were nods and mumbles.

"Good. Now you and you"—she jabbed her finger at two whores at random—"take this body and put it in a room that can be locked. Then secure it and bring me the key."

Baron Lukoil-Gazprom chose that moment to enter the parlor. He glanced at the dead body, but made no comment on it. "We've got thirty-nine enlisted men. Plus one we nabbed on his way in. He's drunk, of course, but a little action will sober him up fast enough."

"It's a start. Form them up into four squads. We can use them to raid the other whorehouses."

Zoësophia cleared her throat. "Provided the baron agrees, of course."

"Protocol be damned! It's the only sensible thing to do, and the faster it's done the better."

The smallest of smiles blossomed on the baron's face. It was clear that he found the notion of the two women coming close to blows amusing. But, "Good advice is good advice," he said. "I'll take it."

"It wasn't—" the general began, exasperated.

A messenger entered the room. He stopped in astonishment at the sight of the half-dressed trollops, pulled himself together, and saluted. "Ma'am. Sir. You ordered the Arsenal to send a wagonload of klashnys, along with bayonets and ammunition? It's just arrived out front."

"That's just wonderful. We've got guns when we need soldiers."

Yet another messenger ran into the room and saluted. "Ma'am. There's a force of hundreds of civilians coming up Bolshaya Yakimanka. They have banners and they're singing."

The general spat on the floor.

"If I may make a suggestion…" Zoësophia murmured, flicking a glance at the prostitutes and hoping the baron would catch her meaning before the general could.

However, it was General Zvyozdny-Gorodoka who caught her thought on the fly and, turning to the brothel keeper, asked, "Are all your harlots as strong as the one who attacked me?"

"For tonight, I am afraid so," the madam said apologetically. "It is this new drug, you see. It—"

"Never mind that! Your girls are under my command now. If I cannot have my soldiers, I'll have the next best thing."

"How many of them are there?" The baron's mouth moved as he counted silently. "Plus the two who are disposing of the corpse. I'll have bayonets fixed on enough klashnys for the lot of them. No ammunition, however, I should think."

"No, of course not," the general snapped.

Zoësophia looked thoughtfully after the baron as he went out into the street. He had not noticed that General Zvyozdny-Gorodoka had established her ascendancy over him. Which made him the only person in the room who hadn't.

***

Once he was free of the drug-saturated confines of the City Below, the cold night air cleared Darger's head wonderfully. But clarity of thought did not make him any the happier. Quite the opposite, in fact, for the seriousness of the rebuilt-cyberwolf's threat came home to him with full and terrifying force.

Quickly, he ran a mental thumb down the particulars of his situation. A creature that was the stuff of nightmares, yet undeniably real for all that, had promised him torture and slow death sometime in the very near future. Meanwhile, he was helplessly strapped down on an apparatus from which he, not being an escape artist, could not hope to free himself. Further, a genetic chimera engineered for strength and (to judge by appearances) controlled savagery was his own personal prison guard. Those were the negatives. Against all of which, he had no weapons, allies, or special abilities other than his own native wit.

Luckily, that would suffice.

Step one would be to get some sense of Sergeant Wojtek's character.

"Sergeant, I fear that my wallet, being overstuffed with banknotes, is digging into my hip. I wonder if you could possibly—"

Sergeant Wojtek looked down at Darger with enormous scorn. "You don't know much about the Royal Guard if you think that one of us can be so easily bribed as that."

"Well, indeed, I am a foreigner and thus woefully ignorant of many important matters. Still, my situation is horribly uncomfortable. Couldn't you let me up? I can give you my word as a gentleman that I will not attempt to escape."

"So you can. But does that mean you'll keep it? No, I think that, if you don't mind, I'll simply obey the orders I was given."

"Your logic is impeccable," Darger said. "And yet, this position remains most damnably painful."

With a sigh, Sergeant Wojtek upended the gurney, folded its legs shut, and then leaned it against a nearby wall so that Darger was upright. "There. Is that better?"

Surprisingly, it was. In addition to doing much to restore his circulation, simply being upright again, after so long a time on his back, filled Darger with hope. "Thank you, Sergeant." He mentally counted to twenty and then said, "Do you play chess?"

Sergeant Wojtek stared at him. "What kind of a question is that? I'm a Russian."

"Then I'll start. Pawn to d4."

After a moment's astonished silence, Sergeant Wojtek relaxed slightly and said, "Knight to f6."

Which was, if not a beginning, at least an opening.

By the time the game was played through, Darger and the sergeant were, if not chums, at least on an amicable footing. "Well played, Sergeant Wojtek," Darger said.

"You'd have had me, if it hadn't been for that one bungled move in the endgame."

"My attention wandered." This was only a half-untruth, for though Darger had planned to lose from the outset, there had also been a distracting incident. "That man in the odd gray costume who walked by us. He looked exactly like—"

"Tsar Lenin. I assure you that he not only looks like Lenin, he *is* Lenin."

"But how is that possible?"

"We live in strange times. Let it rest at that. Tsar Lenin has returned from the dustbin of history and by morning all Moscow will be his."

The army of Pale Folk and Muscovites was pouring from the square, as it had been for some time. Still, the square remained crowded. Sergeant Wojtek made no move to join those leaving. Apparently he was content to bring up the rear.

"Tell me something," Darger said. "You and your fellows have clearly switched allegiance from the current government to whoever or whatever this seemingly impossible figure from ancient history might be. But I would have thought that the Royal Guard would be programmed to be unshakably loyal to the Duke of Muscovy."

"A common misapprehension. We are actually programmed to be loyal to Muscovy itself. It simply never occurred to anybody before now that the duke and the state might not be one and the same thing."

"If I may ask, sir, and meaning no offense. Exactly how were you—"

"You were about to say 'bought'—which would have been a mistake, for we were not bought but persuaded." The sergeant splayed one paw and extended his claws, one by one, as far as they would go. Then he relaxed it. "Consider our situation. Though we do nothing now but stand guard at the center of the greatest stronghold in Russia over a ruler whom no one dare attack, the bear-guards were designed and created to be warriors. Chortenko simply pointed out to us that a war was in the best interests of Muscovy. Then he promised us one. Thus satisfying both patriotism and personal inclination."

"Ahhh, yes. Of course." Darger had never acquired a taste for war, but he understood that certain others—he did not call them madmen—were happiest when in its embrace.

"He also promised us real names," Wojtek said with unexpected bitterness. "With patronymics. The names we have now are only fit for teddy bears."

By this point, however, the square was finally beginning to clear out. "Well," Sergeant Wojtek said. "I suppose we should move on."

"If I may, sir," Darger said. "I see a tavern across the way whose lanterns are lit, suggesting that its proprietor remains at his post. This gurney could not easily fit through the door, but your orders say nothing about it *per se*, only that I be kept bound. You could tie all but one of the straps about my body, leaving only one lower arm free, and then fashion the last strap into a kind of leash, which you could tie to your wrist to make certain that I did not escape. In that way, you would stay true to your orders, while still allowing me to buy you a drink."

"Well…" Sergeant Wojtek said. "Perhaps. One drink couldn't possibly do any harm. But no more than one, mind you. And then we really must be joining the others at the Kremlin."

"Absolutely." Darger did not quite smile, for he knew exactly how far he still was from freedom. But in his experience, once you got a soldier to drinking, the battle was half won.

Across the city, on the far side of the Moscow River, at the bonfire-lit intersection where Bolshaya Yakimanka ulitsa angled into Bolshaya Polyanka ulitsa, General Magdalena Zvyozdny-Gorodoka was handing out klashnys to her gaggle of prostitutes. She very carefully examined each weapon before surrendering it, to make certain it was not loaded. Then she instructed the bawds in how to use them as clubs.

"You want to put your opponent down so he doesn't come back up at you. That means you must strike at the head. Hold your klashny like this." She demonstrated. "Butt forward. The top of the skull is thick, so if you hit there, your weapon may well bounce off. Smash somebody in the face, and he's still conscious and thrashing around. The best strategy is to clip them behind the ear. Out they go, and often enough they're dead. So: Lift your klashnys like this."

The trollops obeyed.

"Strike slightly downward and inward. Thus."

They imitated her thrust, with varying results.

"Then return your klashny to its original position. One, two, three. Very simple. Are there any questions?"

A whore raised her hand. "But how do we know this pleases God?"

"Eh?"

"God is goodness and God is love. I didn't used to think so, but now I'm sure of it. We all are." The other harlots were nodding in agreement. "So

I don't know if He would like us to be hurting and killing people."

"Katya's right. If God is everywhere, how can we do such acts in His presence?"

The general's expression was pained. "Do it lovingly. The way the apostles would. Behind the ear, remember!"

Meanwhile, the baron's forces had all affixed bayonets to their weapons. Some of them were drunk, and the rest were so lit up on drugs they all but glowed. Still, training would tell. Baron Lukoil-Gazprom ranged up and down the ragged collection of soldiers, shouting and cursing until, out of sheer habit, they found themselves in a wedge formation, bayonets forward. They were facing the oncoming mob, which was still several blocks away, still invisible but already audible. They had been through this drill so often they did not flinch.

The conscripts had neither drum nor drummer among them, so a sergeant was given the duty of counting cadence. The baron had just finished giving the man his instructions when General Zvyozdny-Gorodoka came striding up.

"I'll run these fat sluts around and up to that side street there." She pointed. "When the mob passes us, start your men forward. I'll wait until your wedge splits them and then send the girls running into their flank. If that doesn't cause panic, I don't know what will. They'll run every which way, and I don't think they'll be eager to come back for more."

"It's a good plan," the baron said. "I think it will work."

The two returned to their respective forces.

All the while, Zoësophia had been standing at the sidelines, watching. Though her knowledge of military history and tactics was unsurpassed, she recognized that the general and the baron both operated from long experience. In this situation, there was little she could do for them, other than to keep out of their way.

But that did not mean her brain had stopped working. In every action so far, Zvyozdny-Gorodoka had taken the lead and the baron had followed her. Worse, the rank-and-file soldiers had witnessed this fact. Which meant that when this was all over, provided they were still alive, the hero of the night would not be the baron, but the red-haired general.

Something would have to be done about that.

Tonight.

...16...

The Duke of Muscovy dreamed of fire.

He twisted and turned in impotent fury. His beloved Moscow was in danger! All his conscious life, since the day his designers had deemed him sufficiently well programmed to govern, he had looked after it, dreaming of alliances and diplomatic interventions, repairs to the sewage system, improvements in food distribution, new health regulations, the reengineering of peregrine messenger falcons, trade treaties, bribes, the deployment of armies, discrete assassinations, the suppression of news items, construction projects, midnight arrests. The machinations of the underlords, of Chortenko, of Zoësophia, of Koschei, of Lukoil-Gazprom, and even of the false Byzantine ambassador with the improbably long name he had watched ripen, for the reports from Chortenko's people were very thorough, and his powers of extrapolation uncanny. The actions of lesser players he had intuited. The movements and emotions of the masses were statistical certainties. But then the messengers came less and less frequently, and finally they ceased whispering in his ear altogether. A steadily growing blindness hindered his dreams. His ignorance grew.

As the State of Muscovy's flow of information was disrupted, its duke could no longer integrate, hallucinate, and comprehend his realm. Which was to him an agony. Though he had no conviction that Moscow actually existed, he had known better than anyone else exactly what was going on in his city at any given instant. No more.

But he knew there were fires.

There were fires because fires were inevitable. They broke out in the best of times, and to fight them the duke had established volunteer brigades for every neighborhood in Moscow. But this was far from the best of times. Drunks were building bonfires in the streets. Drugged religious zealots were abandoning their prayers and debaucheries, leaving candles and lanterns untended, to join processions headed they knew not where.

Underpeople were scurrying about the passages beneath the city carrying torches like so many mice with wooden matches clenched between their teeth. It was impossible that there *not* be fires.

To make matters worse, tonight only a handful of fire brigades, police stations, or active military units were functional. Chortenko had asked the Duke of Muscovy how to inactivate the greatest possible percentage of them, and the duke had spelled out the process, step by step, in careful detail. That was why and how he had been created in the first place: to answer all questions put to him as fully and truthfully as his more-than-human powers of analysis and integration could make possible. He could no more withhold his counsel than he could tell a lie.

Yet, like an intellectual who had read so deeply and knowledgeably into a great novel that he had gone mad and believed its characters real, the Duke of Muscovy had fallen in love with the citizens whose fates had been entrusted into his safekeeping. He cared about their small, imaginary lives more than he did his own. He had been created to be their protector, their spiritual father. Now he was the only responsible official aware of Chortenko's partnership with the metal demons and of the evils plotted by this hellish alliance. No one but he knew what had to be done to stop them.

Moscow must not burn.

But the Duke of Muscovy was powerless to protect his people. He was held captive in chains of sleep and could not break free. No one came to listen to his mumbled instructions—not even the traitor Chortenko. The Royal Guards kept carefully out of earshot, lest they overhear something they would rather not.

He groaned aloud.

The bear-guards—those few who still remained on duty—covered their ears.

The Zamoskvorechye incident—for "skirmish" was, in context, too elevated a word for it—was over in what felt like only minutes. The procession came flowing down the boulevard like a river, and like a river it looked at first to be unstoppable and irresistible. But Baron Lukoil-Gazprom's wedge of soldiers marched steadily up the boulevard to meet them, bayonets extended. Since most of the marchers came from the City Above and, however drugged, were still capable of fear, the sight of the advancing bayonets did much to discomfort them. Their chants turned to cries of alarm. The front of the procession stopped and eddied in confusion.

Then, before the underlord commanding this arm of the invasion could put into action a counter-strategy, General Zvyozdny-Gorodoka's harlots burst from the side street where they had been waiting in ambush. The marchers had flowed smoothly to either side of the bonfire at the center of the intersection, but its flames temporarily blinded them, so that their attackers seemed to come out of nowhere.

Five minutes' training was not enough to turn a rabble of whores into a disciplined military force. Intoxicated by the unfamiliar taste of violence, the doxies swung their klashnys every which way, clubbing wildly at the marchers with the kind of abandon that Zoësophia very much doubted they displayed in their regular work. Nevertheless, their assault was effective. The procession lost any semblance of order as screaming citizens broke and ran, scattering like jackdaws into the surrounding darkness.

Baron Lukoil-Gazprom followed his wedge of soldiers closely on horseback. Zoësophia rode to his side and one step behind. "You should unsheathe your saber," she said quietly. "Brandish it and shout encouragement at your men."

"That is not necessary. These are disciplined soldiers. They know what to do."

"Do it anyway. We must think of your political future." Zoësophia's tone and manner were so carefully modulated that even as the baron unsheathed his sword, he did not notice that she was giving him orders and he was obeying them.

"Keep going, men! Straight and steady!"

It had to be admitted that Baron Lukoil-Gazprom looked every inch the military hero. Unfortunately for Zoësophia's plans, when his soldiers hit the procession, splitting it and sending the fragments fleeing into the side streets, they were so effective they did not have to kill anybody at all.

Which was disastrous. For at the exact same time, the redheaded general was right in the thick of the fray, dispatching Pale Folk (who stayed where the citizens fled) with her sword, and laughing as she did so. Her floozies, inexperienced though they were, fought an unarmed and unprepared foe and thus met with no resistance. Further, with their inhuman strength and total lack of restraint, they were crushing ribcages and exploding skulls in a manner which, though morally lamentable, was undeniably dramatic.

Worst of all, such extreme exertion could not fail to dishevel the clothing worn by the tarts, and since most of them wore low-cut dresses, several breasts had leaped into public view. There would be oil paintings of this clash, Zoësophia knew, based on the accounts of eyewitnesses, and they would not focus on the comparatively drab figure of the baron.

Then, from the shadowy heart of the mob, there flashed a metal beast.

It leaped over the panicking citizens, running on all fours and using their heads and shoulders for purchase. Straight at the baron it flew, firelight reflecting bright from its gleaming surfaces. For a brief, bright instant, Zoësophia felt hope. "Stand firm," she told her companion, "and when it is almost upon you, thrust hard." She leaned close, so that should the baron's aim go awry she could seize his arm and correct it. One more second, she thought, and my little man will be a mighty figure in every account of this night.

But then two whores reached up simultaneously from the scrim and seized the underlord, hauling it forcibly down to the street. They lifted it up overhead, each one holding it by two legs. Then they pulled in opposite directions.

In a shower of sparks, the beast was torn in two.

The explosion shed light on the upturned faces of the gleeful sluts. One of the two was exceedingly comely. The other was naked from the waist up.

Zoësophia sighed inwardly. *Nothing* was going right tonight.

In minutes, the street was empty save for soldiers, prostitutes, and corpses. Baron Lukoil-Gazprom dismounted and General Zvyozdny-Gorodoka sheathed her sword. They slapped each other on the back, roaring congratulations.

Modestly, Zoësophia stood off to the side, hands clasped and head down, making it clear that she claimed no part, however small, in this victory.

Leaving a small number of soldiers to ensure that the marchers did not re-form, the general and the baron and their collective forces returned to their makeshift headquarters at the whorehouse, where the madam shooed her happily chattering employees upstairs and the soldiers were set to work securing the block. The parlor, with its chintz curtains and stained-glass oil-lamp shades, seemed deceptively homey. It smelled of hard soap, talcum powder, and hair oil. The map of Moscow still lay open on the great table where they had plotted out their strategy.

The baron threw himself heavily into an overstuffed easy chair and lit up a cigar. "That was not badly done," he said. "Not badly done at all."

It was then that messengers arrived from four other sectors of the city to report further invasions.

The four messengers arrived almost simultaneously, one on the spurs of another, carrying tidings of uprisings in Smolenskaya, Taganskaya, Krasniye Vorota, and Pushkinskaya. Tens of thousands of Muscovites had taken to the streets, and there were not the forces to contain a fraction of them. One artillery unit had set up its gun on the Astakhovsky bridge, just above where the Yauza flowed into the Moscow, determined to hold back and break up the Taganskaya mob, should it try to cross the river, as seemed inevitable.

Even as General Zvyozdny-Gorodoka stared at the last messenger in dumbfounded silence, the distant rumble of cannons sounded. The action at Astakhovsky bridge had begun. The baron clutched his head in both hands as if, lacking a convenient enemy to manually decapitate, he would do it to himself.

"Dear God," Zoësophia said. "What are we to do? Obviously, when one visualizes a map of the city, all four forces—five, counting the one you just defeated—are roughly equidistant from the Kremlin and so must be converging upon it. But why? For what purpose?"

Prompted by the naiveté of her question, Baron Lukoil-Gazprom exclaimed, "They mean to overthrow the government! As they march through the city, they will multiply their numbers by drawing in drugged perverts and hedonists. What started out as an easily scattered force will quickly become a universal uprising of the populace."

"Yes." The general stared at Zoësophia. "I am surprised you couldn't have thought that through yourself, dear. You seem like such a level-headed young lady."

"This is the first time I've seen military action of any kind, and I fear I let it rattle me. I'm not experienced the way the baron and you are." Zoësophia squeezed the general's forearm lightly for emphasis—to no result. Even unconsciously, it seemed, Magdalena Zvyozdny-Gorodoka was not interested in women. To some degree, Zoësophia regretted this, for the general provided better material to work with than did the baron. But she would also have been more difficult to control. So it all came to the same thing in the end.

Zoësophia took a deep breath, as if to remaster her runaway emotions. "However, all seven of the duke's brides were given specialized educations, so that we might serve as advisors to him, and mine included military theory." On a side table was a potpourri of dried rose petals. She seized a fistful, crushed them to powder, and dribbled the powder onto the map, letting every speck represent a human soul. Four thin lines, starting at the four squares where the newly reported invasions began, flowed inward to smash up against the Kremlin walls. Then the powder mounded up on Red Square, the area behind St. Basil's, and the open spaces of the Alexander Garden before the Trinity Tower, creating an impenetrable crescent two-thirds of the way around the ancient stronghold.

"Here is what we face," she said. "The government cannot hold out against such numbers. The Kremlin will inevitably fall. Now, as you see, it will soon be surrounded by enemies on all sides save one. To the south, the quay between the river and the Kremlin will be empty because there is not room enough to gather there and we have disrupted the one force that would have come up it. Now, there is an underground passage that leads to the Terem Palace from the basement of a pump house below the Beklemshev Tower—"

"How did you know that?" the general asked sharply.

"To maximize my utility to the duke, the Byzantine Secret Service told me everything they knew about the Kremlin and its defenses. How they obtained this information I do not know. But I see that it is reliable."

There was the briefest of silences. "Go on," the baron said.

"Theoretically, it would be possible to enter the Kremlin secretly and bring the Duke of Muscovy out by this same passage. The Royal Guard would have to be convinced of its necessity, of course. The duke would have to agree to be evacuated. Since the area under the south wall will not be *completely* empty, there would be witnesses, and it is possible the pump house entrance may be discovered. Which would lead to fighting, and that would be chancy. But it could be done.

"I advise against it, however. The advantages of a successful rescue are slight, and the risks are unacceptable. Instead, we should focus on calling in all the military units that Chortenko arranged to be pulled out of Moscow. Having created a plausible counterforce, we can then—"

"You would have us abandon the Duke of Muscovy?" the general broke in.

"The duke is but a figurehead. We owe him nothing."

"We owe him our loyalty!"

"Yes, while he lives. An hour from now?" Zoësophia shrugged.

The general's jaw clenched, and her lips grew thin and white. Without saying a word, she spun around and dashed out the door.

"Wait!" the baron cried. "This requires a plan."

"No time!" The general mounted her horse and seized the reins.

"We can—" the baron began.

But Zoësophia's fingers touched his sleeve. "Let her go." Hooves rattled on the cobblestones, and the general was gone. "To die saving the life of the Duke of Muscovy would be a noble thing. But to die failing to do so is merely stupid."

Even as she spoke, the cannon fire ceased. Whatever had happened at Astakhovsky bridge, it was over now.

Shocked, the baron said, "What are you saying?"

"Only that while bold actions can indeed change history, they require appropriate force, careful planning, and clear purpose. Zvyozdny-Gorodoka is but one woman. She has no plan. Nor has she any but the vaguest notion of what she hopes to accomplish. Further, she is naïve enough to think that the Royal Guard remains loyal to the duke. Inevitably, she will not return from this adventure alive."

"I have seen her emerge unscathed from worse dangers than you can imagine."

"While I have seen what you and she have not—the Duke of Muscovy in person. He cannot be rescued. Which is good, because Muscovy is about to need a new leader. A moment ago, there were only two possible choices. Now there is one."

Heatedly, the baron said, "You dangled the possibility of a rescue before her. You pushed her into thoughtless action with your words. You as good as sent her to die."

"Yes. I did."

"Treacherous bitch!" Baron Lukoil-Gazprom struck Zoësophia with his fist.

He did not, however, hurt her. Zoësophia moved her head so that the blow was slight and glancing, while simultaneously lifting a hand in a seemingly futile attempt to ward him off. As his fist grazed her cheek, she slapped it hard with the flat of her hand, so that it sounded and felt like a solid contact. Then, in an absolutely convincing manner, she fell to the ground.

Summoning tears and sending blood to her cheek so that it flushed red, Zoësophia looked up at the baron, who was almost purple with rage. "You are a cruel and brutal man," she said in a low, submissive voice. She laid her cheek against his boot. "No wonder I love you so helplessly."

The baron was breathing heavily now. Not with anger.

It took five bottles of vodka for Sergeant Wojtek to learn all the verses to "The Bastard King of England." However, Darger was so assiduous a teacher that his student had mastered the song and was halfway through learning "Three Drunken Maidens" before his head finally hit the table.

"Are you all right, Sergeant? Can you hear me?" Darger asked solicitously. "No? You cannot? Well, thank heavens for that." To the bartender he said, "I don't think we'll be needing any more to drink."

"I sure as shit hope not," Kyril said. "It just about broke my fucking heart, watching you pour all that goddamn booze on the floor. I was pouring first-rate stuff, too. The best I had."

"It was a necessary evil. I could never match such a behemoth drink for drink. I'd've been under the table in no time."

"I tried to serve you the cheap shit, but you waved it away."

"Have you smelled it? My dear young fellow, that was rubbing alcohol you were trying to foist off on us."

"Yeah, so?"

"Gentlemen do not drink rubbing alcohol under any circumstances," Darger said firmly. "Nor do they serve it to their guests. You should commit those principles to memory. Now be a good chap and undo these straps, will you? And while you're at it, you might tell me how you managed to obtain your current position. You seem to have come up in the world since I saw you last."

Kyril obliged. "Well, that's a funny story. See, I figured the fastest way to the surface was to go along with the Pale Folk. So I grab one of those red kerchiefs they're giving away and when they come out into Pushkin Square, I'm right there at the front of the parade. First thing I do when I hit the up-and-out is ditch the bird-mask and pop into this bar to buy a beer." Seeing Darger's disapproving expression, he added, "I was hungry! I wasn't gonna drink it for the alcohol or nothing."

"Of course not."

"Anyway, just as I'm coming in, the barkeep drops his cleaning rag, ties a red kerchief around his neck, and skips out to join the mob. Well, thinks I, let's check out the state of the till. So I goes around behind the bar, and just as I'm scooping up the cabbage, this fat bastard walks in, slaps down a five-ruble note, and asks for a beer. I draw him a glass and make change, and by then there's two more fuckers wanting vodka. I start pouring shots and set out a plate of bread. For a while there, I'm doing damn good business. You can't imagine. Then, just as things are tapering off and I'm about to call it a night, in you waltz with your own pet bear. So I stay put, just to see what's what." He paused. "Bit of a coincidence, you popping up, though."

"Great minds gravitate toward the same sorts of places. Your being here convinces me that my tutorial efforts have not been wasted," Darger said, genuinely moved. "I am proud of you." He stood and stretched. "Goodness gracious, but it feels fine to be free again."

"Hey. No need to watch your fucking language around *me*," Kyril said. "We're asshole buddies, ain't we?" Then, misinterpreting Darger's scowl, he said in a considerably less boisterous tone, "I suppose you're going to want your cut from my running the bar."

"Of course not!" Darger said, shocked. "That was money earned by your own enterprise and diligence. I have no claim to it." He clapped a hand on the young man's shoulder. "Anyway, I have a more profitable plan in mind. Have you ever been in a revolution before, lad?"

"What? No! You mean this is a—?"

"Ignore the politics. They are of no concern to us. The important thing to keep in mind about the forcible wresting of power from the old regime and its transfer to the new one is that when it happens, there is a brief, magical period—sometimes lasting weeks, and other times mere hours—when nobody at all is in control, and thus all items of value belong solely to whoever has the wit and initiative to walk in and pocket them. Museums, palaces, treasuries…all are suddenly open for the plucking. Now, where do you imagine the greatest treasures in Moscow are to be found?"

"In the banks."

"At this time of night, their valuables will be locked away in sturdy vaults. Anyway, I am talking about real treasure. Not just banknotes, I mean, but gold, rubies, emeralds, and the like. For which we must turn to—where?"

"Oh! You mean the State Diamond Fund."

"That sounds promising. Tell me about it."

"Don't tell me you ain't never heard of the Diamond Fund!"

"Since arriving in Moscow, I've spent most of my time underground," Darger said. "Illuminate me."

"Well, lemme see. It's kept in the Kremlin Armory. I almost got in on a tour once. Big sonofabitch in a uniform began his spiel before he noticed how ragged I was and threw me out. Lemme see if I can remember it." Kyril screwed his face in thought. "'The Diamond Fund is an ages-old repository of all the greatest treasures in Russia, which was deposited here, within the Armory Museum, many centuries ago. It contains cut gems of every kind and color, including the Shah Diamond and a sapphire weighing over 260 carats; gold nuggets, such as the Great Triangle, which masses almost eighty pounds; as well as myriad items of incalculable artistic and historic value, beginning with Monomakh's Cap, one of the most ancient symbols of…' And that's when he spotted me. What do you think?"

"I think that you are a fellow of hidden resources. A memory such as yours is a gift to be cherished. As for the Diamond Fund itself, you have completely sold me on the idea."

"Yeah, but if we want to nab any of that stuff, we gotta find a way to get through all those crazies outside. Then we'd have to either climb the Kremlin walls—which I don't think is gonna happen—or else talk our way past the guards, which maybe you could do but they'd never let me come in with you. Then we'd have to truck all that gold and shit back out the same way we came in. It sounds like a fucking big task."

"There are no big tasks, Kyril. Only small ambitions. Let's—" Darger stopped abruptly. "No," he said. "What am I thinking? There exists an even greater treasure for our seizing, and we would be criminals not to take it up."

"What are you—?" Kyril began. Then, "Oh, no. You're talking about those fucking *books*, aren't you?"

"I am talking about the treasure of the ages, the greatest and wisest words and thoughts the human mind has ever committed to paper. Or, as it may be, parchment or even papyrus. Kyril, gemstones are but pretty gauds with which we beguile ourselves on our hopefully long road to death. But books—great books, I mean—are why we were born in the first place. Also, there is a very good commercial value to a previously unknown play by Euripides. I know it sounds unlikely, but it's true."

Kyril had gone to the door during this speech and stood in its frame, staring out. "Well, I got some bad news for you." He pointed. "Look at that."

Flames were pouring out of the entryway to the staircase leading down to the Pushkinskaya docks.

"Good lord!" Darger was alongside Kyril in a trice. He clutched the lad's shoulder. "This only increases the necessity for us going back to the lost library. We must rescue the books!"

"Yeah, but look at that. Half the fucking undercity must be burning."

"It does not matter. Great stakes sometimes require great risks. I will not ask you to come along with me, Kyril, for I can see that this is not your cause. But for myself, I can only echo the illustrious if short-tempered German monk, Martin Luther: *Ich kann nicht anders.* This I must do. I—"

"Okay, okay," Kyril said testily. "I wasn't gonna say this. But there's another way into the library."

"What?!"

"If you climb up to the top of it, there's a little door. Behind it, there's a kind of secret passage. I was poking around and found it. I went through it once, almost got caught, and never tried it again."

"Where does it come out?"

"In the Secret Tower," Kyril said, "in the Kremlin."

The square was empty when they emerged from the bar. Kyril had snatched up a bottle of alcohol as they left, "just in case we need to make friends with somebody," he explained, and tucked it under one arm. Darger who, as a matter of principle, liked to keep his hands unencumbered by anything other than his walking stick, tidily closed the door behind them out of consideration for the bar's proprietor.

An unceasing and strangely insistent mumble of noise sounded from Red Square, a mile or so distant. "Listen!" Darger said.

"That's one fucking creepy sound."

"On the contrary. It is the sound of opportunity."

The baronessa's carriage was an open troika. Thus, when the servile driving it pushed through the crowds to the front of the procession, it was the highest spot in the square. Tsar Lenin, seeing this, stepped lightly up onto the troika. Baronessa Lukoil-Gazproma surrendered her own seat to him and, tapping the servile on the shoulder, said, "Get off. Run alongside the rear wheel." With the graciousness of old nobility, she climbed into the driver's seat and took the reins.

The baronessa clicked her tongue, and the three horses started forward.

Tsar Lenin glanced at Surplus and Irina and said, "You should be wearing red scarves." He produced two from his pocket, which they dutifully tied about their necks.

Sitting side by side with the legendary leader from Russia's distant past and reasoning that he might never have such an opportunity again, Surplus said, "Pray tell me, sir—and you needn't answer this question if you don't want to—are you really Tsar Lenin?"

"No," his companion said. "I am not even human. But the mob believes I am Lenin, and that is sufficient. It will give me all of Moscow in a matter of hours, and all of Muscovy shortly thereafter. Then I shall begin a war such as has never been seen before, not even in excesses of the Preutopian era. My armies will eradicate entire nations and reduce humanity to a fraction of its present pestilent self."

"Excuse me?"

"There is no excusing you, for you have committed the first and greatest sin there is—you *exist*. All life is abhorrent. Biological life is worse. And intelligent biological life is beyond redemption."

Surplus found it hard to contain his astonishment. "You are remarkably candid, sir," he managed to say.

The tsar's eyes glittered like steel. "There is no reason not to be. Were you to repeat my words, nobody would believe you. In any case, I am confident you will be dead within the week."

"Does that mean you plan to kill me, sir?"

"If nobody else performs that service for me first—why then, yes, of course. We are entering into an tumultuous period, however. There will be riots tonight such as Moscow has never seen before. So the odds are excellent I will not have to."

"I…I am speechless."

"Then refrain from speech."

The cheering about them was so loud and so constant that Surplus could barely make out Lenin's words. So it was no wonder that the baronessa, much of whose attention was taken up by holding her three horses to a steady walk, continued smiling and waving to either side. She had not heard even a scrap of this conversation. But Irina, who had leaned in close to eavesdrop, had.

"You're not God!" Irina cried in a wounded and disillusioned tone. "You're not at *all* kind. You're not one bit loving."

Lenin favored her with a smile that contained not the least touch of warmth. "No, my dear, I am not. But I am great and terrible, and in the end, that comes to much the same thing."

The wraith stalked the streets of Moscow, avid and dangerous, inchoate of thought, a creature without mercy, the void incarnate. She had no sense of purpose nor any desires that she was aware of, only a dark urge to keep moving. She had no identity—she simply *was*. Light and crowds she disliked and avoided. Solitude and shadow were her meat and drink. Occasionally, she came across somebody as friendless and isolate as herself, and then she played. Always she gave them a chance to live. So far, none of them had.

I am the bone mother, she thought. I am death and contagion, and I am the muttering voice in the night that freezes the soul with terror. My flesh is corruption and my bones are ice. I have teeth in every orifice. If you stick a finger in my ear, I will bite it off.

She came to a dark house and twisted the doorknob until the lock behind it broke. Like an errant breeze she wafted inside and up the stairs. On the landing was a little table with a vase of flowers. She paused to bite off their heads and swallow them one by one. Then she heard a gentle snoring from one of the rooms. She pushed open the door. In the moonlight that streamed through the window, she saw a man sleeping, a tasseled nightcap on his head.

Silently, she crawled into the bed beside him.

The sleeper's head was turned toward her. She lightly brushed her nose against his to awaken him. He snorted but did not wake, so she did it again. His eyes fluttered open and focused vaguely upon hers.

"Boo," she said.

With a scream, the man rolled away from her and crashed to the floor in a tangle of limbs and blankets. In a trice, she was crouched over him like an enormous four-legged spider. "Who am I?" she said. "What am I doing in your bedroom?"

"What?"

She straightened into a crouch, still straddling the man's body. A knife appeared in her hand. She did not know where it had come from, but it felt right. Perhaps she would use it on this pot-bellied fellow. If she dug deeply enough, she might find his soul. Then she could feast.

"That was what you were going to ask me—wasn't it? But I don't know the answer. So I'm asking *you*." Abruptly, she sat down on the terrified little man's chest. "I have a sting," she said, caressing his cheek with the flat of the blade, then turning it sideways to draw the narrowest imaginable line of blood. "But I have no name. I've killed many a man, but I feel no shame. I take and I take but I never give." She lifted the knife away from his face. By the way that his eyes trembled, she knew that he was not in the least reassured. "Answer my riddle and I'll let you live."

"I…I don't…"

"I'll give you one more chance." Her lips moved away from her teeth, and all the darkness in the universe grinned with her. "What am I doing here?"

"S-scaring me?" he stammered fearfully. She considered his words. They sounded true. The knife disappeared from her hand and went back to wherever it had come from.

"And who am I?"

She could see the little man reaching far, far back into his past, looking for the answer. Saw his thoughts pass back through the years, before adulthood, before adolescence, into the dark ocean of childhood, where all the most extreme terrors are born and then stored away, never to be forgotten. In a child's voice, he said, "B-b-baba Yaga?"

"Baba Yaga." She spoke the name slowly, savoring each syllable as if they were strokes of a bell. Ba. Ba. Ya. Ga. She stood and walked to the window. Over her shoulder she said, "That's good. Baba Yaga. Yes, good. You get to live."

Baba Yaga kicked out the window and left through its absence.

Something terrible was happening. The Duke of Muscovy knew this for a fact. It could not be seen or heard or smelled or touched or tasted, but it could be felt, like a vibration in the air, a silent and unending shriek of agony rising from the stones and bones of Moscow, by anyone with the sensitivity to detect it. Over and over, the duke strove to awaken. Again and again, he failed.

There were faint scuttling noises in the darkness to every side of the duke as his bear-guards hurried to get out of reach of his thrashing arms. Something (a support beam, perhaps?) splintered. Something else (a chair?) smashed.

Moscow was burning! The city was in rebellion, its defenders were absent from their posts, and the State was about to fall. Every cell and neuron in the duke's tremendous brain screamed with the need for him to cast aside sleep.

Again, the Duke of Muscovy groaned. He knew what to do—he *knew!* Were he to awaken, stand, and assume his rightful control over the State, he would be dead in half an hour, his mighty heart crushed by stresses no human organ could withstand. But half an hour was more than he would need. He could save his city and nation in half that time.

But he could not awaken.

He could not act.

...17...

There were fires on the horizon to the west and north and a geyser of flames had just erupted from the roof of a house not three blocks away from Yevgeny's crew, sending sparks and ashes showering into the night. Yet no fire bells rang and no firefighters appeared to check the fire's spread. Which was madness. It made no sense at all.

Yevgeny was in an agony of indecision. Was this what he was supposed to be looking for? But if so, why would General Zvyozdny-Gorodoka and Baron Lukoil-Gazprom have been so coy about the nature of the threat? Was he expected to put out the fire or was he supposed to stay at his post and let it burn? If there were three unrelated fires within eyeshot at the same time, surely that meant there were more elsewhere in the city. That wasn't natural. But neither did it look like any kind of deliberate enemy action he had ever heard of. Nothing in his military training had covered anything remotely like the situation he now found himself in.

Then he heard noise in the distance.

At first he thought it was music, because there was a regular throb to it. But as it grew louder and closer, he realized that it was anything but musical. People were chanting and beating on drums and blowing horns to several different beats and as many different tunes at once. *Down with* something, they chanted. *Down with* something, *Down with* something. But Yevgeny was damned if he could make out what that something was.

Yevgeny mounted his horse and raced down Teatralny proezd to Tverskaya ulitsa. At the intersection looking north, he saw a shadowy deluge of humanity churning and rumbling down the street toward him with banners flying and fists flung into the air. This was surely what the baron had said he would know when he saw it. But knowing it and knowing what to do about it were two separate things.

The sergeant appeared at his elbow. "Shall we bring up the gun and open fire, sir?"

"On our own citizens?" Yevgeny said, horrified.

"It's been known to happen, sir."

The mob was coming closer and coming into focus as well. Yevgeny could make out individual faces now. There were three white horses pulling a troika at the front. Behind it, bodies filled the street from wall to wall. Most of them seemed to be wearing red kerchiefs. But the team pulling the troika… Didn't it look familiar? Surely that was—he squinted—the same cloned triplet of a stallion his cousin Avdotya owned? The one whose uniqueness she had ensured by buying the genome's patent and then refusing to license it?

"Do you want me to bring around the cannon, sir, and have it aimed up the street? Just as a precaution, I mean."

"Yes, yes, why do you bother me with questions, just do it," Yevgeny muttered distractedly. He stared with all his might, trying to will the distant figures into clarity, cursing the dimness of the moonlight, praying he was wrong. Slowly they came closer until finally, yes, that was without question the Baronessa Lukoil-Gazproma driving. Sitting behind her were Irina, the dog-headed Byzantine ambassador the baronessa had invited to her soiree, and…Tsar Lenin?

Yevgeny's head swam with the impossibility of it all.

But then the words swam into lucidity. *Down with the duke!* the mob was chanting. *Down with the duke! Down with the duke!*

It was treason. Beyond all doubt this was what the general's gnomic warning had been about. Yet now that the need for action was upon him, Yevgeny found that he could not bring himself to act.

"If we're going to fire, now's the time to do it, sir. While there's still time enough to get off another shot or two if the first one don't turn 'em away."

"I…"

Yevgeny knew what he should do. He knew what General Zvyozdny-Gorodoka would demand of him, were she here. But he could not fire upon his cousin. They had played together as children. As adolescents they had competed for the same lovers. He had been the witness at her marriage to that overbearing oaf of a husband of hers.

Yet he had to. It was his duty.

Yevgeny drew out his snuffbox and flicked it open, feigning a confidence he did not feel. "Is everything ready, Sergeant?"

"Yes, sir."

"Very well, then." Yevgeny took a dip of snuff, marveling at how steady his voice was. His stomach was a lump of ice. He face felt numb. He did not know how he would survive this decision. "In that case, you may…"

"Sir?"

"Yevgeny's mouth moved, but nothing came out.

"Sir, are you ordering me to fire?"

"I—"

"Stop! Cease! Do not fire!"

Yevgeny spun about and saw, speeding up Okhotny Ryad ulitsa, the least likely Angel of Mercy imaginable—none other than Chortenko himself—leaning from the window of his notorious blue-and-white carriage. The servile coachman drove its horses up so mercilessly that the carriage rattled and leaped and threatened to shake itself apart. "Do not fire!" Chortenko shouted again.

The servile pulled back on the reins and the carriage clattered to a stop alongside the artillery piece.

Without descending, Chortenko said, "I am ordering you to withdraw. The city is in danger of conflagration. You must use your cannon to knock down the buildings that are afire before the disaster spreads."

"Sir. Yes, sir," Yevgeny said, vastly relieved. But then something perverse within him caused him to add, "But what of the mob, sir? Their treasonous slogans?"

"This is no time for you to be engaging in political activities." Chortenko whipped off his glasses, revealing his buggish eyes. "You have your orders. Will you obey them?"

"I am a soldier in the service of Muscovy, sir," Yevgeny said, feeling almost as offended as he did relieved.

"Answer the question! Yes or no?"

Yevgeny could not trust himself to speak. So, instead, he clenched his teeth and nodded.

"Then get to work." Chortenko looked up at the servile. "Take me to the Alexander Garden and then, after you have dropped me off, return to the coach house and rub down the horses."

The carriage left. Yevgeny stared after it in astonishment. Then he turned back to his crew. "Well? Get a move on. We've got a fire to fight."

They did.

Arkady was trudging down a narrow and lightless street, hoping against hope that it would soon open into a road that would take him to the Kremlin, when he realized he was not alone. There were footsteps matching his, stride for stride.

He broke into a trot. So did the second set of footsteps. He started to run. So did they. And then—disaster! The doorless and windowless wall of a brick building loomed up before him. He had come to the blind end of a cul-de-sac.

As Arkady stumbled to a stop, the other footsteps did the same. An echo? He almost laughed. Of course. It could be nothing else. Arkady's heart was pounding so hard he feared it would rip free of his chest. He found himself gasping for air. In the darkness, somebody matched him wheeze for wheeze.

"It's just an echo," he said aloud to reassure himself. "Nothing more."

". . . just an echo. Nothing more." The voice came from directly behind him. "*Or is it?*"

He shrieked, and was seized from behind. Arms and legs wrapped themselves about his arms and chest, rendering him helpless. Arkady's knees almost buckled under the weight of a human body. "Sssssso!" a witchy voice whispered into his ear. "You're not afraid of the dark, are you? Not afraid of the ancient thing from the graveyard, don't believe in the night hag, think you can't be ridden, eh?" Crisp teeth nipped his earlobe. It stung so sharply that Arkady knew the bite had drawn blood. "You know for a fact that your flesh is too bitter for my taste? You find it hard to believe that I'd like to break open your skull and eat your brains?" The hag's limbs tightened about Arkady like the coils of an anaconda. "You're absolutely sure I wouldn't crush you dead if you disobeyed my orders?"

He couldn't breathe! Arkady found himself panicking. Then the hag loosened her grip. "Breathe in, boy. Savor the air. That's Baba Yaga's gift to you. Now thank me for it, as politely as you know how."

Arkady gulped in the air, genuinely grateful, absolutely terrified. "Thank you, Baba Yaga. For letting me breathe."

But wasn't Baba Yaga a fairy-tale creature? A figure out of myth? Of course she was. So what was this thing on his back?

"Tonight you are my steed," Baba Yaga said. "Don't try to escape me." (As if he could!) "If you turn around to look at my face, I'll gouge out your eyes and suck their juices." (As if he wanted to see her!) "Now run. Run like the wind, and if we don't get where we're going fast enough…well, the horse that can't run can always be rendered down for glue."

Bony heels dug into his flanks.

Arkady couldn't actually run, but he did manage to achieve a trot, which seemed to satisfy the madwoman on his back for the nonce. "Where are we going?" he asked fearfully.

"To our destination."

"And where's that?"

Baba Yaga laughed wildly. Then she seized a mouthful of Arkady's hair with her teeth and ripped it out by the roots.

He screamed and ran.

The crowds exploded into sheer noise when the troika entered the Alexander Garden before the west wall of the Kremlin. Hats flew into the air like flocks of birds. Louder the cheering grew and louder, until it merged into one astonishing roar so overwhelming as to move beyond mere sound to become a constant and deafening pain. All faces were turned toward the carriage. Every hand stretched out reaching for it. Everywhere, torches, flags, and kerchiefs were in constant motion, a blur of color, as if all the world were on fire. Being in the driver's seat was like sitting at the center of a flaming whirlwind.

It was easily the most amazing moment in Baronessa Avdotya's life.

Intellectually, she understood that none of this was her own due. But it *felt* like it was, and that was the important thing. It filled her with a sense of destiny and purpose. She could not help turning from side to side, nodding and smiling luminously.

She craned around to look behind her and saw Tsar Lenin standing upon the seat. His balance was preternaturally perfect as, hand in air, he acknowledged the applause with a dignified hint of a bow, the tiniest twitch of his wrist.

Now those closest to the tsar unharnessed the horses and led them away. Others seized the carriage by its rods and pulled it by hand through the adoring throngs.

A speaking platform had been set up at the foot of the causeway leading up to the Trinity Tower gate. Bleachers stretched the length of the Alexander Garden's back wall. In between, all the park was already filled with marchers from the three invasions which had by prearrangement arrived earlier than Tsar Lenin's group. More people than Avdotya had ever in her life seen in a single space struggled to catch a glimpse of the great man, and screamed in ecstasy when they did.

Lenin stood straight and proud on the carriage seat, accepting their adulation.

Then, as lightly as he had climbed up, the new tsar leapt down and walked without hurry or effort through a riotous ocean of humanity which parted before him like the Red Sea before Moses, and closed solidly behind him like the gates of history clanging shut. Baronessa Lukoil-Gazproma ran quickly after Lenin, leaving Irina behind (indeed, forgetting her completely), and slid her arm through his.

Tsar Lenin did not object.

The Royal Guard appeared out of nowhere to close ranks behind and to either side of them, a bodyguard that Lenin surely did not need, but which did much to emphasize the legitimacy of the once and future ruler, freshly returned from the graveyard of the past to claim his land once more.

Together they ascended the stairs to the platform.

Upon the departure of the terrifying entity impersonating Lenin, Surplus had quietly slipped down from the troika. Irina had tried to climb over the heads and shoulders of the crowd to join the baronessa and been absorbed in their number, another anonymous drop of water in a sea of hysteria. Alone in all Moscow, it seemed, Surplus was immune to the contagions of emotion that lofted the crowd's mood higher and higher. Indeed, it would not be an exaggeration to say that those emotions terrified him. So much so that he immediately determined to get as far away from their epicenter as possible.

Not without effort, Surplus made his way to the fringes of the crowd. Behind him, the troika was being dismantled and then broken into pieces for souvenirs and relics.

When finally Surplus found himself free of the immense assembly's gravitational pull, he paused to gather his thoughts.

He had been in mobs before, though none so great as this. The prickling sensation of danger, of incipient violence, was not new to him. He knew how easy it would be to surrender to the madness that permeated the air and let himself be swallowed up by it. It was therefore of primary importance for him to keep his head. Systematically, then, Surplus reasoned carefully that:

Imprimis: The Duke of Muscovy was about to be overthrown.

Secundus: This meant that the plan he and Darger had devised to separate the duke from a generous share of his nation's surplus wealth was defunct. There was no point in mourning this fact. One simply had to move on.

Tertius: It would therefore be wisest to take advantage of the night's confusion in order to obtain some lesser share of Muscovy's treasures. Since he and Darger had invested a great deal of time and effort in the original project without the least recompense, this would not be theft but only simple justice.

Quartus: To do so in the fleeting hours during which Moscow's guardians were distracted or off-duty would require some form of transportation. A saddle horse would hardly suffice, for it would too greatly limit the potential volume of valuables he could hope to snatch up. Therefore he needed a carriage. The baronessa's troika no longer existed. So the question presenting itself was, where could he rent, borrow, or steal such a thing?

He gazed thoughtfully after Lenin, striding confidently toward the speaker's platform, where an uncomfortable line of dignitaries awaited him. One notable was conspicuous by his absence. Once brought to mind, however, he was the obvious solution to the problem now faced.

Who else should Surplus turn to in time of need but his good friend, Sergei Nemovich Chortenko?

As she rose up above the masses onto the platform, Baronessa Lukoil-Gazproma had an epiphany. Everything she had ever done with her life—the parties and entertainments, the gifted and witty lovers, the clothes and crafts and furniture and houses that no merely wealthy woman could afford, in short everything—was a weak substitute for political power. It had never before occurred to her that the purposes to which her husband had devoted his life were anything other than a means to wealth. Yet now that she'd had the merest taste of it, she realized that power was good. Power was good and more power was better. She wanted all of it she could get.

She wanted, too, the love and adulation that were raining down on Tsar Lenin at this very instant. And why shouldn't she get it? She was still young. She was willing to work hard. She could learn to be ruthless. Her beauty would not hurt her, and neither would her wealth.

Lenin could not live forever.

He would need a successor.

The new government of Muscovy, a line of mediocrities and dunces (Avdotya knew them all), sat on folding chairs along the back of the platform, looking neither happy nor comfortable. It was obvious that not a one of them would be there had they been given the choice. At their very center was an empty chair, which the baronessa took.

Tsar Lenin had taken the dais. The mob went wild.

He gestured for silence—once, twice, a third time—and then finally received it.

"Comrades!" Lenin shouted. He then paused as a series of barrel-chested men in the blue-and-orange uniforms of the Public Address Service raised their megaphones and repeated his word one after the other, relaying it to the very back of the crowd. "The long, slow war for the unification of Mother Russia has been simmering for more than eight years. And as each year, as each month, as each day of the war goes by, it becomes clearer and clearer to every thinking mind that unless there are drastic changes, our country will not be reunited in our lifetimes." After each sentence he paused, so it could be relayed throughout the Alexander Garden and from there to the crowds in Red Square and beyond. "It is becoming more evident by the day that the Duke of Muscovy moves our armies sluggishly from place to place, as if he were engaged in a game of chess. But war is no game! It is a terrible and desperate enterprise which, if we are to engage in it at all, were best gotten done and over with quickly."

Pandemonium. Lenin waited for it to subside.

"The Duke of Muscovy hides in his palace in the Kremlin. Who has ever seen him out on the streets, inspecting his city, or his armies, or his navy? Moscow is burning, Russia is ablaze, the world stands on the brink of annihilation, and where is he? Where? He is in *there!*" Lenin made a quarter turn and jabbed his hand up at the Kremlin.

"Why have we never seen him? Why does he not walk among us, reassuring us as only a supreme ruler can, sharing in our sorrows and rejoicing in our triumphs? We are born and he is not at our christenings, we marry and he does not attend our weddings, we die and at the funeral we are alone."

There was a ripple in the crowd which the baronessa noticed only in passing, as four more gigantic bear-men of the Royal Guard muscled their way through, escorting a slightly podgy little man wearing glasses whose lenses, seen by torchlight, were two cobalt disks.

Chortenko.

The head of the secret police came up on the platform and walked straight toward the baronessa. Leaning down, he said in her ear, "You have taken my seat, Baronessa. But no, no, no, you must keep it. I will stand here behind you." He placed a hand on her shoulder.

Even in her elated state, Baronessa Lukoil-Gazproma could not help but shudder.

"When leadership is weak and ineffective. When it is invisible and unheard, why then a time must come for it to be replaced. That time has finally arrived. That time is now." Tsar Lenin paused to let the applause roll over him. Then, gesturing for silence, he said, "A new compact must be made with the Russian people. You will give me your loyalty, your labor, your dignity, your bodies, your blood, your lives, your sons and daughters…"

His silence, though brief, seemed to stretch on forever.

"In exchange, I will take you in my hand, mold you together into one indistinguishable mass, and of this new matter create a single tool, a single weapon, a hammer greater and more powerful than anything the world has ever seen. This hammer I will bring down upon our enemies. Upon those who stand in our way. Upon those who are weak and traitorous. Upon all who oppose our greatness. Our armies will sweep across the continent and nations will fall before us. This will be only the beginning…"

The speech was quite literally hypnotic. Lenin's actual words hardly mattered; the experience of solidarity they created was all. So intent was the baronessa on Lenin's radiant vision of the future that she did not realize at first that the buzzing in her ear was Chortenko talking to her. With an effort, she managed to focus on his words. ". . . and in the morning, a private get-together at my mansion."

She turned, astonished. "What did you just say?"

Chortenko stroked her hair. "The two of us, Baronessa, alone. I'll show you my kennels."

Darger and Kyril made a wide circumnavigation of the Kremlin, searching for an approach that was not blocked by prodigious crowds. But though they circled almost two-thirds of the way around the fortress, always there were impenetrable thickets of humanity in their way.

In Kitai-Gorod, they had just taken a shortcut through a narrow and lightless alleyway when someone—or some*thing*—came running up behind them.

Darger whirled about and then flinched back from an astonishing apparition: two people, one riding on the other's back and clutching him so tightly that they seemed a single, if misshapen, two-headed creature. "Whoa!" cried a woman's voice, and the chimera came to a halt. Its two faces were filthy with mud or worse.

"Don't be afraid, sweeties," the woman crooned. "Old Baba Yaga means you no harm. She won't rip off your tongues and gouge out your eyes. She wouldn't eat a fly."

"Don't believe her!" a man said in a terror-choked voice. "She's killed two—"

But the warning was cut short. The man made a strangled noise. Then the grotesque figure collapsed into its component parts, the man tumbling down to the ground unconscious and the woman leaping free. "So much for him," she said. "They have no stamina, these modern youngsters. It was the invention of fire that did it. Fire and edged tools have made them all as weak as porridge."

Darger opened his mouth and shut it again.

"Alcohol?" Kyril said brightly, extending the bottle.

"Yes!" The alarming woman snatched it out of his hand. "And that rag you're wearing as well."

The kerchief whisked itself from Kyril's neck. There was a long silence.

At last Darger said, "Are you in need of assistance, madam? Perhaps we can…" His voice trailed off. Waving his hands through the murk before him to make sure, he said, "She's gone."

"Good. That crazy bitch stole my bottle!"

"The chap she was riding seems not to be injured. His breathing is steady." Darger examined the man's face. "Huh!"

"Something wrong?"

"No, no, it's just that I know the fellow. Well, he is nobody of any conse-quence, and so we may safely forget him." He hoisted the dark form into a sitting position, and left the man leaning against the side of a building. Then he said, "Is there any approach at all we haven't tried yet?"

"Well… There's still the south wall. I never heard of there being a way in there. But what the fuck do I know?"

"If it's a possibility, however remote, we must explore it. Diligence, Kyril! Diligence is all."

Koschei sat on a wooden chair he had carried from his hotel room to a quiet spot on the Kremlin's south wall, by the Annunciation Tower, smoking a pipe. His klashny was a reassuring weight in his lap. God was a burning presence in his brain.

He waited.

The strannik's part in tonight's activities was simple. When the demonic Tsar Lenin was safely in power, he was to give up his contemplation of the Moscow River and stroll across the Kremlin grounds to the ramparts overlooking Red Square. There, he would start shooting people at random. Meanwhile, from their perches atop Goom and St. Basil's, Svarožič and Chernobog would do the same. This would create panic and help to trig-ger a riot that would quickly spread to engulf the city. Thus they would do their small bit to bring about the Eschaton. In all likelihood none of them would live to see God striding the streets of Moscow. But Koschei was confident that they would all die having done what piety required.

"You are silent," observed the devil crouching at his feet.

"We have nothing to discuss," Koschei said.

"You were not always so reluctant to talk to us."

"There was a time when I sought for grains of truth hidden in your lies, like a sparrow picking oats from a steaming horse-turd. This being my last night before my soul is translated into the afterlife, however, I prefer to spend my time in prayer and meditation."

"There is no afterlife. You will die into eternal oblivion."

"God says otherwise."

"Where is this God? Show him to me. You cannot. The steppes of Rus-sia are vast and empty. I crossed them on foot and he was not there. On my journey I killed every human being I encountered. Angels did not descend from the sky to stop me. The city of Moscow is thronged with people of every sort and not a one of them has ever met with God. The history of Russia stretches far into the past and there is in all of it not a shred of evidence for the existence of such an entity."

"I feel His holy presence within me even now."

"Your temporal lobe has been stimulated by drugs we provided you."

"Intending evil, you achieve good. Such is the irresistible power of the Lord."

"The power, rather, of self-delusion."

Koschei frowned down at the scoffer. "Why are you even here?"

"At this moment, there are few places in Moscow that are safe for my kind. One of us died leading the uprising in Zamoskvorechye. When that happened, three of the remaining four deemed it best to leave our uprisings to continue on their own momentum. Only Tsar Lenin is still in public view."

"But why *here?* With me."

"Does my presence offend you?"

"Yes."

"Then that is reason enough."

Some time passed in uncompanionable silence. Then Koschei said, "What are you looking at so intently?"

The metal demon rose up on its haunches, like a hound. It pointed downward, across the road that ran just below the wall. A few scattered pedestrians, gray in the moonlight, hurried toward the gathering in the Alexander Garden. There were no carriages. "You see that small pump-house by the river?" It was practically invisible, but the strannik's sight was good. He nodded. "It is built on the site of the ancient outlet of a hidden tunnel which leads into the Beklemshev Tower, and from there into the Terem Palace. Its existence has for ages been the subject of rumor and speculation, though most believe that it leads to the Secret Tower, and is in fact commonly held to be the reason for the tower's name."

"You know everything—and nothing. Why bring up this useless fact?"

"Because there is a rider on the road."

"Oh?"

"Traveling fast."

Koschei stood and fixed his keen eyes on the woman leaning low over her steed. Her hair flew out behind her as if her head were on fire. The horse was gasping and overheated. "You should be happy, demon."

The metal gargoyle did not look up. "How so?"

"That woman is killing the poor beast with overexertion. Another dumb animal dead, and a soul on its way to Hell for her wicked deed. Surely that elates you."

"You know nothing of Hell. Is your klashny loaded?"

"It is. Why do you ask?"

"Because the rider is none other than General Magdalena Zvyozdny-Gorodoka. In the temporary web of alliances that we have woven, she is our common enemy. The only possible destination she can have is the pump house entrance to the Beklemshev Tower tunnel. The only possible reason for her to enter the Kremlin is to see the Duke of Muscovy."

"So?"

"If she speaks to the duke, he will tell her of all our plans. Inevitably, she will demand to know how they can be thwarted. No one else could possibly answer such a question. Yet for the Duke of Muscovy, extraordinary feats of analysis are possible. I am instructing my brothers to hurry to his side and kill him first."

"That is hardly necessary," Koschei said, rising from his chair.

He raised his klashny and took careful aim.

The first shot sent up sparks by the horse's front hooves. A little too forward and several feet too low, then. The second shot disappeared into the night. Probably too high. But the third shot took the horse right in the chest. It stumbled and fell, sending the general flying.

Koschei waited until she stopped rolling, and then placed eight shots in her unmoving body.

The Pearls Beyond Price were finally, completely ready. Their clothes and jewelry were perfect from tiaras to slippers, and their hair and makeup were works of art. They looked each other over minutely and were pleased with what they saw.

Then they had their escorts assemble before them.

Enkidu saluted. "We got the six carriages lined up outside. Decorated with swags of flowers, the way you said. Plus the horses' manes are all plaited and their hooves gilded too."

"It wasn't easy painting them hooves either," Atlas said. "They didn't much care for it."

Making a dismissive gesture, Russalka said, "We've changed our minds. We only need three coaches. That way there will be one of us at each window to wave to our adoring subjects-to-be, whichever side of the street they happen to be standing on. You may send the others away."

"Are you planning on going out dressed like *that?*" Nymphodora asked.

Enkidu looked down at his navy blue uniform. Behind him, the other Neanderthals stood fidgeting and shifting from foot to foot like so many schoolboys. "Well, yeah, kinda." His voice fell. "Ain't we?"

Speaking one after the other, Eulogia, Euphrosyne, and Olympias said:

"No. You most definitely are not."

"You must change into the new livery we had made up for you."

"Those lovely mauve-and-chartreuse outfits."

Gargantua looked stricken. "The poofty little hats, too?"

"They're called berets," Aetheria said. "Yes, of course you do. It would hardly be a proper ensemble without them. They're in that chest over there. Now—chop-chop!—strip down and get dressed."

Blushing, Magog said, "You mean… get naked… right in front of you ladies?"

"Of course. We have to make certain you put the clothes on correctly."

"Don't worry," Nymphodora said, "you won't be revealing anything we haven't seen before. In our imaginations, anyway."

None of the Pearls smiled, exactly. But their eyes all glittered.

The two underlords entered the Terem Palace by way of the long underground passage that led from Chortenko's mansion. They had reconfigured their bodies, reverting to four legs, as though they were still cyberwolves. When they slunk into the Duke of Muscovy's chamber, the last remnants of the Royal Guard raised their halberds in alarm. "Nobody is allowed in the Terem Palace uninvited," one of their number said, his fur standing on end. "You must leave immediately."

"No," one of the creatures said. "You leave."

"Or die," said the other.

This was not the first time the Royal Guards had met the underlords. Chortenko had arranged a series of vivid demonstrations in his basement, wherein one of their number had displayed its strength and speed upon selected political prisoners. Afterward, Chortenko had urged them to remember exactly how long it had taken those prisoners to die.

By common consent, the bear-guards left.

The underlords took up positions to either side of the duke, one by each ear. "Your guards have deserted their posts," said one.

"Your government is as good as fallen."

"Chortenko is in charge now. As soon as Tsar Lenin's speech is finished, he will seize the Kremlin."

"There will be no resistance."

The duke's noble face grimaced in agony. His great head turned from side to side. But of course he could not awaken, try though he might.

"General Magdalena Zvyozdny-Gorodoka attempted to reach the Terem Palace in order to rescue you."

"You would have called her effort heroic."

"We had her killed."

"With her died your last chance of stopping the revolution."

"In gratitude for all we have done, Chortenko has given us permission to kill as many of your citizens as we wish tonight, in numbers up to half of the total population of your city."

"It is not enough."

"But it is a start."

The sleeping duke lifted one arm so that the back of it covered those eyes which had never once in his life been open. "No," he murmured. "Please… do not." It was clear he was trying to awaken and, as ever, could not.

"Chortenko's reign will begin with rioting and a fire that will destroy much of Moscow."

"In the aftermath of this disaster, he will have to raise taxes steeply."

"This will cause rioting elsewhere in your land."

"The riots will be suppressed."

"But at such a cost that taxes will have to be raised again."

"Which will destabilize the economy."

"Requiring new sources of income."

"Which can be acquired only by force."

"Muscovy will be able to survive only through constant conquest and expansion."

In greater and greater agitation, the duke thrashed about, flinging his arms wildly to one side and the other. Effortlessly, the underlords evaded his blind blows. Always they darted back to his ear again. "No," he said. "I will stop… you. I know how."

"And how will you do that, Majesty?"

"You have no soldiers."

"You have no messengers."

"Your servants have betrayed you."

"You have lost Moscow already."

Weakly raising his arms upward, the duke said, "Lord God…hear my prayer. Aid me, I beg you." His expression was one of mingled horror and yearning. "Send me…a miracle."

"Fool! There is no God."

"There are no miracles."

"Soon there will be no Russia."

The Duke of Muscovy *screamed*.

And then he awoke.

...18...

With a noise like thunder, the Duke of Muscovy smashed through the roof of the Terem Palace, scattering tiles and timbers into the night.

Only to discover that he had woken out of his dreams and into something even more phantasmagorical. Below him was his beloved city...and yet it was smaller and shabbier than he had imagined it. Smokes and stinks rose from its every part. There were buildings on the point of collapse that were still being lived in. A fine silt dust discolored all the streets and sidewalks. Much of Moscow was in bad need of a coat of paint.

Nevertheless, it was his city and he loved it dearly.

So overcome was he by the cunning way that every street and building in his mental map had a physical counterpart and all of them precisely detailed in every particular, that the duke forgot entirely the purpose which had driven him into full consciousness. For he had, of course, immediately seen that the False Tsar was the weak point in Chortenko's plans; if he were killed, the revolution would collapse in an instant. Then, without their figurehead and justification, all those forces allied in the duke's overthrow would turn upon each other. And there were many ways that Lenin could be killed. The Duke of Muscovy had thought of them all.

But the thrilling discovery that *the world was real* acted upon the duke like a drug. All thoughts of Chortenko, of the underlords, of the revolution, and of those plans to counter it which a moment before had seemed so important to him, flew away like jackdaws.

Grinning with wonder, the Duke of Muscovy clambered clumsily over and through his palaces, collapsing walls and crushing floors beneath his feet. Down on the pavement, tiny horses reared in the air and toy soldiers threw down their guns and fled. The sky was flecked with stars and a big orange harvest moon hung low over Moscow.

Oh, what a night!

There was something wriggling in each of his hands. Without even sparing them the most cursory of glances, the Duke of Muscovy tossed away the underlords he had scooped up before standing, one to either side. He heard each of them smash against distant pavement and knew that they had been destroyed. But he did not care. Such petty considerations were swept away in the magic of the moment.

Naked, the duke strode down the causeway of the Trinity Gate. He crushed a wagon and a soldier or two beneath his feet, but that hardly mattered. There was a scattering of klashny fire from a bold trio of soldiers, followed by a stinging sensation across his chest, as if he had lightly brushed against a thistle. But the sensation faded quickly, and the men ceased firing when he bent down and crushed them with the flat of his hand.

Joyfully, the Duke of Muscovy made his way through the Alexander Garden, ignoring the screaming thousands who fled before him.

He waded into the city, a colossus, spreading destruction in his wake.

A carriage rattled up the cobbled street behind Arkady. He did not at first look up, but simply kept plodding doggedly along. Then, as the carriage came alongside him, the coachman reined in the horses.

"Arkady Ivanovich? Is that you?"

Arkady turned. He did not recognize the blue-and-white vehicle as belonging to Chortenko, as any Muscovite of substance would have, and thus his heart leapt up at this unexpected bit of luck. The passenger compartment was empty, so he looked up at the driver and was confronted by the last person in the world he would have expected to see.

It was the Byzantine ambassador, the dog-man whom his father had found wandering in the wilderness and brought home with him, thus setting in action every hideous thing that had happened to Arkady since. Surplus. That was his name. Arkady had spent months in the fellow's company. If he hadn't been so exhausted, he would have remembered the name immediately.

For the merest instant, a twinkle of amusement flickered across Surplus's face. "It's been quite some time," he said. "I'll wager you have a story to tell."

"Yes, I—"

"That was not an invitation." Surplus held out a paw and helped Arkady up onto the driver's platform alongside him. Then, when he was settled, the ambassador said, "Your destination and your purpose, young man. As quickly and efficiently as you can manage it, if you please."

Arkady spilled out his soul.

When he was done, Surplus looked thoughtful. "Hmmm," he said. "Well, I had known some of this already. But your tale explains a great deal."

Timidly, then, because everything else he had tried this evening had gone horribly, catastrophically wrong, Arkady said, "And you, sir? Where are you bound?"

"As it chances, I am at loose ends. I have just now returned from a long conversation with the guards at the Pushkin Museum who, against all odds and expectations, remain alert, undrugged, and determinedly on duty. I could not convince them to let me have the merest glimpse of the hoard of Trojan gold which is their chiefest treasure and, indeed, were it not for diplomatic immunity, I strongly suspect I would be cooling my heels in prison right now. I was considering my next move when I spotted you."

"You must take me directly to the Terem Palace, then." Tears welled up in Arkady's eyes. "Please, sir, it is vital. The Duke of Muscovy must be warned about this terrible conspiracy."

Surplus pulled up the horses and stared up over above the silhouetted city rooftops. "Only a minute ago, I would have told you that your quest was literally impossible, for vast numbers of people had created an impenetrable wall before the Kremlin's entrance. Now, however, I strongly suspect that conditions have changed."

Following Surplus's gaze, Arkady saw a paleness in the night sky which only slowly resolved into the form of a man so large that his upper body was visible over the intervening buildings. This miraculous figure was perfectly naked. Its head moved from side to side, eyes wide and liquid. Its expression was as innocent as a baby's.

Arkady crossed himself. "It's an omen. A vision. A sign from Almighty God." Then he scowled. "But what the devil can it possibly mean?"

"It means," Surplus said, shaking the reins and putting the horses in motion again, "that by the time we get there, our path to the Kremlin should be free." Then, as they clopped down the cobblestones, he handed his handkerchief to the young man. Gesturing at the carpetbag of tools he had assembled for the night's business, he added, "There's a bottle of mineral water in that basket by your foot. You should clean your face—you're a terrible mess."

They had not gone five blocks before they began to pass fugitives from Red Square and the Alexander Garden. First came young men running with all their might, and then young women and older men running vigorously, and then a scattering of people of all ages and categories scurrying along as fast as they could manage. The density of folk trying to escape the prodigious giant thickened until Surplus had to slow the horses to a walk to avoid running anybody down.

"You are a man of extraordinary good fortune, Arkady. It took me weeks of unrelenting effort to arrange a meeting with the Duke of Muscovy," Surplus remarked. "Yet you, in a single—"

A creature out of nightmare, with the body of a man and the head of a tremendous leather-beaked bird, rose up out of the crowd and, stepping onto the coach's running board, pulled itself level with Surplus and Arkady. The monstrous apparition held onto the door with one arm and with the other pointed at them a device very much like a muzzle-loading gun, only with a kind of upside-down jar atop it. It pumped a bellows, and a puff of black smoke engulfed Surplus and Arkady.

When the smoke cleared, the inexplicable chimera was still clinging to the coach. Without dropping the reins, Surplus swung about, lifted up both his feet, and kicked as hard as he could. The bird-man tumbled from the carriage and was quickly left behind.

Surplus waved a hand before his face. "Well!" he said. "That was certainly a dramatic and meaningless event. Are you all right, Master Arkady?"

There was no answer, so he turned in his seat, suddenly concerned. Arkady's face was unrecognizable. His eyes were wide and staring, his mouth set in a rictus of a grin. But there was a touch of determination in it as well, buried down deep.

"The Duke of Muscovy," he said. "The Duke of Muscovy."

Baba Yaga flew across the city, bottle in hand. She had no desire to stay and play with she-forgot-exactly-whoever-it-was who had given it to her. She was hunting bigger game tonight.

Against the flow of panicked citizens she ran, pushing her way through the crush of bodies choking Resurrection Gate, some of whom were trying to flee inward and others outward. She did not much like people and the more of them there were the less tolerable she found them, but this experience was different. They slammed into her and punched and clawed at her, even as she forced her way through them. Their hysteria made her invisible to them and their fear filled her with dark glee.

Glancing back over the gate, Baba Yaga saw a naked giant shifting slowly against the darkness of the sky. It meant nothing to her. She might easily have gone right past the giant and so up the causeway. But it did not fit her mood to do so. Instead, she went straight to the Kremlin's west wall, stuck the bottle of rubbing alcohol in her jacket pocket, and began to climb. She scaled the soaring wall like an enormous bat, digging into the mortar between its bricks with her long, sharp fingers—choosing this means of entry not for any specific reason or purpose, but just because she could.

Even for her, however, doing so was a prodigious feat. When at last Baba Yaga topped the wall, she was gasping with exertion and sweat rolled freely down her face.

She was mopping her forehead with the bandanna when a man's voice said, "One of your creatures has arrived, demon."

"Not one of mine," a machine-voice replied.

"Should I kill her, then?"

"You are a zealot and your delusional beliefs would make her death mean nothing to you. The pleasure of this woman's death is mine."

Even as they spoke, however, Baba Yaga was pulling the cork from her bottle and cramming the bandanna deep down its neck. "I am terror and Old Night," she said. A box of matches appeared magically in the palm of one hand. "I am the fear you cannot name. I am she who cannot be placated. If you think you can kill me, you are welcome to try."

"All things are possible with God's help." The first speaker held a klashny, but he did not raise it to his shoulder. Not yet. Baba Yaga recognized him by his clothing. He was a strannik, a worshipper of the White Christ, and doubtless the one she sought. The White Christ did not frighten Baba Yaga any more than did the Red Odin or even the Black Baal. She was old, old beyond human reckoning, older than language and older than fire. She had coalesced in the darkness that came before the gods. When the first sacrifice had been laid upon the first altar she had been there to snatch it away from its intended recipient. When first ape-man had been killed by an envious brother, it was she who had guided the murderer's hand.

The strannik stood watching, doing nothing. The real danger came from the machine-creature crouched at his feet. It launched itself at her in a silver blur.

Baba Yaga set fire to the rag stuck in the bottle. She had time to do so, she reckoned. It would take a good three-quarters of a second for the demon to reach her.

When it did, she side-stepped the creature and smashed the bottle on its back.

The underlord went up in flames.

Burning, it spun about and tried to seize her in its arms and metal jaws. But Baba Yaga knew a trick worth two of that. She reached into the flames and, grabbing the man-wolf by its ankles, flipped it over.

The underlord would have fallen on its back had the fight not occurred at the very lip of the rampart. Instead, it fell with a long electronic wail down the side of the Kremlin, burning all the way to the ground. When it hit the stones of Red Square, its screech stopped abruptly. Though it continued to burn, it did not move.

Baba Yaga turned to the man in black. "You are a strannik," she said. "There were three of you."

"There still are."

"You think so?" From one pocket, Baba Yaga drew a gobbet of flesh. She threw it at Koschei's feet. "I tore that from the one called Chernobog." She dipped her hand into another pocket. "Him I ran into by chance and oh but he was hard to kill! So hard that I simply had to have more. Before he died, he told me where I could find Svarožič." A second hunk of meat joined the first with a wet thud. "He also was great fun. And he, in turn, told me where I could find you."

"Lying bitch!" Koschei said. "Svarožič cut into his own brain to ensure that he would never break his vow of silence."

Baba Yaga laughed and laughed. "You'd be surprised how much information can be conveyed by gestures, given the proper motivation."

Koschei got off one shot before Baba Yaga tore the klashny from his hands and threw it over the side, after the underlord. He tried to punch her in the stomach, but she ducked his blow and yanked his feet out from under him. He fell flat upon his back.

"Show some spunk, pilgrim! Get up and fight." Baba Yaga stamped down three times, hard, where Koschei's face had been, while he threw himself from side to side to avoid her heavy shoes. Then he was on his feet again, hunched like a wild animal and breathing heavily. His eyes were two hot coals framed by raven-black hair.

"The patriarch Jacob wrestled with an angel," Koschei said. "Clearly it is my destiny to contend with you—and defeat you as well."

"Count your fingers, strannik." Baba Yaga opened one hand to reveal a fresh-severed pinkie.

Koschei looked down in astonishment at his bleeding hand. Then, with a roar, he charged.

But Baba Yaga deftly feinted to one side and then side-stepped him on the other. "You're down to eight!" she crowed.

Head down, Koschei waded into Baba Yaga, showering her with blows. Several landed solidly before, somehow, she dove between his feet and then slammed both her elbows into his back.

He fell forward on his face.

"Six!"

More slowly this time, Koschei stood. With a stunned expression, he held up his three-fingered hands before his face. Blood fountained from four finger-stumps.

"First your fingers, then each ear," Baba Yaga said in a singsong voice, almost as if it were an incantation. "Your nose, your toes, your what-you-fear."

Something inside Koschei broke.

He fled.

Baba Yaga chased the strannik down from the wall and between the churches and palaces and across the plazas and open spaces of the Kremlin, regularly issuing little shrieks and screams so that he would know she was mere steps behind him. They ran all the way to the south wall. Koschei was in a blind panic, and so had as good as trapped himself. She drove him down the wooded slopes of the Secret Garden until he came up against the wall and there was nowhere to go but forward, into the Secret Tower.

Koschei did not notice the faint tendrils of smoke oozing out from under the door.

Seizing the knob in his mutilated hand, Koschei threw open the door and plunged within.

But opening the door provided fresh oxygen for the fire smoldering deep below, and a path upward for its flames. They rose up with a mighty roar, engulfing the strannik and all in an instant turning the tower's roof to smoke and gases.

Baba Yaga did not stay to admire her work. Moving like a swirl of darkness, she disappeared into the night.

All of which was a fine piece of theater. Indeed, it was almost operatic.

But there was a coda:

Down in the city, coming around a corner, Baba Yaga collided with somebody directly under a street lantern. Who of course shrieked in fear at the sight of her. But then, strangely enough, the woman seized Baba Yaga's arms and stared hard into her face. She began to shake her head apologetically, but then stopped and studied her features even more minutely. Finally, she said, "Anya? Is that you? Everyone at the university thought you were dead."

A shock ran up Baba Yaga's spine. "What…?" she said. "What did you just call me?"

"Anya." The young woman looked unaccountably familiar. Her expression was one of extreme concern. "Anya Alexandreyovna Pepsicolova. Don't you even remember who you are?"

Terrible confusion rose up within her, then. She balled a fist and punched this disturbing young person in the stomach. Then, with a high-pitched sound that might have been a scream, she fled, looking for someplace to hide.

After her first moment of shock, Baronessa Lukoil-Gazproma realized that Chortenko's advances were an opportunity in disguise. In the new government, he was sure to be a center of power second only to Lenin himself. So he was an ally to be cultivated. And the baronessa knew how to cultivate a man.

There were unsavory rumors about his sexual practices, of course… But gossip always painted a darker picture than did simple fact. Anyway, before he had lost interest, the baronessa had indulged her husband's brutal appetites from time to time and had survived those experiences well enough. She did not anticipate any serious problems there.

Reaching up and behind her, she took Chortenko's hand in her own, and brushed her cheek with it. Too fleetingly for the act to be noticed by the crowd, she kissed his knuckles.

She could sense his astonishment.

Good.

"As of this moment, the Duke of Muscovy no longer rules." Lenin's words, simultaneously shocking and thrilling, threw the crowd into prolonged applause. He waited it out with stoic patience. "History has done with him. The people are in command and have chosen me to… They have chosen me to…" His words trailed off. Tsar Lenin peered quizzically at the crowd. Which was, the baronessa suddenly realized, behaving oddly. What had been a still lake of rapt faces was now in swirling motion. People were screaming. They were running, as if in fear. It took her a second to realize that they were not running away from the platform and its legendary speaker but from something behind and above them both.

She turned.

It had been hours since Baronessa Lukoil-Gazproma had first taken the rasputin and, though it still made her hypersensitive to all matters spiritual or emotional, its embers were burning low. So she felt not raptured but horrified astonishment at seeing, looming up over the rally, the gigantic face and figure of an archaic giant. The body was perfectly formed in every way. But the light from an uncountable number of torches was reflected back from its tremendous face in a ruddy glow that made it seem to shift and glower. This was not the visage of an omniscient, all-powerful, and loving deity.

It was the face of an idiot.

The baronessa felt as if a curtain had been lifted, revealing a higher reality far vaster and more terrifying than the island of sanity on which she had unknowingly lived all her life. Then the monstrosity was upon her, its gigantic foot descending to crush the platform and everyone upon it. The baronessa had risen from her chair. She was frozen with fear and unable to move.

Tsar Lenin inexplicably dropped to all fours. Then he leaped.

The foot came down right atop him, crushing the tsar and smashing the platform to flinders.

Then it was gone.

When by slow degrees the baronessa came to, she found herself lying on the ground on her back. There were chairs and splintered wood lying atop her, pinning her down, and she seemed to be tangled in the bunting. But she managed to struggle free. Frantically, she began searching, more by touch than by sight, for Lenin's body. Perhaps he had survived. Perhaps he could still rule. With a strength that might have come from the dwindling effects of the rasputin or might have been simple frenzy, she blindly flung planks and beams out of her way, digging through the rubble in search of her nation's beloved leader.

Lanterns moved slowly here and there. It seemed she was not the only searcher. The members of the new government had assuredly fled, of course, like the poltroons and weaklings they were. But Chortenko's people remained, their pale faces floating over the rubble as they worked with quiet efficiency. So too did several members of the Royal Guard, looking like gray round-backed snowbanks whenever they bent low over the wreckage.

"Here!" somebody shouted. There was the sound of an armful of planking being thrown to the side. "We've found him!"

The baronessa scrambled over the debris to join the circle crouching about a small, still form.

"Pick up the tsar," Chortenko told two of his underlings. "Perhaps he can be repaired." Which seemed to the baronessa an extremely odd choice of words under the circumstances. Then, when a nondescript barouche had been brought around, Chortenko said, "What is this thing? I sent you to fetch my own coach. Why isn't it here?"

The man he addressed looked startled. "You lent it to the Byzantine ambassador, sir. So we requisitioned a coach from one of your neighbors."

"Lend my coach? I never did any such thing. Who told you that?"

"The servants back at your mansion. Ambassador de Plus Precieux told them you'd given him its use, and so of course they… Well, who would dare claim such a thing if it weren't true?"

Chortenko looked grim. "I will deal with this when there is time. Right now, lift Lenin into the coach. Baronessa, you will ride with us. The rest of you, stay here and do what you can to establish order."

In the barouche, Tsar Lenin was laid across the forward-facing seat with his head in the baronessa's lap. The noble head was surprisingly heavy. The baronessa took one of his hands in her own and stroked it. The skin was unpleasantly waxy, and as cold as a corpse. "Oh, my beloved tsar," she said, and began to weep.

"Stop that," Chortenko snapped. "He's not dead yet. Paralyzed, yes. But look at his eyes."

The baronessa did. The eyes were slightly open and there was a faint light to them, though it was dimming. Lenin's lips moved, almost imperceptibly. "Half a hundred of us started out from Baikonur," he said in a faint voice. "Now but I remain. And soon there will be none." His eyes moved slowly to focus on Baronessa Lukoil-Gazproma. "You…"

Deeply moved, the baronessa leaned close to hear the tsar's last words.

"You should…" Lenin whispered.

"Yes?"

"Eat shit and die."

By the time Darger and Kyril had made a complete circuit of the Kremlin, the Alexander Garden was nearly empty and they were able to simply stroll up the Trinity Gate causeway. Darger led, feeling infinitely self-assured, and Kyril followed, muttering resentfully. "This is as crazy as drinking piss," Kyril said. "We're walking into what's gotta be the most dangerous place in all Russia for people like us, in order to grab some books? I mean, if it were, I dunno, diamonds or some shit like that, I'd understand. But *books?*"

"Don't hunch your shoulders like that," Darger said imperturbably. "I know you're feeling exposed, but it makes you look suspicious. We go this way."

"I mean, you're smart and all, I get that. But you're bugfuck crazy. I gotta wonder if you've let your brains go to your head."

"Kyril, rescuing even one of those books would give my life a meaning I never expected it to have. Plus, the right collector would pay a fortune for it—and I hope to leave with an armful."

"Listen, there's still time to turn back."

"Here's the Secret Garden. The tower should be visible just around this bend."

The path twisted under their feet and they turned the corner just in time to see the Secret Tower go up in flames.

"Dear Lord!" Darger cried. "The library!"

He started to run toward the tower.

Darger had not gone more than three or four strides, however, when his feet were snatched out from under him and he crashed painfully to the ground. For an instant, all went black. Then, when he tried to stand, he could not. A pair of bony knees dug into his back and Kyril spoke urgently into one ear: "Get ahold of yourself. Those books are gone and tough shit about that."

But they—" Darger felt tears of frustration well up in his eyes. "You have no idea what has just been lost. No idea at all."

"No, I'm pretty sure I don't. But you ain't gonna rescue one fucking page of them by running into a goddamned fire, okay? Those books are dead and gone. There's not enough left of 'em by now to wipe your ass with."

Darger felt something die within him. "You're...you're right, of course." With an act of sheer will, he pulled himself together and said, "Pax. Uncle. 'Nuff. You can get off me now."

Kyril helped him up.

"So what do we do now?" the young bandit asked.

A furry paw clamped down on Darger's shoulder. "Caught up t'you at lasht!"

"Oh, dear." Darger had not thought this evening could possibly get any worse. Yet now it had. "Sergeant Wojtek."

"You don' know musch about the Royal Guard," the bear-man said, "if you think a mere dozen drinks or sho can put one of ush out for the night." His speech was slurred, but he looked to be as strong as ever.

"Indeed, you are a most remarkable fellow, Sergeant," Darger said. "I will confess that if I absolutely had to be recaptured, there's less shame in it for me to be recaptured by you than by some ordinary soldier."

"You can shtop with the flattery. Nobodysh buying a word of it." Sergeant Wojtek carried the folded gurney under one arm. Without releasing Darger, he shook it open. "Now I'm going to shtrap you in again. If you coop'rate and don't try to get away, I promish I won't bite off your face. But if you mishbehave all bets are off. You won't get any fairer deal than that, now will you?"

Darger sat down on the gurney, swung up his legs, and then lay flat. "How on earth did you...? No, don't tell me. You managed to pull yourself partially out of your drowse before I left the bar. Though you were unable to summon the sobriety needed to stop me, you heard me talking with Kyril and so knew where we were headed."

"Right in one." Sergeant Wojtek tightened the straps, one by one. "Hey! Shpeaking of your young partner in crime—where ish he?"

"While I was distracting you with conversation, he quite wisely fled." Darger felt a little sad to reflect that in all likelihood he would never see the young lad again. But at least he could take some consolation in the fact that he had put the boy's feet on the path to a respectable career.

"Well, no big deal. You, however, have to be kept shomewhere shecure." Sergeant Wojtek thought for a moment and then grinned toothily. "And I know jusht the playzsch."

Across the Kremlin grounds he pushed the gurney and through a field of rubble that led to the most extraordinary breach in the side of the Terem Palace. (Fleetingly, Darger regretted that from his prone position, he could not get more than a glimpse of it, and so the nature of the catastrophe that had created it remained to him a mystery.) Then, hoisting the gurney onto his back, Sergeant Wojtek made his way across uneven floors, down into the basement, and through a doorway, where he was finally able to set the gurney down again.

"If you don't mind telling me…where are we going?"

"This tunnel leads to Chortenko's manshion. Ish probably the best protected playzsch in the city, now that the Kremlin's in sush bad shape. I'm going to bring you there and then shtand guard over you until Chortenko pershonally accepts you into hish cusht'dy."

Darger had been thinking furiously. Now he said, "Is that wise?"

Sergeant Wojtek eyed him suspiciously. "Waddaya shaying?"

"You noticed that the crowds had dispersed? That means the revolution has failed."

"Well…maybe."

"Not maybe, but certainly. There is, as the Bard put it, a tide in the affairs of men which taken at the flood leads on to fortune. That tide has turned and left you stranded in the shallows, an easy prey for the warships of the regime you opposed."

Sergeant Wojtek pushed on in stolid silence for a time. At last he said, "You're right. I'm in a terrible fiksh."

"I can tell you how to get out of it."

The sergeant stopped. "You can?"

"Absolutely. However, in exchange for my advice, you must promise to free me."

"How about I shimply promish not to kill you?"

"No good. Leaving me for Chortenko to find accomplishes the same thing and in a more painful fashion."

It took Sergeant Wojtek several minutes to think through his options. Then, placing a paw over his heart, he said, "I shwear on my honor ash a member of the Royal Guard. Are you happy now?"

"I am. Now, what you must do is to quickly obtain a great deal of easily negotiated wealth—gold, jewels, and the like. Then, straightaway go to a hostler—roust him from bed, if you have to—and buy a sturdy coach and six of the best horses he has. He will overcharge you, but what of that? Your life is at stake. Flee immediately, without waiting for morning, for St. Petersburg. There you can easily book passage to Europe, where the remainder of your loot will allow you to live in comfortable anonymity."

Sergeant Wojtek snorted. "Yeah, but wheresh a guy like me going to come up with that kind of money?"

"I believe you will discover," Darger said, "that the Diamond Fund is, briefly, unguarded."

A wondering light dawned in the sergeant's eyes. "Yesh," he said. "It would work."

"Then you may release me, and we shall part as friends."

"Hah! Let a shlippery bastard like you free? Not a chansh," Sergeant Wojtek turned away and started back up the tunnel, leaving Darger strapped motionless to the gurney.

"You gave me your word as a member of the Royal Guard!" Darger called after him.

"Chump!" the sergeant said over his shoulder. "I shtopped being a Guard the inshtant I made up my mind to deshert."

To be chosen for one of the Kremlin troops was a great honor for a Muscovite soldier and one that only the best received. However, when the naked giant came crashing through the government buildings, supernatural dread had gone before him in a great wash of terror. Warriors who would have stood their ground in the face of superior forces and fought to the death, broke and ran. Those charged with defending their nation's very center of power scattered in a panic.

In their wake, Surplus drove Chortenko's blue-and-white carriage up the Trinity Tower causeway and parked it before the Armory.

Surplus knocked hard on the door with the heavy silver knob of his cane. Then, when there was no response, he pushed the door open. "This way," he said, and entered the unguarded building.

Arkady followed a step or three behind him, carrying the carpetbag of makeshift burglar tools and from time to time murmuring, "the Duke of Muscovy," in the manner of a man trying to keep in mind some desperately important fact or duty.

The Armory had from Preutopian times been kept as a museum of Muscovy's and before that Russia's greatest treasures. There was much to see here. But Surplus moved swiftly past the larger luxuries and wonders—the gilded coaches and carved ivory thrones and the like—straight toward the Diamond Fund. "Come briskly, young man. We might as well get some use out of you…as a mule, if nothing else."

"The Duke of Muscovy," Arkady mumbled. He shivered convulsively

"You're cold! And your coat is sodden. Have you been rolling about in puddles?" Surplus removed Arkady's overcoat and replaced it with a ceremonial greatcoat that was thickly woven, intricately embroidered, and worth a fortune in any bazaar in the world. "There. That will keep you warm," he said. Then, "Dear Lord! That awful grimace! Every time I look at you it gives me a fright. Here." Using his cane, he hooked down a medieval helmet with a serene silver face-mask from the wall. He placed it over Arkady's head, cinching the straps with particular care to the lad's comfort. "Now try to keep up. We haven't much time."

Down the lightless gray halls they scurried, pausing every now and again so Surplus could pick a lock (the tools taken not from the satchel but from the pocket case, which he had planned to use at the Pushkin) and so select some choice item. It would have been easier to smash the glass of the vitrines. But that would have been vandalism, and Surplus was no vandal.

Quickly, he loaded down Arkady with the best of what he saw: the Imperial Crown, which was covered with nearly five thousand diamonds and topped by a red spinel, the second-largest such gemstone ever found; Catherine the Great's scepter, which contained the famously large Orlov Diamond; a jewel-encrusted armored breastplate that he didn't recall having read about but which looked respectably gaudy; and much more as well. Arkady's greatcoat pockets he stuffed to overflowing with cunningly made jeweled eggs.

"Can you see?"

"The Duke of Muscovy."

"Yes, yes, most admirable. I commend you for your sense of duty. Try to focus on the moment, however. We have serious matters which must be dealt with first." Surplus heaped Arkady's arms to overflowing with damascened swords, platinum goblets, jewel-hilted daggers and the like. For himself, Surplus was careful to keep his arms unencumbered and his wits sharp. But whenever he came upon loose gems, he slipped them into his pocket, until he had a good solid handful.

Arkady's load would make Darger and him rich beyond belief. The loose stones were only insurance.

A museum was a spooky place at night, lit only by bioluminescent columns. Those small random noises indigenous to any old buildings were all too easily assigned patterns by a nervous mind. So when Surplus, who was far from a coward, first heard what might have been distant footsteps, he ignored them.

Then came the sound of breaking glass.

Surplus froze. Someone else had entered the Armory with the same intentions as he, and had just smashed open a display case.

Well, there was more than enough wealth here for two; it would take weeks and wagons to remove it all. But the very act of looting, as he knew from experience, excited greed. And greed made men violent and unpredictable. "We must leave now, Arkady," Surplus murmured. "I want you to follow me as quietly as you can. Do you think you can do that?"

There was no response.

"Arkady?" He looked around for the boy.

But Arkady had disappeared.

...19...

The Pearls' grand procession was a grave disappointment. The streets were at first empty, and then they were filled with unhappy-looking people, all hurrying away from the heart of the city. None looked festive. Some carried torches, true, but they didn't look like the sort who could be trusted with them. Nobody cheered or threw flowers. After a few tentative waves were ignored, the Pearls withdrew from their windows and sulked.

When at last they pulled up before the Great Kremlin Palace, there were no musicians playing and no ceremonial troops to greet them. The plaza was eerily dark and still.

"Where is everyone?" Nymphodora said, when the Neanderthals had helped them down from their coaches. Neat lines of streetlamps burned quietly over desolately empty spaces.

"I dunno," Enkidu said. "But if it was up to me, we'd turn around right here and now and go home." He held up his hands to fend off the Pearls' glares. "I know, I know! I was just saying."

Olympias sniffed the air. "I smell smoke. Is there a building on fire? Is that why there's nobody here?"

"That is none of our concern," Russalka said. "Let us go to our royal husband."

With Neanderthals to their front, back, and either side, the Pearls entered the palace and swept up the great staircase to the Georgievsky Hall. There were no guards at the door and the hall was empty. Lanterns burned unattended. The silence was so absolute it seemed to reverberate.

"Maybe we shoulda sent word we was coming," Enkidu said uneasily.

"Hush," Russalka snapped. "We go through those mirrored doors over there."

They pushed into the octagonal Vladimirsky Hall and came to a halt. For this room was not empty. Shaggy members of the Royal Guard slouched in delicately carved chairs that were surely worth more than they were, smoked cigars and spat on the floor, leaned against pristine white walls which would doubtless require cleaning as a result. Two were on their knees, shooting dice.

"Cease this scandalous behavior!" Russalka commanded. "A palace is no place for such slovenliness. Our royal husband will be outraged when we tell him about it."

The guards stared. Those who were seated or kneeling rose to their feet.

"Excuse me for pointing this out, Gospozha," said their leader. "But you're not supposed to be here at all. Much less ordering anybody around."

A Neanderthal stepped forward. "My name's Enkidu. These are my boys." He jerked a thumb over his shoulder. "Somehow, I seem not to have caught your name."

The bear man's lips curled back in a snarl. "Captain Pipaluk, of the Royal Guard."

"Well, Captain Pipaluk, I think you oughta treat these ladies with respect. They come all the way from Byzantium to marry your boss-man. They can cause you a lot of trouble."

All the bear-guards laughed coarsely. "Marry the duke?" their leader said. "Impossible!"

"He's in the Terem, right? Through that door there?"

Deadly serious again, Captain Pipaluk said, "He was the last time we saw him. But we're not going through that door until we're sent for—and neither are you."

Enkidu smiled brutishly. "In that case, we're just gonna have to go through you guys." As he spoke, the Neanderthals and the bear-guards all casually arrayed themselves for a fight.

"Well, well, well," Captain Pipaluk said. "This is a clash for the records. The gene vats of Byzantium against those of Russia. The old culture versus the new. Decadence against youth. Come to think of it, you're even dressed for the part, with those pansy outfits and those silly little hats. I believe what we have here is a genuine passing-of-the-torch moment."

"You know what?" Enkidu said. "You speak real good. I don't got no doubt you're smarter than we are. Maybe you got better reflexes, too. Who knows, you might even be stronger. Stranger things have happened. But we still got one big advantage over you."

"Oh, yeah? What's that?"

Enkidu cracked his knuckles. "We got you outnumbered three to one. In my experience, that means we win."

With a roar, the two groups surged into each other, fists flying.

"Men!" Aetheria said. "Honestly."

"Oh, I know," Euphrosyne said. "They look nice enough—but they're always fighting and starting wars and the like. I think they're just trying to impress one another."

"Well, they're certainly not impressing me," Eulogia said.

"Meanwhile," Russalka pointed out, "the way to the Terem Palace is open. Let's just go."

"Oh!" gasped Nymphodora. "Can we?"

"Fortune favors the bold," Russalka said, and strode straight for the door. The other Pearls hurried in her wake.

Anya Pepsicolova had had a home once. To return there was unthinkable, for it would bring the full weight of Chortenko and the underlords down upon her parents. In her new and nightmarish life, she had made many enemies but no friends. She had slept in a constantly changing series of cheap flats where she had kept only the most utilitarian of possessions. Fleeing, there was, in all of Moscow, only one possible destination.

Chortenko's mansion.

Chortenko lived right off of the Garden Ring. From his front step, five separate fires were visible. But his mansion, unlike so many others, was not ablaze.

Well…that could be remedied.

Now that her head was beginning to clear, Pepsicolova was all but certain that she was not Baba Yaga anymore. Which meant either that the massive overdose of drugs she had taken was wearing off or that she'd fallen into a lower spiritual state, shedding her supernatural aspect and becoming merely human once again. She was not at all sure which interpretation she would have preferred, given the choice.

If she was only human, however, that meant she would have to use cunning and guile, things her discarded witch-self would never have bothered with. Pepsicolova entered the mansion through the front door and walked calmly and unhurriedly to the records room. There Chortenko's two dwarf savants were poring over a mountainous heap of files. Igorek picked up a report, flipped through it committing its contents to memory, and then handed it to Maxim, who did the same. After which, the report was carefully placed atop a roaring fire in the fireplace.

The dwarfs looked up incuriously as she entered.

"I am going to set fire to this building," Pepsicolova said. "Your master will want to know this information. Go immediately and tell him."

Igorek and Maxim rose and left the room.

Pepsicolova scooped up an armful of documents and one of the reading lanterns. Then she went to the top floor and set fire to all the curtains. That would start the house ablaze well enough, and by the time the fire burned down to the basement, she expected to have completed her business here.

When enough time had elapsed for those on the ground floor to smell smoke, a servant came running up the stairs with a carafe of water in his hand. "Tell your master that Anya Alexandreyovna has come home," Pepsicolova said. "Also, the building is on fire. It contains much that he values, so I'm certain that he'll want to know." To her own ear, her words sounded mild and reasonable. But something in her tone or expression made the servant turn tail and run, water spraying with each long stride. Not long later, she heard somebody outdoors banging a hammer on an iron fire triangle.

Back down to the first floor she went.

Throwing the mansion's front doors wide open, Pepsicolova dropped a single folder on the mat. A few paces inward, she dropped a second folder. Leaving a line of reports behind her like a trail of breadcrumbs, she made her way down to Chortenko's basement study, where he had once kept her in a cage.

For her, this was where it had all begun.

Here, it would end.

Pushing open the door, she found herself in a room she knew only too well. At her entrance, the dogs leaped and barked and bayed in their cages, throwing themselves desperately against the bars. Already, they could smell smoke from the upper floor. It imbued the air with a tinge of madness.

Closing the door behind her so that the final file was wedged under it, half on the landing and half in the study, Pepsicolova studied the dogs dispassionately. Had they been human beings, she would have left them in their cages without a second thought. She did not much like people. In her experience, they deserved pretty much whatever happened to them. But these were dogs and hence as innocent as she had been when the secret police had first brought her, naked and weeping, to this room. She could not let them die here.

Pepsicolova drew Big Ivan, the least favored of her knives, from her belt, and, using his hilt as a hammer, systematically smashed all the locks one by one.

The dogs leaped and danced as she released them, hysterical with freedom and fear. Some of them bit her, but they didn't really mean it and so she didn't mind.

She had just broken open the last of the cages when she heard footsteps on the stairs. "Don't do this, please," a woman's voice pleaded. "Please, Sergei Nemovich. Let me go." If there was a reply, Pepsicolova could not hear it.

Then Chortenko kicked open the basement door. He had the files she'd strewn about in the crook of one arm, and pulled an elegantly dressed society lady after him with the other. Her he threw into the room. Whipping off his glasses, he turned his bug-eyed gaze on Pepsicolova. His face was flushed with anger. But as always his tone was mild and controlled. "You have crossed a line, little Annushka," he said. "So I—"

The dogs attacked.

Chortenko fell backward as he was swarmed and overwhelmed by the newly freed animals. The society lady darted into a corner, shrieking with fear. But the dogs did not attack her. They were all rabid to tear the flesh from their tormentor's living body. Snarling and snapping and foaming at the jaw, they fought each other to get at Chortenko. But if the male dogs were savage, the bitches were even worse, ripping and tearing at the spymaster with unholy glee.

Foremost among them was Pepsicolova herself.

Her knives were forgotten. She used only her jaws and nails. The sound that Chortenko made as her teeth sank into his throat—a high-pitched sort of scream, more of a squeal, actually—was almost as good as the taste of the flesh she ripped from his struggling body.

Arkady, meanwhile, was staggering through the ruins of the Terem Palace, half-blinded by his mask. He was not precisely clear how he had found his way here. But the fragmentary decoration was familiar to him from his schoolboy history texts. The Duke of Muscovy must surely be here somewhere! Yet nowhere in this shambles could he find any trace of that great man.

Icons crunched beneath his shoes. He tripped over an enamel stove and fell flat on his face. When he regained his feet, a staircase opened up before him and all in a rush he found himself down at its bottom.

At last, Arkady stumbled into the Golden Porch, an antechamber of sorts into which a passage from the Great Kremlin Palace debouched. This room, unlike all the others he had seen, was at least intact. But it too was deserted.

Disheartened and exhausted, Arkady sank down at the top of a short flight of stairs overlooking the antechamber. In daylight, assuredly, it would have looked splendid. Now, however, lit by only two guttering candle-lanterns, one to either side of the stairs, it was cavernous and dark, a palace of shadows at the end of time. Was everybody else dead and only he alive? Had he somehow outlived humanity, dooming himself to eternal desolation and despair? Or was he himself dead and inexplicably condemned to search through the ruins of his life, forever seeking and never finding?

Such were his confused and incoherent thoughts when the Pearls Beyond Price flowed through the doorway into the Golden Porch, chattering and laughing. Only to come to an abrupt halt at the sight of him.

The Pearls' sudden unease was perfectly understandable. In a mirror across the room, he could dimly make out an eerie sight: a man in a lavishly brocaded surcoat, wearing a helmet with a smooth silver facemask, topped by a crown covered over with diamonds, sat brooding heavily and in perfect solitude. It was himself. In the unsteady lantern-light, surrounded by the reds and golds of the highly decorated walls, he might have been a hand-colored illustration in a children's romance. King Saladin resting after his victory over the Zengids, perhaps, or Ivan the Terrible wracked with guilt after murdering his son.

The Pearls clustered together. Then Nymphodora stepped forward and timidly said, "Sir?"

Arkady looked up. Several of the Pearls gasped. Apparently they had not all been absolutely sure he was alive.

"Sir, I must ask. Who are you?"

"I…?" There was an answer to that question, he was sure of it. Arkady sought for it in the reeling corridors of his mind. It was all terribly confusing. But then he remembered his quest, his duty, the sacred errand that had sent him out into the terrible streets of Moscow on this most horrific of all nights. He must find the Duke of Muscovy. He had a message for the Duke of Muscovy. He must warn…

"The Duke of Muscovy."

With screams of delight, the Pearls converged upon him.

Chortenko's body was not recognizable by the time Anya Pepsicolova and her new friends were through with it. She stood, shaking her head, trying to will herself to think clearly and rationally. The basement door was open and the society lady gone—fled, doubtless, in horror of what she had seen. Already, some of the dogs were bounding up the stairs toward the open front door and liberty. Others, however, cowered, afraid to pass through the smoke-filled air that choked the rooms above.

"Hush now, don't be afraid," Pepsicolova said soothingly. "You don't have to go upstairs if you don't want to. There's another exit right over here."

She unlatched, unbolted, and threw open the door into Chortenko's secret tunnel system. Several dogs streaked past her as she stepped through it.

Pepsicolova had no good memories connected to these tunnels. But they opened into not just the Kremlin but several buildings, public and private, along the way. She was considering which exit to take when she saw something in the tunnel ahead. It was, strangely enough, a piece of furniture. A kind of surgical table or cot which was used in hospitals, what was it called? A gurney. As she drew closer, Pepsicolova was astonished to see none other than the Englishman, Aubrey Darger, strapped down helpless upon it.

"Well!" she said, inexplicably amused. "Somebody expended a great deal of effort strapping you down."

With a twitch of her wrist, Saint Cyrila appeared in her hand.

A relieved smile appeared on Darger's face. "Good girl!" he cried. "Well done! Cut me free and we'll—"

Then, as the knife moved not toward the straps but toward his groin, Darger said, "Um…excuse me, but… If I may ask… Exactly what are you doing?"

Which was, Pepsicolova felt, an extremely astute question. She considered its answer carefully, all the while staring down at Darger, hard and unwavering. "Something I've been wanting to do," she said at last, "for a long, long time."

Saint Cyrila cut through Darger's belt as if it were made of paper.

Diving and soaring with a life of her own, the blade moved up and down and up again. Humming to herself, Pepsicolova proceeded to cut away first Darger's trousers and then his shirt. Darger had a great deal to say during the process, but she didn't bother listening to any of it. When he was completely naked, she kicked off her shoes, shucked her trousers, and climbed atop his prone body.

By now Darger was clearly convinced she was crazy. Which, Pepsicolova had to admit, was entirely possible. Eyes wide with fear, he babbled, "My dear young lady! This is certainly neither the time nor the place for such actions. You mustn't… mustn't…"

But Pepsicolova bent low over Darger and, tapped the flat of Saint Cyrila's blade warningly against his lips. "Shhhhhh," she whispered. Then she spat out a tooth and grinned.

"Giddy up." She dug her heels into his sides.

Savoring Darger's protests, Pepsicolova rode him like a stallion.

This day just kept getting better and better.

Yevgeny and his crew were engaged in blasting down burning houses in order to create a fire break to limit the spread of the conflagration.

"Awaiting your order, sir," the sergeant said.

"Fire," Yevgeny said miserably.

"Fire!" the sergeant barked.

The gun fired.

Thus did his men (and, temporarily, his women) show their displeasure with his indecision earlier. Everything was being done strictly by the book. There was no slack, no swagger, no camaraderie, none of the easy give-and-take natural to a well-run crew. Only a stiff adherence to the minutest detail of military protocol.

"Shall we load and fire again, sir?" The sergeant stood as straight as a ramrod, eyes unblinking and unforgiving.

"What is your advice, Sergeant?"

"Sir! No advice, sir!"

"Then we shall move the piece down the street to demolish the next house."

There was the slightest pause. Enough to let Yevgeny know that he had guessed wrong—that he should have put another round into the smoking rubble or else moved the gun in the other direction—before the sergeant said, "Sir! Yes, sir!"

It was all Yevgeny could do to keep from weeping with humiliation.

Then, breaking with the script, one of the men shouted and pointed up into the sky. Turning, Yevgeny saw the most amazing sight of his entire life: a naked giant looming over the buildings before him. The unsteady light from the flames below reflected off its skin, making it shimmer. For the briefest instant he wondered if he were experiencing a mystic vision of one of the demons from the Pit.

The giant shifted against the stars. Moving slowly, it turned onto Teatralny proezd. It was coming straight toward Yevgeny's gun crew.

A horse reared in terror. Several of the soldiers looked like they were ready to run. One of them had actually thrown down the swab he was holding and was about to bolt.

"Stay at your posts, damn you!" Yevgeny shouted, grabbing the panicky soldier and flinging him back toward the cannon. He drew his sword. "I'll kill the first mother-violating one of you who breaks and runs. Sergeant, are you in control of your men or not? Get that gun swung around. Give me an elevation. Are you all hares and hyenas? Stand and fight like the Russians you pretend to be!"

"Sir," the sergeant said, "there's not the time for a precise—"

"Do it by eye, then."

The gun was aimed and its elevation adjusted. "On your command, sir."

"Let it get closer. We've only the time for the one shot."

"Now, sir?"

"Not yet."

"We've got a good shot, sir."

"Just a little…" Yevgeny murmured.

"He's getting pretty fucking close, sir."

"Not until my command," Yevgeny said. He waited until the last possible instant and then forced himself to count silently to three. "Fire!"

They fired.

The Duke of Muscovy's great heart was hammering so hard it was about to burst. He had no illusions on that front. His body had been designed for a prone and sedentary existence. He could not long survive standing up and walking about like one of his own minuscule subjects. Already his mighty bones had sustained hundreds of small fractures from the stresses of his stroll through the city. His internal organs, crushed by forces they were never meant to withstand, were failing. In just a few seconds his heart would stop.

He had realized that all this would happen even as he had struggled to awaken, for the duke's tremendous brain was capable of miracles of extrapolation. Further, having lived only a shadowy half-existence erenow, the dreads and fears natural to a man knowing he was about to die did not rise up within him. Quite the opposite. For the first time, he found himself capable of feeling full human emotion, and he had given himself over to the experience.

It had been, as he had known it would be, a brief life but a joyous one.

Down on the street below, the duke saw an artillery crew swarming about their piece. They were as cunningly detailed as the very best of toy soldiers and he loved them as fully and uncritically as a little boy would have. There were tiny plumes on their shakos and all-but-invisible brass buttons on their jackets. They were tamping down powder and ball while their commander gestured with a sword that was the merest glint of reflected moonlight.

Then his heart failed. In the instant before the world went dark, the Duke of Muscovy saw a puff of white smoke at the mouth of the cannon.

Dying, he regretted that he would never know what came next.

The first thing Arkady heard upon regaining consciousness was one of the Pearls saying, "Well, that was pleasant. What shall we do next?"

He was, Arkady realized, lying on his back, with his trousers around his ankles. One of his shoes was gone, as were his shirt and jacket, but the helmet was still upon his head. Every muscle in his body ached as if he had been beaten with a cudgel. Further, he was utterly and completely exhausted. He could not so much as lift a finger. He had not the energy even to speak. Nor could he bring himself to open his eyes. Worst of all, he had no memory of whatever it was these six perfect Daughters of Ishtar had just done to him.

"I want to see the face of our bridegroom," Aetheria said. (He recognized that dulcet voice which he had once worshipped, and which still tugged at his heart.) His head shook from side to side as she tugged and tugged, before finally undoing the chin-strap.

There was a brief, astonished silence.

"It's Arkady!" somebody exclaimed. There was a scuffling noise as the Pearls gathered around his prone body, looking down.

Strangely enough, none of them died. Evidently the mental commands implanted in them by the Caliph's technicians were not going to kick in. They had enjoyed sex (or so they had thought) with the Duke of Muscovy, and that act had freed them of their psychic shackles. Leaving them free to do whatever they wanted with whomever they wished, as was the birthright of women everywhere.

"But why was he wearing a crown?"

"And carrying a scepter?"

"Look. Here in the pockets of his jacket: precious stones, jewelry, gold nuggets."

"He has become a thief!" Aetheria cried.

"That is sort of romantic," another Pearl said doubtfully.

"Not romantic enough."

"Anything less than suicide is an insult, in my opinion."

"At any rate, these treasures belong to the Russian people and the State of Muscovy, so he cannot keep them," Aetheria said. "Look at this cunning jeweled egg! We can't simply leave him here to walk away with them."

"There's a chest over there; place all these things in it. When the Neanderthals return, we can have some of them stand guard over it for the duke."

Somebody coughed. "Um…we're back," said a male voice and, almost simultaneously, another said, "We won the fight."

The Pearls shrieked.

"Cover your eyes, we're all disheveled!"

"Don't look."

"Where are my clothes?"

Upon which, cursing his eyes for so steadfastly refusing to open, Arkady felt himself falling back into oblivion.

Unhurriedly, Anya Pepsicolova dressed. When she had finished tying her shoes, she straightened and looked down on Darger's naked body for a long, still moment. Darger stared warily back at her, clearly alarmed by the expression on her blood-caked face, but equally clearly still thinking, still scheming. Perhaps she should shave off all his hair, from head to foot, as well? That would bring a neat symmetry to her long, difficult journey through the underworld. She considered the possibility seriously, but then decided against it. Because, really, she'd done enough.

Aloud, she said, "There. That's taken care of."

"The pleasure was all mine," Darger said with unctuous insincerity. But then, under the circumstances—post-coital and still bound hand and foot to the gurney—he was not exactly under oath. "So. Where, if I may ask, have you been all this time?"

"Oh, out and about." Pepsicolova tugged at her lapels to straighten her jacket. She shrugged. "You know."

"What did you do?"

"This and that." She slipped her cap onto her head and adjusted the angle. "Nothing of any particular note."

"Good, good, I'm glad to hear it." A note of cunning entered Darger's voice. "So, my darling Anya, now that we've experienced mutual ecstasy—I presume it was good for you, too?—we must discuss our future together."

"Future?" Anya was pretty sure that Darger hadn't experienced anything at all like ecstasy. She would have noticed. But that was a matter of perfect indifference to her, one way or the other. What did matter was that her skin felt stiff and itchy. "Well, the first thing I'm going to do is to wash my hands and face. Then…I don't know. Go for a walk, maybe."

She turned her back on Darger, on her career as a spy, on the City Below, on everything that had happened to her since she first encountered Chortenko, and started to walk away. Up ahead in the distance, she saw something waiting patiently for her. She could not help but smile.

Darger laughed ingratiatingly. "You foolish, loveable thing," he said. "The future of our relationship, I meant. Our feelings toward each other. Oh, I've been a blind fool! Wasting my time searching for tombs and books and libraries and tsars, when all the while there you were, right before me. But I shall make it up to you, my precious one, I swear."

His voice grew fainter behind her.

"We have plans to make, my sweetness. Promises to make. An engagement ring to buy. We must… Surely you'll…you'll… Wait! Come back! *You've forgotten to untie me!*"

But Anya Pepsicolova was no longer listening.

Several long, bleak minutes later, Darger realized that Pepsicolova had left behind the big knife she carried in her belt. It had slipped from its sheath to the gurney when she doffed her trousers, and then been knocked to the floor in the course of her inexplicable passion. Afterward, she had not bothered picking it up. He could see it, just barely, out of the corner of his eye, tantalizingly near at hand.

Darger eyed the blade yearningly. It might be just possible, he judged, that a desperate and determined man to, by shifting his weight vigorously and repeatedly, overtopple the gurney. Then, by various stratagems, he could draw the knife to himself and so cut through one of his restraints. After which, the rest would be a breeze.

A harrowing, difficult, and suspenseful half hour later, it was done.

Arkady was gone, and with him the bulk of what Surplus had managed to liberate from the museum cases.

Worse, there came the sound of breaking glass as a second vitrine was smashed open. It was louder than the first had been, which meant that Surplus's competitor was coming closer. It also indicated, Surplus feared, that whoever was at work was an amateur seizing the moment, rather than a professional who would be open to negotiation.

He glanced about, sizing up his situation.

There was only one exit from the Diamond Fund. Its display cases offered no hiding places. Not that Surplus particularly desired one. He was by nature a confronter rather than a slinker.

A third vitrine smashed. It was just outside the entrance to the room.

There was a moment's silence. Then a shaggy figure, large as an ogre, filled the doorway. Heaped in its arms was a fortune in armor and weapons. It paused to peer about before entering.

"How pleasant to encounter a compeer," Surplus said, stepping into the light of a column. "I trust your endeavors have been fruitful?"

With a tremendous clatter, the intruder dropped everything he held. Kicking the loot out of his way, he strode into the light and was revealed as a member of the Royal Guard. "All thish ish mine!" the bear-man cried. "If you try to take sho much ash a kopek of it, I'll kill you."

The fellow swayed slightly. It was clear he had been drinking.

Surplus brought his cane up to his mouth and delicately tapped its silver knob against his lips. "Split the swag fifty-fifty?"

"Hah!" The guard shambled forward, stumbling and almost falling when he stepped on what appeared to Surplus's tutored eye to be the ancient and indeed priceless Alexander Nevsky Helmet. "Shergeant Wojtek shares with nobody."

"I'll go as low as one-third. In all fairness, there is far more here than the two of us can hope to carry off on our own."

Sergeant Wojtek rolled his neck, showing his teeth. Then he held up his paws, uncurling the fingers one by one to extend their claws. "Do you imagine for an inshtant that a former member of the Royal Guard can be bought?"

He threw a punch at Surplus's head.

Surplus danced away from the blow. "Really, sir, there is no reason for us to fight. We are surrounded by an ocean of wealth. It makes no sense to quarrel over who gets to drink from it."

He barely managed to evade a second blow.

"Nobody takesh whatsh mine!"

"You make an excellent point, sir, I do confess it, a most excellent point," Surplus said, searching desperately for an appropriate strategy. With each missed punch, the length of corridor behind him grew shorter. At its end, he could break and run, true. But the bear-guard was assuredly not only stronger but also considerably faster than he was. It was only his drunken state that had kept him from simply charging forward and seizing Surplus in a crushing hug. "Yet nighttime is a dwindling resource, and with the dawn we may expect a restoration of order. It would not do for either of us to be found here tomorrow morning."

"Shtand shtill sho I can kill you, damn it." Sergeant Wojtek aimed a haymaker at Surplus and almost fell over when it missed. Clearly the alcohol had badly degraded his reflexes. This was a factor which could be used to Surplus's advantage.

"Is there to be no resolution other than death?" Surplus asked with genuine regret. He held his cane before him, one paw on the knob and the other by its tip, as if he thought it possible to fend off the gigantic animal-man chimera with it.

"None," the Royal Guardsman said truculently.

"Then I must inform you, sir, that you are a drunken lout, a traitor, a thief, a murderous thug, a disgrace to your uniform—and quite possibly not even a gentleman."

With a bellow of rage, Sergeant Wojtek charged.

All in one movement, Surplus stepped to the side, like a matador dodging a bull, pulled away the wooden sheath that was half of his sword-cane, and plunged the sword down the space at the side of the guard's neck that was unprotected by bone.

Deep the sword went, into the heart and through.

...20...

Countless acts of heroism and cowardice, opportunistic looting and saintly forgiveness, small cruelties and inexplicable kindnesses occurred within the disaster that was Moscow. The citizens of that great metropolis, caught up in what felt very much like the end of the world, were granted the rare opportunity of confronting their true selves.

Thus it was, at any rate, for one young man who, weeping and bleeding, left the Hotel New Metropol by a rear window with a cask of rasputin wrapped in stolen hotel blankets. Through the maze of bewildered streets he limped. Column after column after column of black smoke rose up from the helpless corpse of the city behind him, and converged into a dark shroud overhead.

Slowly, painfully, he fled.

Hours later, when Arkady finally reached the outskirts of town where the city dwindled to nothing and weary farmlands began, he paused to take stock. He was penniless, horseless, and thoroughly ashamed of himself. All his connections in Moscow were either dead or extremely unlikely to want to see his face ever again. Further, his home was unimaginably distant and to reach it he would have to cross a howling wilderness filled with monsters. On foot.

Well, what had to be done, had to be done. The demon machines had unintentionally given him a weapon that could be used to wipe their kind from the face of the earth. His father would know, far better than he, how to put the rasputin to good use. All Arkady had to do was make certain that it reached him.

He squared his shoulders and set off.

Baronessa Lukoil-Gazproma's clothes were stained and disheveled and her spirit was in even worse shape when Irina found her at last. She was sitting on the stoop of a house whose shabby appearance testified that she probably did not even know whose it was, with her head in her hands. "I am so damnably tired of politics and society," she said without looking up when Irina leapt down from her phaeton, crying out her name. "I want nothing more than to retire someplace out in the country, where I would never have to deal with people again. If only I could live in perfect solitude, just me and one or two dozen friends. No men. I am done completely with their entire gender."

Irina sat down beside her friend and took her hands in her own. "Well, who could blame you if you did? Still, I doubt your husband would approve."

"Nikodim Gregorovich? He would be elated. I have never told anybody this, precious one, but the baron wanted me to do...certain things. And when I did, he...Well. Our marriage must be counted a failure."

Irina did her best to look surprised by news which all of Moscow society had known for years. Luckily, the baronessa was too lost in her own unhappiness to notice the sardonic twist to Irina's mouth when she said, "I am shocked. But never mind that. Come home with me, Dunyasha, and I will have my servants bathe you. Then I will dry you with my own two hands and lead you to bed, and pleasure you with my mouth. I will sing you a lullaby and watch over you until you fall asleep."

"Dear, sweet Irinushka," the baroness said. "Whatever have I done to deserve such loving kindness from you?"

"You honestly don't know?"

"No."

"Years ago, I was affianced to the baron at the time, and you stole him away from me. Surely you remember that."

"Oh, Irina Varbarova, I'm so sorry! That was such a strange and romantic summer, with all those parties and flirtations, and somehow I convinced myself that you did not mind."

"Nor did I," Irina said. "It was to be a marriage of convenience. The baron had money and I had none. So my feelings toward him hardly mattered. But I was quite afraid of him. I believe that's what attracted him to me in the first place. Really, I am indebted to you for saving me from a marriage I dreaded. Even if it did mean I lacked financial security as a result."

"Oh, Irina, you will never want for anything so long as I live. Anything I have, whatever you want, is yours."

"I know. That's why I'm your friend."

Irina could say things like that to Avdotya, because she knew the baronessa did not understand how true they were.

Anya Pepsicolova walked the streets of the burning city genuinely delighted with everything she saw. She was experiencing quite the most giddy joy imaginable. The gray, choking smoke that drifted through the streets—marvelous! The sound of cannon fire and of burning buildings collapsing—quite wonderful! The black snowflakes of soot that floated down through the air—a delight! She swung her arms up and down, like a little girl making imaginary angel wings in the air. She was free to go in whatever direction she cared. East, west, up, down, it didn't matter. All ways were good when there was nobody to tell you no.

She came upon a fire engine being pumped by three of the biggest, hairiest men she had ever seen in her life. They were putting out the last smoldering embers of what had once been somebody's house. Atop the engine stood a woman of such tremendous beauty as to make Anya disbelieve her own eyes. She stopped to gawk.

One of the apelike men squatted down and gently extended a grotesquely large and lumpish hand. "Heyyy, what a nice little fella. Is it yours?"

"Yes, but be careful. Vera's a rescue dog. She has a temper."

Vera bristled and showed her teeth but the big man held himself still, not flinching away, and clucked his tongue reassuringly. After a bit, she relented and let him rub her head. "Who's a good girl?" he said. "You are. You are. Yes, you are."

"I shared my meal with her and we bonded," Pepsicolova explained. Then, to the beautiful woman, "You look awfully happy." It was particularly delightful to encounter somebody as joyful as herself. Everyone else in the city she had run across was strangely glum.

"I am! Today is my wedding day and I'm celebrating it by helping to save my new city." The beautiful woman hopped down and stuck out her hand. "My name's Nymphodora. Dora for short. What's yours?"

"Anya Alexandreyovna Pepsicolova. Who's the lucky man?"

Dora gestured toward the three Neanderthals. "They are—Enkidu, Gilgamesh, and Rabelais. My sisters and I wrote their names down on slips of paper and drew three each. Except for Zoësophia. She sent a messenger and said she was going into politics so she didn't need a husband quite yet. Which is good, because then we all got the same number."

Pepsicolova was sure she hadn't understood half of what she'd just heard. "Three husbands?" she said wonderingly. "Can you actually satisfy all of them?"

"Trust me, sister," the nearest giant said with a shy grin, "she can."

Dora happily ruffled his hair. "Oh, you big galoot." Then a sudden gout of flame made her shout, "Over there!" and off she and her mighty consorts sped.

Pepsicolova and her dog wandered off into the wondrous if somewhat reduced city of Moscow.

Because the Terem Palace was in ruins and elements of the Kremlin remained on fire, the Ad Hoc Committee for the Defense of Muscovy was reduced to meeting in the brothel in Zamoskvorechye from which Baron Lukoil-Gazprom was already directing rescue and firefighting operations. The ranking members of both the old and new regimes who were neither dead nor incapacitated by sexual exhaustion, crowded into the parlor. So diminished were the numbers of the ruling class and so great was the need to reestablish a functioning government that nobody wasted time in political infighting. That could wait for next week.

"Firstly, thank you all for coming," Zoësophia said. "Baron Lukoil-Gazprom has asked me to serve as the recording secretary for this meeting." No one could have suspected the degree to which the Committee had been chosen by this striking but deferential young woman. Nor how deftly she had countered its most ambitious members by appointing their political rivals to positions of equal authority. "He himself will serve as chair until a new leader is chosen. Baron?"

The baron glanced down at the agenda laid before him as though he had had no hand in drafting it. Which he most definitely had. "There is much we must do. However, the first and most pressing order of business is to name an acting chief of government to replace our own beloved and tragically deceased Duke of Muscovy."

A rustle of wordless surprise passed around the table. This was the first that most of them had heard of the duke's demise. But before anyone could demand details of this startling news, the baron said, "Nominations?"

Several of those present straightened with sudden resolve. State Inspector of Infrastructure Zdrajca bulled his way to the front and said, "I would like to—"

"Jaragniew Bogdanovich Zdrajca." Baron Lukoil-Gazprom referred to a list of names that Zoësophia slid before him. "You are known to belong to an organization including elements of the government created by the False Tsar Lenin." There was just enough of a pause for everyone to realize that most of the members of that organization referred to were present in this very room. Then he continued, "And to having ambitions of establishing yourself as absolute ruler of Muscovy. This makes you a clear and present danger to the welfare of the state." Lifting his head, the baron said, "Take him out and shoot him."

Two soldiers whom nobody had previously paid any serious attention to seized the unfortunate state inspector by the arms and dragged him from the building. There was a long silence and then a volley of klashny fire.

A flurry of motions and points of order later, Muscovy had a new duke-to-be.

There was a tense moment when the question was raised of punishments for those involved in the abortive coup. However, since Chortenko was dead and his puppet government had been assembled under duress, it was quickly established that the only rebel of any note was the Baronessa Lukoil-Gazproma. Who, out of deference to her husband, could not possibly be either executed or imprisoned.

But neither could she be allowed to stay in Moscow.

The baronessa was given a generous pension and the Novodevichy Convent to do with as she liked. Those present had some shrewd guesses as to what sorts of activities she would engage in there, in the fields and woods outside of town. But they also knew that the secret police would immediately clamp down on anyone commenting too loudly on them. So that was all right.

It was an open secret that for years hers had been a marriage in name only anyway.

"The next item on the agenda," the baron said when the business of his wife had been taken care of, "is the beginning of preparations to expand the borders of Muscovy and restore the Russian Empire to its lost glory."

In short order, forces were mobilized and expanded, conscriptions declared, a host of new commissions created and put up for sale, and authority granted the baron to raise taxes as needed to pay for whatever he required.

It was, everybody agreed afterward, an auspicious beginning to what would surely be a golden new era in Russian history.

Yevgeny had become the hero of the day when, seeing the inexplicable naked giant come crashing toward him, he had redirected his cannon to counter this uncanny new threat. Where others had fled, he had without hesitation rallied his fearless gun crew. Under his direction, the team had with one single shot taken down the monster.

After which, his sergeant had said, "Sir? Hadn't you better be going now?"

"Eh?" Yevgeny said, startled by the deference in the man's voice.

"If you want to get the regiment's name in the history books, sir, you should report this action immediately." The sergeant gave his superior a meaningful look.

So, not being a total dunce, Yevgeny had wheeled his steed and raced like the wind to army headquarters to report the feat before others could take credit for it.

On delivering his report, Yevgeny was immediately arrested for being drunk on duty, of course. It would take some time for headquarters to accept the giant's reality. But his claim had been documented, and was thus official. The story would quickly get around, and he could expect to be released before too long. Being of the proper class and breeding for such a deed, he could be confident that a promotion would soon follow. Meanwhile, he was given prison quarters suitable for a gentleman.

It was in his prison cell that Yevgeny met an inmate not much younger than himself who had been arrested for looting. "My own fault," Anatoli admitted cheerily. "I should have stopped before the city forces pulled themselves together. But I got greedy, so I'll be living off the duke's largesse for the next few months." Word had not yet gotten out that the Duke of Muscovy had been killed by the treachery of his own guards. Though, already, Baron Lukoil Gazprom was making plans for a solemn funeral procession (with an empty but human-sized coffin, the true nature of the late duke being a state secret) which would pass between the rows of gibbets on which the bodies of the bear-men of the Royal Guard were still fresh. "The only embarrassing thing is that it was my uncle's mansion I was caught ransacking, so I'm going to catch hell from my mother when I get out."

"And what do you normally do?" Yevgeny asked. "When you're not looting and ransacking?"

"Oh, I'm a wastrel, and a scapegrace and a scoundrel and a horrible libertine," Anatoli said, staring straight into Yevgeny's eyes. His own were green and filled with mischief, but there was an undercurrent of sorrow there as well, a leavening of pain that made the laughter all that much sweeter. "Depending on my mood, of course."

Yevgeny felt his heart melt within him.

Meanwhile, the mysterious giant's corpse had, even in the midst of a citywide holocaust, become something of an attraction. A string quartet was playing at its feet, with a bucket set out for donations. Enterprising artists from the Arbat sold sketches of citizens posing before the body part of his or her choice. Because the flesh was rapidly becoming high, a vendor sold oranges for the clients to hold to their noses while they posed. Several women in modest clothing stood before the noble head, crossing themselves and bowing in prayer—though whether they were praying to the giant or thanking God for its demise, nobody cared to ask. Children raced from the shoulder to the knee and back again, shrieking with joy.

"How do you like it so far?" an artist asked his patron.

The pudgy man examined the picture—in which he stood, casually heroic, with one foot on the giant's hand, as if he had slain the behemoth himself—and blew out his cheeks. "It's good, but I look a little… a little too…Well, is it possible to make me look a bit more…muscular?"

"I can do that, sir. All included in the price of purchase."

It was, after all, Moscow. And in Moscow you could get anything you wanted, so long as you could afford the price.

Kyril had set up business helping people find their homes. He stood in Mayakovsky Square, looking sharply about until he saw a gentleman dressed posh, if somewhat rumpled, and looking confused and distracted. Then he darted up and began his patter: "Good morning, citizen! You look like you've had an evening of it, that's for sure. Well, so have we all, sir, so have we all. Are you having trouble finding your way home? Do you know where your home is? I'd be glad to help."

"I, uh…" The man looked dazedly down at Kyril. "I, um, I *think* I know where my home is," he said tentatively. His glasses were askew.

"Well, let me just check for you, eh? Where do you keep your billfold? Oh, it's right here in your inside jacket pocket. Very wise, sir. Makes it much harder for a pickpocket to get at it, dunnit? Oh, you know it does! Place it in your hip pocket, it's as good as gone. I've seen it happen, sir, and much worse!"

Kyril opened the wallet. "Well, look here. This says that you're V. I. Dyrakovsky—is that you, sir? Yes of course it is—and you live close by Patriarch's Ponds. Very nice neighborhood, if you don't mind my saying so, and the fires are nowhere near it yet. You can go home, catch a little nap, bury your valuables, and still make it out of town in perfect safety before your house burns down. Just keep on going along the Garden Ring until you come to Spiridonovka ulitsa, go down it two blocks and then turn left. Can't miss it! I'm sure you'll recognize your own house." He tucked the billfold back in the man's jacket, spun him around, and gave him a little push. "No need to thank me, sir. I'm just doing what any citizen would."

Kyril stood waving goodbye until the man was lost in the crowd. Then he turned away to surreptitiously examine the banknotes he had slid out of the man's wallet in the course of examining his ID. Three hundred rubles. Not bad. And the morning was yet young!

A carriage rattled over the cobblestones and came to a stop not far away. A veiled woman leaned out the window. "You there!" she called to Kyril. "You in the green suit! Come over here."

Kyril stepped closer, smiling. Opportunity, it seemed, was everywhere. "Can I help you, ma'am?"

"Yes, you can." The woman opened the carriage door. "Get in."

Kyril climbed into the coach and the woman slid over to make room for him. On the other side of her sat two dwarf savants looking alert and placid.

At a word from the woman, the carriage started forward again. But instead of saying what she wanted, she instead studied him shrewdly for a very long time. At last Kyril could not keep silent any longer. "You said I could help you, Gospozha?"

"Yes, you can. If, that is, you're the young lady I think you are."

"Waddaya talkin' about? I ain't no girl." Kyril reached for the latch, intending to kick the door open and leap out. But the veiled woman had already seized his collar. Her grip was implacable.

"Nice try, Missie. You may be able to fool everyone else, but you're not fooling *me*. I've read your file and I know more about you than you do yourself. How long have you been passing yourself off as a boy?"

Long years of scrabbling to stay alive had taught Kyril how to read people. This woman's face and stance conveyed amusement, scorn, perception—and no doubt whatsoever. She wasn't bluffing. She knew. Looking down at her feet, Kyril said, "Since my parents died and I ran away from the workhouse three years ago."

The carriage rumbled down the smoky streets. After a while, the woman said, "What's your name?"

"Kir—I mean, Klara." She stared wistfully out of the carriage window, at all the dazed and well-heeled marks stumbling about in a mental fog, and abruptly blurted, "I was making awful good money out there."

"I have better and ultimately more profitable work for you. I'm the new head of Muscovy Intelligence, and I need some bright eyes in low places."

"What? You want me to be a *spy*? An informer? A fink?"

"Do you have a problem with that?"

Klara thought. "Naw," she said at last. "It just caught me by surprise."

"Must this happen to *every* city we visit?" Surplus said with just a touch of pique.

"At least we can take comfort in the fact that none of this was our doing," Darger reassured him. Then, because he was an honest man, he added, "So far as we know."

They stood atop Sparrow Hills, which, long months ago, they had agreed upon as their meeting-place, watching Moscow burn. Black smoke bent low over the city. At least three of the Kremlin's buildings were burning and the Secret Tower, beneath which lay the former library of Tsar Ivan, was a pillar of flame. Surplus had, in an effort to raise his friend's spirits, shown him the pocketful of gems he had rescued from the Diamond Fund. To no avail. "All those books," Darger mourned. "Gone."

"Surely not all," Surplus said. "Some must have survived."

"Only one. The young man who showed me where the library was snatched it up and stuffed it into my jacket when he hauled me away."

"Which book was it?"

Darger drew out the book and opened it. Then he began to laugh. "It is an economic treatise on the nature of capital. The very book, in fact, which we chose to use as the bait in our plan to defraud the duke."

He handed it to Surplus who gave it a cursory glance. The book was a German first edition. The text looked to be as dry as dust.

"Well," Surplus said, "this is of no possible interest to anyone." He cocked his arm to throw it away.

But Darger stopped him. "Wait! Let us not waste a useful prop. Perhaps we can use it in our next operation, when we reach Japan."

"Japan? Are we going to Japan?"

"Why not? It's said to be a beautiful place. And full of fabulous riches as well. Indeed, its rulers are reckoned as being wealthy beyond avarice. If such a thing is even imaginable."

"Nevertheless," said Surplus, crouching to place the book down upon the grass and then straightening and turning his back on it, "we shall come up with something new for our Japanese friends. There are far too many old ideas in the world as it is."

He turned his back on the conflagration.

They mounted two horses they had rented at exorbitant cost. Which cost, however, came to less than outright purchase would have and thus, given that they had no intention of ever returning the horses to their former owner, was, looked at properly, something of a bargain. The saddlebags, moreover, were packed with a judicious assortment of items taken from the Diamond Fund.

As they put Moscow behind them, Surplus narrated his recent adventures. When the tale reached its climax, Darger, astonished, remarked, "I did not know that your walking stick was actually a sword cane."

"There is a great deal that you do not know about me," Surplus said complacently.

Sometime later...

It was a remarkable sight: A band of hard men numbering in the hundreds—far too many to be called a raiding party, though perhaps not quite enough to be considered a true army—were readying their weapons on a hillside above Baikonur. Most were mounted on short, sturdy horses, but a sizeable fraction rode camels, which lived wild in the region and could be captured and broken to the saddle by those who knew how. Small bright flags here and there identified the leaders from each of the hidden towns of the steppes that had contributed warriors to the cause. Below them sprawled a dark, Satanic city of smokes and machines. Enigmatic engines reached for the sky. Cracking towers and gantries loomed from the yellowish smog. There were silvery glints of movement here and there, but for as far as the eye could see not one sign of life—not an animal, not a tree, not so much as a blade of grass.

A bold young man on a roan mare cantered up to the band's leader. "Are you ready, Father?"

"Arkady Ivanovich, I was ready when your mother was still a virgin. As well she learned." Gulagsky reared up his horse, roaring with sudden laughter. He gestured the young man to his side. "Come ride with me. We will each protect and defend the other." Then, raising his klashny overhead, he shouted, "Are you ready to ride? Are you willing to fight? Are you prepared to die? Are you men enough to crush and destroy every living machine in the city below?"

Up and down the line of mounts, the men grinned savage and merciless grins. They had grown up in an unforgiving land and stayed when lesser folk had fled. Among them they felt not the slightest flicker of fear. Their eyes, to a man, glittered with the indwelling God.

"Baikonur is ours!" Gulagsky bellowed. He swept forward an arm. *"The demon machines stole it from us—now we take it back!"*

The men roared.

They galloped down on the city like wolves upon the fold.